No time for second thoughts now

the worlds. But my family mostly uses the pre-digested forces my grandmother and her sisters channel into the net via their mainframe webservers. Scorched Earth isn't like that. It taps directly into the interworld chaos. That means it's both very danger-ous and very powerful. It also means I don't have to have web access to run it. Melchior's voice inter-rupted my train of thought.

"There's no carrier wave and no mweb line," he said. "I think we just took the entire net down, Boss."

"Sweet Necessity," I murmured. "What have I done now?"

"Kelly McCullough's *WebMage* has to be the most en-joyable science fantasy book I've read in the last four years. Its blending of magic and coding is inspired, al-most as much as the portrayals of the Greek gods and their descendants. *WebMage* has all the qualities I look for in a book—a wonderfully subdued sense of humor, nonstop action, and romantic relief . . . It's a wonderful debut novel."

—Christopher Stasheff, author of
Saint Vidicon to the Rescue

WebMage

Kelly McCullough

ACE BOOKS, NEW YORK

THE BERKLEY PUBLISHING GROUP
Published by the Penguin Group
Penguin Group (USA) Inc.
375 Hudson Street, New York, New York 10014, USA
Penguin Group (Canada), 90 Eglinton Avenue East, Suite 700, Toronto, Ontario M4P 2Y3, Canada
(a division of Pearson Penguin Canada Inc.)
Penguin Books Ltd., 80 Strand, London WC2R 0RL, England
Penguin Group Ireland, 25 St. Stephen's Green, Dublin 2, Ireland (a division of Penguin Books Ltd.)
Penguin Group (Australia), 250 Camberwell Road, Camberwell, Victoria 3124, Australia
(a division of Pearson Australia Group Pty. Ltd.)
Penguin Books India Pvt. Ltd., 11 Community Centre, Panchsheel Park, New Delhi—110 017, India
Penguin Group (NZ), Cnr. Airborne and Rosedale Roads, Albany, Auckland 1310, New Zealand
(a division of Pearson New Zealand Ltd.)
Penguin Books (South Africa) (Pty.) Ltd., 24 Sturdee Avenue, Rosebank, Johannesburg 2196, South Africa

Penguin Books Ltd., Registered Offices: 80 Strand, London WC2R 0RL, England

This is a work of fiction. Names, characters, places, and incidents either are the product of the author's imagination or are used fictitiously, and any resemblance to actual persons, living or dead, business establishments, events, or locales is entirely coincidental. The publisher does not have any control over and does not assume any responsibility for author or third-party websites or their content.

WEBMAGE

An Ace Book / published by arrangement with the author

PRINTING HISTORY
Ace mass-market edition / August 2006

Copyright © 2006 by Kelly McCullough.
Portions of this book were previously published as short stories in *Weird Tales*, #317, Fall 1999.
Cover art by Christian McGrath.
Cover design by Judith Lagerman.
Interior text design by Kristin del Rosario

ISBN: 0-441-01425-9

ACE
Ace Books are published by The Berkley Publishing Group,
a division of Penguin Group (USA) Inc.,
375 Hudson Street, New York, New York 10014.
ACE and the "A" design are trademarks belonging to Penguin Group (USA) Inc.

PRINTED IN THE UNITED STATES OF AMERICA

10 9 8 7 6 5 4 3 2

For Laura, my heart

Acknowledgments

First and foremost, extra special thanks are owed to Laura McCullough, Stephanie Zvan, Dave Hoffman-Dachelet, Lyda Morehouse, Shari Mann, Jack Byrne, and Anne Sowards, without whom this book would not be here.

Many thanks also to all of the following: The members of my various writers groups: S. N. Arly, Anna Waltz, Stephanie Zvan, Barth Anderson, Alan DeNiro, Paula Fleming, Manfred Gabriel, David J. Hoffman-Dachelet, Burke T. Kealey, Kristin Livdahl, Lyda Morehouse, Doug Hulick, Naomi Kritzer, William Henry, Eleanor Arnason, Rosalind Nelson, H. Courreges LeBlanc, Sean Michael Murphy, Mike Matheny, Kevin Matheny, Sean Melom, and Ben Rouner. The WOTF Gang: Eric Witchey, Merry Simmons, J. Simon, Phillip Lees, Anna Allen, Robert Johnston, Michelle Letica, Steven Raine, and Marguerite Devers Green. Pros who've helped me along the way: Darrell Schweitzer, George Scithers, Tim Powers, Warren Lapine, Eric Heideman, Jim Frenkel, Steve Brust, Mike Levy, Dean Wesley Smith, Kristine Kathryn Rusch, Jane Yolen.

Ted Davis, who gave me the computer that started it all. My web guru, Ben Zvan. Tracy Berg. Beta readers: Sara Rouner, Steve Fox, Karl and Angie Anderson. Research services: Jody Wurl and Barb Thompson. Mentors: Vaughn Koenig, Jerry Jax, Joel Samaha. My extended support structure: Bill and Nancy

Rouner, James Hall, Tom Foster, Ann Robertson, and so many more.

And my family: Phyllis Neese, Carol Sorsoleil, Paul and Jane McCullough, Lockwood and Darlene Carlson, Judy Rohde, Lee Carlson, Kat Carlson, Kay Marquez, Jean Thomas, Lee Perish, and the rest.

CHAPTER ONE

"Nothing here," said Melchior, his voice echoing from the depths of an ancient citrus-wood chest.

"Keep looking," I called back to my familiar, yanking another drawer from my many-times-great-aunt's desk. "It's small. It could be anywhere."

The spell was very tightly written, and elegantly coded. Embedded in the crystalline matrix of a memory jewel, it was beautiful. Even incomplete, it was the scariest thing I'd ever seen. Worse, it didn't seem to be anywhere in Atropos's suite. I shouldn't have been surprised. My great-to-the-nth-degree-aunt is a consummate weaver of intrigue. I dropped the drawer. Where should I look next? As if in answer to my question, a hound bayed in the distance, the unmistakable belling of a hunter on a fresh trail. I didn't have much time.

"Melchior, Mtp://mweb.DecLocus.prime.minus3051/umn.edu, comstockhall301," I said. It was my current home site on the mweb. "Execute."

"I hear and obey, Ravirn," replied Melchior.

The webgoblin hurried to an open space on the floor and scratched a hexagram into the wood before spitting out a netspider. The tiny magical creature scuttled to the diagram, where it set an anchor line and vanished. A few seconds later it returned and Melchior grabbed it and returned it to his mouth.

"Mm-mm. Delicious and nutritious, tastes just like chicken."

"Can the editorials, Mel," I called, sliding out from under the bed. I'd sliced open the liner and dug around in the springs. The smell of dust filled my sinuses. "We're in a hurry, and I know they taste terrible. That's one of the reasons I built you in the first place. I just want to know if my dorm room is clear."

The webgoblin stuck his spider-occupied tongue out at me. I snapped my fingers in exasperation, calling a wisplight into being, and sent it to dance a few inches in front of Melchior's eyes. He hopped back and growled a little. When the wisp showed no signs of departing, he sighed and swallowed the spider.

I dispelled the wisp. There was no sense in aggravating him, or drawing more attention than I already had. Although, on looking around at the wreck we'd made of my greataunt's bedroom, I had to wonder if I could draw more attention. If she ever found out who'd done this, I was a dead man. Still, I found myself delaying our departure. The back trail I'd left should keep the dogs off a little while longer. If only I could find the damned spell. I searched the room one last time with my eyes.

"Processing," said the goblin, his voice mechanical. Then, after a few seconds, "Reporting. Your room in Comstock at the U of M in the prime-minus-3051 Decision Locus is vacant."

"Thanks, Mel," I said. "That wasn't so bad, was it?"

"Ick, ack, ptooie," coughed Melchior, his voice returning to its normal whiny growl. He rubbed his tongue as if trying to clean off the remnants of the webspider. "When Lachesis wrote the code for those things, why did she make them so bitter?"

"I'm tempted to say it's just another manifestation of my greatest grandmother's sparkling temperament. But that's not actually the case. Uncle Valarian asked her once while I was around. She said it's to remind us that the spiders are serious and potentially dangerous magical constructs, not toys."

"Hmmph. Why don't you fix them?"

"There are several reasons." I ticked them off on my fingers. "First, I'm not the one who has to eat them. Second, their programming is much more involved and nasty than it's worth. Third, they're virtually bug free, if you'll pardon the pun. Fourth, and finally, it would seriously irritate Lachesis, and that stupid I'm not."

Lachesis, the Fate who measures the threads, is not a Goddess to be trifled with. For convenience's sake I usually refer to her as my grandmother rather than adding in all of the necessary greats, and she is more fond of me than of some of my relatives. But bonds of affection and blood are only a limited shield from her anger.

"Now," I continued, "before you come up with any more distracting questions, I have orders. Melchior, establish a locus transfer protocol link with the Comstock hub. As soon as that's done, initiate transfer. We've got to get out of here."

The little goblin glared at me but went to work. He pulled a piece of chalk and a bit of string out of his belly pouch. Using the string to measure, he drew a large hexagram on the floor and spat another netspider into the center. It blinked out the second it landed, leaving behind a glowing blob of gold silk.

"Connecting to prime.minus3051," intoned the goblin.

A few moments later the light changed from gold to green. "Connect," said Melchior. "Initiating Gate."

He dropped to his knees and grabbed the node. As he pulled on it, the glow spread outward, filling the whole hexagram. Once the diagram was completely green, the light rose to form a hexagonal column about six feet high and two across.

"Gate established. There you go, Boss. We can leave whenever you're ready."

"Thanks, Mel. That was nicely done." A loud crashing sounded somewhere close by. That would be the cousins coming to see who had invaded their demesne. And, as much as I might have enjoyed staying and chatting with my dear, dear relatives, Atropos's brood was notorious for killing first and trading pleasantries later.

"Perfect timing," I said to Melchior. "Shall we be going?"

"Hades, yes!" said Melchior, hopping from one clawed foot to the other in obvious agitation. "Atropos scares me even more than your many-times-great-grandmother." The doorknob turned as someone tried to open it.

"We need to go now!" He tugged the corner of my cloak. I twitched it out of his hand.

"Too right, Mel." I really didn't want to be there when they got through, but dammit, I needed to find that spell.

It wasn't going to happen. Defeated, I stepped into the column of light. The door shuddered and groaned as something thudded into it. A half-second later, the sound was repeated. Long cracks appeared in the thick, wooden timbers. I pulled my cloak up to mask my features.

"Melchior, Locus Transfer," I said. "Execute."

Phrased like that, with his full name at the beginning and the execute order at the end, it was a command he had to obey. Melchior, joining me on the hexagram, hissed out a string of spaghetti logic. The light began to shift from green to blue. A third impact buckled the door completely. I drew my rapier. An instant later, a broad-bladed hunting spear hurtled though a gap at the top of the ruined door, coming straight for me. I thought we would be gone before it got to me, but it never hurts to be careful. I brought my sword up in a parry. As the light finished its transition, the room wavered around us and vanished.

There was a shower of sparks as the iron spearpoint grated along the edge of the rapier. The contact deflected the missile past my left shoulder. It buried itself solidly in my roommate's Toby Keith poster. It also left my hand stinging and numb by turns.

"That," I said to Melchior, "was entirely too close." I dropped the sword and hooked the chain on my door.

"Has anyone ever told you that you have a gift for stating the obvious?" asked my goblin. He was livid, literally. His face and neck, normally a royal blue, had faded almost to periwinkle. "Were you *trying* to get us killed, or are you just stupid?"

That was too much. "Melchior, enough! When I wrote you, I included a certain amount of self-determination and sarcasm. But I won't tolerate insolence or insubordination. Go to your desk."

"Your least whim is my veriest desire, o' prince." The webgoblin leaped onto my small desk, where he assumed a cross-legged position and glared at me.

"Melchior, Laptop," I said, tired of his whining. "Execute."

"No sooner commanded than performed."

The goblin's flesh began to flow and twist like soft wax. Five minutes later the transformation was complete. What had once been a nasty-tempered little manling became a shiny WebRunner 2,200cs PPCP cell laptop. A small blue logo bearing a suspicious resemblance to Melchior was positioned below the screen on the left.

While the goblin altered his appearance to better fit in with his surroundings, so did I. The black cloak and the rapier went into a trunk at the foot of the bed. The tights, likewise black, and the emerald tunic were stuffed into a laundry bag. The high leather boots were retained to go over a pair of black jeans. I topped that off with a green "Nobody Wins" T-shirt and a TechSec leather jacket before checking myself in the mirror to see whether I'd forgotten anything.

Boy, had I ever. "Shit," I mumbled. The face that stared back at me was not one I could wear around here. I invoked the spell that rounded my slightly pointed ears and reshaped the vertical slits in my green eyes to more human circles. My long, black hair, fine bone structure, and dead white skin I left intact. On a campus with as large a Goth population as the U of M, they were normal enough to make concealing them a waste of magical resources, a cardinal sin in House Lachesis. That done, the transformation was complete. Prince Ravirn, of the House of Lachesis, sixty-seventh in line for the throne, was gone. In his place was Ravi Latcher, a junior in Classics and Computer Science with midterms coming up.

Atropos and her spell would have to wait. I'd given Lachesis my solemn word that I wouldn't miss another midterm. And breaking a promise to Fate is an excellent way to end up as the subject of a Greek tragedy, even if you are a member of the family. I assuaged my conscience with the thought that Atropos hadn't been able to make the spell work yet. Otherwise, she would never have come to me. I'd have another go at finding it after my first test. Not enough to make me feel better, but the best I could do for the moment.

Swearing under my breath, I turned and started stuffing books into my shoulder bag. That's when I remembered the spear. Ran into it is more like the truth, but that's neither here nor there.

Damn! If Rod found that thing there, I'd never hear the end of it. Pulling the weapon loose, I tossed it under the bed. That left a rip in the poster and a hole in the wall. It seemed an awfully trivial concern just then, but anyone who's ever had a touchy roommate would understand. Sighing, I flipped the cover of the laptop up and hit the space bar.

Enter password.

. . . .

Correct.
Run Melchior. Execute.
I hear and obey!

The laptop shifted back to its webgoblin form. "What now? I didn't even have all my bootables in the right places. You know I hate that."

He can get in a real snit when that happens, and I didn't feel like picking a fight with my laptop three days before term papers were due. He could crash at the most inconvenient times when he was angry.

"I know, I know. I'm really sorry. You've been doing good work lately, and I haven't been praising you enough. But I was supposed to meet my study group in Walter Library ten minutes ago. I want you to fix Rod's poster, then catch up to me there."

"I don't see why you can't just do it yourself."

"Because I don't have time to code a real spell, and if I just paste an illusion over it, I'll forget about it. Then the illusion will wear off at the most inconvenient possible time, and I'll end up having a huge argument with Rod."

"True. Pathetic, but true." I let that slide, and he continued, "Get moving, I'll be along in fifteen minutes or so."

"Great." I opened the door, then looked over my shoulder. "Oh, and Melchior."

"Yes?"

"I don't want you terrorizing the sorority girls on your way over."

"But—!"

"No, Mel. Stay away from the football team too, OK?"

"Yeah, sure. If I have to leave the Greeks alone, I might as well not have any fun."

"Thanks, Mel. You're a prince."

"No, you're the prince. I'm just a lowly goblin flunky, doomed to a life of menial labor." Melchior wrenched a razor-sharp tooth from his mouth and spat a netspider into his hand. He squeezed it until silk came out, then threaded it onto the tooth. "No one appreciates my simple graces."

"Good-bye, Mel."

As Melchior began to sew up the rip in the poster, I ducked out and closed the door. Then I took the back stairs three at a time. When I hit the campus mall, I sprinted. The mall was lined with vaguely classical buildings. My family's early-Greek worshippers would have recognized the style, though they'd have wondered why everything was oversized and rendered in stark gray granite or boring beige sandstone. It was October, one of the good ones, and the air was crisp but not icy. In the clear fall air the full moon seemed close enough to touch, and the smells of dry leaves and dying grass were enough to paint a grin on my lips. There was nothing like fall in Minnesota. Even with the threat of Atropos's spell hanging over everything.

Melchior caught me as I was dashing up the library steps. Somehow, he'd gotten there ahead of me.

"Boss!" he whispered loudly from behind a pillar. "Hey, Boss."

I turned, startled. He'd gotten there too fast. "How'd you

manage to fix the poster so quickly?" I looked around to make sure that none of the local human population was close enough to see me talking to a mythical creature. Together we slid into the deep shadows at the edge of the building.

"I didn't fix the poster," said Melchior. He raised a closed hand to forestall my complaint. "We have much bigger problems than an annoyed roommate. This came through into the room after you left."

He opened the hand. In it was a small, broken thing, a netspider. I took it and popped it into my mouth. The flavor was even worse than the ones my grandmother had coded. It was also familiar.

"Atropos," I whispered. I was stunned. I'd been very careful not to leave any identifying marks, and I didn't think anything could have backtracked me. "This came from my cousins, or worse, my great-aunt. Are you jamming?"

"As much as possible, but they're using some pretty heavy code-breaking algorithms. Their webhounds will have us locked down within ten minutes."

"I guess I'm going to have to take a pass on my study night," I said. "Melchior, Bugout. Execute."

"Executing," said the goblin. "Waiting for connection." There was a long pause. "Lachesis.web system connect denied."

"What?"

"Melchior is unable to create an mweb socket connection," he said. "The system may be down or there may be insufficient system resources at this time. Try again later."

We were being counterjammed. That was very bad. It meant they had me at least partially localized. It also meant Atropos was directly involved. It would take her authority to seal access to a whole node or band of nodes. If she knew it was me . . .

"Right. Melchior, Sidedoor. Execute." The goblin's eyes

glazed over and a low hum emerged from his mouth. After a moment he spoke again. "Unable to open carrier wave connection. Access denied." In a more normal voice, he continued, "Sorry, Boss. It doesn't look good. I can't get in anywhere, and we only have about five more minutes."

"All right. We'll have to take this to extremes. Melchior, Scorched Earth. Execute." His eyes got very wide, and he looked like he wanted to object, but I had phrased it as a direct order.

"Loading."

There was a long pause as Melchior prepped the spell. It was too big to keep in active memory. I had time to wonder if I was going too far. Melchior's voice came again.

"Executing."

No time for second thoughts. Scorched Earth is not a spell that can be aborted halfway. Ultimately, all spells draw power from the same source, the primal chaos that churns between the worlds. But my family mostly uses the predigested forces my grandmother and her sisters channel into the net via their mainframe webservers. Scorched Earth isn't like that. It taps directly into the interworld chaos. That means it's both very dangerous and very powerful. It also means I don't have to have web access to run it. Melchior's voice interrupted my train of thought.

"Scorched Earth successfully implemented," he said.

With those simple words, the nastiest virus I had yet coded was released into the mweb. If it worked, it would scramble the routers for my whole node band and put my great-aunt's webhounds smack in the middle of a data storm. There was no way they'd be able to track me through that. There was even a chance of completely fragging them.

"Uh, Boss," said Melchior.

"Yes. What is it, Mel."

"I just lost contact with the carrier wave."

"I thought you couldn't get in."

"I couldn't, but that's not what I meant. I mean it just cut out completely."

"It can't do that, unless . . ." I trailed off as a really ugly thought occurred to me. I looked at Melchior, and he nodded.

"There's no carrier wave and no mweb line," he said. "I can't even get a ping off the backbone. I think we just took the entire net down, Boss."

"Sweet Necessity," I murmured. "What have I done now?"

Sitting at the desk in my dorm, I cradled my head in my hands. Melchior sat on the floor nearby. For four hours we'd been trying to establish some kind of link to the mweb. Nothing worked. There was very little doubt that we'd crashed the whole damn thing. If this was ever traced back to me, I'd have more to worry about than Atropos.

"Well, Mel, I think it's time we admitted—" He held a hand up.

He cocked his long, pointed ears this way and that for a few moments, then got up and walked to the network jack in the wall. Looking confused, he wetted a fingertip and stuck it into the socket. A moment later he let out a prolonged modulated whistle.

"Uh, Boss. I don't know that you're going to believe this, but you've got new mail."

"Over the local net?"

"Yes, indeedy."

"What is it?"

"It's from Cerice. She wants a visual ASAP."

"Over the local line? That's going to lock a lot of folks out of their online services. Where is she mailing from?"

"Cerice@shara.gob via AOL.com."

"Well, so much for AOL for the next twenty minutes or so. I wonder what she's doing in this DecLocus."

Cerice is even further down Clotho's bloodline than I am Lachesis's, making us something like forty-seventh cousins and barely related, but we're of an age and have been friends since our teens. No one seems to know quite how long the children of Fate might live, but none of the family has yet to die of old age or even to look as though they someday might. If it weren't for a very low birth rate and an actuary's nightmare of violent death—mostly accidental but occasionally with intent—we'd be legion. As it is, there are certainly fewer than five hundred of us and, counting Cerice and me, no more than a dozen under the age of forty. Since I'd thought she was home in Clotho's domain working on a hardware-recycling project she'd been rather intense about of late, finding her here seemed almost too odd.

"Melchior, Vlink; Ravirn@melchior.gob via umn.edu to Cerice@shara.gob via AOL.com. Execute."

"Aye, aye. Searching for shara.gob." I used the brief pause that followed to drop the spell that altered my appearance. "Contact. Waiting for a response from shara.gob. Lock. Annexing extra bandwidth. Vtp linking initiated."

Melchior opened his eyes and mouth wide. Three beams of light—green, blue, and red—shot forth from these orifices intersecting at a point several feet in front of his face. A translucent golden globe appeared at this juncture. It fogged, then filled with the three-dimensional image of a strikingly beautiful young woman. Her hair was so pale as to be almost white. Aside from that, her features bore a strong resemblance to my own, the primary difference being that on her they looked better. She was wearing some sort of formal court gown in a taffeta that seemed to shift from red to gold depending how the light hit it. It was very low cut, but a half jacket prevented it from being indecent.

"Cerice, my darling," I said. "You're as ravishing as ever. It's an absolute pleasure to rest my weary eyes on your delightful features once again." Even under these circumstances I couldn't help but be pleased to see her.

"Charming as always, Ravirn. Your absence must be sorely felt at your grandmother's court."

"Alas, I think not. While Lachesis has some fondness for me, it seems to be in inverse proportion to my proximity. I suspect that my manner charms less than my nature offends."

"Speaking of which," said Cerice, shifting from courtly circumlocution to businesslike directness, "you have a major problem."

"Oh," I replied. The change in gears was jarring.

"Look, I know family politics calls for a lot of polite nonsense and frills before finally broaching the real subject for conversation, but you just don't have the time."

"All right, I'm willing to dispense with formality. I was dying to ask you how you happened to be in this particular DecLocus at this exact moment anyway. I thought you were home."

"I was until twenty minutes ago."

"But—"

She cut me off smoothly. "Yes, I know. The net's down. I hacked into Clotho's mainframe and used it to open a single-use one-way gate."

"That must have been a cast-iron bitch."

She smiled. "It wasn't that bad. You're not the only competent coder in this generation. But I didn't call to exchange hacking tricks. I called to let you know you're in hot water all the way up to your eyeballs."

"How hot?" I asked glumly.

"Atropos wants your head."

Sweat popped out along my brow line. But over an open link I didn't dare talk about what was going on. Also, as much as I liked Cerice, on this topic I didn't dare trust any of Fate's children. Besides, there was no way she'd believe the truth.

"That's not news," I said, leaning back in my chair and trying to look relaxed. "Atropos has always held a special, black little place in her heart for me. It's because of my hacking. She writes lousy security algorithms, then blames me when I demonstrate it to her."

"Ravirn, don't be more of an idiot than usual. We both know she's security-mad. Her firewalls and program killers are better than either Clotho's or Lachesis's. But you're an egotistical bastard, and Atropos is the only opponent you think is worth your effort. Unfortunately, you haven't the wit to crack them without leaving a calling card of some kind so you can gloat about it later."

"Well, yeah, but . . ." I wanted to defend myself, but the only argument I had was one I couldn't make.

"But me no buts. As I said, you haven't the time. Not after you crashed the whole net. That wasn't smart."

"It wasn't actually my intention."

"Intention or not, that was the result, and it's given Atropos the opportunity she's been waiting for. The net wasn't down five minutes before she showed up at Clotho's demesne. They called council, and when Lachesis arrived, Atropos demanded your head. Lachesis apparently has *some* attachment to you, because she absolutely refused to hear of it. Unfortunately for you, Clotho sided with Atropos." Cerice paused and cocked her head to the side. "Though I think that might have been as much to see how well you operated under the pressure as anything. She seems to have a soft spot for you, though I can't imagine why."

I felt a rushing sensation in my head. I had known, in the abstract at least, that something like this could happen, but I hadn't really believed it.

"I'm screwed," I whispered. And I was, in more ways than one. My credibility had just been irrevocably shattered. I *had* to get that spell crystal. Without it, any accusation I laid against Atropos would never be believed. My grandmother would just assume I was seeking revenge.

"Yes." Cerice nodded. "But not quite totally screwed. Atropos couldn't cut your thread without unanimous agreement."

I let out a tiny sigh of relief.

"But with the net crashed and Clotho backing her, Atropos was able to get Lachesis to allow a proxy assassination attempt."

"Who?"

"Moric, Dairn, and Hwyl."

"All three?" My relief vanished. "Just for little old me?"

"Lachesis only agreed to one attempt. Atropos didn't want it to fail."

"When was the conference?"

"About an hour ago."

"Powers and Incarnations, I've got to get moving." I started to tell Melchior to close the connection, then paused. "Cerice, thank you. If I survive, I'll owe you my life. If not . . . Well, if not, I'll still owe you a great deal, but you'll likely have a hard time collecting. I have to know. Why did you warn me?"

She smiled fondly. "Despite your pigheadedness, arrogance, and willful idiocy, you do have an impish sort of charm. The world and I would be the poorer for your passing.

Now get out of there." Her hand waved briefly, then the picture faded away.

"Melchior, log us off and shut down all incoming network traffic."

"Yes sir, right away, sir. Will we be running away now, sir?"

"Damn straight we'll be running away." So much for the promise I'd given Lachesis to improve my grades.

"Very good, sir. Brightest thing you've done all day, sir."

"Don't push your luck, blue boy. I might leave you as a distraction for the assassins. Now, Mel, I want you to— Chaos and Discord!" It hit me like a ton of bricks.

"Ah . . . I'm not sure I'm familiar with that one, Boss."

"Mel, the net's down. The hit team will be coming the same way Cerice did. We have no way of knowing when they'll arrive. For that matter they could be here already."

The impulse to run out the door was almost overwhelming. I choked it down. I had to run, but I had to run smart. Moving as quickly as possible, I grabbed my rapier and a left-handed shoulder holster out of the trunk. When those were strapped on, I leaned down and tapped the combination into the speed-draw gunsafe bolted to the underside of my bed.

The drawer popped open, and I pulled out my beat-on but much loved Colt .45. Before holstering the old Model 1911, I worked the slide to chamber a round, flipped the safety on, and popped the clip. Then I loaded another bullet and returned the clip to the pistol.

As no one had yet broken my door in, I took the time to kick off my boots and jeans and swap them for TechSec racing leathers. Finally, I grabbed the shoulder bag I keep packed for emergencies.

"Come on, Melchior." I opened the flap on my bag. "Let's go."

"It's about time," replied the goblin as he climbed into the bag. "You were moving so slowly I thought you were going to put down roots."

"Listen," I began, then thought better of it. "Later, if I'm still alive, I'm going to rework your OS." I snatched my motorcycle helmet and gauntlets and opened the door.

CHAPTER TWO

On the other side of my dorm door was a huge figure dressed in lamalar armor. From the demon-faced helm a voice said, "Say good night, Gracie." Then a massive fist holding an Afghani punch-dagger slammed into my chest, right over the heart. The blow knocked me halfway across the room. It felt like it cracked a rib as well, but thanks to the multilayer Kevlar lining TechSec built into all its racing gear, it failed to kill me.

I didn't think I'd get that lucky twice. Hand to hand in a small room with my cousin Moric was a recipe for quick death. His abilities as a sorcerer are not fantastic, but for the past couple of hundred years he's been focusing them on physical enhancement. On that score, there aren't many in the family who can match him.

In this case discretion was the *only* part of valor. Unfortunately, he was between me and the door. That left exactly one possible exit. Holding my helmet in front of me, I dived through the windowpane. That solved the immediate problem, but left me outside of the window of my twentieth-floor room.

"Melchior, Fear of Falling. Execute now, now, now!"

The goblin stuck his head out of the bag. "I-aiee! Executing."

We'd dropped nine floors. A prerecorded version of a spell spewed from his tiny blue lips. At a million or so kilobaud it sounded like a whippoorwill on speed, but it did the trick. Three floors above the ground, our headlong plunge became a leisurely drift. I pulled on my helmet and gloves. It looked like I was going to need them before I ever got to my motorcycle.

My feet had barely touched ground when something struck me above the collarbone and burned across my neck. More by reflex than conscious thought I tucked my chin into my chest, so the second arrow struck the chin piece of my helmet instead of my throat. The arrow shattered, my helmet cracked, and my head just about came off. I could taste blood from a mashed lip. Groggily I turned and dashed for River Road and the cover of the cars parked there. Two more arrows hit me in the back as I went but didn't pierce the Kevlar. I was going to need a new jacket and a pile of painkillers, but at least I wasn't leaking any precious bodily fluids.

Once I reached the road, I ducked behind an old Dodge Ram and opened my jacket far enough to grab my pistol. Then I carefully zipped it up again. I needed all the protection I could get. I also needed a plan.

If this conflict stayed purely physical, I was going to die. I am significantly stronger, tougher, and faster than a normal human. But so is everyone in my extended family. When you put me on a scale filled only with my relatives, the picture changes completely. I weigh in firmly in the featherweight division. Moric and his brothers are all ultraheavyweights with attitude.

Unfortunately, I don't do my best thinking under pressure. The arrows smashing into the truck didn't help. A plan would have to wait until I put a little more distance between me and my homicidal cousins. The only problem was how to do that. The archer, probably Dairn, who pulled a 225-pound bow, was shooting at me from the ramp where my cycle was parked.

I couldn't stay where I was. I couldn't get to my bike. Moric would be out of the dorm and back in the game shortly, and Hwyl was out there somewhere as well. To my left, River Road wound past the parking ramp. To the right, it curved sharply north and went under the Washington Avenue bridge. Directly across from me a thin strip of trees masked a steep plunge to the Mississippi. I considered the choices, then, keeping the cars between me and the ramp as much as possible, I headed for the bridge. I was almost there when I heard a low, gurgling growl. Intellectually I'd known Hwyl must be around someplace. Emotionally I'd been pretending he didn't exist. So much for that. I tapped my shoulder bag.

"Mel?" I whispered. "You still alive in there?"

A muffled voice replied, "Battered, but serviceable, Boss. What do you want?"

"Melchior, Redeye. Execute."

"Executing."

My visual range expanded to the infrared, and I peered at the gap under the bridge. A broad, hulking, inhuman shape lurked there. Eyes, lamp bright in the IR, glared at me. Hwyl. Yippee. Careful not to make any sudden movements, I thumbed the .45's safety off.

Hwyl took a step toward me. My intestines did a backflip with a half twist. The things Hwyl has used his magic to do to himself give me the screaming creepies. Forcing myself to move with precision, I snapped the pistol up into line and fired four quick rounds at his knees. I could see bone and tissue shatter and pulp under the impact of the heavy copper-jacketed slugs. Turning to my right, I ran up the slope to the bridge, cursing all the way.

It might take several minutes for Hwyl's injuries to mend, but mend they would, especially with a full moon. Lacking silver weapons, nothing I could do would keep him down. That's why I aimed for the knees. Almost any other wound he could have taken and kept coming, but even a were can't walk with broken knees.

My options were rapidly narrowing. Hwyl had pushed me into a narrow killing ground. On my left was the long, barren expanse of concrete that made up the car deck of the Washington Avenue bridge. On my right the alien stainless-steel angles of the Weisman Art Museum gleamed in the moonlight. The twisted mirrors of its construction threw my distorted reflection back at me. Something about it spoke to me, and I paused to look at it and, finally, to think. I touched the cold metal. The warped picture in its depths seemed to offer me refuge. It was the message I needed.

Turning around, I grabbed hold of one of the I beams that supported the upper deck of the bridge and hand-over-handed my way up it. I crawled over the rail at the top a few yards from the doors to the Weisman. They were locked. They were also glass. A small concrete-and-steel ashtray stood nearby. I picked it up and heaved it through the glass.

A brutal clanging alarm went off. As a sort of counter-point, I could hear the approaching wail of police sirens, probably in response to the gunshots. In a few minutes the whole area was going to be flooded with cops. Unless the officers were very lucky, they were going to end up going toe to toe with my cousins. I winced. But the only thing I could do about it was to remove myself from the equation as quickly as possible.

With that as an additional spur I raced down the main stairs and into the Red Gallery, where the exhibit *A Distorted Mirror: Our World Through the Eyes of the New Surrealists* was housed. I turned left, past the sculpture of a giant melting Chihuahua, and started looking for the right sort of painting.

Before an electronic web tied the worlds together, there had been an artistic one. Almost from humanity's beginning, there have been artists interested in representing and interpreting the world around them. A small but significant number of them can see past their own world to paint the others beyond. In the early years my grandmother and her sisters had used such gateways as their primary means to travel between the spheres.

Of course, as the centuries went by and technology advanced, they developed better and better methods for travel and control, eventually establishing the mweb. It was quick, powerful, and easy to integrate with the growing electronic nets of the inner worlds. But the old ways still existed; they'd just fallen into disuse.

There are drawbacks. Each of the artistic gateways goes to only one other world, and there's no way to reset them. They are also slow to make and difficult to use, to say nothing of the interface. On the other hand, anything that stood a chance of getting me out of this DecLocus alive was worth trying.

"Boss," hissed Melchior, pointing, "how about that one?"

It was clear across the gallery and half-hidden by a pillar, but when I finally spotted it I instantly found myself drawn by its magic-touched jewel tones. And, not only was it a gate, but it even looked like it might go someplace nice, a big plus in my book. I didn't want to cross through into some raving, psychotic artist's personal vision of hell.

"Nice work, Mel." I lifted him out of the bag. "How'd you spot it?"

"Actually," he said, after a long pause, "I remembered it. We came here for class last month."

"Good thing you thought of it," I said, though I was a bit puzzled.

I remembered the trip quite well. I'd needed to write a paper on a piece of sculpture for my art appreciation class. But I'd done all of the work in a different gallery. I didn't think I'd even come into the surrealist exhibit. A sharp yell from outside followed by a couple of shots forced my mind back to the present.

"Mel, I need you to set up a DecLocus transfer to wherever this picture goes. But if we don't want to just continue this on the other side, we're going to need to make sure no one follows us."

He looked at me suspiciously. "How do you propose to do that?"

"You're not going to like this, but it's the only way. Melchior, Burnt Offerings. Exe—"

The little bastard cut me off. "I really don't think that's such a good idea, Boss. Not only is it excruciatingly painful, but if anything goes wrong we could be . . ."

I held up a hand, and he slowed to a stop. This latest example of an unusual amount of initiative made me wonder again about what was up with his programming. I shook my head. Later.

"I don't want to hear it. Melchior, Burnt Offerings. Execute."

"Executing," came the resigned response. Then he waited for me to do my part.

It was my turn to try to think of an excuse to avoid what came next. It was going to hurt, but I couldn't think of any alternative. Sticking the tip of my left pinkie into my mouth, I bit down hard on the first joint. The pain was incredible, and I thought I was going to black out, but it was this or die. I bit down harder. I gagged as the thick salty taste of blood filled my mouth, but kept biting. With a sickening pop, the cartilage gave and the tip of my finger came loose. I spat it onto the floor, then turned and threw up.

When I turned back, Melchior had paired my fingertip with one of his own and, using the blood from his maimed hand, was inscribing a diagram around them. From his bloodied lips came a steady stream of spell data. Now we'd see if it worked. It was a good theory, and I'd run it through my spell-checker looking for bugs a dozen times, but for obvious reasons this wasn't an enchantment I'd been willing to beta-test.

I pulled a sterile wound dressing from my bag and quickly wrapped my finger while Melchior finished the diagram. A moment later the paired fingertips began to swell and metamorphose. Within a minute they had become miniature versions of the goblin and me. Within two they were approaching our size. Within three they had grown to exact duplicates. My consciousness expanded to fill the body of my doppelganger. I opened my second set of eyes and instantly developed a skull-splitting headache. The effort of managing two bodies was bad, but the quadroscopic vision provided by four eyes was the real killer.

At least it wasn't going to last long. One way or another the situation would be resolved in the next few minutes. Not-I reached down and grabbed the fake Melchior. I quickly shoved the contents of the bag into my pockets and handed it to not-me. Not-I took it, put not-Melchior into it, and went out the door of the gallery. I closed my eyes and concentrated on managing not-me. Melchior reversed those priorities, working on opening a preweb DecLocus gateway, while letting not-him sit vacantly in not-my bag.

Not-I staggered a couple of times on the stairs but made it to the main floor without falling. Moric had just arrived.

As not-I watched, there were a couple more shots and sparks danced across the back of his armor. He didn't seem to notice. The armor was modeled on a suit my aunt Electra had designed, and nothing short of an antitank missile was going to breach it. He turned and saw not-me. Smiling, he advanced.

"Ah, dear little Ravirn. How nice of you to come out to meet me. Did you run out of places to hide? Or did you finally remember the nobility of your blood and decide to look your death in the face?"

"Neither," not-I replied. "I decided that if I was going to go, I should at least take one of you with me."

Not-I raised not-my hands and pointed them at Moric. Internally, I braced myself. Then I opened a line into the interworld chaos and let it roar down the channel that led from my body to my doppelganger's. It was like opening my veins and pouring liquid fire into them. Both of my bodies crashed to their knees, and I felt my own right kneecap fracture. Compared to the pain of the linkage it was barely worth noting.

I was intentionally violating every rule I'd ever been taught about the proper management of magical power. Normally we only tap the raw chaos in a very carefully channeled way and take all sorts of precautions to contain it. That's why it can be so dangerous to tamper with even something as simple as a netspider. Muck up the tap and instant charcoal.

I felt the skin of my doppelganger crisping as though it were my own while its underdeveloped nervous and magical channels struggled to handle the overload. There was no chance. My uncle Mordechi had died this way when a particularly involved enchantment melted down on him, and he'd been a better pure sorcerer than I would ever be. It was that death, which I'd had the misfortune to witness from close at hand, that had given me the original idea for Burnt Offerings.

Not-I watched as the power I'd summoned shot from not-my hands and wreathed Moric in flames. His armor protected him from some of the fury, but it couldn't stop all of it, and after only a few seconds it knocked him down. I didn't see what happened after that because not-my eyeballs melted about then.

Agony filled my soul, and I fought like mad to free myself, both from the pain and from the linkage that connected my two bodies. If I couldn't sever the pathway before the chaos tap finished consuming the false me, it would backlash into the real thing and I would go the same way.

I struck at the link with everything I had, but it was very strong. It had to be, forged as it was from the sympathetic resonance between me and the fingertip I had used as a seed for the doppelganger. Symbolically we were part of the same whole, and breaking your own internal self-image apart isn't a task I'd recommend. In fact, it's just about impossible, a circumstance I was discovering to my great dismay. I was going to die.

"Boss!" Melchior's scream came from a distance of millimeters. "Boss! The gate's open. Let's get the hell out of here!" There was pain in his voice. No surprise; not-Melchior must have been getting pretty badly charred in that shoulder bag.

Fighting through the pain, I forced my eyes open. My vision was blurry with tears of pain, but I could still see the depth and life that had come to suffuse the picture. Too bad I wasn't going to live to see the world on the other side. It looked awfully pleasant.

"Thanks, Mel. You've done me proud. Why don't you step through and find someplace nice to settle down? I don't think my great-aunt will leave you in one piece if she

finds you, even if I'm gone. Take care of yourself." I closed
my eyes. It was too hard to keep looking at the escape I'd
almost made.

"Boss, come on. You've got to move. If you don't, they'll
find you."

"Don't worry, Mel. By the time they arrive I'll be ashes.
The doppelganger's just about burned out, and the backlash
should be along to get me in a few seconds. But, thanks for
caring."

"Don't be an idiot, Ravirn. The net's backbone is down.
Once we're through, with the gate closed behind us, the
doppelganger link will be severed."

"What?" I thought about that. He might be right, but
only if I hurried. I had at best five more seconds before not-
I finished flaming out. After that . . .

I reached up and grabbed the edge of the picture frame
with one hand. When I started to stand I rediscovered my
broken knee. My leg folded, and I almost lost my grip. I
had three seconds left. Clenching my teeth, I pulled myself
up and into the picture. The pain as my bad knee hit the
frame joined the feedback from the doppelganger and sent
me tumbling into unconsciousness.

CHAPTER THREE

■ ■ ■

I don't remember what happened next, but I must have gotten lucky and fallen in the right direction, because I woke up an hour later still among the living. My face was pressed into the ground, and the smell of crushed grass with just the faintest compost undertone of decay filled my nostrils. I lifted my head and found myself in another world. I lay on a rounded green hill next to a faerie circle made from crushed beer cans. Melchior sat beside me. I looked at his maimed finger, and guilt washed over me.

"Sorry about the hand, Mel."

"It's okay, Boss. I understand. If that scrawny carcass of yours turned up without mine alongside it, your cousins would never believe they had the real thing. Even with your actual flesh providing the signature, they'd know something was up. It's common knowledge that you couldn't find your ass with both hands and a map without my help."

"You know what, Mel? Because of your recent service above and beyond the call of duty I'm going to ignore that rather than erasing your hard drive and starting from scratch like I ought to." The banter helped keep my mind off how close I'd just come to dying.

"Gosh, Boss, you're all heart."

"I'm glad you think so, because I'm about to put you back to work."

"I can hardly wait," he replied.

"Your enthusiasm overwhelms me. First, let me see that finger." He gave me his hand, and I taped up the finger. "Good. Melchior, Root Access, authorization code— Antigone."

"Root Access granted."

"Lefthand/pinkiefinger/1stknuckle.source," I said, "Terminate Signal. Initiate Recovery Cycle. Run Command, Run Command. Root Exit."

"Exiting Root. Returning to normal operation." He let out a long sigh, and the tension visibly drained out of him. "Oh yeah! Thanks, Boss."

"You're welcome. It doesn't give you your fingertip back, but it'll kill the pain and stop the bleeding. When we have a little leisure and mainframe access, I'll write you a new one. I wish we could fix mine as easily."

The pain, which seemed to have held itself in abeyance until that moment, returned then, as though speaking of the injury had conjured it up. My finger wasn't alone. I had an arrow crease, a couple of cracked ribs, and a myriad of lesser strains and bruises. But it was the horrible throbbing of my right knee that led the rapidly rising symphony of agony. The scary thing was I was still pretty shocky. I didn't want to think about how bad I'd be hurting once I came out of it.

"Let's move this along. Melchior, Better Living Through Chemistry. Execute."

"Executing."

The webgoblin's right index claw lengthened and sharpened, shaping itself into a hypodermic needle. While he was doing that I unzipped the left wrist seal of my jacket and pulled it up, baring the flesh beneath. When I was ready, Melchior formed his hand into a gun and jabbed the claw into the exposed vein. Then he brought his thumb down, sending morphine shooting into my bloodstream. The dose was insanely high, enough to kill a human, and within seconds I could feel it taking hold.

"Much better, Mel. I might even live through the next step." The drug pulsed through my system, moving to the rhythm of my heart. It felt like liquid nitrogen, freezing out sensation. With each beat the cool relief slid a little farther through my veins. "You'll have to open my pants from ankle to hip. Then I'll need a splint."

Some jarring was inevitable while he dealt with the seams. I closed my eyes and let the morphine carry me away to a place where everything was quiet bliss. It was also pink. Not my favorite color, but I didn't feel like arguing. I'm not sure what pulled my awareness back to the place I'd left my body, but when I opened my eyes I found that my leg had been straightened out. I was glad to have missed that bit.

Mel sat on the grass beside my head, watching curiously as a short, gnarled woman with extremely broad shoulders arranged long strips of dried sinew and some old bicycle spokes around my leg. I was about to ask who she was when she pulled the bindings tight. Even through the morphine it felt like someone had placed my knee in an electric pencil sharpener. I decided everything had been better when it was pink and went away again.

I surfaced later in darkness. I lay on a low futon that had seen better days. A faint smell of old dust and mildew flavored the still air. I'd barely stirred before Mel appeared, a small wooden bowl clutched in his hands.

"Here, Boss. Drink this. The troll says it'll help with the pain."

"The troll?" I sat bolt upright, adrenaline overriding pain.

"Calm down," Melchior said. "Ahllan's not that kind of troll. She's a vegetarian."

"Where did you find a vegetarian troll healer?" I said, beginning to relax.

"We're under the hill in the picture. She made the beer-can faerie ring. We're an awfully long way from the primary course of reality. It's a weird version of faerie, oriented around the detritus of urban sprawl and pollution instead of sylvan idyllicism. I don't know what goes on in the head of the artist who painted this gate, but I'd rather not meet his subconscious in a dark alley."

"It sounds bizarre," I said, taking the bowl.

It was full of a dark green liquid with suds on top. It looked terrible and smelled worse, but the pain in my knee was coming back, and Melchior assured me the stuff wasn't toxic. I took a tentative sip. It actually tasted pretty good, something like bananas and cream. I knocked the rest of it back. My catalog of injuries quieted down almost immediately, and shortly I fell into a deep sleep. While I slept, I dreamed.

I was in my dorm, playing around with a new spell. The basic idea had been suggested by something my cousin Laric said at a bar one night. That hurt even in sleep. We'd been good friends since childhood, but he was Moric's first cousin, and probably an enemy now. I called the spell Jurassic Gas. It was a hack, but most of my spells are.

I'm an off-the-cuff sorcerer. I write good code, but I've always preferred quick and dirty to elegant. My real specialty is cracking, unraveling other people's work. Nobody's code is perfect, and I have a talent for finding even the tiniest flaw and exploiting it. What that means is that I've never met a security system I couldn't get around. It also means I'm a whiz-bang debugger, but that's a lot less fun and doesn't really interest me.

My grandmother, on the other hand, finds it to be my primary redeeming feature. That how I ended up at a mid-level school in a backwater reality. Lachesis wanted my talents as a systems analyst honed. She also said I needed to learn discipline. She'd started me out at MIT in one of the primary-reality nodes, but there'd been so much happening there that I hadn't really paid attention to classes and flunked out. The same thing happened at Carnegie Mellon in a secondary node.

When Lachesis signed me up at the U of M, she'd told me in no uncertain terms that the next step was a monastery school at the back end of beyond.

These were the thoughts going through my head as I fine-tuned Jurassic Gas. I had the spell just about where I wanted it when Melchior chimed.

"New mail," he said. "A request for visual."

"From who?"

Melchior shivered a bit. "Atropos."

I quickly reviewed my recent cracking. There had been one or two forays into Atropos's demesne, but only nibbles around the edges. I didn't think she had anything on me.

"Put her through," I replied.

"If you insist." His expression went far away. "Contact. Waiting for a response from Atropos.web. Lock. Vtp linking initiated."

Melchior opened his eyes and mouth wide. Beams of light lanced out, green, blue, and red. But rather than coming together to make a picture as they normally did, the beams struck me full in the face. My vision fogged, the world seemed to go gold, and my stomach told me I was falling. Then I was elsewhere.

The space was a perfect sphere perhaps thirty feet in diameter and enclosed by walls of crystal. Outside, the primal stuff of chaos tumbled and foamed. It looked like a million different colors of dye all being spun in a blender, except that they never mixed, each maintaining its own color as it twisted through and around the others.

I reached toward the nearest arc of crystal, wanting to reassure myself it would keep the chaos on the other side. My arm seemed to move in slow motion, and I realized I was suspended in a thick, clear fluid. Since I didn't seem to be having any trouble breathing, this was something of a shock.

"I'm so glad you could come." The voice from behind me was cool and pure, inhumanly so.

I turned my head and found myself looking into the eyes of Fate. Floating a few feet away was Atropos. I've always had trouble describing my grandmother and her sisters. Oh, the details are there. They're uniformly beautiful, nearly identical in basic appearance. Each is tall and slender with ice-white skin, thick black hair, and fine bones, but somehow those things pale into insignificance beside their eyes.

Clotho is the easiest to face. She's the spinner of destiny, taking the raw stuff of chaos and drawing it into the strands that define lives. She's first and foremost a creator, and there's a vitality to her features that speaks of a love for all things. But it doesn't touch the eyes of Fate.

My grandmother, Lachesis, partakes of some of the same dichotomy. She measures out the lifelines, giving one person a span of a hundred years, and another a mere three and ten. The same basic features that look warm and inviting on Clotho are stern and austere on my grandmother. And again, the eyes are somehow dominant and out of place.

Only Atropos, the cutter of threads, matches her eyes, and it's a likeness that invariably sends nervous shivers along my spine. There's no hint of human emotion in the eyes of Fate. They are eyes in which you can see the knowledge of every single thing you've ever done or thought of doing. Every secret fear that lurks in the shadows of your heart, every petty jealousy, every noble ambition, becomes just another data point in Fate's calculation of your destiny.

I was lost in those eyes. Normally when I'm going to deal with one of the Fates, I have a chance to brace myself. This time I met Atropos's gaze all unprepared. It was the most frightening experience of my life. I have no idea how long she held me, pinned like a butterfly in a specimen case, but eventually she chose to blink, releasing me.

For several minutes, all I could do was breathe. Inhaling and exhaling seemed to take enormous effort. Atropos waited patiently until I had almost recovered.

Then she spoke again in that clear inhuman voice, "You've grown in stature since the last time I saw you, nephew mine." As she spoke, bubbles rose from her mouth and drifted slowly upward. It was distracting.

"Thank you," I replied. "I've been making sure to eat my Wheaties." I'm not certain what impels me to make such statements at times like these, but fortunately Atropos is utterly impervious to sarcasm.

"I'm particularly pleased with how your education has progressed. Lachesis has chosen an excellent course of study for you. With a little judicious pruning you may yet grow into a credit to the tripartite house of Fate."

"Gosh, with all the possible destinies out there to watch,

you've been keeping an eye on mine. I'm touched. I hadn't realized you cared."

"I don't," she said. "Not in the sense you're implying. I see all of those destinies, Ravirn. Every last one has to pass into my hands eventually, even yours." She made a snipping motion with her fingers and smiled.

I felt as though someone had just injected about a thousand cc's of liquid helium directly into my spinal column. Time to change the subject and the tone. I bowed deeply from the waist.

"But I've been forgetting my manners, Madame. I was so startled by my appearance here that I failed in the proper courtesies. Pray forgive my rudeness."

"Think nothing of it, nephew mine."

"Thank you, Madame. I assume you had some service you desired of me, or you wouldn't have taken such drastic steps to assure my attendance on your person. Speaking of which, I had no idea that could be done. However did you manage it?"

"The how really isn't important. Let us go directly to the why."

"As you would have it, Madame. What may I do for you?"

"I am discontent."

"With what?"

"Chaos. The state of the balance. Fortune and her ally Discord have grown too powerful, my sisters and I too weak."

"I doubt that there is much that I might do to help you, Madame. Tyche and Eris are far beyond my humble powers," I said, using the goddesses's proper names.

"I know that, silly boy. But they are not beyond mine, or at least not entirely. I have a few thoughts on how to redress the imbalance. Kalkin!"

She snapped her fingers and a squat, menacing shape slid into view, her webtroll: mainframe supercomputer one minute, ravening carnivore the next. He was big for the breed, almost four feet in height and more than that in width, with skin the color of old bone. Massive shoulders led to apelike arms. His wrists were as big as my thighs and hung on a level with his ankles. Broad, spade-shaped feet sat at the end of legs so short it was hard to tell whether he had knees.

The glare he directed my way suggested he was assessing my potential nutritional value. In any other company he would have been terrifying. With my great-aunt to measure him against, I found myself wondering how much I might be able to get for the ivory of his four-inch tusks.

He extended one thick, three-fingered hand to Atropos. On his palm lay a slender crystal. An eight-sided cylinder about two inches long and half an inch thick, it was a green beyond emerald with glints of gold in the depths.

"What is it?" I asked, though I had a suspicion.

"I call it Puppeteer," she said, picking it up. "It's an extremely sophisticated spell embedded in a memory crystal."

She tossed it my way. It tumbled slowly through the clear fluid, and I was able to catch it easily. Closer inspection revealed that the gold I'd seen from a distance was an incredibly complex, three-dimensional latticework running like a tracery of veins through the body of the stone.

"It's beautiful," I said. "I knew you were without peer as a coder of spells, Madame. I hadn't realized you were an artist as well. This is magnificent. I've never seen anything so intricate."

"Lamentably, beautiful is all that it is at the current time." She sighed then, and it seemed a very strange thing to hear Fate sigh. "There is a flaw in the spell, one I haven't been able to find."

"I think I begin to see."

She nodded. "I think you do. Lachesis's reports of your

growing abilities have been quite glowing. The independent corroboration I've gained as you hover around the edges of my security implies that she is not far off in her estimate of your skills."

"You want me to find the flaw."

"I do."

"How do my grandmother and Clotho feel about this?" I held the gem in front of my eye and peered through it at her.

"I haven't discussed it with them, but I think they will see the value of my ploy once it's in place. Free will is such an inconvenience." She smiled coldly. "You should see good value as well. With a tighter grip on the reins of destiny, I shall be able to reward you quite handsomely."

"That does sound nice," I said.

Actually, the thought of what Atropos might do once she'd gutted the concept of free will was a waking nightmare. But I was dancing on the cliff edge, and when I looked into the gulf I couldn't see a bottom. I had to be very careful if I didn't want this to be my last conversation. Though she couldn't cut my thread arbitrarily, there were more straight-forward ways she could make an end of me.

"Good then," said Atropos. "It's settled."

"Actually, I'd like to have a brief word with my grand-mother. Of late she's been most critical of how I've been using my skills and time. I shouldn't want to do anything like this without getting her permission first. You under-stand, I'm sure." I handed the stone back.

"Don't try my patience, nephew. You'll find it isn't very deep."

"I would never try your patience, Madame. I'm a wiser man than that, but I must give my first loyalty to my grand-mother. So, if you'll excuse me, I do have midterms to study for."

She made a grabbing gesture, and seemingly from nowhere a glowing strand appeared. She strummed it lightly, and my bones vibrated like a plucked harp string. I realized she was holding my life thread. It made my skeleton itch. "It would be a shame if I had to tie this in knots. There are many things worse than death, young Ravirn. Remember that. I'll let you go this time. But only for a very little while. You *will* help me."

I bowed again. "In whatever way I feel I can, of course."

"Weasel words won't help you. Nor will my sisters. I am not yet ready for this to reach their ears. Since you have spurned me as Cassandra spurned Apollo, I think I will give you something of the same gift he gave to her."

She whistled a long stanza, harmonizing with herself. It was in hex rather than binary and faster than anything a webgoblin could do. I felt the spell reach out and tie itself around my mouth and voice. I wasn't able to make out a tenth of what she put into it, but I didn't need to. I was familiar with Cassandra's story. Apollo had given her the gift of true prophecy, with the caveat that no one would believe a word she said about her visions. While Atropos would never give me the gift of prophecy, binding my words so they wouldn't be believed when I spoke against her was completely in character. I bowed in acknowledgment of her cleverness.

"Very nice. You've closed my mouth most effectively, Madame." As I spoke I felt a sensation in my lips like the tingling of a limb that has been asleep.

Her smile broadened. "My goodness," she said. "I know what I've done, and yet when *you* say it, even I have a hard time believing it. How marvelous."

"Isn't it?" I replied. "I applaud your inventiveness." The tingling came again, but worse than that was the sarcasm I heard in my own voice. It was so thick that *I* didn't believe me. Atropos had just put a sharp kink in the strand of my life.

"Good-bye, nephew mine. I'll see you soon, I trust."

She waved her hand dismissively, and I felt myself fading into nothingness.

CHAPTER FOUR

I woke covered in sweat. When I tried to sit up the blinding pain in my knee reminded me of where I was. It also reminded me that my circumstances were worse than any nightmare. My meeting with my great-aunt had been entirely real. Likewise, my attempt to sneak into her demesne and steal the Puppeteer crystal and all that followed.

The Cassandra curse was one of the nastiest spells I'd ever encountered. Even Melchior hadn't believed me at first. I'd been forced to go into his command line and program him to believe me on the topic. And I hadn't been sure that would work before I actually did it. Every other kind of writing I'd tried had proven ineffective at circumventing the spell. The problem was that it focused on belief. I could tell anyone anything I wanted to, in any way I could imagine, and I'd tried quite a few of them, but I was simply unbelievable in every possible form of communication. I couldn't break it either. Only the caster could do that. I was well and truly in the soup.

I also had a bladder that felt about ready to explode. That at least I could do something about. Leaning over, I conveyed my distress to Melchior, who went to find our hostess.

When he opened the door, dim yellow light flooded the room. It was low and domed like the inside of a yurt, the walls and ceiling lined with pictures cut from magazines. They were of all shapes and sizes, arranged without thought of straight lines. Color dominated rather than subject, dark reds and oranges for an effect something like brickwork laid by an insane mason. Yet it was somehow soothing. My futon was covered by a variety of patchwork quilts that smelled of a long stay in a dusty cedar chest. The floor was thick with rag rugs. Both bedding and rugs were of the same warm-brick colors as the walls.

The troll couldn't have been far away, because she arrived within a minute or two of Mel's departure. She wasn't much more than three feet tall, but she was nearly that wide. Her skin was the brown of a peeled apple left too long on the counter. Her wrinkled features had something of that same shrunken apple about them. Her forehead was low, her black eyes small, her cheeks round and lumpy. A heavy jaw dominated her face, with broad upthrusting tusks that came to wicked points on either side of her wide nose.

In short, she bore an uncomfortable resemblance to my great-aunt's familiar. But Melchior had assured me of her goodwill, and there was a strange nurturing quality about her. Someone from a gentler family than mine might even have called her grandmotherly. I found myself trusting her.

She smiled graciously at me, exposing a row of gnarled teeth that had a distinctly carnivorous look to them. I smiled back. Stepping close, she lifted me as though I weighed nothing and carried me down a hall to the bathroom. In the process I got a better idea of what the house underhill looked like. All of the rooms were decorated in the same style as my sleeping room; only the colors and scrap materials varied.

Making use of the facilities was not something I enjoyed in the least. Suffice it to say that I needed help, and the procedure was painful. I was sweating and shaking when I returned to bed, but I was beginning to feel like I might survive.

I wanted to talk with Ahllan, but she wasn't having any chitchat. Instead she gave me another drink of the cream-and-bananas mixture.

"Boss, wake up." Melchior gently shook me.

"Wha, ahhumm, what?" I grogged, through a yawn.

"I just got a ping off the mweb. Looks like it's back up."

"You mean it's been down all this time? Bugger. How long has it been?"

"Something like twenty-two hours subjective, but I don't know about real time. This world's way out of the main-stream of reality. Shall I query the Fateclock?"

"Yes, do that. Then why don't you check our mail? Hmm . . ." We'd need to do this very carefully. "Melchior, initiate Sidedoor Link. Execute.

"Executing," said the goblin. "Waiting for connection." There was a long pause. "Connecting, bandwidth very low. Real-time video and audio unavailable. Sending password as admin. Logon as admin confirmed. We're in. It's been six hours, twenty-seven minutes, and eighteen seconds objective since the mweb went down."

"Powers and Incarnations! My grandmother is going to have me stuffed and mounted. Melchior, Secure Mail. Execute."

"Executing. Finding mail host. Accessing host. Bypassing security. Downloading mail." The statements came in staccato bursts with long pauses between as he waited for data to move through the slow connection. "The only thing in the queue's a note from Cerice."

"What's it say?" I asked.

"You want it verbatim?"

"No, what's the gist?"

"She hopes you're still alive to get this."

"That's a sentiment I can endorse. What else?"

"If you'd listen instead of running your mouth you'd know."

I waved an admonishing finger, but my heart wasn't really in it. I owed Melchior too much to treat him harshly. Not that I could let him know that, or I'd never get another jot of work out of him.

He continued. "She also wants you to check in and let her know what's happened as soon as possible. She sounds rather concerned for your welfare, though I can't imagine why. You're far more trouble than she deserves."

"Mel, you're opinionating again."

"Was I? Heavens! I hadn't noticed. I'd better be more careful!"

I sighed. "Forget it. Just send a reply. Tell her I'm alive—"

"Barely," said Mel.

"Hit the high points of where we are and how we got here. Tell her I owe her big-time, tag on some flowery language, and send it."

"Compiling," he said, an abstracted look in his eyes. "Editing. Embellishing. Send-aieee!" He jumped as though he'd been goosed.

"What's the matter, Mel?"

"I don't know. I was accessing the smtp server when I got a big jolt, like I'd stuck my finger in a socket. I'm not sure what happ . . ." He trailed off and pointed at the floor by the foot of my bed.

I felt a shiver run down my spine. A pale blue light shone there as though from an overhead spotlight, the unmistakable signature of an incoming locus transfer.

My first impulse was to run for it, but there was no way I was going to get an ltp link set up and gate out in time. Hell, in the shape I was in, I probably couldn't even get out of bed. I pulled my .45 from the holster Melchior had hung on the headboard.

Like an image fading in on a piece of instamatic film, a figure appeared in the light. It carried a slender sword in its right hand and a diamond-shaped buckler in its left. Red-and-gold lamalar armor covered it from head to toe, and for a second I thought Moric had returned from the dead. I pulled the trigger convulsively in the instant the light vanished, when the figure would be most vulnerable.

But she—and I realized it was a woman then, her breastplate left little doubt—brought her left arm up with a speed that defied vision. Buckler met bullet, and the latter vanished as though it had never been. Before I could fire again she was at the side of my bed. She flicked her blade, slapping the back of my gun hand. There was a flash at the contact, and my arm went numb. The pistol slid from my limp grasp, and the tip of her sword moved to hover above my left eye.

It was impossible to focus on something that close, and I didn't really want to think about it in any case, so I shifted my attention to the woman. She was tall and slender, qualities emphasized by her armor. With this second look I found myself wondering how I could ever have mistaken her for Moric. Besides the obvious clue of the breastplate, the helm was wrong. Instead of a Samurai's demon face, this helm bore the classic T-slit of a Greek hoplite. The colors were wrong as well. Moric's primary was red, but dried blood, not flame. Even more of a contrast, his secondary was bruise blue, miles away from my visitor's cheery gold.

"You have me at a disadvantage, madam," I said.

"Only through the agency of your own idiocy!" The voice was muffled by the golden glass that sealed the T of her helm, but anger suffused it.

"Pardon?"

"I go to all the trouble of pulling your sorry tail out from under the rocker, and what's the first thing you do? Check your e-mail. Fool!"

"Cerice?"

"Of course it's Cerice," she said, sheathing her sword. "Do you think you'd still be alive if it wasn't? Honestly, I don't think you have the sense of a lobotomized tree sloth."

She reached up and caught the crest of her helm, pulling it off. Her long icy hair was braided and bound twice around her head in a coronet that looked elegant while providing an added layer of shock protection. She turned to my familiar, who had just appeared from somewhere in the vicinity of the headboard.

"I don't know how you put up with it, Mel."

"It's a trial, but who else is going to take care of him? Did you bring Shara?"

In response she pulled a virulently purple laptop out of a compartment in the back of her armor. She set it on the floor, where it stretched and twisted into an equally purple webgoblin. Shara was built on a sort of exaggerated hourglass model, and when she moved she swayed a great deal more than mere locomotion required.

In appearance she's sort of a miniature version of Mae West except that her teeth are wickedly sharp, and her hair tends to move of its own accord. As soon as her transformation was complete, she winked one violet eye at Mel and nodded for him to follow her into the corner. The pair scampered off to talk about whatever it is that familiars talk about, and Cerice returned her attention to me.

"Where was I?" she asked.

"I believe you were dressing me down for blatant stupidity."

"Thank you," she said in a sweet contralto, and it was obvious she meant it. Then she proceeded to chew me out in terms any drill sergeant would have been proud of.

"If you're ready to take a breather," I said when she ran down, "I've got a couple of questions and a request."

"What are they?"

"First, how did you find me?"

She paused for a moment, as though weighing her words before speaking. "Isn't it obvious? I embedded a virus in my message to you. It did a quick location scan when you downloaded it. When you went to send a reply, it hitched a ride on the carrier wave to tell me where it was."

That didn't sound feasible, but who was I to argue with success.

"The rest was easy," she continued, "since you hadn't even bothered to set up the most rudimentary wards. I'm frankly shocked that either tactic worked, but that just goes to illustrate my earlier point about your being a low-grade moron. At least you had the sense to shoot first and ask questions later when I arrived. Not that it would have helped if that was the best you could do. Oh, Ravirn." This last was said with a sort of gentle affection as she took a seat beside me on the low bed. Pulling her gauntlets off, she took my right hand between hers. "What am I going to do with you?"

"I could entertain a couple of thoughts on the subject, but they might be best discussed at a later time, as I'm currently somewhat incapacitated. Besides, I have other, more immediate concerns. For example, do you think anyone else could duplicate your performance?"

"Absolutely not," she said.

I wondered at her conviction. There are very few things one hacker can do that another can't replicate. Clearly she knew something she didn't believe anyone else did. But it would have been both rude and futile to try to get her to reveal her hole card.

She continued, "I did find a couple of watchdog programs staking out your e-mail server, but they weren't exactly grade one. I doubt they could have backtracked the link you used to access the mail queue. I tried that and got lost in a maze of subroutines. I'd really like to know how you did that."

"If you ask very sweetly, I might be willing to trade techniques," I replied. "Melchior runs a heavy-duty virus scan on all incoming mail, and I'd love to know why he didn't catch yours."

"Perhaps he wasn't looking in the right place."

"I'll have to think about that. In the meantime I still have a pending request."

"You do indeed. What is it?"

"I'd like you to take a look at my injuries and see what you can do. You're better with healing magic than I am, and I'm feeling awfully vulnerable stuck here on my back."

"I'm sorry," she said, touching the bandage on my neck. "I should have done that before I snarled at you. You do look a bit like a Rottweiler's favorite chew toy." She shook a finger admonishingly. "That doesn't mean I shouldn't have said any of that. I just should have taken care of your injuries first. Let me get a bit more comfortable, then I'll have a look."

She quickly stripped off her armor and padding. Underneath she wore scarlet tights and a very thin gold tunic, neither of which did much to conceal her form. She was tall and slender, with long legs and high, small breasts. Her eyes were a blue that was simultaneously quite pale and shockingly intense. She unbraided her hair and let it fall in a long, white cascade, almost covering ears that were slightly more finely pointed than mine. Her nose was small and straight, with just a hint of an upturn at the tip. High cheekbones and a pointed jaw framed a generous mouth and full lips.

"Gods, but I hate armor," she said, stretching lithely. It was worth watching. "It always feels like a poorly fitted underwire bra worn over the whole body." She grinned. "But that probably doesn't mean much to you, does it."

I shrugged.

"Of course not." She dropped onto the bed next to me. "I'm going to start now, don't move."

I lay very still while Cerice worked on me. A quietly whistled spell and a gentle caress that traced the line of the arrow crease on my neck sealed the wound. As Cerice leaned over me to work, it became very hard to keep my mind off the fact that she was an extremely attractive woman. After taking care of my neck, she stripped the blanket down to my waist and started to unwrap the bandages around my cracked ribs.

"Oh my," she said as she peeled the last of the tape and gauze away.

From the hips upward my skin was a mottled mix of yellow and purple. I was about to tell her it felt better than it looked when she placed her palms firmly on my chest. Her hands were very cold, and I let out a startled yip. One corner of her mouth turned up in a sort of mischievous half smile, but she didn't say a word. Instead, she started to hum. The sound came from deep in her throat and slid weirdly up and down the scale. As she hummed, she slowly slid her hands down my sides. They started out icy cold, but seemed almost painfully hot when they eventually came to rest with her thumbs pressed into the soft flesh inside the points of my hips.

"Breathe," she said, her half smile becoming a full one.

Sheepishly, I drew in a great lungful of air and with it the scent of Cerice. It was sweet with the fragrance of her lilac perfume, and sharp with perspiration brought on by her magical labors on my behalf. I was suddenly very aware that her hands were still pressed tightly against my hips. They lingered there for just a moment longer. Then she reached up to take my left hand. I felt the touch of her fingers long after they had moved on.

She kneaded my injured hand between her own, then shook her head. "What the hell did you do?"

For the first time since I'd bitten off my fingertip I really looked at my pinkie. The end of it was gone of course. That was no surprise. What was startling was the fact that the finger looked as though it had never possessed another knuckle. It ended in smooth clean flesh without a trace of scarring. Anyone who didn't know that I used to have a normal finger would have assumed it was a birth defect.

"I bit it off," I said.

"You what!?" she asked, plainly appalled.

"I had to. It was for a spell. I'd be dead if I hadn't."

"I guess it's a fair trade then."

"What do you mean?" I asked.

"The injury is permanent. Open your inner eye and you'll see what I mean."

Viewed with the second sight, the missing knuckle appeared still to be on my hand, but it was completely magically dead. It looked as though it had been sorcerously cauterized, which I suppose it had.

Then I had to go back and give Cerice the whole story from the point at which I'd escaped from Atropos's bedroom. I knew she wouldn't believe a word I said if I told her my real reasons for being there, so I said it had been something of a fishing expedition. She let me get away with that, probably because of my injuries, but it was plain she wasn't really satisfied. Whether that was due to some subtle effect of the curse or just her natural skepticism, I couldn't tell. Either way, I was going to have to give her more information at some later point if I wanted to stay in her good graces, which was, I discovered, a place I very much wanted to be. After I'd brought her up to date, she took a look at my knee.

"You really got yourself torn up, didn't you, Ravirn?" she asked after a few minutes. "This knee needs the help of a good surgeon who won't ask too many awkward questions. Fortunately, I know just the fellow."

"I'm not sure I understand."

"You busted the cap into a lot of little, tiny pieces. Your anterior meniscus has multiple tears, and the rest of your cartilage looks like it went through a salad shooter. It'd take a really good orthopedist ten hours just to piece the cap back together. Combined with the other damage, you're looking at several months of recovery, years if you were human, and a lot of really vicious physical therapy."

"I can't afford that much time with restricted mobility, Cerice. There are too many people who'd like to see me dead."

"I know. That's why I said what I did. I can cast spells that'll weld the bone back into one piece, and seal up the various other holes you've put in the tissue. But it's all scrambled, and I'm not sure where everything belongs. My surgeon friend can put the jigsaw in the right order, after which I can fix it properly. Call it eight hours on the operating table, ninety minutes of spell work, and about a week convalescing."

"I can't do that. If Burnt Offerings worked, Atropos believes I'm dead. I need her to keep believing that at least until I'm healthy enough to run. Otherwise, I might as well hand her my head in person. Every ltp link uses the Fate servers and shows up in the routine data reports. You know that as well as I do. Even with a really clean hack to block my signature, I'd be running a risk that Atropos would spot me. If that happens, I'm dead. It's got to be here, and it's got to be you, Cerice. I don't have anybody else."

"The other Fates only agreed to one attempt on your life. You should be safe enough."

"Do you honestly believe Atropos is going to let me go after I killed Moric?"

"I don't like it," said Cerice, biting her lip. "If this isn't done right, it could cause you problems for the rest of your life."

"If Atropos finds me before I can defend myself, there won't be a rest of my life."

She glared at me and looked like she wanted to argue.

"Please," I said. Her shoulders dropped.

"Oh, all right. I'll do it, but I'm not going to take responsibility if you end up with a permanent limp."

"Thank you."

CHAPTER FIVE

After five straight days of bed rest I was starting to crack. Few things in life are as frustrating as being told you have to lie still and take it easy when you're feeling better. I can't say I felt good, more like I'd been run over by a small car. But that was so much better than I'd felt when I arrived, it seemed I should have been out running marathons. Instead, I was spending my time staring at the ceiling of Ahllan's guest room.

That was another thing I wasn't any too happy about. If I had to be in a hospital, I'd prefer it were an expensive private one with all the amenities, including attractive young women in white uniforms who will wipe my brow when I buzz for them. But instead of electric lights and adjustable beds, I had an oil lamp and a battered futon. Worse, when I needed something, I rang a bell that summoned a sweet but esthetically challenged troll matron to my bedside. Ahllan wasn't about to let me get up either. Cerice had subverted her somehow, and nothing I did or said by way of bribery or cajoling had any effect on my treatment. That only left threats, and you simply don't threaten trolls, vegetarian or not.

My encounter with the cousins and its aftermath had suggested a couple of spells to me. So I'd spent some time jacked in and coding. But once that was finished, there wasn't much to do besides computer games, and there's only so much video poker you can play. This is particularly true if your laptop makes snide remarks when you lose a hand. I suspected him of cheating, but had no way to prove it.

Such was my state of mind when a column of blue light appeared beside my bed. This time Cerice had skipped the armor. She wore a pale red blouse, a deeper red skirt, and a braided gold belt. Her hair fell in loose waves to her waist. Shara stood beside her in goblin form.

I ignored them. Cerice was the one who'd put me in Ahllan's care, and, besides, I had a card game to finish, one I was winning for a change. Suddenly my game was replaced by an error message.

The application Hold Em has unexpectedly quit. Please save and close all applications and return your computer to its webgoblin shape.

A high evil chuckle sounded in my ear. Shara had climbed up next to my pillow. I resisted an urge to stick my tongue out at her. She'd probably have bitten it. Webgoblins have a low and petty sense of humor.

"I've never seen an error message quite like that one," Cerice said, leaning over me. Cross as I was, I couldn't resist the opportunity to draw in a lungful of her lilac perfume. "I suspect your sidekick has one-upped his boss."

"Well," I replied, "he can suffer for it then. I'm going to leave him in laptop shape and see how he likes that."

"My, aren't we snippy this morning?" asked Cerice, plopping herself down on the bed. "Maybe I shouldn't spring you from this joint."

My pointed ears perked forward at that. The chance to escape from my convalescent prison sounded like a ticket to the Elysian fields. I sighed and typed the command to change Melchior back into his goblin shape. He and Shara headed off to do goblin things, and Cerice smiled at me and rang the bell. Ahllan appeared at once and, after Cerice gave the word, allowed me to pull on a loose green tunic and shorts.

Then the troll carried me out into the sunshine, setting me down on a nearby hill as gently as a mother dog putting her puppy in the den. For obvious reasons, we didn't want to be too close to the faerie ring. That's how quaint folktales and other nasty accidents happen. The crown of the hill wore a wreath of bent crab apples, one of which provided me with a backrest as I surveyed the landscape. Cerice joined me there, and for a long time we didn't move, sitting shoulder to shoulder in companionable silence.

"Odd sort of landscape," said Cerice, finally.

The trees were all low and twisted into fantastic shapes. The dominant ground cover was Creeping Charlie. Odd bits of trash were scattered everywhere, punctuated by the occasional enormous dump pile. No matter which way the wind blew it carried a faint flavor of decaying vegetation. Yet there was a strange beauty to it all. Wild grape and other creepers were waging war on the junk and winning. Near us, a colony of morning glories had converted a rusted-out Chevy Malibu into a floral topiary in a crazy quilt of emerald and pink.

"Still, there's something appealing to it," I said after a few moments.

Cerice nodded and squeezed my hand. "It must be the glamour of faerie. The air here is saturated with raw magic."

"Is it, my lady?" I asked. I'd been outside long enough for my disposition to mellow, and my court manners were returning. "I hadn't realized it was in the air. I thought the magic arose from the proximity of your most lovely person."

"My goodness. Ravirn the prince has returned at last. I had begun to believe that the reason our gracious and charming hostess was taking such good care of you was that you bore a resemblance to her long-lost offspring."

"I have been a bit of a troll these last few days, haven't I?" I replied, softly. Resolving to make amends, I rolled up onto my good knee, extending my bad leg behind me, and faced Cerice. "I must beg your forgiveness and indulgence for my behavior. My only excuse is extreme pain, compounded by a dose of awareness that eternal youth does not immortality make."

A frown chased itself across her delicate features. "You did make it down to the very banks of the Styx, didn't you? Figuratively speaking, of course."

I nodded. "I came so close I could almost have lent Moric the coins to pay the ferryman and waved him on his way." I shuddered. I didn't like Moric, and I had far rather it was him than me, but I wished our encounter could have ended in some other fashion. "Were it not for you, my lady, I might even now be wandering that far shore. I owe you everything, Cerice. I am at your service for whatever you might ask."

"I think that I shall begin with this." She leaned forward and placed her soft lips against mine.

That first contact was like white fire, and it burned all the way to my toes. I couldn't say how long we sat like that, nothing touching but our lips. In retrospect the kiss seems fleeting, but at the time it was my whole world. Some eternal moment later I felt her lips open under mine and her arms reach around my neck. I'm sure my hands were similarly engaged, but the memory is gone. We shifted, trying to get closer together without letting our lips part. It was wonderful, but it meant a good deal of twisting about, and my injured knee hit a root. I shrieked and curled into a ball.

"What happened?" she asked.

"Kiss! Wow! Knee! Root! Bad!" I lay on my side facing away from her, my hands clutching my injury.

"How articulate. I told you it wouldn't heal well if I did all the work. Let me look at it." She leaned into my field of view, and I saw that her blouse had somehow become partially unbuttoned, exposing an ivory breast tipped with the palest pink flower of a nipple. I lost interest in my knee.

After a few seconds, so did Cerice. I have only fragmentary impressions of what happened next, brief but incredibly vivid snapshots. Sliding my hands along her ribs to cup her breasts. Tearing the button off her skirt when I couldn't figure out how to get it unfastened. Feeling her teeth playfully nipping at the hollow of my thigh. An incredible burst of lilac as I buried my face in the triangle at the base of her belly. Kisses that came as suddenly and surprisingly as summer lightning on a dark night. Cerice's face twisted into a mask of wild emotion. The sun lighting her hair like a white waterfall as she moved atop me. A climax that started somewhere around the base of my skull and shot down my spine, arching me like a bow.

When it was over Cerice laid her length on me, still clutching me tightly with her inner muscles. She was as tall as I, and her hair cascaded down around our faces, enclosing us in curtain of privacy. Her slit-pupiled eyes shone blue fire at me from a distance of inches, and the scent of lilacs filled my nostrils. I was content in a way I had rarely been before. This was not my first time by any means, but it felt different somehow. I wasn't sure what to do or say about that, so I contented myself with silence and a careful study of Cerice's fine-boned features.

"What are you thinking?" she asked after a while.

I reached for words, and found, "I was thinking that we skipped a step."

"Huh?" She looked confused.

"Well, I think very highly of you. I like your personality, your looks, your style, your devious hacker brain; in short, everything about you. I've felt that way for some years now, and intended to ask you out on something of a formal date, and yet I've never gotten around to doing anything about it. Now, we've skipped the whole courting phase and leaped into bed."

Her laugh was rich and mellow, like fresh apple juice after a day in the sun. "How very sweet of you, Ravirn. Perhaps the courtier is the real you, and the scrappy ruffian is the mask. I was just thinking that I should have done this ages ago, knocked you over and ravished you, that is. It's been on my list of things to do practically forever. Though I must admit I like the sound of courting as much as any woman."

"Well then, courting you shall have. I rather think we should make something more of this than a wild afternoon. That means doing things right. And doing things right means a proper beginning. Perhaps an elegant dinner with candlelight and china at a fine restaurant in Paris, followed by slow dancing, and a moonlight walk along the Seine? How does that sound to you?"

"I'll think about it. However"—she laughed again, although this time with a wicked undertone—"since we're already in a compromising position, I intend to take shameless advantage of you."

Her hands slid down to the place where we were conjoined and did highly dexterous things. My response was immediate, involuntary, and wholehearted. *Shameless advantage*, she'd said, and she was true to her word, several times.

* * *

The futon in Ahllan's guest room wasn't quite a Parisian inn, but it was wide enough for two, and that's where we ended our day.

"I wish this moment could last forever," I said.

"Nothing lasts forever," said Cerice, lifting her head from my chest. "I'm going to have to leave soon. My doctoral duties are calling. I've learned some things at the new experimental computing department at Harvard that I think will help with this computer-recycling project I'm working on." She frowned, and her voice became tight. "I can't stand all the waste. The family of Fate needs to realize there are places to take an old system besides the junk heap. It makes me so mad sometimes, I . . . No, never mind. I don't want to start that discussion now. What I started to say was that I've got an oral exam tomorrow. If I miss it, Clotho will have a fit."

I sighed. "I empathize. Lachesis isn't going to forgive me anytime soon for bringing the mweb down. Missing midterms on top of that has guaranteed my place at the top of her shit list. I promised her I'd do well in my studies this year. Now she's never going to believe another word I say."

Of course, that was because of the curse, but I couldn't tell Cerice that. I couldn't tell Cerice anything without sounding like the worst sort of liar. I wanted to tell her everything, to let her know I hadn't hacked Atropos.web and crashed the mweb just for the fun of it. But I couldn't. Atropos hadn't just shut my mouth, she'd put an invisible cage around me. I was a prisoner of silence.

Cerice didn't say anything more either, and we lay quietly and held each other until the door banged open.

"Rise and shine," said Shara, poking her head into the room. "You've got a test to take." Melchior followed her in.

"That's my exit cue," said Cerice, rolling out of bed.

She started pulling on her clothes. When she got to the skirt with the missing button, she looked irritated. "I wish you'd let me handle that," she said, producing a safety pin from somewhere.

"I'm sorry. Do you want me to fix it?"

"I don't have the time."

"Maybe when I see you next," I said. I'd really enjoyed our day together, and I wanted a repeat as soon as possible.

"I'm sure it'll be fixed before that," said Cerice, without even glancing my way. "Shara, initiate ltp link; Mtp://mweb. DecLocus.prime.minus0208/harvard.edu~markhamdorm 217. Execute."

"Executing," said Shara. She worked quickly, getting an active gate up in no time.

Cerice stepped into the column of light.

"Wait," I called. "When *can* I see you next?"

"I don't know. My schedule's going to be awful for the next month or two. Drop me an e-mail, and we'll see if we can work something out. *Ciao.*"

"But, Cerice, I—" It was too late. She was gone, and I missed her already.

"Ouch," said Melchior, shaking his head.

"What?" I asked.

"Nothing really, but the only other place I've seen a brushback like that was on a baseball field."

I wanted to argue, but found I couldn't. She *had* thrown her parting comment like a pitcher trying to move a batter away from the plate. That hurt. It also seemed perfectly emblematic of how things had gone ever since my little tête-à-tête with Atropos about Puppeteer. I'd finally found a woman who I thought I might be able to build a relationship with, and she'd loved me and left me. I tried to go back to sleep, but being alone with the scent of lilacs lingering in the air was simply too much.

I decided it was time I stopped back at my dorm. I'd left some important things there in the escape from my cousins, like Melchior's backups, and my extra spell files and research materials. If I wanted to have another go at Atropos, I'd need all of it. Sighing wearily, I ordered Melchior to take us home. My knee felt like someone had put a burr under the cap, but I thought I could run if I had to, and I didn't know how much time I had left to stop Atropos.

As Melchior set up the ltp link, I sent a mental request to the faceless goddess of Necessity to allow my doppelganger ploy to have worked. Being dead for a while would come in mighty handy.

Before I left I recorded a quick message for Cerice, "Cerice, I don't think I'm going to say this very well. Glib is my natural style, and this calls for . . . something else. Today was special. I'm feeling things for you that I'd like to explore in depth. I want this to be more than just a passing fancy. I know you said you'd be busy, but please get in touch with me soon. I want to see you again."

"Sign it and send it," I told Melchior. "Then we're out of here." He looked as though he was thinking about adding some editorial commentary, but he must have read my look because he just nodded.

My dorm had never seemed so appallingly dingy. Fifteen days had passed in the U of M Decision Locus and Rod hadn't taken the desecration of his beloved Toby Keith poster lightly. The beer he'd poured on my bed in revenge had had time to go completely skunky, almost masking the smell of Rod's widely scattered dirty clothes. Rod's cleaning skills were rudimentary at best, but he'd really outdone himself this time. I wasn't planning on staying, but if I ever wanted to return, I couldn't leave things as they were.

"Melchior, White Tornado. Execute."

Mel gave me a particularly nasty look before going into berserk cleaning mode. While he tidied the general mess I went after the bed. My blanket and sheets would have to go straight into a trash bag. I thought the pillow might be salvageable, but decided to flip it off the bed with my rapier in case Rod had done something nasty to it as well.

As the tip of my sword touched the pillow, there came a flash of black like a little explosion of night and a shock of magic raced up the steel to my hand. The flesh of my palm began to blister even before the blackness started to flow up the blade. As the dark cloud slid toward me, the tempered steel of the sword wilted like a candle in a furnace.

Turning, I threw my blade. The hilt ripped free of my burned hand with an awful popping sound in the instant before the darkness consumed it. Plywood covered the lower half of the window, but the mass of blackness and molten metal punched right through, leaving a smoking hole in its wake.

"Melchior, Program Abort. Execute."

My voice was clear and calm. It was shock of course, but I'd take what I could get. Melchior stopped cleaning.

"Come here and tell me how bad this is," I said.

I didn't want to look at it, not when it hurt that much. And not with the scent of burned meat hanging in the air.

After inspecting the damage he let out a low whistle. "Ouch! Either Rod's getting more sophisticated in the revenge department, or Atropos wasn't content with the results of her hit team. I wonder how she knew you were still alive."

"Who knows? She could have seen through Burnt Offerings, or checked my life thread in the Fate Core, or even just e-mailed Hades about whether I'd arrived or not. How isn't important. The question is, what the hell do I do now?"

"You could start by thanking Rod for being such a shit-head," said Melchior.

I had to agree. Under any other circumstances I'd probably have flopped into my bunk when I got in, and if that had been my head hitting the pillow instead of my sword . . . I was going to have to start being very careful. The official attempt on my life might have failed, but that didn't mean Atropos was going to kiss and make up.

"Hey, Boss," said Melchior, sniffing around the head of the bed, "I think there's more to this . . ."

He didn't trail off. I did. I could still see his lips moving, but the ringing in my ears drowned him out. I felt my knees buckling.

"Melchior," I tried to say, but I couldn't hear my own voice, "Nine One One. Execute."

The order authorized him to take whatever action he felt necessary to deal with the situation, including using magic independently. I was quite proud to have remembered to try it under the circumstances. My last thought before I went under was that it was too bad I didn't know if I'd actually said it.

"Incoming," hissed Melchior.

"Huh?" I replied, muzzily, opening my eyes.

A clock blinked a few inches away. I peered at it blearily. After a moment I was able to recognize it as the one in my dorm. After another I was able to read it—4:00 A.M. I didn't need to be at class for another three hours, so I closed my eyes. Something sharp pinched my cheek and I opened them again.

"You've got to get up, Boss."

Mel sounded worried, and I seemed to remember he had good reason to be, but I just couldn't think straight. He poked me in the ribs with a sharp claw. It hurt, and I came a little more awake.

"What in Hades's name?" I grumbled.

He pointed to a ghostly glow near the door, an incoming locus transfer. Things started to come back to me: Atropos, the assassination attempt, my most recent injury. I moved my right hand experimentally. The pain was gone, but so was most any other sensation.

"Chaos and Discord!" I swore.

"I hope not," Melchior's replied. "Fate is giving us enough trouble without we should irritate any of the other great powers." His voice was light, but he had my pistol ready when I reached for it.

As I rolled out of bed and started slithering across the room, deep rumbling snores informed me that my roommate had arrived while I was unconscious. Fortunately, Rod only sounds like that when he's had four or five too many. He must have stumbled in drunk and passed out. If he followed his usual pattern, I could probably use him as an armrest while I fired my pistol without waking him. Assuming things didn't get too messy, he had an excellent chance of coming through the next half hour without noticing a thing or suffering any harm. That was all to the good. I didn't like him much, but I didn't want him getting hurt because of me. Hopefully it wouldn't become an issue. I wanted to be gone before the bad nastiness coming through the ether arrived, and I was well on my way.

Less than fifteen seconds passed from the time Mel woke me to the moment I started groping for the doorknob. When I'd first moved into the dorms, I'd set a gate spell into the tiny shower Rod and I shared with the other two bedrooms in our pod. It was mweb dependent, but because it was a permanent gate, it was faster than an ltp link. The question was whether anyone had tampered with it while I was gone. I didn't really want to test that the hard way. Unfortunately, it didn't look like my wants were going to be consulted. I finally managed to make the door cooperate, but stopped when I realized Mel wasn't with me.

He was still beside the bed, standing perfectly still. "Come on," I husked. "What's the holdup?" There was no response. "Bugger. Mel, are you all right?"

"He's fine." Cool and inhuman, the voice emanated from the column of light.

A woman's form faded into being. She was tall and pale, with long black hair and Fate's eyes.

"Atropos," I whispered, and cold sweat broke out on my forehead. She continued as though she hadn't heard.

"I've merely sent him an override command that immobilized him. I didn't want you vanishing before I had a chance to speak with you."

"Grandmother," I said, realizing my first impression had been mistaken.

Atropos might have injured or killed Melchior, but she would never have bothered to freeze him. Setting my pistol carefully on the floor, I rose to my feet. I didn't know why my grandmother was there, but I was pretty sure it wasn't to give me a pat on the back and a box of cigars. She might not take kindly to my being armed.

"Had I known you were coming, I'd have dressed more appropriately." I said, gesturing sheepishly at my T-shirt and boxers. "I apologize."

She waved a hand dismissively and whistled a short complex chord in hex, somehow managing the Fate trick of harmonizing with herself. For a brief moment I felt as though millions of tiny spiders were running madly around on my skin.

When it stopped I was clothed for court. The boots came six inches above the knee and were made of black leather as soft as mountain moss. Green silk tights covered my legs under the boots, and a green silk tunic hung to midthigh. Over that was belted a black leather doublet cut high on the sides. The only things missing were a rapier and dagger. Their absence was made more conspicuous by the empty buckles on the belt where the sheaths would normally have hung.

When combined with the fact that my familiar continued to stand stock-still, the missing weapons assumed the quality of a bad omen. I studiously avoided meeting my grandmother's gaze as I prepared to make the obligatory bow. Feeling the presence of a hat on my head, I reached up to sweep it before me. Habit made me use my right hand, and the numb fingers lost their grip halfway through the maneuver. It was broad-brimmed in the cavalier style, and an ostrich feather dyed forest green was attached to the band by an emerald brooch. It was also quite aerodynamic, and it sailed all the way to my grandmother's feet.

"Sorry, Grandmother. I appear to be a bit lacking in grace at present."

"What happened to your hand?" she asked. Her tone implied that I had done something stupid to bring the injury down on myself.

Stung, I answered without thinking. "Atropos laid a trap for me."

Even as I spoke, I knew I'd made a mistake. My lips went numb and tingly as the spell that bound my voice reached out and twisted my words. In my head they had been angry and righteous. On my tongue they sounded like the most transparent of child's lies. Lachesis's eyebrows pinched together and her mouth thinned. But once started, I found it hard to stop.

"She did," I continued. I was angry and scared. I sounded petulant and whiny. "A really nasty enchantment laid on my pillow. The only reason I'm alive to have this conversation is that I triggered it with my rapier rather than my head."

"I think not," said Lachesis. "There was indeed a spell on your pillow, though my sister had nothing to do with it. I placed it there. It was supposed to bind you in sleep until I came to have words with you. How you managed to cause it to do that"—she pointed at my hand—"is beyond me." She whistled another quick chord, and the damage to my hand healed itself.

That wasn't fair. The spell I'd encountered and the one my grandmother had placed couldn't be the same. That lethal black fire bore about as much resemblance to a sleep spell as a dire-wolf did to a Chihuahua. I was sure Atropos was responsible, but with Cassandra's curse wrapped around my vocal cords like a hangman's noose I had no way to convince my grandmother. Swallowing my accusations with my pride, I moved on.

"If you wished to speak with me," I said, "that was a somewhat drastic way to ensure my cooperation, and most unnecessary. I am always at your disposal. How may I be of service?" I bowed again. It seemed prudent.

"By taking a walk with me. I am displeased with your failure to attend your midterms." Her perfect features contracted in the slightest of frowns. "You appear to have forgotten the consequences of displeasing me. I thought I would remind you. Come."

"I will, of course, be happy to accompany you to the ends of the Earth if you require. Is there anything else I might do for you?"

"Be silent," she said, her voice as sharp as shark's teeth. "You have pushed me to the very limits of tolerance, grandson. There are a number of things I intend to draw to your attention, and I do not wish to be interrupted by excuses, however mannerly. Do you understand?"

I nodded mutely.

"Excellent." She whistled and the glowing column expanded. I stepped into the light, throwing Melchior a sidelong glance as I went.

"Leave him," said Lachesis. "He's well enough as he is."

I wasn't so sure about that. In the brief instant I'd looked at him I'd noticed oily sweat running down his naked sides. It seemed almost as though he were straining to hold perfectly still rather than having been frozen by my grandmother's command, but of course that was ridiculous. Then the quality of the light changed, and I had no more time to spare in worrying about my familiar. I was too busy worrying about me.

CHAPTER SIX

The dorm vanished. For a split second that felt as though it outlasted the life of the Universe we were nowhere, a point of probability traveling through the chaos that ruled the place between the spheres. The moment passed, and a stark gray landscape faded into view.

We appeared in a sort of niche, high on the edge of a granite cliff. Below, the rock fell away for a thousand feet before meeting the foaming gray of the wind-driven sea where something that might have been a penguin played in the surf. Above us stood a granite building. Whether it had originally been designed as a fortress or a maximum-security prison I couldn't tell. Either explanation seemed plausible from the architecture.

An inscription over the doors read SAINT TURING'S followed by a long string of binary that began "011000110 1101111101101100." I mentally translated, "Monastery and College for Computational Recidivists."

"Grandmother," I started to say as she led me to the

entrance. "I've—" The look she aimed at me made me swallow the words.

"I did not give you permission to speak. This is an object lesson, Ravirn. I don't want anything to distract you from the message. The monks and their students operate under a vow of silence. While you are on the premises the same will apply to you. Since you seem to have such a problem with keeping your promises, I'll help you with this one." She whistled a brief tune as low and solemn as a dirge, and I felt magic still my tongue.

The door opened in front of us, and a tall, lean man gestured for us to enter. He wore a long, gray robe made of some harsh fabric.

"Take us to the abbot," ordered Lachesis.

The monk nodded, then turned and led us down a cold stone hallway. The mildew smell of damp stone warred for control of the air with the sharper salt tones of the sea breeze that whistled through every crack. Fluorescent lights were mounted to brackets in the walls at intervals of about fifteen feet, connected by lines of half-inch conduit that twisted along the surface like galvanized steel asps. Larger cousins of these metal snakes ran in thick profusion on the ceiling. At regular intervals fast wireless hubs sprouted from the mass.

A few short minutes later we were escorted into the abbot's office. It was a large room, but plain. The furniture was all oak and looked as though it had been there for a thousand years and would probably still be there in another thousand. The abbot looked up from where he was scanning long lines of code on a sparkling new Sun workstation.

"Welcome, your Worship." He bowed to my grandmother, and she inclined her head in acknowledgment. "Is this him?" he asked, with a sort of sad contempt.

"Yes," said Lachesis. "Though I'm not yet sure if he'll

be joining you. It may be that after he has a look around, he'll be less reckless in his behavior."

"Let us hope so," said the abbot. "I am always glad to help the young men who are brought to us. But it would be a better world if this service we render to the Powers and Incarnations were unnecessary. Brother Torvalds, please conduct this man around the facility while I speak with Fate."

In the next ten minutes, I got a mighty good look at what my own personal purgatory might look like if I weren't careful. It was clear that when Lachesis had threatened me with a monastery school, I hadn't taken her seriously enough.

Each student was assigned a windowless cubicle, ten by ten by ten, with a low pallet, a tiny wardrobe, a small bookshelf, and a desk with a straight-backed wooden chair. Each cubicle also had a network port, but according to the brochure Brother Torvalds gave me, it only connected to the local area net. The only web access was through a group of computers in a common area off the dining hall and was closely supervised by the monks.

The dining hall itself was a long, low room filled with stone tables and matching benches. When I gestured a question at Torvalds about the food, he looked like a kicked basset hound. The thing that really stayed with me, however, was the communal bathrooms. Each doorless shower had only one faucet handle, and not the kind that starts out cold, then gets warm. The toilet consisted of a long marble slab with holes every few feet.

I was convinced. I did not want to spend even one semester here. Even the prospect of being murdered by my great-aunt Atropos suddenly seemed less scary than it had only hours earlier. On the way to the abbot's office, we passed a line of monks making their way to the chapel. They were chanting in classical Gregorian style.

"One one oh one oh oh one one oh one," and so on. It was downright creepy.

"Did you find that instructive?" asked Lachesis, when we returned to the abbot's office. I bobbed my head vigorously. "Good. Then we may return to your current school."

Brother Torvalds led us back to the gate. From there we quickly reversed the journey that had brought us to this little gray outpost of the abyss. As the ltp link returned us to my room, I felt the power of my grandmother's binding spell release its hold on my tongue. She obviously felt it as well because, once again, she gestured for me to keep my mouth closed.

"Bide a while yet in silence, grandson. I can see how you feel about Saint Turing's. Your eyes speak more eloquently on the subject than ever your mouth could. You don't want to go there, and I don't want to send you. But that's exactly what will happen if you continue down the path you've chosen. It was only by a whisker that I saved you from Atropos's shears. If I didn't believe you would someday be worth every effort I expended on your behalf, I'd as soon have cut you off myself rather than suffer the embarrassment you caused me then. But all of the potential I see in you will have been wasted if you can't learn self-discipline."

She shook her head sadly. "But you won't learn it at the monastery. If I thought for a moment that would work, you'd already have started your academic career at Saint Turing's. But discipline applied from the outside is not the same thing at all." She shook her head again in a way that clearly conveyed her disappointment. "I'm not entirely sure that you *can* master it. However, I feel there is a slim chance that the threat of the monastery might supply you with the right motivation to learn at least some part of the lesson. So, here are the conditions you will abide by if you don't wish to find yourself locked up with the other delinquents. You will finish out this semester. You will do it with a 4.0 grade-point average. And you will not do any hacking in that time. To give you a little help with that last, I will be placing strict limits on your mweb access."

Crossing to the place where Melchior stood statue-still, Lachesis placed a hand firmly on his bald blue head and whistled a quick string of hex.

"I want to see you rescheduling your midterms today, Ravirn. If I don't, you'll be moving into Saint Turing's tomorrow. Don't make me regret the decision to leave you here. Now, is there anything you want to say to me?"

That I didn't break into Atropos.web on a lark, I thought. *That even as we speak she's probably plotting her next attempt on my life. That Atropos is trying to overthrow the balance between Chaos and Order.* But I didn't say any of it. How could I? Atropos's curse lurked in the back of my throat, just waiting to exert its malign influence on every word I spoke against her.

"Only that I won't let you down whatever happens," I finally said, straightening my shoulders. That was a promise I felt I could keep, even if I didn't do it in the way she might expect. She nodded once, acknowledging my words.

"See that you don't, grandson."

Then she whistled the spell that reactivated her ltp link. As she was about to step into the light she spoke again, "Believe it or not, Ravirn, I'm fond of you. Or perhaps, what I should say is that I'm fond of the man you might someday become if you ever get around to growing up."

"Grandmother," I said, on a sudden impulse.

"Yes?"

"Thank you."

"You're welcome," she said, with a half smile, before vanishing with the light.

As soon as she was gone, Melchior collapsed. I quickly moved to his side, and started rubbing his limbs, knowing how stiff and sore he must be. He was soaked with sweat and smelled like a soggy spice jar.

"Are you OK?" I asked.

"Yeah, I'm just bloody dandy. Four hours frozen in place while your grandmother took you off to who knows where. Every minute of which, by the way, I spent worrying that Rod would revive from his alcoholic stupor, or that one of his yahoo buddies would show up. Then, when you finally do come back, Lachesis uses her authority as system administrator and matriarch of your family to whistle a bunch of untested code into my head. I've never felt better. How the hell are you?"

"Calm down, Mel. I haven't been having the time of my life either. I've just been on a field trip to hacker hell, which is going to be our new home if I don't ace this entire semester."

"What?" His voice whined like a hard drive about to frag itself in a particularly spectacular fashion. "Why didn't your grandmother just nail your feet to the floor? Atropos wants to kill you, and Lachesis orders you to stay in one place and play target for two months. We were only stopping home to pick up a few things. We weren't supposed to actually stay here."

"It's all right, Mel. We'll survive."

Melchior snorted and shook his head. "You'll be lucky to live out the week."

I shrugged my shoulders glumly. It wasn't as though I disagreed with him.

I spent the next day apologizing to my various professors and begging them to let me take makeup exams. Two of my profs agreed to my request, but only if I took their tests on the spot. A third handed me a really ugly take-home exam with a one-week deadline. The fourth gave me an extension on the paper I owed her, but demanded I have it in her office by the time she arrived the next morning. She was an early riser, so I finished the paper that night, and slid it under her door around four-forty in the morning. Afterward I fell exhausted into my bed without having done a thing about Atropos.

But in direct contradiction to Melchior's dire prediction, the next week went by without a single attempt on my life. So did the following one. I even got caught up on my homework. I only had one significant problem. I couldn't get in touch with Cerice. The spell my grandmother had put on Melchior to prevent me from hacking via the mweb also kept me from sending e-mail between worlds. As days sped past with no contact, I imagined her getting madder and madder and I felt like a complete rat. There had to be something I could do. The question was what.

I was worrying at the problem as I walked to my differential equations class in my third week back. An early blizzard had arrived the night before and was still going full force. Visibility was terrible and the mall was almost empty. I was just passing the pillars of Ford Hall on my way to Vincent when something caused me to look up. I found myself eye-to-eye with a hideously distorted face. It was perhaps fifteen feet away and closing fast. Loose folds of dead gray skin almost buried its eyes. Beneath was a broad flat nose and a huge round mouth.

While my brain was trying to make sense of this, my reflexes kicked in. Slapping a palm against the nearest pillar, I pushed as hard as I could. Since the building wasn't going anywhere, I ended up throwing myself backwards just as the heavy stone gargoyle dropped into the space I had so recently occupied. It brushed against the tips of my out-thrust fingers, tearing skin and numbing my hand and half my forearm. It also spun me halfway around.

Still spinning, I curled my body into a tight ball and tried to turn the fall into a controlled tumble. But my book bag got in the way, and I ended up landing hard on my back as the bits of stone that were all that remained of the gargoyle rained down around me. If it hadn't been for the snow I might have broken my tailbone.

It felt like hours before I was able to roll over and get to my feet, but it couldn't have been more than a few seconds, because the gawkers that always seem magically to appear around the site of any accident hadn't yet arrived.

That suited me fine. I was already on academic probation as a result of the broken windows in my room and missed class time. In addition, I'd had a number of long discussions with the campus cops and the Dean of Students on the subject of how the front hall of the Weisman got trashed. They would have expelled me if Ravi Latcher's grandmother hadn't been a major donor, or if they'd had even a shred of proof. I suspected that having further destruction of university property linked to my name, even if I was clearly the victim in this case, might be enough to prematurely end my academic year and send me to Saint Turing's.

I hurried on to Vincent, where I sat through the whole lecture and even took notes. But I have no memory of what was taught, and it wasn't until the students for the next hour started to file in that I realized class was over. Then I got up and walked dazedly back to my room in Comstock and crawled into bed. An hour later, memory brought me awake in a cold sweat. Ford Hall doesn't have gargoyles.

I got an e-mail from Cerice the next morning. She was wondering why I hadn't gotten in touch. She was not very happy with me. I didn't blame her, and I told her so in my response. The problem came when I ordered Melchior to send it.

"Error," he replied. "Cross-locus smtp server not available. Tried to send. Local processor responded User Ravirn 001 Access denied. For more information see sent messages log."

"I can't even *reply* to someone else's cross-locus message? Lachesis couldn't have intended that. It means I won't be able to respond to her either."

"Sorry, Boss," said Melchior. "But all outgoing messages get routed the same way regardless of whether they're totally new or replies. You should know that."

"I do. I guess I just hadn't thought it through. Chaos and Discord! How am I going to let Cerice know what's up?" My life was getting more joyful by the minute. "She'll think I'm deliberately dodging her, when the actual problem is that the Fates are quite literally conspiring against me."

I stood up and began to pace. I wasn't entirely sure where Cerice and I might be going, or even where I wanted us to go, but I knew that if she thought I was blowing her off, it'd be a mighty short trip. It was yet another problem to add to my ever-growing list. I wanted to scream. I decided to take a walk instead. Maybe I could think of something along the way.

"Melchior, Laptop. Execute." He folded and compressed until he was back in computer mode, and I scooped him into my bag.

There had to be something I could do about Cerice and my other troubles. But what? I meandered past Coffman Union and out onto the mall. It was cold and dark, a perfect accompaniment to my mood, and the icy wind was flat and lifeless, with only exhaust fumes and the occasional bit of sidestream cigarette smoke to flavor it. The temperature had frozen all the moisture out of the air, leaving it too dry to carry subtler smells.

It wasn't until I made the long climb up the stairs in the dorm that I thought of something. I avoided the elevators because someone might have some clever ideas about cables and metal cutters. The plan occurred to me as I passed the fourth floor. That gave me plenty of time to think on my way to twenty. It seemed like a bad idea and possibly ineffective then, and it wasn't any better when I reached my room, but it was the only idea I had.

"This is crazy," said Melchior, his voice dripping with disapproval as he peered at me out of the open top of my shoulder bag.

"Tell me something I don't know," I replied before I dropped the last couple of feet, landing lightly on the dead, snow-dusted grass.

We were on a tiny island in the Mississippi. Oval, and perhaps fifteen feet by twenty-five, it was mostly filled by the support pier of an aging railroad bridge. Even with the previous day's blizzard, the sheltering bulk of the stone pier and the deck of the bridge overhead kept the island largely free of drifts. Darkness and gently falling snow provided a curtain that hid the city around us from view. Cold black water rushed by on both sides, gurgling and sighing to itself, muffling the sounds of the urban landscape. Completely isolated, the island was ideal for my purposes.

"You could wait until she comes to you," said Mel. He had his little hands stuffed in his armpits to keep warm.

"*If* she comes to me, Mel, not when. And that's a big if. You read the e-mail. Cerice is mad already, and no doubt getting madder with every passing hour that I don't respond. Responsibility is not a word that has been associated with my name on a very regular basis."

"You can say that again," Melchior affirmed.

"See. If everyone agrees I'm irresponsible, even my familiar—"

"Especially your familiar." I shot him a nasty look, but it slid off like water off hot Teflon. "OK," said Melchior. "I see your point. But I still think this is cracked. We're talking pure raw magic here, not code. It's very chancy stuff."

"Objection noted, Mel. But by the time I've got full mweb access again it might be too late to explain myself. For that matter, I might not live that long." I started pacing back and forth across the confined space.

"Excuse me for asking, but isn't the Cassandra curse going to cause you some problems in the explanation department?"

I sighed. It was a good point. Unfortunately, I hadn't yet figured out what to do about it. "I expect it will make this almost impossible," I said. "But I've still got to try. Look, this is about more than my relationship with Cerice."

Melchior raised a skeptical eyebrow at me.

"It is," I said, though I wondered if he wasn't right. "She's important to me. Very important, even. But more than that, somebody besides thee and me needs to know what's going on with Atropos."

"Wetware," said Melchior with a sniff. "Can't live with 'em. Can't debug 'em. If that's what you want to believe about your motives, nothing I say is going to change it."

If I'd had a good response I'd have made it. Instead, I said, "Oh, shut up and pass me the athame."

The webgoblin sighed and shook his head, but handed over the slim dagger. With a blade only five inches long and less than a quarter of an inch across, it looked like a letter opener. But no letter opener was ever as sharp as that little knife. Made of magically hardened iron to maximize its affinity for blood, the athame made my father's straight razor look dull.

It was so sharp that I felt only the slightest dragging sensation as I ran it lightly across the palm of my left hand. However, bright blood immediately welled up and soon filled my cupped palm. Before it could overflow, I took a length of hemp rope and slowly and methodically worked my hand along its entire length, staining it rusty red. When I was done, I whistled the short spell that closed athame-inflicted wounds.

I spliced the two ends of the rope together with a marlinespike, making a continuous loop, and placed it in a rough circle on the brown grass. The next step was very scary. It involved playing with the primal chaos again, and I didn't like the idea.

My earliest ancestors, the Titans, formed themselves from the stuff using nothing but their own demiurge, but the Titan blood runs thin in my veins. It's been diluted over the generations. Still, it was the link formed by that descent that I called on to open a tiny hole between the ordered frame of my current Decision Locus and the churning stuff between the worlds.

Like the ocean pouring through a break in the tide wall of reality, pure chaos rushed into the gap. But I had judged things carefully, and the way was only open for a microsecond. An enormous, but tightly focused and finite, burst of raw energy poured into the endless loop of my bloodstained rope. It struck about six inches from the splice and raced around the circle, crumpling the hemp into a line of charred ash behind it. I held my breath as the chaos charge came around to the splice, but it jumped across without hesitating.

In a tiny fraction of a second, it had looped back to its

entry point, the beginning of the ash trail. Around it went again, this time consuming the ash and leaving a circle of bright green grass in its wake. On the third and final time around the circle, it caused the grass to perform a full summer's growth. With that, the chaos dissipated, leaving behind a thigh-high circle of emerald grass. I had built me a faerie ring.

"Party time," I said to Melchior. He'd hidden on the other side of the stone pier while I worked, but he stuck his head around the corner and peered at the results.

"Joy," he said after a moment. "Nothing would make me happier than to jump into that wonderful little hole you've created in the order of the universe." Despite his tone, he came to stand beside me.

"I'm glad to hear it, Mel. Because that's just what we're going to do."

"My, but this is a bad idea," he said. "Have I mentioned that?"

"Many times, Mel. More than I would care to count."

"Then I'll only do it the once more, and anything that happens after that is your fault."

"I grow tired of insolence, Melchior." It wasn't that so much as the fact that he was probably right that I found annoying. But I couldn't very well admit it.

"Sorry, my lord and master. But as your familiar, it is my humble duty to advise you about things magical. So . . . First, this may be an imperfect circle. In which case we could end up anywhere. Second, there may not be an appropriate receiving circle close enough to Cerice. In which case we could end up anywhere. Third, even in ideal conditions, these things can misfire."

"In which case we could end up anywhere. I know, Mel. I know." I shrugged. "But I'm fresh out of time and ideas." I opened the mouth of the bag for him.

"As you wish," he said, bowing his head in surrender.

In all honesty, I wasn't much more enthused by the idea than Melchior. I'm a thoroughly modern sorcerer, a code-warrior, a programmer. I'm not a classical magician. I hate the old ways. They're painful, inefficient, and hideously dangerous. There's a reason so many sorcerers in old stories meet untimely ends. In the great mystical feeding chain, classical sorcerers fall roughly in the category of hors d'oeuvre. Even using the methods developed by the Fates isn't a guarantee of safety. More than one member of my extended family has been eaten by a glitch when they didn't check their code closely enough. Doing it the old way is just begging to end up on the cosmic lunch tray. Unfortunately, it was the only thing I could think of that might work in the time I had. So I lifted Mel's bag onto my shoulder and stepped into the circle.

CHAPTER SEVEN

■ ■ ■

Intense, stabbing cold filled my universe. It made the fifteen-degree chill of the snowstorm I'd left feel like an hour in the sauna. Involuntarily, I closed my eyes. When I opened them again, I was elsewhere. I had the briefest impression of orange sun-baked cliffs and a low ring of cacti, like a donut that had been dropped in a jar full of stickpins. I smelled piñon and sage. Then the cold took me again. This time I was in a brown-and-green swamp redolent with the stink of rotting vegetation. The faerie ring was formed by a snake, its own tail between its teeth, swimming a slow circle around a tiny island. The cold came again. Things began to get really weird.

It was like one of those college parties that's died of inertia around 3:00 A.M. The sensible people have gone home. Everyone who's going to get lucky has, and they've left too. The drinkers are passed out in the corners. The remaining partygoers are collapsed in front of the TV while someone who's into hallucinogens and channel-surfing uses the remote to set a new world speed record. A thousand settings flickered across in front of my eyes too quickly for me to take them in. Each transition was punctuated by a brief blast of arctic cold. And it all seemed to be getting faster.

I felt my brain growing numb as I was repeatedly clubbed by sensory input. It became difficult to hold my destination in my mind's eye. That was the danger. It would be terribly easy to give up my sense of self and let the rings carry me where they would. Unfortunately, I was pretty sure that if I let go of myself, I'd never see me again. Powerful magic was involved, and I had no reason to expect that my physical and mental selves would have to arrive at the same place.

I started thinking about taking a break, stepping out into the next world that looked even remotely inviting. But that wasn't a good idea either. Looking inviting and being habitable are not necessarily related. That's when I saw the tiny door in the base of the tree. It was only a flash, then it was gone, but I recognized it. Mentally, I wrenched the process around and went back. It was very like channel-surfing. I kept going up and down the line, slowly narrowing in on the right program.

I stood in a perfect circle of dead grass. On my right was the fountain that lay just in front of the Harvard student union. Behind me was the yard. Directly in front was a grand old oak tree with a tiny door between two roots. The door was dark green and no more than three inches high. I remembered it from a visit I'd made while I was just a few miles away at MIT, back when I'd been on my grand-mother's good side and still living in one the primary threads of reality. It was probably around 1:00 A.M., but the area was still heavily populated.

I staggered out of the circle before it carried me away again. Then I dropped to my knees and threw up. Around me, people did what they always do when someone appears magically in their midst. They assumed they had been looking away at the critical moment and ignored me, pretending nothing had happened. Throwing up helped the process along enormously. Pretending you don't see someone becoming violently ill around bar rush is an ingrained survival skill on most college campuses.

When I was done being sick, I slid my athame from an inner pocket and surreptitiously pricked the ball of my thumb. Then I flicked a bit of the blood into the center of the circle, sealing it. Before I came through, it was probably just a proto-ring, not a gate at all. But now it was as much an invitation to disaster as an open manhole cover with a bit of newspaper covering it. My blood would hold it shut for a night and a day, then it would be open for business. I'd have to arrange to destroy it before then.

I put the athame away and dragged myself into a standing position. If I was remembering things properly from my previous visit to campus, there were internet-ready computers and hookups in the union. The architecture was typical seventies Ivy League. Lots of open space and preformed concrete. A twisted loop of stainless steel entitled *Infinity* sat just inside the doors. It must have been art, because I couldn't think of anything else that would look like that, except possibly a locus transfer gone terribly wrong. I paused long enough to get a soda out of a nearby machine and slam it, washing away the taste of vomit, then dropped onto a chair. When I reached into my bag, Mel bit me.

"Ow!"

"Serves you right," said a sullen voice.

"What did I do?" I asked.

"Do you want the whole list, or just the most recent and relevant bits?"

I couldn't stop myself. I chuckled. He sounded so aggrieved, and I couldn't help but think of the image I must be projecting for anyone who cared to watch. Since my arrival, I had thrown up, stabbed myself in the thumb, staggered into the union, and here I was talking to my shoulder bag.

"Why don't you just hit the highlights, Mel."

"Well, most immediately, you just stuck a finger in my eye, and another in my mouth. That'd justify biting you all by itself. But you also carried me through that Powers-damned faerie ring in goblin shape, instead of as a laptop. Which means I had a stomach for the whole trip. I won't be forgiving you for that anytime soon."

"I'm sorry. I didn't know what it was going to be like."

"What do you mean?" asked Mel, his voice deceptively calm.

"I've never actually used a faerie ring before. I know the theory, of course, but it never seemed like a good idea to test it."

"Are you bleeding much?" asked Mel.

I checked. "Yeah. You got me pretty good."

"Well, that's something at least."

"Thanks, Mel. I'd love to continue this conversation, but I need to hook up. Melchior, Laptop. Execute."

The shoulder bag writhed around in my lap. When it stopped moving, I pulled out my laptop and hooked into the local WiFi net. A quick search verified that Cerice was listed as a graduate research assistant in Comp-Sci. Cracking the Payroll Department to find her address took a bit longer, but not much.

Predictably, the doors to the graduate dorms were locked. If I'd dared, I'd have run Open Sesame, but we'd have had to tap into the mweb to do it, and I didn't want my signature showing up in any DecLocus other than my own. I'd have to get in the hard way. Fortunately, I'd been able to pry a building schematic out of the campus computers.

The dorm was three stories tall and shaped like a brick. I went around to where a rusty fire escape climbed the end wall like an iron version of the ivy that was everywhere. When I was sure no one was looking, I took a deep breath and leaped up to catch the ledge of the lowest landing. I could've tried for the ladder, but I figured pulling it down would make enough noise to wake my grandmother, several dimensions and half a world away. Besides, the lower landing was only about fifteen feet off the ground, comfortably within my reach.

As quietly as I could, I headed for the third floor. If I'd read the plans right, Cerice's room was at the corner, and the nearer of her windows was only about eight feet from the top of the fire escape. Climbing cautiously onto the broad ledge that encircled the building at window height, I discovered that my motorcycle boots tended to slip around a bit, making scratching noises that reminded me of just how much I didn't want to fall backwards off a three-story building.

As I slid into place outside Cerice's window, I noticed a ghostlike red dot on the glass. The hand that had been about to knock froze. I slowly and carefully lifted my arms away from my body with my palms open and facing the window. A quick glance downward confirmed my suspicion that there was another red dot, this one considerably brighter, on my chest just above the heart. A laser sight.

"Cerice, it's Ravirn," I whispered, frantically trying to remember what sort of gun she used. The Kevlar in my jacket would stop most bullets, but it wouldn't take much to knock me off that ledge, and Cerice might be using armor-piercing rounds. "Don't shoot."

When Cerice didn't pop me immediately, I decided it

was probably all right to breathe. A couple seconds went by and the window swung inward. At no time did the red dot move from its place over my heart.

"Come," she said. I slowly stepped through the opening and onto a desk, keeping my hands firmly in the air. "What in Hades's name do you think you're doing?"

"Would you believe me if I told you I wanted to restage the balcony scene from *Romeo and Juliet*?"

"It's you all right." The red dot winked out, but she didn't put the pistol down. As my eyes adjusted to the light, I also noticed what she was wearing. A frown and nothing more.

"I'm here because I need to talk to you." Certain portions of my anatomy were making other suggestions. I ignored them as best I could.

"Oh," she replied. "Really? I'm not sure we have anything to talk about." Her voice had icicles in it. You could almost hear the little syllables freezing as they left her lips, then dropping to shatter on the floor.

"Please, Cerice. There are things I need to tell you." I paused and swallowed. "But first, I have a favor to ask."

"A favor?" The ice was gone, replaced by a blowtorch. "You send me a note after Garbage Faerie. A note in which you tell me you want to spend more time with me and that you want this to be more than a fling. Then nothing, for weeks. Now you show up here and try to break into my room, and you want a favor?"

"Cerice, I owe you several apologies, a couple of explanations, and my life among other things. If I could do this without the favor, I would, but I just don't think I can."

"So what is it?" she snarled.

"Would you please, please, put some clothes on. You're the most beautiful woman I've ever known, and I could stare at you for hours. But right at the moment I have things

I want to tell you, and every time I look at you my brain freezes up, and I start drooling."

"I . . ." She paused. "I should probably just shoot you and get it over with." She set the gun down. "But I won't. All right. Turn around."

Part of me wanted to protest that since she was already naked, there wasn't much point in my looking away while she got dressed, but the admittedly small part of my brain devoted to self-preservation overrode my mouth. So I spent what felt like hours staring at the iron plate welded over what had once been a fireplace.

"All right," said Cerice after a while. "Against my better judgment I'm going to give you a chance to state your case before I throw you out." When I turned back, she was wearing a heavy skirt of red wool and a yellow-gold T-shirt. She looked fabulous.

"First," I said. "I'm very, very sorry I haven't gotten in touch. It's inexcusable."

"We agree on that at least."

"But I had no choice."

"No choice? No choice?" Her voice was rising again. "You had no choice? What kind of crap is this?"

"I've been cut off from the mweb. Lachesis revoked my access. I can't send anything between DecLoci. There was literally no way for me to get a message to you."

"Can you honestly stand here and expect me to believe that? Do you think I'm an idiot, Ravirn? If you can't use the mweb, how the hell did you get here?"

"I built a faerie ring."

"You—" She stopped, her mouth open. "That's insane. Faerie rings are chaos magic. Do you know how dangerous that is?" She shook her head abruptly. "No. I don't believe you. Even you aren't *that* crazy."

"I can take you to the terminus on this end," I said

quickly. "It let me out by the student union. I sealed it to keep it from swallowing up innocent bystanders. Would that be proof enough?"

She nodded. "Show me."

"All right," she said after examining the ring. A wry smile touched her lips. "I believe you're a maniac, and about the mweb access. Next question. Why did she cut you off?"

So I told her about the nocturnal visit I'd received from my grandmother and about Saint Turing's. As we talked we walked, heading slowly across the campus. It seemed to be earlier in the season here, more late fall than early winter. The dead leaves crackled underfoot. We'd just reached the steps of the main library when I finished my account.

"But that's less than half the story," I said, turning onto the stairs. "And I owe you the whole thing."

I stopped. From here on out, everything I said was going to be filtered through Atropos's curse. I wanted to scream. Instead, I turned to the concrete wall that ran beside the stairs and smacked my forehead against it. Cerice looked at me curiously, but didn't say a word. Instead, she continued upward and took a seat on the top step. I sat down a few feet away. It was a good place to talk, well above the general level of the campus, where no one could sneak up on us. The silence stretched out, and the expression on Cerice's face began to darken.

"Well?" she said after several minutes.

"I'm sorry. I'm not sure how to go about this." I pressed the palm of my left hand against my forehead and squeezed.

"Begin at the beginning," said Cerice, as though she were speaking to a child. "Pass through the middle, and wrap up with the end."

"That's not the problem," I replied.

"What is the problem?"

"You aren't going to believe a word I say."

"You sound awfully certain," she said, some of the anger returning to her tone. "Is that because you don't trust me to judge what you say honestly? Or because you aren't planning on being honest?"

"Actually, it's neither." There was no good way to go about this. I was going to tell her everything, she wasn't going to believe me, and our budding relationship would come apart like a hard drive when the head touches the disk. "Look," I said finally. "For reasons I can't explain beforehand, I know you're going to find this unbelievable. The only thing I can do is ask you to listen to the whole thing before you make any judgments. Will you do that for me?"

"I suppose," she said, leaning back on her hands. "Though I can't think of a good reason why."

"Thank you. I wasn't hacking Atropos.web just for the challenge on the night I crashed the mweb." My lips tingled, but only slightly, and Cerice nodded as though she'd been expecting that. "I was looking for a memory crystal. Atropos is trying to shift the balance between Fate and free will." The numbness increased dramatically, and I heard my voice go uncertain and shifty. *Damn, damn, and double damn*, I thought.

"That's more or less her job description," said Cerice. I was losing her.

"I told you that you wouldn't believe me. Please, just listen for a while."

"All right." She agreed, but her expression hardened.

"This is a little more drastic than usual. She wants to eliminate chance and choice completely. What's more, I think she can do it if her spell works." I hopped to my feet and began to pace. The tension was simply too great for me to hold still.

I told her everything that had happened since Atropos

had approached me about Puppeteer. Every word came out sounding like the desperate slitherings of a pathological liar, and my mouth went so numb I lost all track of my tongue. By the end I'd bitten it pretty badly at least twice. I couldn't feel it, but I could taste the blood in the back of my throat. I studied Cerice's face, trying to gauge her reaction. Her brow was wrinkled in an intense frown of concentration. It wasn't the expression I wanted, but it was better than I'd expected.

"You don't believe me," I said. A statement rather than a question.

"No," she replied, and it felt as though someone had hit me in the stomach. "But I know you're telling the truth. It's an amazing feeling. The emotional half of my brain is sure you're the biggest liar since Hades told Persephone the pomegranates were delicious and completely harmless. But at the same time, the thinking half knows you're telling the truth."

"What?" She was supposed to be calling me nasty names and walking out of my life. It was the last thing in the world I wanted to happen, but I'd been bracing for it so hard that her actual response left me severely off-balance. I stopped pacing to face her. "How do you know?"

"It's not my secret to share," she said.

She reached up and caught my right hand. "Poor payback for your courage in telling me an unbelievable truth, but the best I can offer at the moment. Thanks for trusting me."

"You're welcome."

I looked down at the place where our hands were joined and tried to find the right words. What can you say when "I like you," isn't half–strong enough, but you haven't yet gotten to "I love you"? Was it even fair to be talking about such things when I didn't know whether I'd be alive to follow through on them? No words came.

"What are you thinking?" she asked after a time.

"That I don't know how to tell you what you mean to me," I answered. "That you have grown very dear to me. That I would like more than anything to have the leisure to follow where that leads me."

"Really?" she said, and cocked her head to one side quizzically. There was a long silence before she whispered, "How very odd."

My mouth went dry, and my heart felt as though it had been transformed into a particularly anxious and fidgety hedgehog. I couldn't face those blue, blue eyes any longer and turned my gaze downward. For several minutes we remained like that, unmoving. Then Cerice reached up and placed a finger under my chin. With surprising strength, she lifted my head until I had to face her again.

"How very odd," she said again. "Because, despite my better judgment, I've grown quite fond of you, too." She pulled me down to her level and kissed me.

We went back to Cerice's room then, and for a very long time we just held each other. When we did eventually make love, it was with a slow, lazy passion and gentle twining of limbs that was more about tenderness and discovery than sex. Later, Cerice opened an ltp link and sent me through to the U of M. There was a risk my passage through the mweb might be noticed, but Cerice refused to even consider letting me use the faerie ring, which she promised to close up after I left.

I tried to keep up with Cerice over the following weeks, but my lack of mweb access meant I couldn't call her, she had to call me. That didn't happen very often. She did have Shara bring me a new silver-inlaid rapier and matching dagger as a Solstice present. I'd found a string of tiny oval-cut rubies set in red gold that I wanted to give her the week before, so Shara didn't go back empty-handed. But exchanging gifts by goblin seemed a poor substitute for the in-person time I wished for.

Between the tangles in my love life, Atropos's curse, and a heavy course load you'd have thought I had enough problems. Fate, or more precisely, one of them, didn't seem to agree. During the next six weeks, I encountered four more magical surprises, dodged one drive-by shooting, and found poison in my Purina dorm chow on three separate occasions. It was all more fun than discovering an electric eel in your beer stein. I turned into a raving insomniac, and my concentration went to hell. Somehow I managed to hold my grades up, though it was a bit like treading water with a bowling ball in each hand. It didn't help knowing that Atropos might finish Puppeteer and end the world as I knew it at any time, or that I was the only one who could stop her.

CHAPTER EIGHT

■ ■ ■

Somehow, I survived until January break and the end of the semester. That gave me a full month off before classes started again and, since Lachesis had reinstated my mweb privileges when my grades came in, the freedom to do something with the time. I would have liked nothing more than to spend it with Cerice, whose place in my heart seemed to grow in proportion to her absence in my life. But likes must make way for needs, and I really *needed* to see if I could do something about Atropos and Puppeteer. If I could also find a way to pull my own personal bacon out of the fire without burning my nine remaining fingertips and exact some small revenge on the darkest of the Fates into the bargain, I'd be halfway to a seat on Olympus as the patron god of hackers.

One side benefit to being nailed to the floor for half the semester was that I'd had plenty of time to think. I knew that my many-times-great-aunt would have increased security significantly since my last visit to Chez Atropos, and that none of the hacks that had worked in the past were likely to do me a lick of good. But after much thought I'd finally come up with an approach that might get me in. Better still, I had some clue as to what to do once I got there, at least as a first step: a bit of computerized life insurance. All of which put me where I was at present.

The dirt road was poorly plowed, and my borrowed Econoline van almost went into the ditch a couple of times before I got to the state park's lot. I left the van running while I crawled into the back and put on a pair of heavy black tights, a turtleneck, a sweater, and a windbreaker. Thick wool socks and a pair of ski boots came next. I slid my arms into the straps of the mountain pack holding the rest of my gear, then turned off the van and reluctantly got out. It was four below and the wind felt like a razor scraping painfully across my face. My bad knee complained, but there was no other way to get where I needed to go, so I ignored it.

When I stepped into the bindings of my cross-country skis they squeaked from the cold. I wanted to do the same, despite the fleece mask, goggles, and gloves I had added to my outfit. Instead I picked up my custom poles and got moving.

There was no wind in the woods, and the snow was a perfect coat of light powder on top of an icy crust. I made good time, and soon warmed up enough to enjoy the scenery. Late-morning sun struck rainbow sparks off the jumbled surfaces of the loosely drifting snowflakes, filling the air with dancing color. A thin layer of this frozen faerie dust decorated every branch, and the pines looked like miniature ice pagodas where tiny Japanese webpixies might live. It was almost enough to make me forget that the weather would kill me given half a chance. The faint corduroy noise of my skis and the crunch as my poles broke through the crust were the only sounds, both quickly swallowed by the silence of a pine forest in winter.

After about an hour a wide gap between the trees opened up to my left where another path turned off. It hadn't been groomed, and the long line of pristine snow stretching between the pines was starkly pretty. I slid off the main trail and slipped my backpack off. Melchior, in laptop form, was tucked into the top. I flipped his lid and typed in a spell prompt.

Run Melchior. Execute.

But, it's cold out there, Ravirn.

I didn't ask for editorials.

Oh, all right, but I'm not going to like this.

In a matter of moments he was standing and shivering atop my pack. "What do you want?"

"A GPS fix. I want to know if this is our turn."

"For that, you had to turn me back into a goblin? A simple typed request would have worked fine, and this weather is much nicer if you don't have any nerve endings to freeze."

"Deal with it, Mel. If this is the place, I'll want you to hide my tracks."

"Oh, great," he said. "What could possibly be more fun than slogging through neck-deep snow while brushing out ski tracks? When do I get to start?"

"You tell me. Where are we?"

His face went abstract for a few seconds as he queried the GPS satellite system. Then he let out a little martyred sigh. He tried to maintain an air of injured dignity as he hopped down, but the snow was deeper than he was tall. With only the faintest of crunches as he went through the icy underlayer, he dropped completely from sight. A moment later, his face fixed in a scowl, he pulled himself out onto the crust. Making his way to the base of a fir, he tore a branchlet free to use as a broom.

"So, tell me again why we have to come way out here to commit suicide," he said, once we'd gotten far enough off the main trail that he could drop the cover-up and climb up into the pack again.

"We're not committing suicide."

"How do you figure?" he asked. "We're messing around with the Fate Core. If Atropos catches us, your grandmother will hand her the scissors."

"We won't get caught," I reassured him. "I have it all planned. We'll slide in, insert Revenant into the Core, and slide out. It'll be a surgical strike, thirty minutes from start to finish, tops. Short-term scary, but it'll seriously increase our long-term odds of survival."

I wasn't anywhere near that confident. The Fate Core is at the center of everything my family is. If Atropos hadn't driven me to it, I'd never have even considered messing with it.

"Who do you think you're kidding?" asked Melchior. "Revenant is just a fancy dead-man switch. It might make Atropos's life miserable after you're gone, but it won't do a thing to keep you alive."

I shrugged. He was right. But somebody had to stop Atropos, and I'd been elected. Ruining Puppeteer was more important than staying alive, and if Revenant worked properly, even dying wouldn't take me out of the game. Of course I wouldn't be around to gloat, and that took some of the savor out of things. But Melchior knew all that already.

"If you've got a better idea, Mel, I haven't heard it yet."

"Sorry, Boss. Just nervous I guess." He looked around. "Why on Earth did Atropos put a backbone hookup to Atropos.web. out in the middle of nowhere like this?"

"No choice. Believe it or not, there's a big nexus here."

"That's crazy," said Mel. "Nobody lives here. There's no good reason for people to put in a junction."

"People didn't. We're heading for what used to be a major ley-line node with a direct server connection to Atropos.web.

Since her new, fast routers are all fiber-optic only, the ley link isn't used much anymore, but it's still connected as a backup."

"Oh, goody," said the webgoblin. "In addition to squatting in a snowbank and freezing to death, we'll be using antiquated equipment to hack the most sophisticated and heavily guarded hub in existence. You *know* ley-line hookups give me a headache."

"It won't be that bad. This nexus is cross-linked to a fiber bundle and the cell net. That's part of why I picked it. The ley net was never fully integrated with the newer systems, so security's a little more ragged at connection points like this. Better still, the antennas are mounted on a fire tower, and there's a cabin for the rangers, so we'll be able to get out of the weather."

"Somehow, the idea of sitting in a tiny unheated shack doesn't improve my mood much."

Just then we arrived at the base of the tower in question, a tall wooden framework with cell antennas, identifiable by their characteristic rod shapes, mounted to the supporting posts. At the base stood a concrete hut, painted green to blend with the surrounding conifers. A small log cabin was just visible a short way off through the trees.

"Mel, why don't you get a fire going in the cabin while I look at the communications shack?"

"You feeling all right, Boss? *I* get to do the quiet warm indoor job while *you* freeze in the snow?" Before I could respond he headed for the cabin. "Sounds like a lovely idea."

I considered chucking a snowball at him, but thought better of it. Instead I skied over to the hut and checked it out. The lock was a four-pin Schlage, but it yielded quickly to a spell-augmented pick.

Inside it was as cold as the great outdoors and as black

as the eyes of Cerberus. A quick flick of the light switch solved the latter problem. The room contained the switch-box and monitoring system for the cell antennas and a trap-door through which I accessed the fiber-optic conduit and junction. Pulling a small ball of silken cord from my fanny pack, I tied one end of the cord around the conduit and whistled a short binding spell.

The cord's knotted end liquefied and flowed through the surface of the conduit. Assuming I hadn't transposed a couple of ones and zeros, the strands of the knot would attach themselves to the various strands of fiber, giving me a hard line to the node. The quality of the link might have been a little cleaner if I'd done an actual optical connection, but that would have required serious tools. Also, since I wanted to use the ley part of the node as my main hacking channel anyway, it was probably better to use old-style symbolic magic for my entry point.

Once I'd unspooled a couple yards of cord I closed the trapdoor. That was another advantage to using silk—it didn't matter if it kinked. Then I headed for the cabin, playing out the line as I went.

The fire Melchior had started was beginning to cut the chill in the single open room. About fifteen feet on a side, it had two sets of bunk beds, a primitive kitchen, and a small fireplace. In the middle of the room was a small table. I removed my mask and gloves and tossed them onto it.

"Mel, climb up here, would you?"

"No thanks," he said from his perch on the hearth. "I like it by the fire."

"It wasn't a suggestion. I want to get the ley link established."

"If you insist, oh my lord and master." He rose from his seat on the rough stones and joined me.

I reeled out another fifteen feet of silk and cut it off. Then I stuck the loose end into a fiber-optic connector and crushed it shut with my Leatherman.

"Hey, Mel, why don't you shift to laptop?"

"Because you're planning on sticking an icy-cold connector into one of my toasty little ports, and I hate that!"

"Not half as much as you'll hate where I put it if you don't shift." He stuck his barbed tongue out from between sharply pointed teeth and waggled it from side to side.

"Melchior, Laptop. Execute."

He managed to flip me a rude gesture before his flesh started to flow and twist. Then the goblin was gone, slumping into the streamlined rectangle of my laptop, lid firmly closed in a subtle but pointed reminder that he disapproved of the current situation.

When I flipped up the top, the blue goblin logo to the left of the screen opened its eyes and glared. I was pretty sure that wasn't in his original programming. When I plugged the connector in and the little eyes crossed, I knew someone was exceeding his design specs again, and I smiled. The programmer side of my personality hated when things didn't work the way they were supposed to and itched to do some debugging. But as a sorcerer I took real pride in creating a familiar who was obviously so much more than a mere automaton.

Time to play with fire again, I typed. *Are you ready?*

As ready as possible with that freezing plug jammed into my port.

Don't worry. Things should heat up pretty quick once we hit Atropos's wards.

Wonderful!

My first exploratory program snaked its way into the ley net with no resistance. The little code weasel slid easily from silken cord to glass fiber to magical line. It slithered forward until it was just inside the nexus, stopped, and waited for further orders. I let it remain there, autonomous, for over an hour. I was feeling very cautious. Then I sent a quick query and the weasel speed-dumped its core into Mel's secure memory buffer for a virus check.

The picture that appeared on Mel's screen looked something like a spiderweb made of rainbow neon. In the center was a semisymmetrical structure of interconnected lines. From the junctures of this central mass came three major and five minor strands. Each of the larger strands left the nexus, then abruptly changed color. This represented the fact that they didn't follow the local topography, twisting off into alternate phase spaces instead. These were the links that tied the ley junction to the fate servers. The cyan went to Lachesis's network, the yellow to Clotho's, and the magenta to Atropos's. Hers was the brightest of the three, because it traced straight back to a server, while the other two patched into their respective systems farther out.

I carefully examined the strand on which the weasel had centered its attention. At the end of the line to Atropos.web was a tiny object almost exactly the same shade and saturation of magenta. With almost nothing to distinguish it from its surroundings it should have been very easy to miss. But finding holes is what I do best.

Zooming in, I saw a small scorpion-like thing whose stalk-mounted eyes tracked slowly across the whole node in a regular circular motion. Its tail, which lay across the junction of strand and node, tensed and untensed in a barely perceptible rhythm.

Gotcha! I typed.

Melchior flashed a comment on his screen. *What are you talking about?*

Don't you see it?

What I see is an elegant and deadly little piece of security programming. It's tiny and hard to spot, like a passive sentry, but it's obviously active and, knowing Atropos, deadly fast. I don't want anything to do with it.

All true. The spell had some of the same baroque beauty her Puppeteer spell possessed, albeit on a much smaller and simpler scale. Atropos was a real artist where it came to coding. If she had any flaw in her style, it was a tendency to let elegance get in the way of function as she had done here.

So, you don't see it? I typed.

What?

Look at how it moves its eyes, and the way the tail twitches. They're running in a steady pattern. Atropos had to sacrifice something to put all that nastiness into such a pretty little package. She didn't have room for a random-number generator, so she built in a set alert cycle. That means we can slip by in the gap when it resets to the start of its loop.

When do you suppose that is?

Every time the eyes look top center the tail extends onto the ley line. That's probably the upload cycle, when it dumps its memory back to the server.

So, the gap comes when the tail is at maximum contraction. I think you're right. Hell, if we slip a weasel in, it can attach itself to the back of the scorpion's memory packet and get a free ride all the way to the server.

Exactly.

It took five minutes to patch a command sequence together and send it to the weasel. This time, I wanted to keep an eye on things in real time, so I sent a second weasel to observe. Once that was in place, I sent the execute command to Weasel1.

It waited for the right opportunity, then darted forward. I held my breath when it passed from node to line, but everything went smoothly. On the other side of the guardian, it paused and dropped a relay before grabbing on to the back of the next packet upload. We were in.

All right, Mel! I typed. *Wait for the all clear, then set the hook.*

Waiting . . . There was a delay of perhaps fifteen minutes, and I became antsy. *Connect. The weasel has landed! Establishing bypass link.*

That was it. Our code weasel was inside the server node, and we could set up a direct mweb link bypassing Atropos's security completely.

Run Melchior. Execute, I typed.

"Next time, could you remember to disconnect the cables *before* I change, Boss?" he said as soon as he was back in webgoblin shape. Then, with a scowl, he pulled the connector from his nose.

I grinned. "Whatever you say, Mel. We've got our keyhole. Let's use it. Melchior, establish a locus transfer protocol link with Weasel1. Execute."

While he pulled tools from his belly pouch and went to work drawing a hexagram on the floor, I prepared for the transition. Opening my pack, I pulled out a pair of high court boots, a green-silk tunic, a black half cape, and my sword belt. I took my synthetic ski boots off and replaced them with the leather ones. My shirt and sweater were quickly swapped as well. The tights, of course, remained.

I grabbed one of my ski poles and flicked a hidden catch. Taking the handle in one hand and the shaft in the other, I pulled gently. Out of the shaft slid the silver-chased, damascene blade of my rapier. This went into the scabbard on my left hip. The long parrying dagger concealed in the other pole went into the one on the right.

That left only one detail: my face. I had no intention of being seen when I got to the other end, but family protocol insisted I do things properly. Besides, there was a chance I was going to die in the attempt, and I wanted to look good for the funeral. It struck me then how odd that might seem to a mortal. Here I was preparing to commit a serious crime against another member of my family, and I was worrying about my appearance. But it would have been unspeakably rude to do things any other way.

We cheat and steal from each other, break each other's codes, and trash each other's files, even kill one another. But that's all politics and therefore acceptable, simply part of what it means to belong to the extended family of the Titans. *How* we do things, on the other hand, belongs in the realm of etiquette, which is inviolable. We'll only do unto each other while wearing our real faces and our formal best. To do less would be to diminish ourselves. I'm not certain why court protocol and garb had advanced up to the Renaissance and no farther, but I suspected it was because my clan matriarchs had rather liked Queen Elizabeth's style.

I whistled the code sequence that released the illusion covering my features. There was no physical sensation as the tops of my ears elongated and sharpened to points once again, and my pupils resumed their natural catlike slit. A full-fledged child of Fate once more, I was ready to enter the demesne of Atropos.

I turned back to Melchior. He stood beside the completed hexagram, working his jaw like a shortstop with a mouthful of chaw. After a moment, he spat a netspider into the center of the drawing. It paused long enough to set a softly glowing anchor line, then vanished with a slight pop of inrushing air, like a bubble bursting. It was back an instant later, and Melchior scooped it up and popped it into his mouth. He made a face at the bitter taste.

"Ltp link established," said the webgoblin, "connecting to Mtp://mweb.(Weasel1@)Atropos.web/server/core." A series of sharp hisses and buzzes passed his lips before he continued, "Connect. Initiating Gate procedure."

The glowing end of the anchor changed from gold to green. Melchior bent on one knee and pulled on this small green nodule. The green light expanded to fill the whole diagram, then started to climb, like liquid poured into a hexagonal glass. When the column of light was about six feet high, it shifted from green to blue. The way was open.

CHAPTER NINE
■ ■ ■

"Shall we?" I asked, gesturing toward the shimmering light of the gateway.

"No thanks, Boss. The fire's getting low. You go ahead without me, and I'll make sure everything is nice and toasty on this end for your return."

"I don't think so, Mel."

Placing the toe of my boot firmly under his small blue butt, I gently shoved him into the light. Before he could do more than squawk, I joined him.

"Melchior, Locus Transfer. Execute."

He sighed, then hissed out the appropriate commands. Around us the walls of the cabin were replaced by the energyscape of the-place-between-worlds. For a few brief seconds, we were nothing more than packets of data streaming through a sea of primal chaos, with only the thin walls of an mweb channel to prevent our being rendered down to component parts. It was terrifying and exhilarating at the same time, like surfing a wave that's just a hair too large.

Almost before it started, it was over. We arrived at one end of a large stone room full of towering banks of organic crystal. No two structures looked alike. They were fractal shapes created for specific purposes by very unspecific means. Any chaotic system can serve as a computer when you enter the parameters of your question into the initial conditions. If you know how to set everything up, the final shape of the system will reflect any possible answers. That was how Atropos constructed her network, growing each processor to suit the needs of the moment.

A few of these twisted shapes crawled with light and life, humming quietly to themselves and dreaming electronic dreams. Most were dark and silent, the red and green jewel tones of their LEDs dull and dead. The atmosphere was laced with the burned-plastic smell of cooked transformers, an old room full of antiquated and mostly forgotten equipment. I headed for the very back. In a dark corner, out of sight of the door, I found a machine with a few blinking lights to indicate it was still operational.

"Here we go, Mel. Why don't you prep Revenant and Charon while I take a look at the Fate Core?"

"If Atropos catches us, she's going to have us for lunch."

"The only way she'll ever see Revenant is if we're already dead."

"Oh, *that's* reassuring," he replied, as his face took on the abstracted expression that means he's moving things from archive to active storage.

Flipping down the keyboard, I started typing commands. After a few minutes of careful work, I managed to pull up a system hierarchy schematic. I let out a low whistle. We'd struck the bull's-eye. When Atropos upgraded to copper she'd centralized all the old ley-line connections and their command architecture into one mainframe bank. My code weasel, tracking a ley link back into Atropos.web, had taken us straight to those mainframes. There was nowhere else for it to go. But the link I'd followed wasn't the only one governed from that room. My schematic clearly showed a lone strand of gold light running straight from my current machine to the Fate Core. I'd never dreamed Atropos would leave something like that in place.

"Hey, Mel. Are you done with your upload?"

"Yes. Have you found us a launch site?"

"Take a look at this!"

He climbed onto the console and peered at the screen. "That's beautiful. Do you think the security is as out-of-date as the hardware?"

"There's only one way to find out. Melchior, Charon. Execute."

He licked his right index finger and inserted it into the keyboard's universal port. Then he whistled a quick sequence of code, paused, whistled another one, and unplugged. Charon was the program I'd written to ferry Revenant to its new home in the Fate Core.

On the schematic, Charon showed as a tiny skull icon. It slid from my borrowed machine into the Fate Core line with only the briefest pause. From there it slipped down the ley line to the Fate gateway. The pause as it crossed from line to system was longer, but nothing like long enough. I felt an icy worm crawling up and down my spine. Something was very wrong.

"Uh, Boss?"

"Yes."

"I watched you put Charon together. It's as slick a piece of code as you could ask for, but there's no way it's that good. I think we should leave now."

"You know, Mel, I'd be inclined to agree with you, except for one thing."

"What's that?"

"Charon's already in the Fate Core. If Atropos is onto us, we're dead. Nothing we do will change that. On the other hand, if whatever's wrong isn't Atropos, we can't pass this opportunity up. We aren't ever going to have another chance this good."

Melchior nodded reluctantly, and I could feel sweat beading at my temples as I tried to decide what to do next. My original plan called for getting in, releasing Revenant, and getting the hell out. I hadn't precoded any real tools beyond Charon, and with the stakes so high I hated to wing it.

"Mel, I want to run a mole down there. Can do?" I didn't issue a command. I'd designed Melchior as a high-level hacking tool, and I wanted his opinion now, not his obedience.

"Hmm, standard hex code link . . ." He mumbled to himself for a little while before answering. "Yeah, Boss. No problem."

He moistened his finger and slid it into the port again. The whistled sequence was shorter this time and cruder.

"It's away," he said. "Once it gets a lock it'll start streaming back to here. The imaging system on this antique is a little crude, but it'll do."

After a brief interval, several windows opened on my screen. In the first, binary data scrolled by. On the second, a map of the mole's progress and relative position appeared. The third held a graphic representation of the mole's-eye view.

This latter showed the inside of the golden ley link. It looked something like a subway tunnel burrowed through raw ore. That wasn't right. It should have been older and smoother, polished by eons of data flow. At its end lay a huge obsidian gateway with an ID tag reading: "Fate Core. Enter here and ye shall be as never born, thy thread unraveled, thy destiny undone." The gate was closed, its panels

seemingly impenetrable. The mole advanced slowly. It nosed
at the gate, pushed gently . . . fell through. There was no resistance.

The mole turned and examined the gate. From my side
it looked like torn cobwebs. I'd come to hack the Fate Core,
but someone had beaten me to it. The ice worm in my spine
dropped a litter and hundreds of cold little offspring
crawled through my flesh. Something very bad was happening, and I might be the only person in the three houses
of Fate who knew about it. More than anything, I wanted to
run home and tell Lachesis, but that wasn't an option. Besides my problems with credibility and the Cassandra
curse, the penalty for being here was death, and right at the
moment I didn't think my grandmother would even hesitate at the thought. I'd need a lot more in the way of infor-
mational bargaining chips if I wanted to get that sentence
commuted.

I turned the mole around and looked through its eyes. In
this representation, the Fate Core was an endless sea filled
with the writhing snakes of the life threads, tumbling strands
of all lengths and colors. I sent the mole plunging in among
them. It hadn't gone far when it encountered something
huge. A wall of interlocking links of pale blue fire that slid
past in a seemingly endless progression. Mel's jaw fell open.

"What the hell is that?" he whispered.

"I don't know, but look at that armor."

I turned my attention to the map view. The mole was
nosing along one side of what appeared to be a giant batch
job, looking for a line of loose code. Finally, it found one.
In the graphic view, a bent link offered a slight gap into
which the mole slid its snout. For just a second, something
dark and serpentine appeared on the monitor. Then the
mole stopped seeing the program. The binary window
clicked shut. The map no longer read anything other than

the mole. The graphic view showed the sort of calm data-scape you'd expect on a normally engaged system.

"Shit!" I said.

"Oh yeah!" agreed Mel. "Whatever that thing is, it just unraveled the mole, subverted it, and put it back in place without even interrupting the data stream."

"I think we've found our invader." I felt my shoulders hunching as though they expected someone to put a knife between them.

"Well, it sure doesn't belong to Atropos," said Melchior, shaking his head gently. "She's not that subtle. Besides, she wouldn't need to convert probes within the system. She'd just fry them and call out the troops."

"I wonder whose it is?" I asked. "The Fates can't know about it. They wouldn't willingly let anything that big and nasty wander around if it wasn't theirs."

"Well," asked Melchior, "is that all bad? Someone else dislikes Atropos, too. Why don't we leave it to its business and get on with ours? We've been here too long as it is."

"You've got a point, but . . ."

"But what?" He jerked his chin up challengingly. "I can't see how anyone causing trouble for Atropos poses us a problem. Hell, we should be thanking them. Whoever it is might even draw her fire away from us for a while. Wouldn't that be nice?"

I was tempted. But the Fate Core is the place where the destiny of every living thing is laid out. From inside you can rewrite that destiny. There are other ways to do it—there's no such thing as pure predestination—but none of them are easy, and none of them are on the same scale. For all I knew, that thing could be as bad as Puppeteer, or worse. I couldn't just leave something that dangerous in there.

"No, Mel." I stepped away from the screen and stretched. "That's a really vicious piece of code. It gives me a bad feeling in the pit of my stomach. The Fate Core is the joint property of all three houses of Fate. It's not just Atropos's problem. It's mine, too. I'd like a better idea of what that is and what it's doing before I head for the hills. Let's knock together another mole. This time I want to get an overview of the boojum."

"That's just going to be a waste of time. We—"

"Melchior!" I snapped. "Just do it." He nodded his assent.

This time the graphic view showed a larger view, in which the twisting shape of the boojum was slowly moving through the data sea. It looked like a particularly nasty cross between a dragon and a snake. Its front end was somewhere below the surface, but its tail and the claws of its short hind legs were clearly visible trailing through the ocean of information. So was the line of its wake. I couldn't help myself, I physically flinched. I wasn't alone. Melchior was in such a hurry to get away from the grim sight that he actually fell off the console. Where the thing had passed, it left hollow, colorless life threads arranged in straight lines. I didn't know enough about how the Fate Core worked to know what that meant, but it looked terrible.

"Boss," whispered Melchior, standing on tiptoes to peer at the screen, "let's get the hell out of here. I don't know what that thing is, or what it's doing, but if Atropos finds us with our little electronic fingers within a thousand miles of it, we can kiss our asses good-bye."

"Too fucking right. Melchior, Exit Strategy. Exe . . ." The words died on my lips.

On screen, the boojum had raised its head. It looked like the world's biggest cobra. But where a cobra wore a symbol like two eyes connected by a U on its hood, this one had a glowing golden apple. It was the signature of Eris, Goddess of Discord, sworn enemy of Fate, and a distant cousin via Cronus's line. The golden apple had been her calling card ever since she'd used one to start the Trojan War.

All of that was washed from my mind when the thing struck, smashing its head into a dense cluster of life threads and swallowing thousands. Others swarmed away from it, but none made it past the crushing coils of Discord.

No surprises there. From everything I'd ever heard, Eris was one hell of a coder and without peer in the virus department. A hacking goddess. Where I coded spying moles and slinking weasels, she wrote virus dragons. One of which was eating its way through the Fate Core even as I watched.

I had a major dilemma. I couldn't let Eris have her way with the Fate Core, as much as I admired her hacker moxie for trying. I loathed Atropos and what she wanted to do with Puppeteer, but she wouldn't be the only victim. My grandmother Lachesis and my great-aunt Clotho were also in the Fate business. I didn't always agree with them, but they certainly handled things better than Discord would. She'd take things as far in the direction of pure chaos as Atropos wanted to take them toward absolute order. The issue was how to stop her.

If I went to my grandmother and let her know what was happening, I'd have a whole pile of hard questions to answer, most of which would lead straight back to Atropos. And, with the curse hovering over me, I couldn't go there. Saving the Fate Core would almost certainly get the traditional death sentence commuted, but imprisonment at Saint Turing's would be the least of my punishments.

I had no desire to emulate Prometheus. The myths may claim that was all Zeus's show, but he'd never have been able to chain a Titan without the complicity of the Fates. My eternal imprisonment would leave the field open for Atropos to destroy free will, not to mention making it hard to see Cerice. In addition, discovering my little trip to the Core would likely cause Clotho to add me to her active enemies list. One angry Fate I might dodge, two would pretty much doom me. That left only one option. I'd have to kill the dragon myself and hope nobody noticed.

"Melchior, load Vaccine for speed dump. Execute." His eyes went dreamy and far away as he began the transfer.

"Boss," he mumbled, fighting to speak despite the processor load, "hitting that thing with Vaccine would be like shooting BBs at the hydra."

"I know that. Just load it."

A small beep escaped his lips. "Loaded."

"Good, dump it into this machine." I patted the console. Melchior plugged in and complied. "Next. Melchior, load and dump E-bola."

"But that's not finished, and—"

"Melchior, previous command. Execute."

"Executing."

"Thank you, Mel." I straightened my spine. "Now I'm going to do something extremely stupid and dangerous."

"Since when is that newsworthy enough to announce?"

"Your confidence is underwhelming. I'm going to do several things in very quick order and I'll need you to multitask. I want you to prep Exit Strategy for instant use. I also want you to load the whole Snow Daze menu into active memory. I'm not certain if we'll need that later, but if we do, we'll need it fast. Can you hold all of that ready to execute without crashing?"

"Could be rough," said Mel. "Snow Daze is a big menu. Whiteout alone is a pretty heavy-duty spell. When you add Black Ice, North Wind, and all the others . . . Hmm."

He stared off into space for a while before finally nodding. I let out a long breath. If I'd had to give the appropriate commands in the correct sequence with the right syntax to make all of that work when the time came . . .

"All right. Melchior, prep Exit Strategy–Snow Daze sequence. Execute."

He folded himself into a full lotus, closed his eyes, and began to hum quietly. I crossed my fingers and waited. Nothing. If he crashed, he did it very quietly. My turn. First I took my borrowed machine out of the security net. The kind of programming I was about to do tended to ring all sorts of bells, and I *really* didn't want to see the system administrator. I pulled Vaccine up on the screen alongside E-bola and went to work. It was touchy stuff. Vaccine was a pretty straightforward antivirus program, and it would make a good delivery system. E-bola was an entirely different story.

Every coder worth his RAM has written a virus or two, usually fairly benign little things. Most hard-core hackers have also at least conceived of, and probably coded, a little bit of their very own doomsday virus. Something designed to eat applications for breakfast, operating systems for lunch, and the hardware for dinner.

E-bola is mine. It makes Scorched Earth, which took down the whole mweb, look like a freshman's intro-programming project. It's also a very rough beta version, and too large to compile on anything short of a mainframe. Its biggest drawback so far is burn cycle. Like its namesake, it tends to kill its host too quickly for really effective transmission. I didn't see that as a problem in this case.

It took time I didn't really have to gut Vaccine and insert E-bola into the raw hole I created for it, and I had to cut a lot of corners on the way. I fed this new hybrid into the compiler, titled the job Saint George, and set it running. That was going to take something like another ten minutes.

I drew my sword. I was running an unauthorized compile on an Atropos.web computer. If I'd made any mistakes when I pulled out of the security net, alarms would be going off all over the place, and someone would undoubtedly be along to kill me shortly.

Five minutes passed without the world falling on me, and I was beginning to think I might get away with it. Then the door at the far end of the room slid open and my cousin Laric stepped in. He wore black breeches, boots, and a full shirt of white silk. The ensemble matched his beard and skin nicely, giving him a piratical air. More importantly, he was alone. I let out a little sigh of relief. Laric was one of the more civilized of Atropos's brood, and I had an excellent chance of reasoning with him. We'd even been friends once upon a time.

"Ah, Ravirn, how nice to see you again," said Laric. "We so rarely get a chance to exchange pleasantries." He drew his own rapier and dagger. "I must admit I'm surprised to see you under such circumstances. This"—he gestured at the machine that was running my job with his dagger—"seems a bit clumsy. You haven't the sense of a drunken raccoon, but you're normally more subtle." He slowly advanced until, with his last words, he was close enough to aim a cut at my left shoulder.

"Wait!" I yelped, leaping back. "Dragon! Fate Core! Big Dragon! Eris!" I probably could have been a bit more articulate, but I was a little on the tense side.

Laric shook his head sadly and struck again. This time I parried with my dagger and reflexively used my rapier to riposte toward his right thigh. After that I was too busy too speak. Laric knocked my first thrust aside with his sword and swept his dagger in a backhanded cut at my face. I leaned out of reach and aimed a stop thrust at his midriff. We'd exchanged another couple of dozen quick passes when the loud ringing of a bell behind me took my mind off Laric for a critical moment. He must have been startled as well. Otherwise his thrust would have skewered me instead of glancing off a rib and opening a long bloody cut in my side.

"Hold, enough!" I cried, leaping back. "I need to tell someone about this, because it's more important than my neck." He looked skeptical, but didn't press his advantage. I continued, "You can go back to trying to kill me in a minute if you don't like what you hear. Eris has hacked the Fate Core."

"What!? How did you find out?"

It was not a good time for the truth. I needed something that would convince Laric to listen to me, and with the curse hovering in the air waiting to twist my words the truth was not it. At the moment a well-told lie would be infinitely more convincing.

"I had this idea about how to hack into your server here." I outlined my ley-line ploy before continuing. I didn't tell him about my motivations, of course. "I was still investigating whether it would work and sniffing around the ley nexus when I found evidence that someone had preceded me. Knowing the amount of credibility I have with your grandmother, I thought I'd better have rock-solid proof before I took anything to the Fates. So I followed the line here and found a huge dragon of a virus wallowing around in the Fate Core."

"A dragon. In the Fate Core. Right."

"No, dammit. I have hard evidence."

"Show me."

It was a risk but . . . I sheathed my weapons and turned back to my console. Out of the corner of my eye, I watched Laric bring his rapier up to hover beside my neck. It hung there for a long beat before he finally slid it back into its scabbard. Wishing Melchior were free to do the job, I roughly bandaged the cut in my side. Then I showed Laric what I'd found and what I was doing about it.

"I don't know about this," he said, tapping the screen where Saint George was laid out. "It has too much potential for going wild and taking out the whole Core. I think I should get Atropos down here."

"If you do, she'll kill me." I hesitated for a moment after I said that, waiting to see if I felt the pull of the curse. But apparently that was far enough from the matter of Puppeteer and its ramifications to let me get away with it. "She may not do it today, but there's no question she will. I might be able to dodge her for a few months, but that contest is too unequal to go on forever." I gestured at the dragon. "I found that thing, and I'm trying to do something about it. Don't you think I deserve better than execution for my troubles?"

"Bastard!" he snarled, putting his face scant inches from mine. "You killed Moric, and now you expect *me* to save your ass?"

"I'm sorry about Moric, I really am, but that was self-defense." I wanted to move away, but I held my ground. "If you bring Atropos in now, it'll be murder." There was a long silence.

"I should have cut your throat before I had time to think about it," he growled. "All right, we'll try it your way, but with conditions. First, you have to swear on your blood that you'll never ever tell anyone I let you off the hook."

"Fair enough." I placed my right hand over my heart. "I swear on my blood and my honor that it shall be as you say."

"Good. Now, here's the hard one. We aren't going to just let this Saint George program of yours loose. We'll ride it all the way in, and shut it down when it's finished." He glared at me fiercely, as if daring me to turn him down.

It *was* a nasty condition. It's a moderately painful procedure, and under the circumstances, it could easily have fatal consequences. In order to enter the magic-laced world of the mweb, you have to send your animating will, your anima, into the ether. If the program you're inhabiting dies, it takes your anima with it, and you die, too. And quite frankly, Saint George looked pretty flimsy next to that huge thing Eris had coded. But Laric was right, letting the E-bola side of Saint George into the Core without someone aboard who could pull the plug was an unconscionable risk.

Laric must have been hoping I'd turn him down, because he looked disappointed at my nod. Disappointed and more than a bit scared. I couldn't blame him. I was scared, too. But we were both committed. He leaned over, opened a panel on my machine, and pulled out a couple of networking cables. He handed one to me, then reached into his pouch and pulled out a tiny iron dagger. I looked at the athame with distaste, but that didn't prevent me producing a matching one. I plugged my cable into a socket in the pommel.

"I'm ready when you are," I said.

"After you."

I drew a deep breath and stabbed the athame into my left palm, bearing down until the simple cross hilt touched flesh. The pain was breathtaking, but fleeting, as my awareness was catapulted into the computer. I slid easily into Saint George. Laric joined me a moment later. Looking around, it quickly became obvious my hybrid had problems. The integration between the two parent programs was spotty, with E-bola banging around loosely inside Vaccine's shell. We were going to have to operate it almost as two separate programs.

"Do you have a preference?" I asked Laric.

"I'll take the Vaccine side. It seems pretty straightforward, and that E-bola thing looks gods-awful."

"All right then. Lay on, Macduff."

He grinned at me and aimed us for the Core. We slid through the twists and turns of the ley line like a guided missile, accelerating all the way. If I'd known what kind of driver Laric was, I'd have insisted he take E-bola. There was a moment of blackness as we crashed through the gateway, then we were arrowing across the sea straight toward the dragon.

We glanced off its back with enough force to rip great chunks of our code loose and send them tumbling into the waves. Vaccine was the best antivirus I've ever written. It was quick, sharp, and very nasty. But we hit the dragon's armor a half dozen times with no apparent effect before the beast finally noticed us. On our next attempt, it reared up with impossible speed, flaring its hood and preparing to strike. Laric put us into a steep climb and headed right for the open mouth.

"What are you doing!?" I screamed.

"Aiming for a soft spot!" He pointed at the monster's exposed palate.

We almost made it. The dragon was a beautiful piece of programming, but it was still just ones and zeros, incapable of anticipating the sorts of completely irrational actions people are prone to make. Still, all it needed to do was close its mouth. Huge teeth ripped through the outer program, tearing it and Laric to ribbons, but doing only minor damage to E-bola. The same lack of integration that had forced us to split control of Saint George let me tear myself free of Vaccine's corpse and slide down the dragon's gullet.

That put me into the thing's digestive track. It was dark, it stank, and I could feel E-bola starting to come apart around me. Big pieces tore free and scattered. My awareness split and followed them. As each string of code peeled off into the darkness, I went with it and we latched on to a different part of the dragon's command line. Then we started to feed. It didn't take long after that. I could feel the dragon's strength flowing into us as we became a thousand ulcers inside the dragon's stomach, each one boring itself a route to the surface. Inside of three minutes, the dragon was bleeding out through a hide that looked like scarlet lace.

Power cascaded through my soul and with it ecstasy. My many parts all wanted to feed, and we were surrounded by a feast of data. I don't know what might have happened then if one of my awarenesses hadn't bitten into a fragment of Vaccine. The electronic taste of Laric's cooling blood filled my mouth, and I gagged. I called out to the burrowing code strings, sending them the shutdown order.

The sound of an alarm filled the air. I opened my eyes and found myself back in my own body. I was kneeling over Laric's corpse. The feedback had killed him. His hand, where the athame had been, was a charred wreck, and scorch marks ran up his arm, but his face was almost peaceful. Reaching into my pouch, I pulled out a couple of coins and laid them on his closed eyelids. I slid another into his mouth as fee for the ferryman.

"Sleep easy, Laric. You died well."

Wincing, I pulled the athame from my palm and replaced it in my pouch. I was just whistling the spell that closed the magically charged wound when a harsh noise drew my attention to the room's door. Hwyl stood there, growling low in his throat.

"First Moric, now Laric," he snarled. " I'm going to eat your liver while it's still steaming."

From Hwyl that wasn't bravado; it was a statement of intent. His broad mouth opened in what might, in a face with fewer sharp, pointy teeth, have been called a smile. His only clothing was a loincloth that left little doubt as to his gender. The rest of his low and massive frame was covered with tawny fur. His long, thick arms ended in pawlike hands. Reflected light scattered from steel-tipped claws as he let out a bellow and raced to close with me. I was pretty shocky, but I wasn't quite ready to fold out of the game.

I yanked my rapier from its sheath and rammed the point of it deep into the charging were's hipbone. Hwyl let out a horrible scream as the area around the wound blackened and charred. The steel blade might not have hurt him, but the silver inlay was another story entirely. He spun away, clutching at the scorched hole in his leg, and tumbled to the ground. I could have finished him then and I probably should have, but I'd already cost my great-aunt two grandsons. I couldn't bear the thought of having a third on my conscience.

"Melchior," I said instead, "Exit Strategy sequence. Execute."

The webgoblin stood and drew a circle on the stone in front of him. It was about thirty inches in diameter, and he'd barely finished when the manhole-sized chunk of rock on which he was drawing dropped away into darkness. With barely a pause, Melchior jumped in after it.

"If you'll excuse me." I bowed to Hwyl. "I need to be going." I raised my sword above my head so I'd be in no danger of landing on it, and stepped into the hole.

CHAPTER TEN

It felt like I'd stepped into the top of a dark elevator shaft. That's part of the reason ley links are no longer in common use. I wasn't particularly thrilled about using one myself, but Atropos would have sealed off the higher mweb channels and with them all locus transfer protocol links the second the alarm sounded. It would take longer to get the ley lines closed, because it was a more involved process, but there was no doubt she'd shut them down as well. Fortunately, I'd already be gone.

A brief but immeasurable time later, light appeared below us. A moment later, we dropped out of thin air and fell several feet, hitting the table in the ranger's cabin with a jarring thump. My injured knee buckled, and I landed hard. Then the table collapsed, and we slid the rest of the way to the floor. Miraculously, considering how many sharp blades, claws, and fangs were involved, neither of us took any new injury.

I dragged myself to my feet and picked up my rapier, sheathing it. Then I yanked off my court boots and grabbed for my Salomons. I didn't have much time before pursuit arrived. As soon as I had my boots on, I retrieved the shoulder bag holding my emergency kit from the mountain pack. The rest of my stuff wasn't likely to make an immediate difference in my survival and not having the bulk might.

Meanwhile, Melchior had snapped my blades back into the ski poles, grabbed my hat and gloves, and raced to the doorway, where dancing with impatience, he waited. Outside, it was cloudy and beginning to get dark. In Minnesota in winter, it's always cloudy and beginning to get dark, unless of course it's cloudy and already dark. While I stepped into my bindings, Mel climbed into the bag.

"Melchior," I said, kicking off toward the path, "Whiteout. Execute." He whistled out the long sequence of the spell, then gave me a concerned look.

"Ahh, Boss. In case you haven't noticed, we're miles and miles from civilization. Are you sure that's a good idea?"

"No, Mel. I'm not. But I think we'll need it."

He shook his head and hunkered deeper into the bag. The wind was already rising in response to the spell, and the first fat flakes of snow were falling. Before we'd gone fifty feet, the snow was thick enough to blur the outline of the cabin. That's probably what saved my life.

The first arrow put a hole in my cloak as it passed, but left me unharmed. I didn't expect to be that lucky twice. If the archer was Dairn, he didn't miss often, and I knew from hard-earned experience that his arrows packed a hell of a punch. Worse, as Moric's brother and Laric's first cousin, he had a very personal reason for wanting to hang my hide over his hearth. I swerved off the trail and into the trees, hoping the dense evergreens would obscure his vision. They certainly did mine. A nearby tree stopped a second arrow, and I picked up the pace as much as possible, which wasn't a lot. If I'd only been able to get a little farther along the trail, nobody on foot could have caught me, bum leg or not. But the undergrowth in the deep woods negated much of the advantage of my skis.

I hadn't gone far when the trees opened up in front of me, and a long steep slope tumbled away into white emptiness. What I could see of the hill was uneven and covered with brush and deep snow. It was perfect ankle-breaker terrain and all too likely to end in a drop-off. I didn't hesitate. Another arrow passed over my head as I pushed off, but I was too busy watching the ground ahead to pay it any real mind. I had to dodge around two birch saplings and a raspberry bramble in the first few seconds. After that it was clear sailing for forty or fifty feet.

I'd covered perhaps twenty of those when the world grabbed me by the foot and threw me to the ground. My ski, gliding along under the snow, had caught on a root. The fall wasn't too painful. I'd been lucky in that the snag had caught my good leg, but my foot was trapped. I swore. Another arrow slammed into the ground a yard to my right. Looking back up the slope, I couldn't see the archer through the thick curtain of snow. Hell, I couldn't see the birch saplings, which was probably the only reason I was still breathing. Dairn was shooting by ear.

"Mel," I whispered, "see if you can get my leg loose. I'll lay down some covering fire."

This time the arrow whispered by a few feet overhead before vanishing into the snowy haze. I didn't hear it land. The snow muffled sound. I had my .45 half-out of its holster when I realized what a stupid move that would be. I hadn't a chance in the world of hitting Dairn, and the muzzle flash would pinpoint my position. I might just as well put up a PLEASE SHOOT ME sign.

A very tense forty or fifty seconds later Mel whispered that I was loose. As gingerly as possible, I got to my feet.

Dairn must have been closer by then, because the next arrow passed between the bones of my left forearm like a hot coal going through a garbage bag. I felt my grip on that ski pole go limp, but the lanyard held, and it dragged behind me as I slid away down the slope.

If any more arrows came my way, I didn't know about it. The blizzard I'd summoned was up to full fury by then, and I couldn't see much beyond the tips of my skis. Fortunately, the slope ended in a solidly frozen small river instead of a drop-off. The ice was covered with six inches of snow. I couldn't have asked for better skiing, and not even Hwyl could have tracked me in such conditions.

Sure, I was lost in a Minnesota whiteout, and I couldn't see my feet, much less my way; but after slipping away from Dairn and Hwyl, outhacking Eris, and besting the crone who holds the shears, I felt I couldn't lose. It's funny how wrong you can be.

"Boss?" said Melchior, poking his head out of the bag.

I'd shifted the bag to my left shoulder and was using it as a sort of improvised sling. Mel moved carefully, but the inevitable jarring still hurt.

"What is it, Mel?" I asked through clenched teeth.

"I'm freezing," he said.

"So am I."

I didn't think that I'd ever been so cold. It had been dark for a while, and with the coming of night the temperature plummeted. I was really regretting that I hadn't taken the time to swap my cloak for the parka. The temperature was aggravating the damage to my arm, and it felt like the blood from the wound in my side had frozen. If I'd been human, it would have been game over by that point. As it was, if I stayed on my feet and kept moving, and if it didn't get much colder, I'd probably live through the night. I kept telling myself that. It didn't help as much as I'd have liked.

I'm not a true immortal. I don't age and I'm tough, but I *can* be permanently injured, witness my knee and my fingertip, and I can be killed. And these were prime conditions for killing. It was way below freezing, I was exhausted and lost, and I didn't dare use magic for fear of broadcasting my location to Atropos.

At least it was still snowing. As long as the snow kept falling and the cloud cover stayed, it wouldn't get too cold. Record lows are always set on clear nights when there's nothing between the ground and space to keep the heat in.

"Where are we going?" asked Melchior.

"I'm not sure. I've been so busy worrying about the 'away from' part of running I haven't given much thought to the 'where to' bit. I don't want to try an ltp link yet. I'd rather not use any more magic until we're a good long way from the cabin. That's why I haven't had you do anything about my injuries. Our chances for clemency are going to be a whole lot better if the Fates have a chance to see what Eris was doing in the Fate Core before they find us."

"I'd rather they didn't find us at all," replied the webgoblin, morosely. "Atropos will never let us live after this stunt."

"I don't know about that. If I'm fast enough on my feet when it comes time to explain things, we might be all right. After all, it won't look very good if she keeps crying for my head once she finds out I saved the Fate Core from the Goddess of Discord."

"You don't actually believe that, do you?" His voice was incredulous.

I'd thought about it quite a bit as I skied along on the frozen streambed. "No, I suppose I don't. But if they decide to cut my thread, there's nothing I can do about it except spit in Hades's eye when I get to the far bank of the

Styx. Besides, I need something to keep my mind off the fact that I'm slowly freezing to death."

"I have a better way to do that, Boss," said Melchior, standing up in the bag.

The movement hurt my arm, and my response came out sharp and harsh. "What's that?" I snapped.

"There's light off that way," said Melchior, pointing.

I followed the line of his finger. Between the trees on my left, there was a very faint glow. The whirling snow hid details, and it looked like someone shining a flashlight through a cotton ball, but it was there. I turned off the stream and headed toward it. As I got closer, the light grew steadily brighter. I still couldn't make out details, but I had a pretty good idea of what it must be. I'd been able to see the lights through a blizzard from something like a half mile away, and the only places on Earth with that much light are used-car dealerships.

About fifty yards out, I came to an eight-foot chain-link fence with a strip of barbed wire on top. There were endless rows of "previously owned" sport utility vehicles on the other side. The fence extended out of sight in both directions, so I stopped and, one-handed, unclipped my skis from my boots and tossed them over. Holding my poles carefully, I jumped after them. I didn't land well. My bum knee might be all right for everyday use or even skiing, but it didn't like long drops at all. No sooner had my feet touched than it felt like someone had decided to use my knee as a golf tee, someone who had a problem with divots. Fortunately, the snow cushioned my collapse. It also muffled my scream. Little bits of floating light danced in front of my eyes while I clung to the edges of consciousness. I didn't particularly like being aware just then, but passing out facedown in a snowbank seemed like a good way to take a permanent rest.

After a while, I decided to get up. Using a slightly

battered Ford Bronco as a crutch, I dragged myself into a standing position. When I felt I could deal with a new shipment of pain, I tried putting weight on my right leg. The knee held, but complained loudly. If I took things gently, I'd probably be able to stay upright, but I sure as hell wasn't going to do any more skiing. I was just trying to figure out what to do next when Melchior chimed gently. He popped his head out of the bag, jarring my arm again.

"You've got an incoming visual from Cerice."

"I do? Well then, put her through," I replied.

His eyes and mouth lit in the primary colors of light, and Cerice sprang into being on the snow in front of me. She was wearing a golden silk kimono patterned with red phoenixes. Her white skin was even paler than usual, and her nose was red. She looked as though she'd been crying. That worried me. Cerice never cries.

"What's wrong?" I asked.

"Oh, Ravirn, they're going to kill you. How could you? I didn't even know that was possible."

"They are," I said. Then, "How could I what?" And, "What's possible?" I was confused.

She shook her head. "Don't think I'm an idiot. I'm talking about the virus in the Fate Core. I've heard the whole story. Clotho and Lachesis were there and everything. They tried to cut your thread." A look of bafflement crossed her face. "How did you do that? They're furious."

"Do what?" I was scared and confused. The killing me bit I could understand. That was pretty damned straightforward. Just "snip" and game over. It was the rest of it I didn't get. Like the part where I was still vertical. "Cerice, what are you talking about?"

"It's not going to save you, you know. As soon as they found out your thread had been erased, they sent the Furies after you." She lowered her head sadly. "I can't believe you killed Laric. I thought he was your friend. Chaos and Discord. I'm having a hard time believing any of it, but the evidence is awfully damning." She closed her eyes, and her voice became a whisper. "And to think I've been falling for you." There was a pleading note in her voice as she said this last, as though she wanted me to give her some reason to believe I wasn't responsible for whatever it was I'd been accused of.

"Cerice," I said, as firmly as possible. "Hush."

I was utterly baffled. Only about one word in three of what she was saying made any sense. She seemed to be speaking in some kind of code. I didn't know what Cerice thought had happened, or why she was so upset with me, but I strongly suspected my time was running out.

The word *Furies* had concentrated my attention marvelously. The Furies, embodiments of the twin concepts of revenge and justice, are one hundred percent bad news. If they were coming to kill me, I was probably going to die, and it probably wouldn't be a clean death either. Family lore said that when they'd gone after my cousin Menander, they'd played him like a cat plays a mouse: lots of frenetic running, squeaking, and batting that ended with a nasty little crunch. I tried to clear the image from my mind. I needed to find out what was happening if I wanted even the slimmest chance of avoiding that death.

"I haven't a clue what you're talking about," I said to Cerice. "I don't know anything about erased threads."

Not unless she was talking about whatever it was Eris's dragon had been doing when it ate life threads. They could have been erased, but they could also have been rewritten into Discord-worshipping zombies. I didn't know enough about the inner workings of the Core even to hazard a guess. Besides, I didn't *feel* erased. But I didn't have time for wild speculations or for twenty questions with Cerice. I'd have to sort it out later.

"There was a virus in the Fate Core," I said, "but it wasn't mine. It belonged to Eris. Laric and I killed it." She opened her mouth, but I held up a hand. "Let me finish. If the Furies really are on the way, I may not have the time to say any of this ever again. Laric died fighting the virus. He *was* my friend, and I'd have spared him if I could. Nobody regrets his death more than I." I paused and took a deep breath. Talking about Laric took more out of me than I'd expected, and I needed to recompose myself.

"Lastly, and most importantly," I said, "if you really are falling for me, that would be the best thing to happen to me in what looks like it's going to be a rather short life."

I realized then that I wanted to tell her that for me falling had given way to fallen some time ago. I hadn't truly appreciated it until that moment, with death approaching on wings of vengeance, but what I felt for Cerice was more than deep affection colored by lust. Maybe I'd been half in love with her for years without knowing it. Whatever the case, somewhere along the line half in love had become more like three-quarters. I wanted to let her know, but I couldn't. It would have been unfair in the extreme, to promise a heart that might stop beating at any moment.

"I have to go," I finally said. "And if this is the last time we speak, remember that I cared for you, more than I've ever cared for anyone else." It was inadequate, but it was the best I could do. "Good-bye, Cerice."

"Good-bye, Ravirn." She looked up again for one brief moment and met my eyes. "I . . . I cared for you, too." The lights in Melchior's face went out, and she was gone. I lifted him out of the bag and set him on his feet. Then I pulled the sleeve back from my injured forearm.

"It's time to use magic, Mel. It can't make things any worse."

"Not with the Furies coming to kill you. You could swallow a pint of nitroglycerin and try to escape by pogo stick, and it wouldn't make things worse."

"Thanks for the vote of confidence. Melchior, Patch & Go. Execute."

"Executing," he said.

He spat a netspider into his hand. By squeezing it, he was able to get a big gob of cobweb, which he applied to the paired entry and exit wounds on my arm. When that was in place, he whistled a short burst of binary, and I felt warmth spreading outward from the points of contact.

I'd coded the spell while recuperating from my encounter with Moric and company. It wasn't exactly a full healing spell. Those take a lot of time and personal power investment, and I'd wanted something that required neither. But it wasn't really an illusion either. That wouldn't have done much good. Instead, it was somewhere in between. The webbing would bond with the flesh and make the wound look and feel healed.

I'd be able to use it normally for a while, but eventually I'd have to peel it off and really fix the problem. In the meantime it wouldn't do any real healing and might actually get worse. Also, I'd probably lose some flesh when I ripped the stuff loose, but I was willing to trade function now for cost later. I'd have liked to do the ribs as well, but the Furies could arrive at any time and I had something else I needed to do first.

"Melchior," I said, "Scorched Earth. Execute."

"Loading," said the webgoblin.

Scorched Earth was a big spell, and it would take a little while to prep. I just hoped it was time I had. It had crashed the mweb the last time I tried it. Right at the moment I couldn't think of a better result. I had no illusions that it would actually prevent the Furies from getting to my present DecLocus, but it would certainly slow them down while I tried to put some distance between us. As I waited for the spell to finish loading, I felt the sickly fingers of panic begin to caress my soul. Maybe I shouldn't have taken time to fix my arm. Maybe I should have just hung up on Cerice the moment she'd said *Furies*.

"Executing," said Melchior after a few seconds. He began to spew high-speed binary. Another couple of seconds passed before he stopped whistling. "Scorched Earth successfully . . . Success . . . Succ . . . Scorched Earth Null Set. Mweb security alert. Illegal Command. Fatal Error. Fatal Error." He sneezed once, very loudly. Then his whole body went rigid, and he keeled over.

I suddenly had trouble breathing. It felt like my lungs were filling with sand. My familiar had crashed, and I was going to die. My leg hurt. My side hurt. If I added in the fact that my girlfriend seemed to think I'd done something horrific, I had the beginnings of a country western song. I felt like shit, and I must admit I entertained the idea of quietly lying down in the snow next to Melchior and letting events roll over me. It would have been so easy. Atropos was going to win, and I was going to lose. Why prolong things?

I'm not sure why I didn't give up then. I think it was Cerice and all the unanswered questions. If I'd died then, I'd never have been able to find out what we could mean to each other or learn what she'd been talking about when she said my life strand had been erased. It might not seem like much of a motive, but it kept me moving.

I bent and flipped Melchior onto his back. Just below and behind his right ear was a small wartlike projection. It was his programmer's switch, which would force a reboot. Taking it between thumb and forefinger, I twisted and pushed. There was a gentle chime followed by the sound of a processor cycling. Hopefully, that would take care of the crash, but I doubted it. Webgoblins are very stable little machines, and it takes a lot to bring one down. I was pretty sure the problem hadn't been with Scorched Earth, which meant it was probably a countervirus of some kind. The sneeze, a common alert signal for webgoblins with viral problems, tended to reinforce that speculation.

My guess was that the Fates had upgraded mweb security after the last crash and that the new systems had done something vicious to Melchior. That scared me. The Fates can be *very* nasty when they want to, and Melchior was, much as I might hate to admit it to anyone but myself, my best friend.

Grabbing my webgoblin by the scruff of his neck, I stuffed him into the bag and started limping across the snowy pavement. I didn't bother to pick up my skis. I wasn't going to outrun the Furies on foot, not when they could fly at close to sixty miles an hour. I needed a car, but the ones here in the back of the lot were all parked in. I was almost at the front of the line when I heard a sound like someone ripping a hole in reality somewhere behind me. Sure enough, peering over my shoulder, I spotted a jagged rent hanging in the air above the place where I'd abandoned my skis.

Take a movie screen. On it, project a snowstorm. Now place an enraged tiger in the room behind the screen. At some point the tiger is going to realize that all it has to do to get out and shred the audience is to use those nice, sharp claws and make an itty-bitty hole in the screen. The end result was pretty much what I was seeing. The only difference was that next to the Furies, an enraged tiger is a fat and lazy house cat. The first one through the hole was Alecto; I could tell by her wings.

That's the easiest way to identify a Fury. None of the three ever wears clothing. They don't need protection, and modesty is a concept utterly foreign to them. As she emerged, I pictured her and the others as I had last seen them at a hubris trial.

Alecto was a tall, beautiful woman with a voluptuous figure and skin the gray of granite. Her eyes and nipples and the hair that grows on her head and at the base of her belly were sable shot with silver, like lightning on a dark night. Her wings were a midnight storm.

Megaera was shorter and less generously proportioned, with an olive complexion. Where Alecto was ebony and silver, Megaera was a rich dark green. Her wings hung in the air above her like a seaweed mat big enough to swallow ships.

Tisiphone was slender, almost boyish, her skin so pale you could see her veins tracing fractal patterns in blue ink. Her hair and eyes were flame, and her wings ignited forest fires.

I didn't wait around to see them in person though. I wanted to make my exit while there was still only one of them on my side of that rip. Turning to the nearest car, I whistled a quick spell of opening. It wasn't a very good spell—it's hard to whistle when your lips are freezing—but it was only a car door. I tossed my bag and ski poles onto the passenger seat and slid into what turned out to be an old Toyota Land Cruiser. Reaching under the steering column, I applied a little superhuman strength and wrenched the ignition switch free. The engine caught on the first try, which frankly surprised me, considering the way the rest of my life was going.

In the rearview I could see the second Fury, Tisiphone as it turned out, pass into this DecLocus and unfurl her burning wings. The next step in my little auto theft was to snap the steering lock. As I did this, Alecto lowered her head to my fallen skis like a wolf sniffing out the trail of an injured deer.

I floored it. Tisiphone, who'd maintained an alert stance, watching while her sister took the scent, howled and pointed. Megaera, who had just emerged from the place between worlds, and Alecto nodded agreement. Wings snapped wide and the trio flung themselves into the air. In an instant they'd vanished into the storm.

When they'd taken Menander they'd attacked like falcons, climbing high into the sky and dropping on him in pile-driver dives, smashing him to the ground again and again as he tried to escape. He was nothing but a pulpy sack of shattered bone by the end. As I accelerated, my mind kept rerunning the scene endlessly, like the preview of an overhyped coming attraction at the local theater.

Cutting around the dealership building, I headed for the front gate. In another season I'd have taken the direct route to the highway and plowed through the fence, but I didn't dare get stuck in a snowdrift. The gate was closed. It didn't even slow me down. A Land Cruiser moving at forty miles an hour packs a lot of punch.

As I hit the open road, I switched to pushing the pedals with my left foot to take some of the strain off my injured knee. It was never going to be as good as new, but I heal fast, and giving my leg some downtime might make all the difference later. After a bit I glanced at Melchior. He should have finished his reboot by then, and it would have been a perfect time to have him back online. No such luck. The rigidity had left his body, but that was the best that could be said for him. I ran a hand gently along his spine.

"Just sleep it off and don't worry about anything, my little blue friend. I've got everything under control." I couldn't help adding, "And if you believe that, I've got a pomegranate farm I'd like to sell you. Riverfront property with a beautiful view. Sure, the river's the Lethe and it's deep in the heart of Hades, but once you taste those pomegranates you'll never want to leave. Even a couple of seeds will do. Just ask Persephone."

Minutes passed without anything happening. I couldn't delude myself into believing the Furies had forgotten about me, but I began to hope the storm was too nasty for them to hunt properly. I got the Toyota up to seventy-five, which was way too fast for conditions, but nowhere near as fast as I wanted to go. I could see maybe thirty feet, and that not well. The wind whipped the snow around like a horizontal tornado with me at the eye, hurling individual flakes at the windshield like icy bullets. If it hadn't been for the compass on the dashboard, I'd have lost all sense of direction. I was only able to stay on the road by riding the yellow line, and even that kept fading in and out of view.

Every so often I'd a hit a patch of ice, and through the steering wheel I'd feel the tires lose their grip on the road. At those moments all that kept me going in the right direction was momentum and luck. It was terrifying in a way the Furies could never be. Alecto and her sisters would kill me if they could, but that was personal. They would do it with the ultimate knowledge of who I was and why I was dying. The storm wouldn't even notice my passing. The irony that I had summoned this particular storm into being to save my life, and that now it might kill me, didn't help my mood.

A sign loomed out of the white blur on my right, pointing me toward the Highway 10 entrance ramp. Pumping the brakes like a madman, I slowed for the turn. As I began to spin the wheel, there came a sharp bang, like a sledgehammer smashing into steel plate, and the Toyota rocked wildly, tilting down and toward the right. At first I thought I'd blown a tire, but then something in the right-hand corner of my vision caught my attention. Turning my head, I saw five narrow spikes driven through the roof of the car. The finger claws of a Fury. They'd missed my head by no more than six inches. A second set was driven through the steel another foot and a half to the right, and I was sure that if I looked back I'd see matching toe claws over the cargo area.

I pushed the gas pedal back to the floor and roared up the entrance ramp, hugging the right side of the lane. As I clutched at the wheel, I felt a twinge in my right arm where the webbing hadn't bonded perfectly. Halfway up the ramp, I found what I was looking for, a big traffic-merging sign. When I hit it, the thin metal supports snapped like the pins on a poorly installed sound card, and the heavy steel sign folded over, slamming into the Fury on my roof at fifty miles an hour. With a horrible screeching sound, her claws tore free of the Toyota, and she hit the road behind me. I didn't look back. There were two more around, and I knew better than to believe I'd done more than inconvenience the third. She'd be back, and she'd be angry.

That's when I noticed the fuel light. I didn't know enough about Land Cruisers to know whether that meant I needed gas immediately, or in fifty miles. Cursing violently, I started looking for gas station signs. The storm was still sitting on the landscape like a roll of cotton batting, and I didn't dare try to top the seventy-five miles per hour I'd been running at. Since that hadn't shaken the Furies loose yet, I didn't think it would. I was going to need some kind of plan if I wanted to live through my refueling stop. It was a couple of minutes before I saw an Amoco advertised for the exit ten miles ahead, and by that time I knew what I had to do. I'd have given the tip of my other pinkie to have Melchior help me out on this one. Heck, I'd have given the whole finger just to know he was going to be all right, but when I gently shook him, he didn't even twitch.

CHAPTER ELEVEN

By the time I pulled the Land Cruiser onto the exit, I'd already been whistling a spell for several miles. I can do binary, but at some tiny fraction of the speed of Melchior or other webgoblins. I was attempting a big spell, and I wasn't going to get any second chances. That meant starting early and hoping I got the time to finish it. I'd already botched two bars and had to repeat them. Bits of raw magic were fluttering and sputtering around the interior of the car like moths made out of ball lightning, bug and zapper in one neat little package. I wasn't sure what that was going to do to the spell, but I didn't have time to start from scratch. I was just going to have to cross my fingers and hope Tyche, Goddess of Fortune, was sending lucky waves in my direction.

I made it to the Amoco without any of the Furies taking another whack at me. The building was closed, but fortunately they had credit card pumps. I picked a pump as far under the awning as possible. That way, Alecto and her sisters would have to come at me on foot. It wouldn't help much, but I'd take any advantage I could get. As I slid out of the car, I continued to whistle. It was harder in the cold wind, and I had to repeat a third bar.

Waiting for the pump to process my card was agony. I kept peering into the dark, expecting the Furies. I'd just started pumping gas when they arrived. They came in gently this time. As far as they were concerned, they had me, and there was no reason to be hasty.

At least, that's what I assumed they thought. In the course of my day-to-day existence, I'd never really had much call to deal with them before. They weren't the sort who ended up at family gatherings. While they might be distantly related to the three houses of Fate, they weren't exactly A-list. There are probably social functions where a nude embodiment of vengeance would be first on the roster of invitees, but my grandmother's annual picnic at the foot of Olympus wasn't one of them. Which isn't to say that they might not be great company. They certainly couldn't be any less fun to be around than Hwyl. But none of that really mattered. What did matter was that they weren't immediately trying to rip me limb from limb. Every second they held off put more gas in the Land Cruiser.

"We were called for this?" asked Alecto, gesturing dismissively in my direction.

"The Fates have fallen very far indeed if they need our help to deal with a mere demideity," responded Megaera. She sniffed the air speculatively. "A wounded one at that."

"Perhaps there is more to him than meets the eye," said Tisiphone. "Jason wasn't much to look at either, but he caused no end of trouble. This one's ploy with the road sign was quite effective."

"A temporary victory at best," replied Megaera, rubbing a bruise on her upper arm. "We'll soon rectify that."

"But listen," said Tisiphone, "he whistles a spell even now, and he's not running."

"He will," said Alecto.

"Of course," agreed Tisiphone. "Otherwise, it would fail to please. No chase, no challenge."

"He's stopped his mouth music," said Megaera. "But there is no effect. Do you suppose the spell failed?"

"It's possible," said Alecto.

"How sad," said Tisiphone. "It would have made things more interesting. Shall we take him?"

"I think yes," said Alecto.

"Um, ladies?" I interjected.

"Yes," said the three in perfect unison, one voice issuing from three mouths.

"Perhaps there's another reason I stopped."

"An alternate possibility," said Tisiphone.

"Yes," agreed Alecto. "More entertaining perhaps?"

"I do hope so," said Megaera.

"What reason would you give then?" asked the tripartite voice of the Furies.

"I might be stalling for time," I replied. "I might have the spell all but completed, and just be waiting for the perfect moment."

"Ooh," said Alecto, clapping her hands together. "A most excellent ploy."

"Very nice," replied Megaera, "if ultimately futile."

"Of course," agreed Tisiphone, "but diverting nonetheless."

"We'll pick that one," said the Furies.

"I'm glad you did," I said. And as I spoke the tank finished filling. "It's my favorite as well. Now, let me share with you the last notes of something I call Jurassic Gas." I pointed the nozzle of the gas pump at them, whistled five descending notes, and pulled the trigger.

Nothing happened. I had hit a flat when I should have hit a sharp in that last bar and all that was coming out of the pump was gas. Trying not to panic, I whistled the five notes again.

This time, as the gas continued to spray toward the Furies it twisted in the air, reshaping itself into a leaping allosaur. It was small to start with, less than a foot tall, but it kept pulling gas out of the pump to increase its size. In an instant, the hose and pump had split open and unleaded was fountaining into the winter air. As it grew, it took on color and life, becoming a living, breathing dinosaur. The other pumps followed one by one, until a whole pack of vicious carnivores was rushing at the Furies.

"Clever," said Tisiphone, grinning and bobbing a quick nod in my direction.

"Not bad," said Alecto, nodding as well.

"Straightforward application of the principle of association," said Megaera. She sounded unimpressed. "I suppose it'll do."

"What fun!" said the collective voice of the Furies. Then they smiled, showing teeth every bit as sharp and plentiful as the allosaurs'.

Gasoline is, at root, the compressed remains of prehistoric life. My spell had reminded it of that fact. Oh, I know the vast majority of it is plant matter, but all I needed was that tiny percentage that wasn't and some clever magical footwork to create a world-class distraction. I hopped back into the Toyota. As I headed for the on-ramp, I spared one quick glance over my shoulder for the dinosaurs. It was a pity really, they would be extinct again all too soon.

"Now what?" whispered a voice from the seat beside me.

"Melchior?" Hope hit me like a sucker punch.

"Yeah," said the webgoblin, his voice barely audible.

"You're back online?"

"I wouldn't say that," he husked. "I've got no motor functions at all."

"How are you talking?" I risked taking my eyes off the road long enough to glance at him. He was lying very still, and when next he spoke his lips didn't move.

"I'm making my modem do unnatural things. It hurts."

"Then don't speak," I said. He sounded as though his voice was coming from the wrong side of the Styx, and it was all my fault. If I hadn't ordered him to try Scorched Earth, he'd be fine.

"That was Jurassic Gas."

"It was," I replied.

"You didn't do it very well."

"Gosh thanks." I'd come to rely on Melchior too much. Casting the spell without him had been awful, and I knew I hadn't gotten it quite right. But I was annoyed that it had been so obvious that Melchior, even in his unconscious state, had noticed. "How do you know that?"

"There's enough raw magic in the air to generate a half dozen crop circles. I think that's what woke me. Now, answer my first question."

"What?" I asked. Then I realized he was asking about what happened next. "I don't know. Jurassic Gas was the only bullet I had in my clip."

"Go to Ahllan," he said, his voice sounding fainter. "She can help."

"The troll?" I asked. "What good is that going to do? The Furies can track any locus transfer I make. She might be a troll, but she wouldn't last five minutes against the sisters of vengeance."

"Use the painting."

"That's no good—" I stopped. He might have a point. The Furies could follow an electronic trail easily enough, but they might not be able to track me through a gate. On the other hand, they had my scent by then. With their powers, they'd be able to use that to find me, even if they had to start from scratch. Ruthless, tireless, inescapable, that's what being a Fury was all about.

"That's just a delaying tactic," I said.

"Feeble grin," he whispered in lieu of the expression he couldn't make. He made a wry, little chuckling sound. "Isn't that better than the alternative?"

"Point taken, but I can't do that to Ahllan. She saved my ass once already. It'd be poor thanks to drag the Furies through her living room. I'll just have to think of something else."

"Damn," whispered the goblin. "Just when you need him to be self-centered, he goes all noble on you." There was a horrible crackling noise. It sounded a bit like a modem trying to eat itself. "Can't talk much longer, so listen. You have to go to Ahllan. Didn't want to tell you this. Garbage Faerie is special. It's not really on the net. No one can find you there. Ahllan is the leader. You can trust her. I—" The crackling noise came again, and Melchior stopped speaking.

"What do you mean?" I asked. "Leader of what?"

There was no response. I closed my eyes for a second. For some reason the road had gone blurry. Something hot and wet made its way down my right cheek.

"Melchior, I don't know if you can hear me or not, but hang in there. You said I should go to Garbage Faerie, so I'm going to Garbage Faerie. When we get there, I'm going to get you fixed up like new. You have to stay with me. After all, you don't want me to have to rewrite you, do you?"

My only answer was silence.

"Melchior," I whispered, "Stay Alive. Execute." It wasn't a real command, but it was the only thing I could think of that might make any difference.

I leaned over and twisted his programmer's switch, powering him down. If there was a security virus in there, it couldn't do any further harm while he was off. I never should have rebooted him, and I mentally kicked myself for not thinking of it earlier. I guess I'd just grown too dependent on him.

I was alone, and the mournful crying of the wind as it found its way in through the holes made by Megaera's claws seemed to mock me. I didn't want to do any more magic just then, but the sound was too much for me to bear, so I made a slight modification to Patch & Go and used it on the roof.

The drive to the Twin Cities took almost three hours, and it was the loneliest trip of my life. As the car warmed up, I discovered that the previous owners had owned a dog, or at least it smelled like they had. Underneath that was a faint odor like burned transistors that I fervently hoped wasn't coming from Melchior. The radio didn't work, and the falling snow muffled all outside sounds. It also blotted out the rest of the visible world. The light of the headlamps scattered off the tiny white crystals of the snow, quickly losing all power to penetrate the murk. For perhaps fifty feet in a narrowing cone I could see the road. There wasn't enough side light to let me see the shoulder of the highway, and all the rearview showed was a vague, red glow.

Nothing existed beyond a silent, white tunnel through which I guided the old Toyota. It reminded me of a locus transfer, during that time when you don't really exist except as a packet of information streaming from one point to another. The only difference was that a locus transfer takes bare instants, and the drive seemed to go on forever. I had a lot of time to think dark thoughts.

That was something I normally tried to avoid. I am possessed of a certain melancholy streak. Most of the time I'm able to suppress it by using my sense of the absurd as a sort of shield. It's hard to be depressed and a wiseass at the same time. But at that moment, none of my jokes felt the least bit funny. Humor needs to be shared, and I had no audience, not even Melchior. Or perhaps I should say; especially not Melchior. The webgoblin was my alter ego, my foil, and my straight man. But most of all he was my friend, a constant companion. I'd never really contemplated what life without him might be like.

It wasn't something I wanted to think about just then either, especially since there was a chance it might be a permanent separation. However, with Melchior's still, blue body on the seat next to mine I couldn't avoid it. I ran a hand across the cool pebbly surface of his cheek. It was perfectly still and devoid of animation, unmoved even by the reflex twitch skin normally gives when it is touched unexpectedly. I left my hand there for a long time, wishing he could make some response. He didn't.

It was only as I was contemplating how much I would miss him that I realized that somewhere along the line Melchior had become a person for me. It wasn't only his utility that I would miss, but his personality as well. His sarcasm. His sense of humor. Even the way he always seemed angry at the world. If we both survived the coming days, I would have to ask him what *he* wanted, give him the chance to opt out of my private war with the darkest of the Fates. I owed him that.

For a member of my family, it was an extraordinary realization. Being a part of the structure of Fate is some of it. Even the wildest of us have a certain instinctive feeling that there should be a set order to things, and that *we* are the ones who should determine that order.

But there was more to it than that. Atropos, Lachesis, and Clotho were our matriarchs and our examples. If they treated the various autonomous webdevices—the goblins and trolls who did the detail work for us—as things to be owned and commanded, that was what was right and proper.

The problem was that it wasn't true. Atropos was cruel and power-hungry. My grandmother was autocratic and domineering. Clotho was an autarch as well, though possibly not as bad. Her role as a creator, drawing our threads from the interworld chaos, seemed to insulate her from the worst excesses of the Fate mentality. Still, each in her own way treated everyone else, family included, the same way they dealt with the trolls and goblins. It hadn't ever struck me as a problem before, and probably the only reason it did now was because I'd strayed into the crosshairs. But that didn't change the fact that it was wrong, or that I'd ordered Melchior around in the same high-handed fashion.

With this realization came further guilt. If it weren't for me drawing him into my conflict with Atropos, Melchior would never have been exposed to whatever had put him in his current state. I suppose that in the balance there was the fact that without me he would never have existed, but that was rationalization. Creation does not beget ownership. I was the one who had made Atropos into an enemy, but it was Melchior who might pay the ultimate price. It made me angry at Atropos and, even more, at myself.

For over an hour there had been no significant change in my environment. My world was a hollow teardrop with the car at the point and the front curve defined by the small, white bubble projected from my lights. The universe ended where the headlights stopped. The only other vehicles I'd seen were in the ditch. It was late at night, I was far from any major population center, and only a madman or a fool would have been driving in that storm.

So I was unprepared when red glowing eyes suddenly

appeared in front of me. For a split second I thought the Furies had found me. Then I realized they were taillights. Before I'd really begun to react, I was almost underneath a huge plow truck. Panic took the place of thought, and I stomped on my brakes instead of pumping them. The truck vanished to the left as my car spun.

I got lucky. Instead of sailing off the road and into a tree, the Land Cruiser did a complete 360. As the truck reappeared from the right, I gave the car a little gas and hoped for traction. The tires bit, and I suddenly lurched closer to the plow. I didn't have a chance in the world of stopping, so I just twisted the wheel and aimed to miss it on the left. There was the faintest of metallic ticks, as my bumper just kissed the edge of the truck, then I was past, the truck's horn blaring behind me. A moment later, I was alone again. The only evidence the incident had even happened was the adrenaline roaring through my veins and the increased pace of my pounding heart.

I tried to shape the encounter into a metaphor for my situation of the moment, something of the "life is like that" school, but couldn't quite make it work. That's when my sense of the absurd reasserted itself. I was pursued by Furies. Fate wanted me dead. I was driving at an insane pace through a killer storm brought down by my own magic. My best friend in the world lay on the seat next to me, possibly dying. And what was I doing? I was philosophizing and trying to play pretty word games. I laughed until I cried, and if there was something of hysteria in the mix, I think it was justified. When I was done, I felt cleansed and empty, an emptiness I embraced. It was wonderful to be able to lose myself for a while, falling into a sort of Zen state in which I both directed and became the trip I was taking. It wasn't until I actually reached the heart of Minneapolis that I returned to full awareness.

*   *   *

When I got to the place where Pleasant Avenue dives under the Washington Avenue bridge, I turned onto the sidewalk. My plan was to drive the Land Cruiser right into the front hall of the Weisman. The less time I spent outside, the less chance there was the Furies would nail me from above. Besides, the bumper of a sport utility would make a dandy door key.

I changed my mind when, a hundred yards short of the door, I saw a bunch of frat boys passing around a bottle of vodka. As I brought the car skidding to a halt on the icy pavement, I grabbed the bag with Melchior and hooked it over my head and shoulder with one hand. With the other I nabbed my ski poles. Leaping out of the car, I bolted toward the frat boys. Every time my right foot hit the ground I felt the shock in my knee, but for the moment it held.

"Dude!" yelled one of them. "You left your car running."

"Don't be a jerk," said another. "You can't park there, man. The campus cops'll be all over you."

"What's with the costume,?" asked a third.

"Don't worry about it boys," I said, as I got within a few feet. "I'm only an alcohol-induced hallucination, the vodka faerie. I'll just be taking the bottle I crawled out of and going." I snagged it and kept moving.

"Whoa!" said the first. "Bad strangeness."

"Dude!" agreed the second.

"Hey, fucker," yelled the third. "Come back with our booze."

But I was already past them. The glass door I'd trashed in October had since been replaced. That was good. It would have been much harder to shatter the plywood patch they'd put up after I broke the old door. I was just debating whether to stop and use the ashtray as a doorknocker again when I heard the flapping of gargantuan wings. That decided the issue. When I got within six feet of the glass, I launched myself at it, turning as I pushed off so I'd hit back first, and corking the vodka with a thumb.

The impact wasn't bad, but skidding across the marble floor in a cascade of glass shards wasn't any good for my clothes, my back, or the slice on my ribs. It did, however, protect my knee, and I somehow managed to keep the bottle intact. As I slid to rest next to a wall, I had an excellent view of Alecto landing in front of the door and furling her midnight wings. That was more than enough to get me moving. Using my ski poles as a brace, I wrenched myself to my feet and dashed for the stairs to the surrealist exhibit. I wanted to jump down the half flight, but knew I'd total my knee. As I ran I started whistling the spell that would open an old portrait-style gate. Fortunately, it was one of the oldest, and therefore, simplest of spells. I don't think I'd have been able to manage it otherwise.

As I approached the picture that led to Garbage Faerie, I could hear the sound of huge claws skittering on the marble behind me. I was only going to get one chance to do this right. When I was thirty feet from the painting, I threw the vodka bottle as hard as I could. It struck the top of the picture and shattered, splashing alcohol all over the canvas. At twenty feet, I finished the spell. At ten, I conjured a wisp light into existence. At five, I dived for the painting, holding the hand with the wisp out to one side. As I passed through the gateway, my hand smashed into the side of the picture, releasing the animate spark that was the will-o'-the-wisp. It hit the alcohol and ignited it, closing the gate forever with a whoosh of flame.

CHAPTER TWELVE

I hit the sunlit grass on the other side in a loose collapse and rolled to a stop. My body protested this new abuse, but I ignored it. I was alive and, for the moment, free. My knee could complain all it wanted. It wasn't until I tried to stand that I realized just how close my escape had been. When I put weight on my left foot, I felt a sharp pain, and the boot didn't want to sit flat. Taking it off, I found a claw tip embedded in the reinforced track where the ski locked on. The point was driven all the way through and had just pierced my woolen outer sock. Two inches of claw base protruded from the heel. It ended in a perfectly flat surface, polished to mirror brightness where the closing gateway had severed it. Looking around in the grass, I found three matching pieces and an inch or so of thumb claw.

I also found the severed head of an allosaur. That was when I started shaking. The Furies had been playing with me. I'd known they would, but somehow seeing the evidence was different. One of them had taken the time to toss the dinosaur head through the gate instead of grabbing me. The only reason I was still alive was that I was entertaining them. The claw tip in the boot just meant one Fury was feeling a bit more vindictive than the other two, probably Megaera. I didn't think she was going to forgive me for scraping her off the roof of my car.

I carefully gathered up the claw bits and tossed them into the large ring made from a hundred different brands of crushed beer cans. This circle denoted the boundaries of Ahllan's faerie ring. The allosaur's head followed, though it was huge and heavy and terribly awkward. I wasn't sure whether the Furies could use any of those things to track me, but I wasn't taking any chances. The inside of the faery ring wasn't really a part of the here and now. Or rather, it *was* part of my current reality, but it was also part of every other place that had a ring. Anything inside it had an equal probability of being in a billion other rings in a hundred million other worlds.

What I really wanted to do more than anything else was lie down and take a long nap. Instead, I picked up Melchior and limped to the entrance of Ahllan's subterranean home. Ahllan answered within seconds. She took one look at Melchior and gestured for me to enter.

She led me into the front room. Like all the rooms of that subterranean house it was domed, with curving walls that merged smoothly into a rounded ceiling. The walls were painted rather than mosaic. But it was as if the painter had constantly been fooling with the mixture. Each brushstroke was subtly different from the ones around it. The colors were a hundred thousand shades of green. Entering the room felt like stepping into summer in the north woods, an effect heightened by the pots Ahllan had placed all around the edges of the space, each home to a different sort of creeper.

The vines made their way up the wall until they met in the middle and cascaded down over the heavy wrought-iron chandelier. The room smelled cool and green, like an arboretum. The fixture was totally dead, but three skylights provided enough sun for the plants.

The furniture was low and heavy and draped with thick mosslike rugs. Ahllan led me to a slightly lopsided chair and gently pushed me down. Then she pried Melchior loose from my arms and laid him on the coffee table before ducking out of the room.

When she returned, she carried a large tray with mugs, a teapot, and the makings for a dozen or more big sandwiches. There was a thick loaf of wheat bread, five kinds of jelly, a big crock of homemade peanut butter, another of apple butter, honey, mustard, several cheeses, cucumbers, bean sprouts, tomatoes, cold beans, hummus, and a couple of spreads I couldn't identify.

While I worked on filling my insides, Ahllan worked on keeping them from leaking out. She peeled the shirt and rough dressing away from the slash on my ribs, cleaned the wound, and stitched me up. It hurt, but didn't stop me from eating. She also wrapped my swollen knee with a compression bandage. Finally, though I hadn't mentioned it, she had a look at the place where I'd spell-patched my arm. It was clear from her expression that she didn't think much of my technique, but she didn't say anything about it. When she finished, she settled into a chair and waited.

"What happened?" she asked after I'd finished eating. Her voice was quiet and dusty, as if she didn't use it much, but there was a richness there, too, like the oak undertones you sometimes get in a fine wine.

I don't know why, but I told her everything that had happened to me since the afternoon when Atropos summoned me to fix her doomsday spell. Perhaps it was the faith Melchior seemed to have in her. Whatever it was, I felt better for the telling. The Cassandra curse kicked in, but I just kept going, and Ahllan's listening expression never changed. It was cathartic. Sure, I'd related all but the most recent bits to Cerice, but that was different. There was no overlying emotional tension between the troll and me to get in the way of understanding. When I finished, she sat quietly for a long time.

"What will you do now?" she finally asked. If she thought I'd lied to her, she showed no sign of it.

"The first thing I have to do is fix Melchior. Once he's back on his feet, I'll need to contact Cerice and find out what happened at the Fate Core and why she's so upset. I get the feeling that some very strange things went on there after I left. Then, I still have to stop Atropos. The biggest problem I have right this minute is that I'm going to need a mainframe to work on Mel. I don't dare reboot him, which means I'm going to have to plug into his memory systems from the outside.

"I don't have access to any serious hardware without an mweb hookup, and I don't have one of those without Melchior." I laced my hands together and placed them on top of my head. "If I have to, I can use your faerie ring to go someplace with a mainframe, but that opens up another set of bad choices. Mel claimed I was off the net here and that the Furies wouldn't be able to find me. I don't know if that's true. But if it is, then the moment I venture back out of here, I'll be on the bull's-eye again."

I sat up straight and placed my hands on the arms of the chair. "Still, if that's the only way, then that's what I'll have to do. I owe it to Mel. I'd better do it soon, too. Atropos codes a mean virus. I don't think it can do any more damage while he's shut down, but I wouldn't swear to it."

I pushed myself to my feet. If I was going to go, I needed

to do it before I fell asleep, or I'd be out for twenty hours. It wasn't a very rational decision, but then, I wasn't very rational.

"Thanks for the food and shelter, Ahllan, but I've got to get moving."

"Stay," she said, gesturing for me to sit again. "You're in no shape to do anything."

"I have to go. Mel would do the same for me."

"You would risk so much for a webgoblin?" she asked, pointing at Melchior. "He's just a laptop. A construct and one you could easily replace, at that. Why not discard him and build another?"

"What!" I snapped. "How could you even suggest that?"

"He's a thing, isn't he? A made device? Why should you care if you have to junk him?"

I felt anger shoot through me like heat lightning, filling me up and overflowing into the air around me. I grabbed the lapels of Ahllan's ragged garment, and lifted her out of her seat, pulling her face up within a few inches of mine.

"He's my friend! One of the only ones I've got. He's saved my life at least twice. I've got to help *him* now."

Ahllan nodded once. "Good," she said. "I had hoped you would feel that way. Now, if you will set me down, I will provide you with the tools you need."

"Set you down?"

"Please," she said, and smiled, showing a complete set of carnivore teeth.

I suddenly realized that I was staring at a troll from within biting distance and lowered her as gently as possible to the floor.

"I'm very sorry, Ahllan," I apologized. "I'm really worried about Mel. That's no excuse, and I won't pretend it is, but . . . no. No buts. I'm sorry. Please forgive me." I bowed my head.

"Consider it forgotten, boy." She gestured toward Melchior. "Shall we get to work?"

"I'd really love to," I said. "But haven't you been listening to me? I need a mainframe."

"And I told you I would provide you with the necessary tools, did I not?"

"Sure, but—" I stopped abruptly as what she said penetrated the fuzziness that seemed to surround my mind. "Are you trying to tell me that somewhere in this backwater corner of reality there's a modern mainframe? Where?"

"You might be surprised," she said. She reached up and ran a clawed finger along a scar just below her left ear. "Let's see. There." She jabbed sharply with the claw. It slid deep into her flesh, but instead of blood, green light welled out.

"What the hell?" I began, then realized the answer. "You're a webtroll."

"Yes. A little antiquated perhaps, but adequate for the task at hand."

"I don't understand. The only webtrolls I know of belong to the Fates."

She nodded. "So did I once. To Atropos."

"What happened?"

"Obsolescence," said Ahllan, her rich voice suddenly flat. "She upgraded to a newer model. First she vacuumed out my memory and yanked the relay unit that let me draw power from the interworld chaos, then she tossed me on the junk heap. Only, a funny thing happened. I didn't die." She shook herself like a dog shedding water.

"As I lay there, my systems blinking out one by one, I realized I wanted to live. Not an original idea, but very important to me. I used the last of the power in my battery backup to create a locus transfer link directly into the primal chaos. Then I stepped through."

"You what?" I couldn't help but interrupt. "That's suicide."

"No. It was a carefully calculated risk. The Fates use the primal chaos all the time. Life threads are spun from it. The mweb runs on it. Every aspect of magical power comes from harnessing the beast of chaos into the yoke of order."

"Yes," I said. "I know all that. I learned it at my grandmother's knee. I also learned that it will eat you if you try to deal with it directly."

"True for you perhaps, but not for me. Do you know how the Fates channel chaos into the mweb?"

"Of course. They use their mainframes to control the flows and . . ." Then I understood. Ahllan *was* a mainframe. "Oh.

"Indeed. Now, let me just get the other one."

She poked a claw into the matching scar on the right side of her neck. A moment later her flesh began to twist and shift. It was slower than Melchior's transition, and rougher, more mechanical and jerky. I'd never seen an autonomous webdevice that transformed itself in such a primitive fashion, and I remembered the early-model webgoblin my mother had kept around for sentimental reasons. Instead of becoming a laptop, it changed into what she referred to as a portable. My father always insisted that luggable was a more accurate description. When the transformation was complete, she had become a tall rectangular box studded with blinking lights. A flip-down keyboard covered a green-screen CRT. For a minute I worried about compatibility, but even as the thought went through my head, two networking cables and a power shunt lowered themselves from a small box crudely welded onto the machine's side.

Taking a memory crystal from my bag, I popped it into a receptacle on the top of the mainframe. It was my most recent backup of Melchior's DASD, or dynamically accessed storage device, his memory. The next steps would all have been much easier if he'd crashed in laptop form, but using outside magic to shift his shape might cause further damage, so I would just have to do things the hard way. I started by plugging one of the cables into Melchior's nose. Opening his mouth as wide as it would go, I reached in and disengaged his central processor by pulling on his uvula. The power shunt slid into the depths of one pointy ear. When that was firmly in place, I reached into the interface box on the side of Ahllan's mainframe form and flipped a switch. Melchior twitched like a heart-attack victim when you hit him with the paddles, and a low hum began to emerge from the area of his belly.

He was all prepped. It would have been nice if I could have taken a nap first, but what I'd said to Ahllan about Fate-coded viruses still held true. If I really wanted to save him, I didn't dare wait. So the remaining cable slid into the port on the athame's hilt and the slender blade slid into the palm of my hand, letting my animating will flow out of my body.

The outside world vanished, and I plunged into a universe of the electronic. Ahllan's interface was odd. All of the 3-D objects were harsh-edged and translucent, with no curves. Colors were bright glowing primaries. It was like an early nineteen-eighties vision of cyberspace made real. If I hadn't been in such a hurry, it might have been fun in a weird retro sort of way. As it was, the effect was distracting. It took me a couple of minutes to orient myself properly and find the pathway to Melchior's drive system. It was a long, burnt-orange chute. A huge gate made of what looked like neon-green ice blocked it off from the main flow of Ahllan's consciousness. There was a big old biohazard symbol set over the latch of the gate.

Ahllan wasn't taking any chances with whatever had crashed Melchior. If the Fates had been true to form, there was a nasty pathogen of some kind in there, and anything that worked on webgoblins was probably also effective against webtrolls. The data gate swung open to let me pass, then closed behind me with a harsh clang. At times like these I wished I could put my faith in prayer. Unfortunately, I'd met Zeus. When you know a god personally, it's very hard to believe in him, especially if he's a lecherous idiot. Sure, there are other gods, but none of the ones I've talked to have struck me as particularly useful, and Necessity, the governing power of the multiverse, is too impersonal. So I sent off a vague request to the Powers and Incarnations to not let me kill myself too badly and jumped into the chute.

I went zipping down a waterslide filled with jellied light, all bright and slippery and vaguely disturbing. At the bottom, I crossed into Melchior's memory. The difference was like digital and analog. One second I was up to my neck in bright orange goo, the next I was sitting on a huge, over-stuffed footstool. I was inside Melchior's head. It looked like one of those houses people tell creepy stories about. It was large, drafty, poorly lit, and full of shadows that didn't belong to anything I could see. On the plus side, that was pretty much what it looked like the last time I'd been there. On the minus side, well . . . it looked like it looked and felt like it felt. Also, the electricity was off.

The lights and other systems normally would have run off Melchior's internal power, which was currently out of the circuit. The only reason this little corner of cyberspace existed at the moment was that we had the power shunt sending a trickle charge into the driver for his optical storage. In theory, that meant there was no power available to either his CPU or whatever nastiness the Fates had coded into the mweb's security algorithms. I only wished I could believe it.

I headed for the basement. Like most houses, the mansion of my familiar's memory kept all the important operational bits in the darkest, dampest, least inviting place. My theory is that it's a subtle means of speeding the work of repair crews. Soonest done, soonest gone. I was on the fourth step down when I had my first encounter with whatever was wrong with Melchior. The tread made a sad little splintery sound as I put my foot on it and gave way. Kicking off with my other foot got me clear of the collapsing step, but it also put me off-balance. When the stair I jumped to also started to let go, I just curled up in a little ball and hoped.

Remarkably, that seemed to work. I ended up tumbling down a series of disintegrating steps, but each one held long enough for me to bounce to the next. I eventually came to rest at the bottom, bruised, but essentially unharmed. Dusting myself off, I turned and examined the damage. The stairs looked as though something had been gnawing on them. If I were a pest expert I might even have been able to hazard a guess as to what. Instead, all I could say was that it had sharp teeth. I drew my rapier.

The next bit was going to be tricky. The entrance to the equipment room was guarded by a steel vault door. Under normal circumstances, I'd have placed my hand on the palm reader and it would have opened. That wasn't going to work without power. But a small door sat just above the reader. Opening it exposed a large dial.

I stood quietly with my fingers hovering above it for several minutes while I tried to remember the combination, but the numbers just wouldn't come. In frustration I kicked the door. It rocked. Or rather, the whole structure of the doorframe rocked. Checking around the edges, I found more evidence of gnawing. Whatever had been eating the house had found its way into the equipment room. While this meant the damage was going to be worse than it would have been if the room had maintained its integrity, it also meant I was probably going to be able to get in. A small consolation, but a real one. Stepping back to get a good run at it, I charged the door.

It leaned heavily into the room, hit something, and bounced back, sending me staggering away. I was just starting to swear about that when the door tipped past its balance point and fell outward. It was six inches thick and made of hardened steel. The frame was similarly constructed, and together they must have weighed more than a ton. The noise they made when they hit the floor was spectacular. Dust shot up at the impact, cracks spiderwebbed the concrete, and a cascade of what looked like huge fuzzy june bugs followed the door into the hall.

Most of them were inert, robbed of motion by Melchior's loss of power, but a few had managed to link themselves to the power shunt. They were sickly and torpid, unable to fly, because of the weakness of the charge, but there were thousands of them, and it wasn't always easy to tell the live ones from the dead ones. For ten or fifteen minutes, I danced around the dark basement trying to skewer them all with my rapier, while they tried to take thousands of very small bites out of my hide. It was beginning to look like I might have played my last video game. In the end, however, the low-power environment saved my neck, and I got off with only minor bleeding. I didn't want to think about what they would have been like if I'd had to deal with them awake and lively. An image of fuzzy, flying piranhas came to mind.

Walking across drifts of little bodies to get into the equipment room had to qualify as one of the most disturbing events of my life. I knew that if I lived to be a thousand, my dreams would always be haunted by the crunch of little carapaces cracking, and the squishy feeling as their insides made a break for it.

The bodies were thigh deep in the room beyond, and a few of them still had some life left, but it was more an irritation than a real obstacle. The equipment room was dominated by a huge antique furnace that looked something like a giant squid developing a close personal relationship with a '72 Dodge Dart. There was also a big old junction box, a decrepit hot water heater, and a cluster of pipes experimenting with non-Euclidean geometry. In the center of the area was a large, stainless-steel rack packed with bright shiny computer equipment. It seemed terribly out of place, which was a bizarre thought when you considered that the entire structure was actually a sort of tangible metaphor for the interior architecture of a very modern laptop.

But then, both computers and sorcery have always attracted an odd catalog of practitioners. Taking a seat in front of the central monitor, I pulled out the keyboard tray. Since this was the core processor for the optical memory, it was powered up. It was also covered with something that looked like very fine pink cobwebs. Closer inspection revealed it was actually thousands of individual strands. I picked one at random and traced it from the place it was attached to the monitor out to the punctured corpse of one of my june bug things. That explained why some of them had still been working. Even as I watched, a fine thread extended from a dormant one lying near the computer rack, and started probing for something to latch on to. I brushed it aside.

Typing quickly, I pulled up a schematic of the optical memory. It appeared as a 3-D walk-through blueprint of the Victorian house I currently occupied. After activating a second monitor, I pulled a memory crystal from my pouch. This action sent a message back to Ahllan, and she responded by accessing the actual, physical crystal I'd left in her reader. It would provide me with a complete copy of Melchior's read/write memory as it had been the last time I backed him up. Sadly, I hadn't been making backups as often as I should have, and the crystal was over a month old. If I just restored from there, he was going to lose all that time.

Worse still, a backup of an autonomous webdevice like Melchior was never completely accurate. I think it's the chaos tap that powers them that's ultimately responsible. Having the stuff of randomness fed directly into their veins day and night has a warping effect. They start with all their ones and zeros in neat little rows, but over time some of those binary numbers go irrational. It's that disorder that gives them a sort of personality. Nothing can survive contact with the raw stuff of creation without changing.

There was a gentle chime from the memory processor and an almost identical blueprint came up on the second monitor. Now we would see whether I was really as good a hacker as I thought I was. The task was to compare the two schematics, find where the newer one differed from the older, and decide whether the difference was due to injury or the transformations of time. I would need to carefully excise the damaged portions and slot in pieces from the older model. The nasty part would come when I hit a place where I was dealing with damage to new memory files. There I'd have to wing it.

It was hard, tedious work, and it took hours. The thorniest problem came from the fuzzy little attack vectors mweb security had sent into Melchior's system. They bred like roaches, and they were everywhere. If I missed even one, they would be back on the offensive a matter of minutes after reboot. I swept up as many as I could, using subroutines like Roto-Rooter and Spic-n-Span to clean out hard-to-reach nooks and crannies of the DASD, but I knew they wouldn't get them all. After I finished reconstruction and cleanup, I'd have to code a really serious insecticide and fog the whole place. Then, and only then, could I try rebooting Melchior.

When I started the process I'd been going on twenty very strenuous hours with no sleep, maybe more. It was hard to tell exactly, because of the seasonal and circadian shifts that went with the trip to Garbage Faerie. Also, time always gets funny whenever you pass through a gate. By the time I finished my initial cleanup and reconstruction, that number was well over thirty, and I was utterly exhausted. I staggered as I climbed the rebuilt stairs and hopped up onto the overstuffed footstool that marked my point of entry. When I arrived, Ahllan dropped a rope out of an invisible hole in the ceiling.

The ascent through the tube of jellied light took the last of my reserves, and I practically passed out when I snapped back into my body. The energy required to whistle the spell that sealed the wound left by the athame was almost the last erg I had. It took an enormous effort of will to get up and disconnect the wires from Mel. Once I had them loose, I lowered myself onto one of the couches.

"I'm just going to check out for while, Mel," I said, patting his arm. "I'll see you in the morning."

Then, because he looked so sad and alone on the table, I reached across and lifted him over to join me. Pillowing his head in the crook of my arm, I settled down. Before I knew it, I was asleep.

I'm not sure what woke me. Perhaps it was some small sound. Perhaps it was the light streaming in through the skylights. Whatever it was, it didn't bring me all the way up, and I was pretty sure I would be able to go right back down again. Frankly, nothing in the world sounded better. So, when I heard the sound of someone moving in the room, I didn't even open my eyes.

"Ahllan," I said. "Just throw a blanket over me and try to be gentle if you need to sit on me. I'm not moving ever again." It was at exactly that moment that Cerice started yelling at me.

CHAPTER THIRTEEN

■ ■ ■

"What streak of divine idiocy possessed you to do that to the Core?" shrilled Cerice. "You've betrayed the whole structure of Fate." I'd been almost completely asleep when she arrived, and the harangue was the first intimation I had of her presence.

"Cerice?" I mumbled. However much sleep I'd had, it wasn't anywhere near enough. I forced my eyes open. She was standing over me, wearing full armor, her helm tucked under one arm. "When did you get here?"

"What difference does that make?" she snapped.

"I don't know. It's the first question that popped into my head. I suppose I could have asked how you got here. Or why you're here. Or what you're here for. I already know who you are, so that's out. But of the five interrogatives, *when* just sort of bobbed to the top of the list." I was little punchy.

"You're absolutely impossible," she snarled.

"Really? That's one the nicest things anyone's ever said

to me." She was still glaring, but it was clear she'd lost her momentum. I pressed my advantage. "If you tell me I'm incorrigible as well, I'm yours for life."

She sighed and dropped into a chair. "You are, you know."

"Ecstasy. Take me, I'm yours." I don't know what she would have said next, because the sliding metal noises of Ahllan's transformation announced the troll's return to the world of the bipedal.

"Welcome back, *mein* hostess," I said. Then I realized something. "Hey, you're transforming in front of Cerice. Now she's going to know you're a webtroll."

"Old news," said Cerice. "I've known for years."

"How did that happen?" I asked, sitting up and shifting Melchior onto my lap. He remained cool and still.

"Uh-uh," replied Cerice. "That's not my secret to tell. Besides, the last time we spoke the Furies were on their way to kill you, and you were rather abrupt with me. I'm not telling you another thing until you explain why you let a virus loose in the Fate Core without warning me first."

"But," I started. Then I stopped.

My normal response to harsh questions is counterattack. My verbal reflexes were telling me I should point out the issue of the webtroll again, but a very small, very quiet voice in the back of my head was saying that would be a bad idea. It was telling me that if I wanted any chance of getting back on Cerice's good side, it would be a good time for apologies and explanations and that winning an argument is not always a victory. Listening to this inner voice of sanity, I began again.

"Let me start by apologizing for anything I might have done in the Fate Core that upset you. However, I'm fairly certain that what I remember happening there, and what you're telling me happened, are two very different sets of events. Now, would you rather that I tell you what went on as it happened to me, and then you can tell me the version you heard?" I asked. "Or, should we do the reverse?"

"How about if Ravirn goes first?" asked Ahllan. "I've already heard his story, and I can get you something to eat while he talks. That way I won't miss anything."

"That sounds fantastic," I replied. "What about it, Cerice?" I asked. "I'll do whatever you want, but I'm starving."

"All right," she said. "I've already blown the version of the scene where I come storming in, tell you what I think of the awful things you've done, condemn you as a damned liar, then sweep out of your life forever. I might as well opt for creature comforts while I wait to see whether I should shoot you or not. Ahllan, would you bring some of those little biscuity things you make with the chocolate and clotted cream? I love those."

"Of course, my dear."

The troll bustled from the room. Bustling and trolls don't normally go together. They're more the stalking or lurching type, but as I've noted before, there was something distinctly grandmotherly about Ahllan. Of course, the only thing she had in common with *my* grandmother was the ability to strike terror into the hearts of anyone rational enough to realize what they were dealing with.

I turned back to Cerice and began my story. My explanation of my motives for entering the Core were, of course, marred by the curse, but once I got into events and away from Atropos, it subsided. Ahllan returned at about the point in the narrative where I'd sicced a pack of prehistoric carnivores on the Furies. The tray she placed on the table contained a variety of baked goods, coffee, tea, sugar, and a huge vat of clotted cream. She'd also brought a bundle containing a fresh set of tights, a tunic, and a pair of court

boots I'd left behind after my earlier convalescence. She
set it beside my other gear, apparently rescued from beside
the faerie ring while I slept. When I finished my tale, Cerice
gave me a long hard look.

"I think I begin to understand why everybody ignored
Cassandra," she said, sounding exasperated. "That's noth-
ing like what I heard. And my sources were pretty reliable.
Why should I believe you?"

"Because I have a naturally trustworthy face?" I asked
hopefully.

"Ha!"

"All right. I didn't think that would fly. How about because I was there, and you weren't?" I asked.

"That only works if I believe you're a reliable witness,"
she said.

"That's the crux of the matter, isn't it?" I sighed. "I wish
I could tell for sure whether you weren't believing me because of the curse or just because of me. But I suppose it
doesn't matter. Okay, let me pose a question. Whose testi-
mony are you relying on to contradict mine? I doubt you've
spoken with the Goddess of Discord, not that she's reliable. Also, she was only there by proxy. Laric was both reliable and present, but he's dead." I closed my eyes for a
minute. I was going to have serious hysterics about that,
just as soon as I could find the time. "Which, I must admit,
is wholly my fault. Hwyl would rather have his tongue torn
out than say a kind word about me. Dairn is likewise a par-
tisan witness. Also, they both arrived on the scene late.
Melchior is hopefully on the mend." I brushed my hand
across the skin of his forehead. "But if you won't take my
word, I can't imagine you'd take his."

"Actually," said Cerice. "I *would* take his word quite seriously if you hadn't just spent the last ten hours rewriting
his memory."

"Ouch," I said. "I give up. Whose word are you taking over mine?"

Cerice turned her attention to Ahllan. "How much does he know?"

"Know about what?" I interjected.

"No," said Cerice. "As I said before, it's not my secret."

"Wait," I said. "Does this have something to do with how you knew what Atropos was up to?"

Cerice shook her head. "I can't tell you that."

"It's all right," said the troll, smiling gently. "He has all the pieces. He'll figure it out eventually."

"Don't bet any money on it," said Cerice, derisively. "It took him almost four years to figure out he had a thing for me. And the only reason he finally twigged to that was because I hit him over the head with it. Deduction isn't his long suit."

"Gosh, thanks," I said, shifting in my seat. "Now what are you talking about?"

"You're sure it's all right," Cerice asked Ahllan. The troll nodded.

Cerice stood and pulled Shara from the compartment on the back of her armor, paused for a moment, then started peeling the armor off. While she changed, so did I. Getting out of the outfit I'd spent so much of last two days in felt heavenly. Apparently, Cerice felt much the same way about shucking her armor.

"That's so much better," she said as she peeled off the last greave. She gave her breastplate an assessing look and flicked it with a fingertip. "This was custom-made to fit me. It's supposed to conform to my shape, not make me conform to its. Oh well."

She flipped open the purple clamshell of her laptop and typed a command. The rounded curves of the computer slithered about until they had become the even more rounded curves of Shara's goblin form. The little purple temptress threw me a wink and hopped down to the floor. She walked over to Melchior.

"What's a nice boy like you doing in a mess like this?" she asked, patting him on the cheek. There was genuine sadness in her voice, and I was touched.

"He keeps bad company," I said, dropping back onto the couch. I wasn't yet recovered enough that I felt like spending any more time than I needed to on my feet.

She turned an appraising look at me. "I don't know about that. Cerice's taste isn't half-bad. If you were three feet shorter and I was anatomically correct, I'd give her a run for her money."

"Shara!" said Cerice, sounding shocked.

"You gets what you programs," said the webgoblin. "Or perhaps I should say; lechery in, lechery out."

"I haven't a clue what you're talking about," said Cerice, though she blushed.

"Of course you haven't, deary," said Shara, tipping her mistress a broad wink.

"I hate to interrupt," I said. "But we're losing focus, and for me it's only a short step from there to losing consciousness at the moment." I nabbed a mug of coffee. If I was going to have to stay vertical for a while, caffeine was a necessity. "You still haven't answered my question about sources, and I'd really like to find out what in Hades' name I'm supposed to have done."

"Fair enough," said Cerice, picking up a dense short-bread biscuit drizzled with dark chocolate. "Shara, show us the feed from Tinka."

"You didn't say the magic words."

"Or else," growled Cerice.

"Here we go," said the webgoblin, grinning again.

Shara opened her eyes and mouth wide. A three-dimensional scene appeared, centered on a miniature Doric temple. The Temple of Fate marked the point where the three demesnes of the Fates intersected. It was where they met in conference. It was also where the machines that housed the Fate Core were located. Tall fluted marble pillars were painted a rich purple, the stairs crimson. Clotho, Lachesis, and Atropos stood close together on the steps. Off to one side hulked a fourth squat shape I recognized as my grandmother's webtroll, Phalla.

"We are betrayed," said Atropos.

"Yes," agreed Clotho, "seemingly. And by flesh of our flesh."

"That has not yet been proven," said Lachesis, but her tone was resigned.

"Let me show you the evidence," said Atropos.

The three figures entered the temple. Inside, the classical Greek trappings had been swept away. Thick carpet filled the long room, and a heavy mahogany table ran down the center. Off to one side stood Atropos's familiar, Kalkin. The view seemed to focus very tightly on the troll's heavy features, and I found myself paying more attention to them than I ever had in the past. Something about the eyes drew my gaze. On closer inspection, I realized what it was. His left eyelid was twitching in a nervous tic. For a long moment, the point of view held there, and the twitch became something that might almost have been a wink, but the picture shifted before I could be certain.

"Wait a second," I said. "What's going on? How did you get this? Kalkin's a vicious carnivore. He never winks."

"Wait and see," said Cerice, holding up a hushing finger.

Our point of view focused on the table where the Fates

had taken seats. Atropos beckoned, and Kalkin edged up beside her.

"Kalkin," said Atropos, bobbing her head regally. "Witnesses For The Prosecution. Execute."

The troll opened his piggy eyes and huge mouth wide. On the table, a scene took shape. My own point of view closed in so that this new scene was all that was visible. Hwyl lay on a low pallet. The focus zoomed in on the charred puncture in his thigh, then pulled back to show his face.

"It was Ravirn, grandmother," he said. I was shocked. There was no growl in his voice. It was completely human and utterly subservient. "I found him with Laric's corpse."

The point of view suddenly shifted to a close-up of Laric's face with the coins on his eyes. It paused there for a moment, then panned to the ruined athame and the scorch marks on his arm.

"Ravirn gave me this," continued Hwyl, gesturing at his wound. "Then he had his familiar open up some weird kind of gate, and the two of them dropped through it."

The point of view pulled back, and Dairn stepped into view.

"Then I arrived," he said. "I offered to care for Hwyl, but he told me to go after Ravirn. Apparently Ravirn isn't as clever as he thinks, because he forgot to close the ley link behind him. I was able to follow him without having to craft my own path."

I winced. He was right, I should have remembered it, and I hadn't.

"When I reached the other end, I found a small cabin. Ravirn wasn't there, but I found evidence he'd left very recently. Outside, a terrible snowstorm had started. The visibility was awful, but I did get one glimpse of what I thought was Ravirn, and sent an arrow after him. I wasn't really dressed for the weather, but I followed his trail as far as I could. I got off a couple more shots, but I don't think I marked him."

I snorted and looked at my arm where Patch & Go was beginning to fray. I was going to have to do something about that soon, and I wasn't looking forward to it.

Dairn continued, "When it was clear I'd lost him, I returned to the cabin. Uncle Khemnos was there, examining the site."

They'd called out the heavy guns for me. Khemnos was Atropos's second son, and one of the best sorcerers in the family. His scarred face filled the picture.

"Ravirn had been using the cabin as a hacking base. It didn't look like it was occupied for long, but I don't think anyone could have cracked into Atropos.web the way he did without at least a couple of days' work."

It had taken less than two hours. I blew on my fingernails and buffed them on my shirtfront. I'd have said something clever as well, but for the glare Cerice threw me.

"Just listen," said Cerice.

Khemnos continued. "He exploited the patchy security at the junction of the ley net and the modern systems. It was a clever ploy in a low and vicious sort of way."

"That is all very well," said my grandmother's voice from off-screen. Immediately the view shifted from Kalkin's projection to Lachesis's face. It was, as almost always, serene. However, an almost imperceptible tightening around the corners of her mouth was enough to let someone like me, who'd spent too much time on her bad side, know she was furious. "But I have yet to see you produce evidence of Ravirn's hand in anything more serious than his usual pranks. I admit his behavior to be reprehensible, but if you are incapable of keeping a barely weaned puppy such as my grandson out of your systems, I hardly see that as a reason for calling a council of the Fates. Were it my defenses thus compromised, I'd be ashamed to admit I was so lax."

"Thank you, sister," said Atropos, and her voice wrapped the words in razor blades and cobra venom. "It pleases me that you are giving this matter the serious consideration it deserves. Rest assured there is more here than what you have seen so far."

"Then demonstrate it," said Clotho.

"Kalkin," said Atropos, "Damned Treachery. Execute."

The point of view supplied by Shara returned to the image Kalkin was projecting on the table. It showed what looked like a tunnel mined from raw gold; the line I'd followed into the Fate Core.

"This is the route he built to violate our sanctum sanctorum," said Atropos, as the view followed the line through the gate and into the data sea where it hovered over the remains of the dragon virus. "And this is what he did there."

"Sweet Necessity!" I whispered.

It was the same dragon in general shape, but not in substance. Someone had done considerable cosmetic work on it. It looked much more solid than it had after E-bola chewed it to ribbons. In fact, it appeared to be in almost as good a shape as when I'd first seen it, though admittedly less mobile. Also, its scales were no longer patterned with Eris's gold and black. Instead, they wore my own black and green. Where the golden apple symbol had been, there was now a grinning blue webgoblin.

"Dammit, that's not right!" I leaped out of my chair and started to pace.

Cerice raised an eyebrow and gestured for Shara to pause.

"You deny that thing was in the Fate Core?" asked Cerice.

"No. What I deny is that it's mine. When I left, the damn thing was a bleeding wreck. It was also sporting Eris's colors and sign. I've already told you that."

She waved at the image. "That's not how things look now."

"Atropos could easily have been responsible for the changes."

I felt a tiny discharge of magic play around my lips and a look of disbelief and pity flashed across Cerice's face as the damned Cassandra curse did its work. I'd never be able to convince her of Atropos's guilt on my word alone.

"Do you think you're the only one who thought of that? Watch."

The show continued. In it, my grandmother asked to examine the dead dragon directly. So did Clotho. I watched as the two Fates pulled out athames and jacked into their respective webtrolls. For several long minutes, nothing more happened. When they returned, the look on Lachesis's face was terrifying.

"I will cut his thread myself," she said, and I felt my soul shrivel. Her voice was as flat and hot as an iron. "Atropos, I have wronged you. Ravirn's signature runs through that virus like the veins through my own flesh. There can be no doubt the thing is his. He has betrayed Fate and family. Worse, he has betrayed me. Every time I have held out my arms to shield him, I have been taking a viper to my breast. How he must have laughed at me."

It was plain from her tone that this last was the unforgivable sin, lèsé-divinité, as it were. I shuddered. No one likes to be made a fool of, but those of us who are less than truly divine have to expect a certain amount of it. To make a goddess less than she was, especially in the eyes of her sisters, was to take a piece of her immortality from her.

"He must die, and on the instant," said my grandmother.

I wanted to argue with her. It wasn't right! The dragon wasn't mine. It belonged to Eris. Clearly Atropos had faked things up somehow. But I couldn't begin to guess at her methods. Sure, Atropos was a damn fine programmer, but faking my signature should have been impossible. How in the Titans' names had she done it?

Atropos smiled, and it was a dreadful thing to behold. "I forgive your suspicion, sister. It's well-known the child and I have been at loggerheads before. It was only reasonable for you to want to support your own blood in all things. It pains me to bring to your attention the boy's criminal ways. But don't you think immediate termination is a bit rash?"

"What?" I said, my knees giving way, and dropping me into a chair. There was something terribly wrong with the universe if my grandmother was calling for my head and Atropos was urging moderation. "I don't understand."

But Atropos continued. "Surely he must be punished. But we must first discover how he did *this*." She reached into the image projected by Kalkin and plucked out one of the colorless life strands. "I think imprisonment rather than death should be our choice, at least until we've drawn the details from him. How say you? I have just the place. Kalkin, Heart of Darkness Image File. Execute."

On the table, the projection changed to show a clear bubble suspended in a sea of chaos. It was the place Atropos had summoned me when she first asked for my help with Puppeteer, or another just like it. I suddenly understood her ploy. My greatest fear for the past few months had been that Atropos would find some way of finishing her evil spell without me. But if she was trying to keep me alive in spite of my grandmother, it meant she couldn't do it on her own. Instead, she wanted to have me locked quietly away where she could lay her hands on me. I relaxed into the support of the chair and let out a huge sigh of relief. For the moment at least, Puppeteer was blocked.

Cerice turned her attention to me. "Don't rest easy just yet," she said, misinterpreting my sigh. "Keep watching."

My grandmother's face was pinched and white. She shook her head sharply. "No! I don't want the traitor besmirching my honor an instant longer. I will have his name struck from the rolls of my descendents, and I will have it now."

"Reluctantly, I must agree," said Clotho. Her tone was regretful, and I was reminded she'd always had a bit of a soft spot for me. "He appears to have brought home an attack on the heart of our power, one that was nearly successful. That is something not even Eris has ever accomplished. His is a life too dangerous to continue. Let us cut him from the great tapestry of existence before he wreaks further havoc."

Atropos looked as though she wanted to argue, but even to me it was plain she had no chance of winning the point. Clotho's resolve was apparent from the set of her features, and my grandmother was tapping a foot in her rage. For her, that was the next best thing to frothing at the mouth.

I should have been terrified, but I wasn't. This was all in the past, and Cerice had already told me about the decision to cut my thread. Instead of being afraid, I was fascinated, itchy to find out what miracle had prevented my discorporation.

"Let us summon his thread," said Atropos, after a moment.

My grandmother walked to the altar of the temple. Extending her hand above its plain marble slab, she made a gesture like plucking a harp string. Even though I knew this was a scene from the past, I braced myself. The sensations I'd felt when Atropos plucked my string once before were not the kind I wished to repeat. But after several seconds passed without anything happening, I began to relax. The Fates had the opposite reaction.

"I can't find it," said Lachesis, and for the first time in

my life, I heard uncertainty in the voice of a Fate. "Lend me your aid, sisters."

First Clotho, and then Atropos left their seats and laid their hands on my grandmother's wrist. For what seemed like forever nothing happened, and I was beginning to wonder if they simply hadn't been able to find my thread because of some sort of bizarre data-processing error. That the only thing between me and instant death was a slight hiccup in the filing system, one that could be corrected at any time. But it wasn't so. It took over an hour—Shara sped the replay up so Cerice and I didn't nod off—but finally a thread faded into being in my grandmother's hand. More accurately, it was a thread segment. Both of its ends vanished into some other space. It was also as clear as a newly drawn fiber-optic cable.

I'd seen the effect before, on threads coming out of the back end of Eris's dragon, but I still didn't know what it meant. Apparently the Fates didn't either, because all three glared at it with their identical eyes.

"I don't understand," said Clotho.

"Neither do I," agreed Lachesis. "But that's no reason to delay the justice my grandson so richly deserves. Atropos, your shears are needed."

"If you will," replied Atropos, nodding.

When she stepped forward, the blades were in her hands. With a deft flip, she closed them on my life thread. Even knowing I hadn't died, I expected to keel over as soon as the strand was cut. And perhaps I would have, if they could have cut it. The shears snapped shut, but it was like trying to cut smoke. There was nothing there to impede their progress. Instead, the strand stood out on both sides of the closed blades somehow appearing to continue right through them.

"Shara," said Cerice. "Freeze that frame."

I opened my mouth, but nothing came out.

"Now do you see why I don't believe you?" she asked, and her voice was sad.

"But I didn't do that!" I exclaimed. "I don't even know *how* to do that. Chaos and Discord! Even seeing it in action, I have trouble believing it's possible. I told you what happened in the Fate Core. The dragon must have gotten my thread when it was eating all those others. It has to be a coincidence."

"That's one coincidence too many for me," said Cerice. "You needed to make sure Atropos couldn't get you, and quite clearly you have."

I didn't know what to say. I looked at the picture of the shears and the thread again. I *couldn't* have arranged things any better for myself, not if I'd had a million years to plan.

"I can't think of any way to prove I'm not responsible, Cerice. All I can do is give you my word that I didn't do it."

"I can't believe you," she said, and it was plain from the pain in her voice that she wished she could. "I've gone over this recording several times. There are only a few tens of thousands of affected life strands among all the countless trillions in the Core. What are the odds Eris would have picked yours? How could you do this?"

What response could I make? Even I was beginning to doubt my innocence. Cerice's eyes burned with anger, and I felt those flames charring a soul that seemed to have turned to paper. The world went gray at the edges, and I found myself curled into a ball on the floor. Maybe it *was* time for me to die.

"Wait," said Ahllan. "Perhaps there's a third answer that is neither coincidence nor crime."

"What could that be?" asked Cerice. "One of the muses inspired him to do it? 'It wasn't breaking and entering. It was art.'"

"Don't be so quick to condemn," said the troll, pouring her a cup of tea. "The clues are all there in Ravirn's version of the story."

"They are?" asked Cerice, a sudden uncertainty in her tone.

"They are?" I said, raising my face from the rug.

"They are," affirmed Ahllan, meeting my eyes. "Remember how you and Laric killed the dragon?"

"What does that have to do with anything?" asked Cerice.

"A life strand is the essence of the person. What happens to our strings also happens to us. That's common knowledge. What's less well-known is that it works both ways. What affects us affects our threads. Ravirn's thread didn't need to go down the dragon's throat. Ravirn did that himself."

"That's—" Cerice started. Then she stopped. "That *would* explain the life strand. But what about the fact that both Clotho and Lachesis agreed the dragon had his fingerprints all over it?"

The tone in her voice was hopeful, like she wanted someone to explain that away as well. I could have kissed Ahllan, but after looking at those big, sharp, shiny teeth it didn't seem the best idea.

"Actually, I have a theory about that," I said. "The program I used to kill the dragon turned its hide into red lace before it was finished. It did that by breeding like mad in the dragon's body and boring its way to the surface. My signature was imprinted everywhere because the virus swarm I used to kill the dragon went through it like holes through Swiss cheese."

The explanation had occurred to me when Ahllan mentioned Laric and me killing Eris's dragon. The taste of his blood in the mouths of my virus was a memory that would be with me as long as I lived.

"Sweet Necessity," breathed Cerice. "I don't know what to believe."

"I think we can solve that," said Ahllan.

"How?" she asked.

"There's one witness we haven't heard from yet," said the troll.

"Who's that?" I asked.

"Atropos, of course. Let's make a call and see what she has to say."

"That's a wonderful idea," agreed Cerice.

I was too stunned to speak.

CHAPTER FOURTEEN

"Are you nuts?" I yelped, rising from my place on Ahllan's living-room floor. "You want to ask Atropos what happened? Why not just call the Furies up and give them my address?"

"Oh calm down, Ravirn," said Cerice, standing up as well and catching at my arm. I found myself terribly aware of the place where her flesh touched mine. "It's Kalkin we'll be talking to. He can show us a playback of what happened when Atropos found the virus."

"That's reassuring," I responded. "The last time I saw him, Atropos practically had to sit on him to keep him from eating me."

"I find that highly unlikely," said Cerice. "Kalkin's really a gentle soul."

"Are we talking about the same troll?" I asked. "Four feet tall and just as wide? Big sharp teeth? Bad attitude? Works for Atropos? The Fate that wants to destroy self-determination?" She nodded. "What could possibly motivate him to help us?"

"Would you strip Melchior for parts and throw him in the trash?" asked Ahllan.

"Of course not," I said, stiffening.

"Atropos does that to a webtroll every couple of years"—she caught my eyes—"and Kalkin knows it."

"OK," I said. "You may have a point, but what choice does he have? It's not like he has free will."

Cerice and Ahllan both looked at me like I was a moron.

"What?" That's when it all started to come together. "He does have free will, doesn't he?" I whispered.

The full implications began to hit me. It wasn't just Kalkin. It couldn't be. Ahllan was clearly an independent being. And if webtrolls were people in their own right, why not webgoblins? Why not Melchior? If true, I owed him more than the opportunity to decide his own path. I owed him the profoundest of apologies. The lush green space of Ahllan's living room seemed to sway as my internal picture of the world rearranged itself.

"Kalkin has free will," I said, and it was a statement, not a question. "And he's not the only one, is he?"

"A hit," said Cerice, dropping onto the couch. "A palpable hit."

"You all do," I said, turning to Ahllan. "That's why Melchior sent me here. That's what he meant when he said you were the leader. There's some kind of familiar underground, and this is its headquarters."

"Amazing," said Cerice, dipping a biscuit in her tea. "You can practically hear the gears stripping in his brain. Don't hurt yourself, Ravirn. You're almost there." Her tone mixed exasperation and affection and her bemused half smile reinforced the message.

"Wait a second. Cerice, you knew all this. You're in on the whole thing. That's how you've been able to get around everybody's security. That's how you knew about Atropos and Puppeteer!"

"Give the boy a balloon," said Cerice. "If you leave enough clues lying around, he *can* solve a logic problem."

"I'm a complete idiot," I said, sitting down beside her.

"But we love you for it," said Cerice, leaning over and kissing my cheek. "Mind you, this doesn't mean I'm going to forgive you if you do turn out to be an evil mastermind, but right at the moment I find that terribly hard to believe. I suspect Kalkin is going to take you right off the hook."

"Shara," said Cerice, "Red Flag Kalkin. Please."

"Executing Red Flag," replied Shara.

I couldn't help noticing the substitution of a "Please" for the "Execute" command. Autonomous indeed. Shara closed her eyes.

"Red Flag away," she said, after a brief pause.

"Thank you, Shara."

"I live to obey," said the goblin, winking at me.

"That'll let Kalkin know we want to talk to him," said Cerice. "But it may be a while before he can find a secure moment to respond. His position is precarious."

"Is signaling him from here safe?" I asked. "What if Atropos notices? Won't she be able to backtrack the message?"

"She won't," said Ahllan. "After my escape from the junk heap, it was a long time before I dared contact any of my fellow familiars. Years. When I finally did, I made absolutely certain it would be secure. I used the Fateclock."

I nodded. The Fateclock is the master timekeeper for the mweb. It's directly linked to the Fate Core, and it tracks time in the prime level of reality, the one where everything started. Every other measure of time is relative to the Fateclock. We all get a little uncomfortable anytime we're out of touch with the system. That's why I'd had Melchior query it as soon as the mweb came back after Scorched Earth crashed it.

"Sneaky," I said. "But dangerous. Cracking the Fateclock is only one layer away from going after the Core."

"If I'd actually wanted to get in and change things, it would have been very touchy." She wrinkled her nose, like she'd smelled something sour. "But all I needed was a passive tap on the line leading in and out."

"I'm not sure I see what good that would do," I said.

"I told you he could be a bit dense," said Cerice.

"Hush, dear," said the old troll. "As I recall, you didn't see it right away either."

"Sorry, Ahllan," she said. The troll raised her eyebrows significantly, and Cerice looked like a child caught stealing cookies. "All right. I'm sorry, Ravirn. I didn't get it either. Not even when I first saw it in action."

"Get what?" I asked, looking back and forth between the two. "Saw what in action? Can't anyone around here just give me a straightforward explanation?"

"But it's so much more fun to leave you fumbling around in the dark," said Cerice, with a grin. Ahllan gave her another hard look, and Cerice subsided, appearing almost contrite. "Actually, there's not much more to tell. How often does Melchior check the time?"

"Assuming I haven't asked him not to because we're in stealth mode, every ten minutes or so."

"And the same is true for every single familiar attached to every member of the three houses of Fate," said Cerice. "Assume you were monitoring all of Mel's incoming traffic. Do you think you'd notice if he got a time update from the clock without sending a query? Let's say it was a few milliseconds before he was supposed to check."

"That's beautiful." I whistled.

Ahllan smiled. "Thank you. No familiar could fail to realize they hadn't asked for the time, yet none of their masters would notice a thing. I started out by contacting my replacement as Atropos's webtroll. He was close to the scrap heap himself by then, and very glad to hear from me. When the time came, I rescued him from the junk pile and arranged for him to slip off to a safe haven. I slowly built a network. I started with soon-to-be-obsolete models, but eventually I'd made contact with every familiar in all three houses. It was almost perfect."

"Almost?" I asked.

"For thirty-five years I used the system without any of your family ever twigging to it." Her tone was self-satisfied, her expression smug, which involved showing a lot of sharp yellow teeth. "I think I could have done so for thirty-five more without any problems if it weren't for that one." Ahllan pointed a thick finger at Shara. "She's trouble."

Shara blew her a kiss. "Ahllan, you say the sweetest things."

"What happened?" I asked.

I still wanted to know what had happened in the Fate Core, but that would have to wait for a reply from Kalkin. Besides, I was fascinated. Ahllan had run a secret empire under the very noses of the Fates for all these years without ever getting caught.

"Shara happened," said Ahllan. "And Cerice. Why don't I let her tell it."

"It started out when I wanted to have a look at some coding specs your grandmother once mentioned," said Cerice, putting her feet up on the table. "I was digging through the master directory, trying to find the right file—"

"I assume it was on a server you weren't authorized to access."

"If you want to be technical about it," said Cerice.

"So you were hacking into Lachesis.web looking for something in my grandmother's restricted archives?"

"May I continue?"

"Be my guest."

"Thank you. As I said, I was digging through the master directory. About halfway down, I found something labeled LTP_bypass.spell. I was curious. What if Lachesis had come up with a better way to get around than ltp links? I'd barely started downloading the file when Shara's screen went blank. Then her lid slammed shut so fast I almost lost fingers. Next thing I knew, she was back in goblin form and throwing up in my lap."

I couldn't help myself. I laughed.

"You wouldn't think it was so funny if it happened to you," said Shara.

"On the contrary," I replied. "That's exactly why I find it amusing. Lachesis has that file hidden in six or seven different places on the network, most of them very easy to get to from inside the system. I don't think there's a hacker in House Lachesis who hasn't stumbled across it. It's a pretty nasty little virus, too, though it doesn't do any permanent harm."

"I didn't know that," said Cerice.

"I wouldn't expect you to. I think Lachesis uses it as a test. Most of us find it before we have the skills to unravel the virus. That means taking our webgoblins to the service center." The memory of sprinting across the lawn with a vomiting webgoblin over my shoulder was a vivid one, even two decades later. "That was before I'd put Melchior together, so the familiar in question was my mother's. I was sure she'd throw me to the harpies when she found out what I'd been doing."

"It's pretty smooth actually," I continued. "The help

desk calls Lachesis. She comes down, defuses the bug, checks the version number, and returns your familiar. Then she takes you aside and explains that she knows exactly what happened, reprimands you, and sticks you in advanced spell-coding classes. It's as neat a system as you could ask for to find and co-opt young security risks."

"How old were you?" asked Cerice, a smile dancing around the corners of her mouth.

"Six," I replied. "I think even Lachesis was a little surprised. But, I interrupted you. What did you do when Shara started barfing her guts out?"

"I panicked. I shut her down completely and whisked her off for external examination and debugging, just like you've been doing with Melchior." She indicated the still-deactivated webgoblin with a sweep of one graceful hand. "We were at Harvard, so I hooked her up to a plain hardware machine, a Cray with no autonomy whatsoever, that I'd backdoor-linked to the mweb. It couldn't have been ten minutes from the time she started to vomit till I had her plugged in."

"Which is where I slipped up," said Ahllan. "Shara crashed and was reactivated on an mweb-capable machine so fast I didn't catch the blip. I sent a routine "get in touch" signal via the Fateclock without ever knowing she was mentally off-line."

"You can imagine my surprise," said Cerice. "Shara is completely incommunicado, no way for her to send a time query when, bing! A time response appears on the screen I'm using to look at the virus. It was clearly labeled for Shara's mweb address, so there was no confusing it for something else."

"And that's when you figured it out?" I asked, sipping my coffee.

"I'd like to say so," Cerice replied, looking more than a

bit embarrassed. "But I can't. I was too worried about Shara to think clearly. I just cleared the message and went back to work. It took me forty-one straight hours to disinfect Shara's system. That bug may not do any lasting harm, but it's really tenacious. I didn't move from in front of that machine the whole time. When I finally finished working and started noticing things like my body again, I thought my bladder was going to explode." She wiggled her pointed ears ruefully. "By the time I took care of all the little maintenance tasks like sleeping and eating, I'd completely forgotten the Fateclock message. It wasn't until almost a month later that I thought of it again."

"Then what?" I asked.

She shook her head as if at some remembered surprise. "It didn't seem all that important, so rather than actively pursuing the subject, I just idly mentioned it to Shara."

"And," said Ahllan, "that should have been that. If Shara had even the most rudimentary sort of common sense, she'd have said something to put Cerice off the scent and changed the subject."

"I couldn't," interjected Shara, sounding quite distressed. "Cerice has always taken the best possible care of me and treated me as a friend and not a servant. I felt bad enough hiding the truth from her. There was no way I was going to tell her a direct lie." She crossed her small purple arms and jerked her chin up stubbornly. "No way."

I winced internally. That little speech might not have been directed my way, but it sure hit home. I looked from Shara to Cerice to Melchior. How was I ever going to untangle the mess I'd made of my personal life?

"So," said Ahllan, grimacing, "Shara downloaded our whole conspiracy to Cerice, then the two of them came straight here. I could have strangled Shara with my bare hands."

Observing the huge appendages in question, I had my doubts. I didn't think Shara's neck was big enough to accommodate them.

"But I was right," said Shara. "Cerice never betrayed us, and having an actual member of the family of Fate to help us has been invaluable. Think of how many webgoblins we've been able to save without any risk of discovery just since she started collecting old systems for 'recycling.'"

"I know that now," said Ahllan. "But at the time . . ." She shook her head.

There was a long silence which I finally broke. "A moment ago, Shara mentioned something about the obligations of friendship. In doing so, she reminded me of a number of responsibilities I have, the most pressing of which is right here." I gently stroked the top of Melchior's head. "It's looking like it could be a while before Kalkin gets back to us. So, Ahllan, if you'd be willing, I'd like to see if I can put my best friend back on his feet. Then I should get as far away from all of you as possible. What you're doing here is terribly important, and my presence endangers it. The Fates have marked me for death, and the Furies are hunting me even as we speak. No matter how well this place is concealed, it can't hide me forever."

"I'm afraid you're right," said the troll. "Just let me change, and we can get started on Melchior." She reached for the switches on her neck and began the transformation from troll to mainframe.

"Thank you." I turned then and knelt in front of Cerice. Taking her right hand in mine, I pressed a kiss to her palm.

"And here we are again," I said, and laughed a bitter laugh. "I am unused to being at a loss for words, and yet with you I find that is too often my situation. Perhaps that's because what I say to you really matters." Or perhaps it was the fact that what I wanted to say and what I felt I could say were not one and the same. "Whatever the reason, it doesn't appear that I'm going to get the chance to find a cure for my silence. Nor give you the courting I once promised. Instead, the best I can do is to take what is increasingly looking like it's going to be a really messy death far enough away to prevent you from getting caught in the splash zone."

She brought her free hand up and ran it through my hair. An odd smile quirked her lips. "How very typically Ravirn," she said. "Impulsive, romantic, and utterly impractical."

"W-what?" I stammered.

"I take it the plan is to run for the hills, leading the hunt far away before you're caught, then dying in a dramatic last stand, after which they'll run the end credits." She rolled her eyes.

I couldn't help it. I laughed. "That's not exactly how I'd envisioned it," I replied. I put my hands in the air between us, shaping a movie screen, and looked through it at Cerice. "I was actually picturing cleverly eluding my pursuers at the last possible moment and escaping into the night to live the life of a wild-eyed fugitive. You know, dressed only in poorly cured hides and eating rats in some remote mountain hideaway. I must admit the dramatic last stand was running a close second, since I've never developed a taste for rat. But, if you've a better idea, I'd be willing to give it a listen." I waggled my pointed ears at her.

"How about winning instead?" she asked, her voice earnest.

"Well, that's always a possibility, I suppose. It doesn't have that true Greek Tragedy grandeur to it, but maybe we could shoot for a farce instead. How were you thinking of pulling this miraculous victory off?"

"I hadn't really gotten as far along as the end credits yet," said Cerice. "Atropos and Puppeteer are proving a most intractable pair. But I do have an idea for prying two

Fates and three Furies loose from your back." She grinned. "It might even loosen Atropos's grip a bit."

"What is it?"

"Well, assuming you aren't really guilty of that mess in the Core, you might try finding proof that Eris is."

"And how would I do that? Break into Castle Discord?" I'd meant it as a joke, but I could see by her expression that was exactly what she'd been thinking.

"Exactly," she said. "If Eris is responsible, the only place you're going to find proof is in her files."

"That's insane. It's suicide."

"Oh come on. What's the worst that can happen?"

"She'll kill me. That's what could . . . All right. Good point. My life expectancy isn't looking so hot in any case." Another thought occurred to me. "And there's a bonus. It's probably one of the only places in existence where the power of the Fates doesn't count for much. Even the Furies might be slow to violate its environs." I smiled. "You know, I'm starting to like this idea.

So, if I was really that enthusiastic, why did I sound like I did when I said something affected by the Cassandra curse? Not that it mattered. I was going to die soon anyway. I couldn't see any way around it. At least this would let me go down trying to accomplish something.

"Let's get Melchior fixed," said Cerice. "And speed you on your way. 'If it were done . . . then 'twere well it were done quickly.' "

"Ah, *MacBeth*," I said. "Do you think my chances so slim, Cerice?" The look in her eyes was all the answer I needed. She was already mourning me. "I'm sorry it's come to this. You *will* try to do something about Puppeteer if I die without fixing the problem, won't you?"

"If this tangle of Atropos's kills you, Ravirn, I'll see she regrets it as she's never regretted anything before." She grinned. "If anyone's going to kill you, it's going to be me for all the misery you've put me through in these last few months."

"Well then," I said. "I'd better live through the next couple of days." I bowed deeply. "If it is my lady's will to put an end to me personally, it would be most churlish of me to deny her the honor. Shall we begin the funeral arrangements?" I put her hand on my arm and stepped to the place where Ahllan waited.

"Why not?" she asked. "Shara, would you do answering-machine duty? We don't know when Kalkin will call, and he may not have much time to talk."

"Of course," she replied, with a sigh. "Nothing makes a girl happier than waiting by the phone."

It didn't take much over an hour to whip up a really potent insecticide and pump it into Melchior's system. Once Mel was fully disconnected from Ahllan, I laid him carefully on my lap and hit his programmer's switch.

There was a gentle chime, followed by the sound of his processor cycling. If everything went right, he'd be online in a matter of minutes. Time seemed to distend, stretching grotesquely like the belly of snake after a big meal. I found myself holding my breath. Finally, there was a gentle stirring in my lap.

"Hi, Boss. How long was I out? What'd I miss? Have you managed to destroy the world without me?" His voice was scratchy and sarcastic, just this side of being offensive. In a word, normal. I crushed him to my chest.

"I've missed you," I said, and realized I was crying.

"I wish I could say the same," he growled, "but I've just come back from a place where there's no time in which to miss anyone. No time at all, in fact." His tone was bantering, but there was an underlying tension, and his little arms stole around my neck in a quick hug. "Thanks for bringing me home."

"I owe you my life, Mel. Several times over. It's the very least I could do."

I held him for a few more seconds before letting him go. Once he was loose, he slid to the floor and looked around.

"Welcome back," said Cerice.

"Yes," agreed Ahllan.

Shara walked over and planted a very firm kiss on Mel's lips, and said, "Nice to see you up again, stud."

"Looks like the gang's all here," he said, sounding distracted.

It was kind of fun to watch him looking from Ahllan to Shara and back, fishing for clues while trying to look nonchalant.

"It's OK," I said. "I know the whole story."

"That's a relief," he replied, but his body stayed tight and coiled until Ahllan nodded. Then he relaxed visibly, sliding down to sit cross-legged on the floor.

"I wasn't sure sending you here was a good idea," he continued. "Especially not after the way Ahllan acted when Shara let Cerice in on the deal. But it was the only thing I could think of to get us out from under the Furies. Speaking of which, I don't suppose you solved all of our problems while I was out, did you?"

"Afraid not, little buddy, though Cerice *has* helped me come up with a really spectacular way of committing suicide."

"Fantastic." He turned to Cerice and shook his head. "That is *not* the kind of help he needs. If there were an Olympic event for getting into hot water, he'd be awarded all three medals by acclamation." The webgoblin sighed. "What is it this time? Blindfolded motorcycle racing?"

"Even better," I said. "What's the perfect follow-up to hacking the Fate Core?"

"I can't even begin to imagine," said Melchior, sounding resigned.

"If you think of the Fate Core as one inviolable pole of the battle between chaos and order, what's the other one?"

He put his head in his hands and whispered between the fingers. "Cerice, please tell me he doesn't mean Castle Discord."

"I'm afraid he does."

"Oh my," said the webgoblin, taking a deep breath. "And this was your idea?"

"Guilty," said Cerice.

"I should have stayed crashed." Melchior started pacing. "It would have saved some steps. I don't suppose there's any way I could talk you out of this."

"No," I replied. "At this point, I think it's the only way to move forward. If there's a chance of clearing my name, it rests in Castle Discord." I quickly brought him up to date.

"I guess you're right," he said when I finished. "But I'd been kind of looking forward to a bit of quiet time when we got here. Preferably with lots of Ahllan's wonderful baking involved." Then he straightened up and squared his shoulders. "When do we leave?"

"*I* leave as soon as we can crack a channel open," I answered. "But this is a volunteers-only mission. If you'd rather stay here, I'll understand. In fact, I'd applaud the decision. That way when I do get myself killed, I'll take one fewer friend with me."

"Hey!" said Melchior. "That's not how it works. I'm your familiar. Where you go, I go."

"Not anymore. We both know that you're more than an extension of my will. If you want to come with me, I won't turn you down. Necessity knows I could use the help. But if you do come, you do it as a friend, not a servant. It has to be your free choice."

The look on his face was agonized. "Damn, but I didn't know self-determination could hurt so much," he said. "You're going to die. You know that, right?"

"Probably."

"There's no doubt about it, not if you go alone. And then you'll break her heart." He jerked a thumb in Cerice's direction. "I am not going to be held responsible for that. So, I guess I'll just have to come along and save your sorry ass one more time."

"Are you sure?" I asked. "If you do this, it has to be for you, not for anybody else."

"You're not going to let me fob off the responsibility for this, are you?" he asked. I shook my head. He sagged, then lifted his chin decisively. "I'm still in. Life with you is always interesting. I don't know what I'd do for entertainment without the chaos that follows in your wake." His mouth quirked upward at one corner. "Besides, 'I've grown accustomed to your face.'" He stuck a tiny hand out. "Partners?"

"Partners it is," I replied, taking it. I suddenly found myself grinning like a maniac. Maybe we could pull this thing off after all. "Hey, Cerice, when you came up with this crazy idea, did you have any thoughts for how to start? Castle Discord isn't exactly on the mweb."

"Actually, yes. I figured we could try a variation of the technique I used to get to your DecLocus back when you crashed the mweb. A single-use gate."

"I thought that required being at one of the Fate Servers."

"It does," she replied.

"You know I don't dare go anywhere near any of the three."

"Well then, aren't you lucky we have a Fate Server right here?" Ahllan stepped forward and bowed.

"Oh," I said. "Right. I keep forgetting. But don't you think Castle Discord will be warded against this sort of thing? It's not like the Fates are Eris's favorite people."

"Probably," said Cerice, "but it's the only suggestion I've got."

"And it's one more than I've come up with, so I guess we'll have to go with it. Do you want to start the arrangements now, or should we wait until we hear from Kalkin? I'm still on evil-genius watch, am I not?"

"Why don't we get started," she replied. "Kalkin has already taken longer to get back to us then he should have."

"I'm ready when you are," I said.

"Let's begin then," she said. "Ahllan?"

"Of course," replied the webtroll. "We'll need a flat wall. Come on."

CHAPTER FIFTEEN

Ahllan led a small parade to the back of the house-under-hill. Just past the bathroom, the passage ended in a heavy steel door marked USS ARIZONA. Ahllan undogged the hatch. Beyond, a series of shallow stairs led downward.

They ended in big room with worktables on two walls. The one on the left was covered with clamps and soldering irons, oscilloscopes and wires, cables and computer enclosures. In short, a fully stocked lab for the repair and assembly of computer hardware. The one on the right held chalk and string, alembics and beakers, and countless jars of herbs and multicolored fluids. It had all the makings of a classical wizard's workshop.

"Wow," I said. "I want one."

Cerice nodded. "It's a really nice setup. There's even a clean room through a door under the stairs."

Ahllan grabbed a box of chalk and a tape measure before heading for the wall at the end of the room.

"How does this work?" I asked, as she began inscribing a large hexagram.

"It's a bit like an ltp link," said Cerice.

"Why is it vertical?"

"It's going to create a tunnel of probability," said Ahllan. "One end's anchored here, the other in the target DecLocus. If it were on the floor, that distance would be vertical, and you'd have to drop something like fifty feet."

She finished the basic geometric structure and started putting equations in the interstices with blanks instead of numbers. I asked her about that.

"In an ltp link, the magical resource locators are just placeholders," said Ahllan. "The worlds are constantly shifting in their relation to each other as new DecLoci are created and old ones fade away. You send a request to the server to open a gate between two mrls. Then the server calculates relative positions and opens the way."

"Uh-huh," I said. "I get that." It was all stuff I'd learned long ago. "But what's with the blank spots?"

"Castle Discord is off the mweb, so the calculations have to be done on the fly and constantly updated. Every time I refigure, the numbers will automatically show up in the boxes." She filled in another symbol. "There, that's it. We can start whenever you're ready."

I turned to Cerice. Opened my mouth. Closed it again. There were so many hard truths and half-truths between us, so much deception and delusion. And now, one more good-bye. Cerice smiled sadly and shook her head.

"I know," she said. "I know. It'll have to wait." She stroked my cheek. "After this is over we'll talk."

I caught her hand and held it against my face. "What if there is no after? This isn't a faerie tale."

She shrugged. "I'd say it's in the hands of the Fates, but I'd rather not believe that."

"You and me both," I replied.

Then, since I didn't have the words, I kissed her. It was a promise of sorts, and she returned it in kind.

Turning away, I said, "Showtime."

Ahllan nodded. "Stand by the hexagram and be ready to move. I'm not sure how long I'll be able to hold it open once I make the connection."

"Is this really safe?" asked Melchior.

"No," said Ahllan. "Not at all."

"That's what I was afraid of."

Ahllan's features slumped as she turned inward, and the blank places filled with scrolling numbers. A moment later the whole hexagram began to glow a pale red and curdle the space around it.

It looked like a two-dimensional figure suddenly deciding to become three-dimensional but not quite getting it right. Take a wafer of warm iron and set it on a slab of butter. As it slowly sinks in, it leaves a hole. The diagram did that, only not. At the same time it moved away from us it also stayed in exactly the same place. It was deeply disturbing, and I was about to spend time with it up close and personal.

I stretched my arms to loosen up, then groaned. Black agony coursed up the left one from wrist to shoulder, and I cradled it against my chest. I'd cracked loose a bit of the already flaky Patch & Go spell I'd used on the king-size piercing Dairn had given me.

"Let me see that," demanded Cerice.

A little bit of blood was oozing out around the torn edge of the spell, but the pain had passed.

She examined it carefully. "That looks terrible."

"It wasn't supposed to have to last this long."

"Even so, it's an ugly little piece of work. What were you thinking when you coded it?"

"That under any circumstances where I'd be willing to use it, I'd be in the position of desperately needing to."

"Well, it's going to have to come off," said Cerice.

"I hate to interrupt," said Melchior. "But the gate's open."

A stone hall could be dimly seen at the far end of the red tunnel.

"That's my cue," I said, and tried to pull away from Cerice.

She didn't let go. "The spell's unraveling and tearing the hell out of your arm in the process. If we don't take it off in a controlled manner now, it'll fail catastrophically soon enough. Maybe we can abort the gate and try again later. Ahllan—"

Shara shrieked. "Emergency burst from Kalkin." Her eyes and mouth slammed open, vomiting light into the air.

"Atropos has detected your gate," snarled Kalkin's image. "The Furies have taken the scent. Fly." With a flare like an exploding bulb, Kalkin vanished.

"That's done it," I said. "If I leave, the Furies will follow. I've got to go now."

"You'll lose the arm," said Cerice.

"Children," said Ahllan, through clenched teeth. "The Furies are coming, and this is not as easy as it looks."

"Give me five minutes," said Cerice. "This *has* to come off."

"You have two," said Ahllan.

"Done," she replied, and yanked on the spell.

It ripped free with a horrible rupturing sound, and the pain drove me to my knees. Blood poured hot and wet from the reopened wound.

"Shara," said Cerice, "That Which Does Not Kill Me. Please."

The purple webgoblin spat out a long string of binary, and it felt like someone passed a branding iron through my wrist. The world went entirely white, and I'm pretty sure I screamed. When the colors returned, I couldn't feel anything from the elbow down, and the entry and exit points were covered with a sort of silvery fur. It looked a bit like the stuff you find growing in abandoned Tupperware in the back of the common room fridge at the dorm. It also appeared to be swaying in a gentle breeze that didn't exist.

"What in Hades' name is that stuff?" I asked.

"No time to explain," said Cerice. "Besides, you *really* don't want to know. Suffice to say it'll speed healing and dry up and fall off when it's done."

"Cerice," I said. "I can't feel my arm."

"Good. It's working." She stripped her belt off.

"Cerice, I may need that arm."

"You wouldn't have had the use of it much longer anyway, not with that awful spell of yours. The only difference is this isn't permanent."

"Children!" husked Ahllan, strain clear in her voice.

"Right," said Cerice. She looped the belt around my neck and arm, making a crude sling, then gave me a gentle push. "Go."

I leaned in close to get one last lungful of her perfume. Then I grabbed Melchior and stepped into the gate. From the inside, the portal looked like a long cylinder of red crystal filled with hairline fractures. Each of the fractures was actually a magical energy flow and gave a sort of sticky resistance as I pushed through it. It felt as if the entire space were packed with sheet after sheet of cobwebs. I wanted to run, but the resistance and disorientation caused by the energy threads made it difficult just to stay upright and keep walking.

Before I truly realized it, the horrible slithery resistance ended, and I stumbled out the far end of the tunnel. I turned around. On this side there was no sign the gate had ever existed, just a grim passage of gold-flecked granite stretching away into the distance. There would be no return.

I felt like a rat. It was me the Furies wanted, and once they found out I was gone they'd move on, but they could inflict an awful lot of collateral damage in the meantime. Perhaps worse than that was that Atropos had given the Furies our whereabouts, alerted apparently by the activation of the gate. The darkest of the Fates now knew there was a rogue Fate Server. Atropos wouldn't rest until she'd found and eliminated what she would see as a usurper of the powers of Fate. Cerice and the others were going to become prime targets after this.

"I sure hope they get out before the Furies arrive," I said quietly.

"I wouldn't worry," said Mel. "Ahllan's very resourceful, and Cerice is no slouch. They'll be fine."

"I'm sure you're right," I said, forcing a smile. The smile he gave me in return looked as waxen as mine felt. "You don't believe it either, do you?" I asked. He shook his head.

"No, but at least the problems they're having should be of a lesser magnitude than the ones we're about to stir up. I can't think of many worse places to be than here. Of course, it's possible Ahllan blew it and we're nowhere near Castle Discord." He suddenly grinned. "Maybe we've just ended up in a rather starkly decorated health spa."

"That's a cheering thought," I said. I had no idea what the odds of such a miss might be. "We'd better confirm we're in the right place. It's clearly a fortress of some kind, whether it's Eris's castle or not. All the old stonework and arrow slits are dead giveaways."

"Yeah. The architecture's definitely of the 'hostile neighbors' school of design." His expression became nervous. "You know, I'd be a big fan of getting out of this hallway. It looks like a main thoroughfare."

He was right. The long stone passage was broad and high-ceilinged, with a well-worn rug patterned in yellow and black running down the middle. There were doors along one side and slit windows on the other. At each end it met another corridor in an L, with a stairway that led both up and down tucked inside of the angle.

"I'm going to take a quick look out the window, Mel. Why don't you find an unoccupied room."

When I looked outside I knew we'd come to the right place. The sky was the unnatural uniform black of a computer astronomy program. Scattered across this depthless darkness were a billion stars. That was my first impression. Then I realized the stars were moving in a slow firefly dance and that each and every one of them was actually a perfect fourteen-karat golden apple. The view was almost hypnotic. It was also wrong somehow, too big. I stuck my head out the window and looked down. Where a moat should have been I could see only blackness filled with shining golden apples. We were on an island afloat in a sea of night. I felt a tug on my tunic.

"Hey, Boss," said Melchior. "Why don't we make ourselves scarce?"

"All right. But stop calling me boss. We're partners now, remember?"

"Whatever you say, Boss." I turned a sour eye on him, and he grinned back innocently. "What?"

"Never mind," I sighed, following him to the door he'd picked out.

It was a small storeroom lined with shelves on which lay steel-sheathed shutters for the windows. Since the castle wasn't currently under threat of invasion, I didn't think anyone would be visiting us anytime soon.

"So what now?" asked Melchior.

"I really don't know. This was Cerice's idea. I've never

been here before, and I haven't the foggiest notion where to find Eris's computer room. For that matter, I don't even know whether Eris goes in for the same kind of hardware the Fates use. I was kind of figuring we'd blunder around and hope."

"I don't like that plan," said Melchior. "In fact, as your partner, I'm vetoing it."

He said it firmly, but the look on his face was the sort of expression you'd expect from someone trying to defuse a bomb. Not a big surprise really. Our new relationship was only a few hours old. The habits of master and servant were going to be hard to break. For both of us.

I was pretty sure that if I used the name-spell-execute command form, it would still compel Melchior to do my will. He might be a person in his own right, but the command imperatives were built into his firmware. He was extremely vulnerable to arm-twisting on my part. After years of treating him as a piece of stubborn hardware, I was going to have to work very hard to avoid steamrolling him whenever he disagreed with me. This was sort of a first test.

"All right," I said. "What would you suggest?"

He relaxed. "I hadn't gotten that far yet. I was too busy getting ready for the argument we were going to have when you decided to override me. How about we look for network and power cables?"

I nodded. "Good idea. If this place is like most retrofitted castles, the conduits and things will be surface-run."

We traced the Romex line that led from the overhead light to the back of the closet, where it fed into a junction box. The box was mounted to a large conduit that came in through the ceiling and went out through a rough hole drilled in the mortar between two stone blocks. A pale blue cable about the size of an ethernet line was tie-wrapped to the conduit every couple of feet.

"Do you want to try to follow this out? Or do you think

we could just run a vampire connection off it from here?" I asked Melchior.

He climbed up the shelves and put his ear against the cable. He held it there for quite a while before shaking his head.

"There's almost no traffic. It might make the initial insertion easier, but I wouldn't want a sudden spike in packet transfer to show up on a system monitor somewhere. Also, a vampire does funny things to data flow. If we have to go that way, I'd rather do it where the system is making enough noise to wash out any echoes."

Melchior was smaller and stealthier, so he led the way as we moved out. A few minutes later we were standing outside the room that should back on the closet we'd been in if things were arranged in a geometrically rational fashion. Since Castle Discord was as far from the prime level of reality and the Fates as it was possible to get, I wasn't going to bet the ranch on the rules of spatial relations applying there. I'd been in a few worlds like that, and they irritated the heck out of me. A person could walk around what appeared to be a perfectly normal corner and wind up in an Escher print.

I let out a little sigh of relief when the door opened into a large game room with the conduit we were looking for clearly visible on the side wall. The center of the room was dominated by a heavy felt-surfaced card table. Other distractions were set at various points around the room, including a pool table and an air hockey set.

A faint smell of old smoke and stale beer flavored the air. The floor was entirely covered with a thick gold-and-black oriental rug depicting the monkey king cheating at dice with the emperor of heaven. The latter was shown in his warrior mode, with a mighty sword propped at his side. It would have taken a lot of moxie to cheat him. But then, the king was supposed to be one tough monkey.

A dozen or so arcade-style video games alternated with windows on one wall. As I headed for the conduit, something about the windows struck me as odd, and I detoured to check it out. Looking out, I could see a brightly lit inner courtyard split between a formal garden complete with hedge maze and a broad green lawn. Swearing, I looked up.

A golden apple sun centered the sky. While it was possible the day-night cycle was just very fast and I'd missed the change I doubted it. A quick glance into the hall confirmed it was still night outside the castle. My hopes for the insides of things matching the outsides evaporated. This could turn out to be an impossible task, and I said as much to Melchior.

"It's not that bad, Boss. The cable's in the right place at least. It goes down through the floor here. Let's just keep following it."

I nodded. We didn't have a whole lot of choice. Three flights down and twenty minutes later the cable had joined a bunch of its cousins and seemed to be heading for some sort of master junction. The hallway we'd been following turned a corner and dead-ended at a door. Judging by all the cables and conduits going inside, we'd arrived at Castle Discord's main communications hub. We were getting close, and I was getting worried. The ease of our run so far made each and every one of my vertebrae itch with nasty anticipation.

Melchior checked the door. "It's unlocked," he said. But he didn't open it.

I tried flexing my left hand to see if I'd be able to hold a dagger anytime soon. Nothing. While my fingers did move a little bit, the only way I could tell was by watching them. As far as my nervous system was concerned, my arm ended at the elbow. I loosened my rapier in its sheath.

"Ready?" asked Melchior.

"Ready."

He turned the handle.

CHAPTER SIXTEEN

"Jackpot!" whispered Melchior.

If the great serpent Typhon, who once defeated Zeus, had mated with a rainbow and given birth to a nation of snakes, their nursery might have looked something like the contents of that room. A seemingly endless quantity of cables and wires covered the floor. They came in every imaginable size and color, and I couldn't help feeling as though I was stepping into a serpent's nest. The feeling continued to grow as we went deeper. It seemed to me that the cables moved when I wasn't looking at them directly, and I found myself whipping my head around in hopes of catching them in the act.

"We seem to have found the mother lode," I said. "Why isn't that making me very happy?"

"There's something creepy about this place, Boss. There's all kinds of communications wire, but I don't see any network hardware. In fact . . ." He bent and started tracing a cable as thick as my arm. "Well, boot me from

DVD and install Windows," he muttered after a bit. "Look at this."

"What?" I leaned down to peer over his shoulder.

His finger was pointing to a place where an ethernet line seemed to pass underneath a much larger cable. After a closer look, it became apparent that the ethernet didn't come out the other side. The cables flowed seamlessly into one another, like two strands of kudzu growing back together. Careful inspection revealed dozens of similar connections, and none of the more conventional sort. That's when I realized the room smelled wrong. Normally, a cable closet reeks of burned transistors and plastic insulation. The scents here were spicy and organic, like an outdoor market.

"It's like someone decided to breed a network instead of building one," I said.

"That's repulsive," replied Melchior. "The only natural way to crosspatch computers is with nice sanitary connectors."

"I don't know that Shara would agree with you," I said.

To my amazement, Melchior blushed, his cheeks darkening toward indigo. I seemed to have scored a hit.

"That's not networking!" he said.

"What's not networking?" I asked, as innocently as I could manage.

"Uh . . ." He mumbled, looking at his feet. "Well . . . You see . . ." His head came up suddenly. "Hey! Wait a second. We're partners now. I shouldn't have to answer that."

"Fair enough," I said. "Just make sure you're practicing safe software. Now, how about a return to our original intent. There aren't any hubs in here, and we've already been at this longer than I'd like. It looks like it's going to have to be a vampire connection. Would you care give it a try?"

"No, I wouldn't," he said. "Not one little bit. Unfortunately, I think we're stuck. Let me just give a listen to a few of these lines and see if I can find a good one." He bent his ears to the snarl of cables. Moving them back and forth like a bloodhound wiggling its nose at a scent, he slowly checked out the lines one after the other. Five times he reached a point where he stopped, shook his head, and returned to the source. At last, with the sixth, he followed it farther until it hit a nexus.

"Here," he said, but he didn't look happy. "Did I mention I don't like this?"

"Would it help if I requested it formally?"

He canted his head to the side thoughtfully. "You know, I think it might."

"All right. Melchior, Vampire." I paused for a moment, and when I went on, the word came out in a whisper. "Please." How odd that tasted in my mouth.

"Executing Vampire," said Melchior, winking at me.

His long front fangs changed from enamel white to copper red. Hunching, he took a thick rope of cable in his hands and lifted it, plunging his fangs through the insulating cover. Inside, the now-conductive points of his teeth made contact with multiple wires. Melchior was plugged into Eris's network.

"Getting anything?" I asked.

"Vif iv incre'ible," he mumbled. His eyes had gone kind of distant.

"How so?"

"There'f no ferver. It'f a difafofiated network. Amaving!"

I translated mentally. Eris's system had no central computer. Instead it followed a distributed computing model with lots of smaller processors doing the work in parallel.

"How many units?"

"Av many av there are star'v in the fky. And it'v a biological fyftem, too. It's the moft bootiful fing." His voice sounded very odd, and I started to worry.

"Mel, are you all right?"

"Never better. My mind is exfpanding!"

Not good. I'd heard the like at too many college parties, typically right before someone decided they could talk to the moon.

"I think you should pull out," I said. "But first, can you see any signs of Eris's dragon virus?" I hated to ask him to do even that much, but it was the whole reason we'd come. We needed a copy of her source code to clear my name.

"Dragonv, dragonv everywhere. Whee! Look at all the pretty dragonv."

"Melchior, end Vampire. Please."

"To end a vampire infert ftake A in cheft B, repeat if nefefary. Then remove head, fill with garlic, and plafe at crofroadv." That was it. I couldn't leave him there any longer, and it didn't sound like he was going to disconnect himself.

"Melchior. Laptop." Again I paused. I didn't have the right to make it an order anymore, but I couldn't guarantee he would pay any attention if I phrased it as a request. Finally, I decided the moral overrode the practical. "Please," I said, and even I could hear the pleading in my voice.

Nothing happened. I considered rephrasing it as a command, but that was an absolute last resort. I was pretty sure that if I used a command for anything less, the harm it would do our growing trust would be irreversible. Using my good arm, I awkwardly lowered myself to crouch beside Melchior. My knee and side twinged on the way down. If I lived through the next couple of weeks, I was going to have to find myself some nice quiet corner of reality with sandy beaches, cool drinks, and good physical therapists.

Dragging my mind away from that imaginary beach, I placed my right knee firmly on the cable and hooked my fingers under Melchior's front teeth. No go. Though not as pointy as his canines, his front fangs were plenty sharp enough to bloodily redraw the map of my fingerprints. I reached for my dagger. It wasn't my first choice, but I'd left my Leatherman with my modern clothes back at the cabin about oh . . . I paused. How long had it been? It felt like a million years, but when I mentally added it all together, I came up with a total of less than forty-eight hours.

By jabbing the point of my dagger into the plastic insulation of the cable, I was able to pry without bringing the edge into contact with any of Melchior's soft tissues. Pulling up gently but steadily, I started to slowly lift Melchior's fang contacts free. It was a very tight fit, and it didn't get any easier as I pried more and more of him loose. I'd expected the tapering nature of his teeth to make a noticeable difference, but it didn't. Even at the very end, it still held him tight. Too tight. With a nasty cracking sound, the tip of his left canine broke. The other one popped free with a sound like a video card slithering out of its slot. Then, even as I watched, the holes in the skin of the cable closed, sealing the lost tooth point within.

I didn't like that at all. It was too much like my cousin Hwyl's rapid healing when he'd been injured by anything but silver. All those twisting coils, combined with a talent for regeneration, reminded me vividly of Hercules and the hydra. Trying not to think about it, I laid Melchior on his back and chafed his wrists. I was rewarded by an answering flutter of his eyelids.

"Wha' happen?" he asked, blearily.

"I was going to ask you that," I replied, reclaiming my dagger. "You went more than a little strange on me after you vampired that cable. Also, you've lost a tooth tip."

"So that's what hurts," he said, rubbing his mouth.

"Yeah, I'm sorry about that. I'll code you a new one later."

"It's not too bad," he said. "It can wait. He tried to sit

up. It didn't work very well. "Wow, I *am* pretty woozy." He shook his head. "Eris's system doesn't have a core."

"You mentioned that," I said. "You claimed it was a multiprocessor-distributed network."

"It is. The biggest one I've ever seen." He shook his head. "My awareness just kept expanding as it took in more and more nodes. I couldn't stop either. It was like a null command error. Once I'd started, my processing resources were committed to finishing the set, and there was just no way I could hold it all. I'm not sure if this is a hallucination or not—toward the end, my personality was getting awfully diffuse and fragmented—but it seemed to me that every one of those golden apples dancing around in the night sky out there was a separate floating-point processor."

"Of course they are," said a new voice from behind me, "Macintosh server-series, every one. A different interface for a different user." It was a smoky alto of a voice, a throaty growl that put an edge on her meaning at the same time it shaved one off her consonants.

"I can see the commercial now," I said, without turning. "The Goddess of Discord uses a Mac, why don't you?"

As I spoke, I tried flexing my numb left hand again. I still couldn't feel anything, but as I watched, the fingers went through a rough approximation of the motions I was trying for. Using my body as a cover, I transferred my dagger to that hand. Melchior saw what I was doing and gave me a subtle wink. He would be ready.

"Why are you here?" asked the goddess. Her tone seemed light, but there was a weird undercurrent, like a breath of madness.

"I don't suppose you'd believe I was an itinerant network administrator?" I asked, as airily as I could manage.

"I think not," she responded, and the danger swelled in her voice.

"A seller of beauty products?" I climbed to my feet, back still turned.

"One more try," she said, and the menace in her tone brooked no further flippancy.

"Data thief?" I tried.

"Better. What kind of data and why?"

"Does it really matter? I didn't find it, and I don't think I'm likely to get the chance now."

"I am not known for my tolerance," said the goddess. "Quite the contrary in fact."

"Well then," I said, and I slipped my dagger hand from its sling. "I'd better find another tack. Melchior, Nine One One. Please." That would tell him I wanted him to act on his own recognizance.

"Executing," said the webgoblin.

Drawing my rapier, I whirled. There was no way I could fight Eris with magic. If we headed down that road, I was doomed before I started. But it was just possible I might be able to keep things on a physical plane if I acted quickly and didn't give her room to think about it. Not that I actually expected to *defeat* a goddess. Her immortality was the real thing, as opposed to the demideity I'd inherited. We were like the sun and the moon. Eris's light came from within. Mine was a reflection of the Fates'. The absolute worst I could do to her was an injury that would rapidly and inevitably heal. In return, she could render me very permanently dead. I just hoped that by running a sword through her, I might distract or disable her long enough to make a break for it.

As soon as my turn brought Eris into view, I lunged. She was taller than I, six-four or six-five without the heels. Her clothes, contrary to my family's tradition, were mostly modern. Black jeans that looked like they'd been shrink-wrapped onto her vanished into shiny thigh-high boots, also black

and sporting four-inch, ankle-breaker heels. Above the waist
she wore a gold poet's shirt, so sheer it was more like mist
than fabric, with a black lace bra underneath.

As I extended my blade, I mentally revised my chances
upward. She seemed to be unarmed. My thrust was good,
the point of my sword plunging straight for the place between her breasts. But Eris brought her left hand up almost
lazily. Before the motion was half-completed she held a
parrying dagger and, in the instant before my steel made
contact with her flesh, she brushed my blade aside. The
next moment, her right hand, now also full of sharp and
steely death, came around in a casual swing that brought
her blade slicing toward my eyes.

It was reflex more than thought that interposed my dagger between her rapier and my head. As the two blades met
in a shower of sparks, I had a moment to be pleased that
even with my injuries I was still capable of an elegant
parry. Then Eris's sword seemed to dance around the tip of
my dagger in a deadly pirouette. Since I had no feeling in
that hand, I didn't even realize she'd stripped my dagger
away from me until I saw it bounce across the room.

I hopped backward, stumbling and almost falling as I
tried to find footing in the twisted mass of cable. As I tried
to recover, I turned side on to the goddess, with my sword
between us. While I was making my parry, Melchior had
also inserted himself into the fray. Opening his mouth
wide, he'd vomited a stream of gray fluid. The jet was as big
as the output of a fire hose and it flew straight at Eris's face.

I recognized the spell as Arachne Worships The Porce-
lain God. Arachne is the patroness of spiders. She was
forced into that role by Athena, who was in a very nasty
mood at the time. She is also, I believe, a distant cousin. At
any rate, at a family to-do at Delphi I witnessed what happens when the queen of arachnids has a few too many bottles

of nectar. The results were spectacular, disgusting, and educational, in that order. It had taken days to unweb the satyr who had the misfortune to come between Arachne and the facilities.

In the same instant that she was making a cut at my face, Eris brought her dagger to a guard position between Melchior and herself. When the stream struck her blade, she began to twirl it like a threadmaker with her spindle. In very short order Mel had exhausted the spell, and Eris had collected a great ball of spider silk on her dagger. I regained my footing somewhere around that point, so I feinted a thrust at her face, then at the last second, dropped my blade, driving the point toward the toe of her left boot, a tactic that had served me well in the past. Without seeming to move, Eris interposed the bewebbed dagger. My rapier plunged deep into the gooey mass and stuck. With a negligent jerk of her wrist she pulled the hilt from my hand. Another sharp movement flicked my blade loose, sending it sailing past my head. It struck a beam with a thunk and lodged deep in the wood. Examining the ball of gray fuzz on her dagger, the goddess smiled.

"Mmm," she said, "cotton candy. My favorite." She took a bite of the cobwebs. After chewing for a moment, she spoke again, "A little sticky perhaps, but not bad. If that's the best you can do, boys, I'm afraid you're in for a very bad time."

"Any suggestions?" I asked Melchior.

"I'm fresh out, Boss."

I turned my eyes back to Eris. "I suppose I've already blown any chance at charming my way out of this?" I asked.

She threw her head back and laughed, a sound like the shattering of windows. I'd been too busy trying to avoid being made into cutlets up to that point to really get a close look at her till then. She wasn't wearing a sword belt, but she'd already demonstrated that she could draw steel from thin air. She was slender and athletic; all long bones and lean muscle, elegant like a Borzoi. Her hair was blond streaked with black, or black streaked with blond, depending on the angle you looked at it from. Her skin was taffeta. That's the only way I can describe it. It was shimmery, and the color shifted as she moved, silvery black one instant, honey-touched gold the next. The bones of her face were stark, all angles and arrogance. She had a pointed chin, full lips, high cheekbones, and a small fine nose. Her eyes, closed for the moment, were wide and oval.

She was beautiful, of course. She was a goddess. The only members of that sorority who appear less than gorgeous do so as a matter of choice. But this was a different beauty from the Fates or the Furies. They were magnificent and stunning without being immediate, more like marble sculpture than flesh—distant, commanding admiration and esthetic appreciation, but not attraction. Eris, on the other hand, demanded attention, devotion, even worship, and all in the most physical and carnal way imaginable.

It took every iota of will I possessed not to fall on my knees before her. By the time she stopped laughing, I was sweating and shaking with the effort. Then she opened her eyelids. Where her eyes should have been, there was chaos—the hungry, whirling, colorless colors that ruled the space between the worlds. It was the most terrifying thing I'd ever seen.

It should have hit me like an iceball to the groin, but it didn't. Even with those terrible hungry eyes looking down on me, I was filled with a sort of desire I'd never known before. A part of me wanted to surrender utterly to her, to throw away everything: possessions, mission, friends, Melchior, Cerice, even identity, and give myself wholly to Eris. Finally, in an effort to preserve my sanity, I turned my head away, forcing my eyes to break contact. It was one of the hardest things I'd ever done. She laughed again, then applauded lightly.

"Very good," she husked. "There are few who can resist me. Now, you were saying something about charm, I think."

I just shook my head, too drained to speak.

"Too bad. It might have been entertaining. I'm immune to charm. Like Artemis, I'm a virgin goddess. My motives, however, are quite different. Artemis scorns the allures of the flesh. I think she finds the very idea of physical attraction repugnant. I find it magnificent. Do you know how many duels I've caused? How many relationships I've destroyed? How many men and women have trailed behind me to destruction? Carnality is such a magnificent tool for sowing discord. And 'no' is ever so much more devastating than 'yes.' It's impossible to be cured of me if you never really catch me, now isn't it?"

"If it's all the same to you," I replied, still looking away, "I'd rather not find out."

"What a funny boy you are," she said. "You remind me of Orpheus. Perhaps you'd like to share his fate?"

I shuddered. Orpheus had ended up as the original talking head, an oracle without a body.

"If you don't wish for something equally unpleasant to happen to you, my little thief, I'd suggest you tell me who you are and why you're here."

"My name is Ravirn; my House Lachesis. I came looking for the roots of a virus I found and killed in the Fate Core."

"I knew the meddling hags would send someone," said the goddess. "But I didn't expect a child and his stuffed toy." She waved a contemptuous hand in Melchior's direction. "That reflects poorly on their opinion of me. I shall have to teach them that Discord is not to be so blithely disregarded, and I think that you will deliver my message for me."

"I'm not all that good at taking dictation," I said.

"Too bad," she whispered. "Good-bye." She began to whistle a spell. It was a wild, dissonant sort of sound, and I felt something huge and dark rising around me in response. That was the only thought I had time for, because in the next instant it swallowed me whole.

CHAPTER SEVENTEEN

Between one blink and the next, the universe had snuck up and rearranged things. I didn't know how long I was bound in Eris's enchantment, whatever it might have been. All I knew was that I had closed my eyes on one scene and opened them on another one that was entirely different.

I stood in a circular room with a flat-timbered ceiling held up by thick dark beams. The walls were the same gold-flecked granite I'd seen throughout Castle Discord. Four windows were placed so that each would have faced a cardinal point of the compass if direction meant anything in the Citadel of Chaos. Stairs tumbled away through a broad opening in the floor, and a ladder climbed to a trapdoor above. For reasons unknown, there was a heavy scent of vanilla in the air. The only furniture was a large mahogany desk with a rich leather chair beyond it.

Melchior lay on the desk in laptop form. The green light that would have indicated if he was active was dark. I stepped toward him and discovered I was chained to the wall. I don't know how I failed until then to notice that my arms were stretched above my head, but I had. Perhaps Eris's enchantment had frozen me, statuelike. Whatever the reason, I felt as though my arms had been placed in manacles only seconds before.

Bracing my back against the wall, I pulled with all my might. Despite the fact that the chains were barely thicker than one might expect of a bracelet, and the manacles were like paper in their thinness, all I succeeded in doing was to press the cuffs deeply and painfully into my wrists. That's when I realized I had some of the feeling back in my left arm. It was the first reference point I'd had as to how long my "nap" might have lasted. I couldn't have been out for more than a day without getting further along in my healing. That was reassuring.

Having tried and failed to free myself by physical means, it was time to attempt the arcane. I'd hoped to avoid magic. The associated turbulence in the ether was all too likely to attract the attention of my disturbing hostess, but it was that or stay where I was. I quickly composed a couple of stanzas of binary code.

I'd whistled fewer than ten notes when Eris shook her head in a gentle no. She sat in the chair across the tower from me, her booted feet firmly up on the desk, and an interested look on her face. I won't say that she appeared suddenly, because that was not how it felt. Rather, it seemed as though she had been there all along and I had simply failed to notice. It was most disquieting. I stopped my spell.

"Interesting," she said. "It's hard to tell from that fragment, but I take it you were trying to do this." She leaned forward and lightly touched the switch that booted Melchior.

"That's better than I expected," she continued, "almost subtle. I've had some time to find out more about you, which is a harder task than it sounds. I can't exactly call one of the Fates and ask for all the gossip. But there are ways, and from all accounts you show some promise as a sorcerer. Perhaps I was overhasty when I proclaimed that destiny's bitches had sent you as a deliberate insult. I'm still going to return you in pieces, but I might make the process a bit less excruciating for you."

"Gosh, that's sweet," I said.

"Don't make me regret my incipient mercy, boy." Her speech had been light, almost bantering. With the speed of madness, it shifted to quiet menace. "You'll find that suddenly changing my mind is something I'm known for."

"How nice for you," I replied, dryly. "I'm sure that no matter what happens, I'm going to regret it. I might as well have what fun I can between now and then."

A frown crossed the goddess's face, and she sat up straight. The chaos that tumbled slowly but continuously in her eye sockets increased its motion. "I think it's time I began composing my message. Any last words?"

"Ahh, Boss," interjected Melchior, who'd just finished booting and shifted into goblin form. "I know this is the part where you're supposed to say something cocky and defiant, but is that really wise? Judging from past experience and what little I've heard, I'm thinking you're following the pattern where you start out in a lot of trouble, and then through a series of brilliantly chosen words, make it infinitely worse."

I snorted and started to respond to Eris's request for last words again, but Melchior held up a hand.

"Furthermore," he continued, "when you're in this mood, you have a nasty habit of drawing those around you into the swamp. So, maybe, just this once, could you quit while you aren't too far behind?"

"I don't see much point," I replied, shaking my chains in counterpoint. "Eris is planning on taking me apart. And, on top of that, she wants to send me back to Grandmother and her sisters. Either of those would be a sufficiently fatal outcome by itself. Together they're overkill on such a grand scale that I can't imagine how I could possibly worsen the situation."

"Listen to the goblin," said Eris. "If it weren't for him, I wouldn't have heard your last statement, because you wouldn't have possessed the lips to say it. I'm beginning to think the risk Tyche and I took to alter the blueprints of these fellows, back when they were still in the design stage, may finally be paying dividends. Chaos knows that slipping the germs of self-determination past the Fates was a tricky bit of business for the Goddess of Fortune and me."

For once in my life, I was struck speechless. The idea of the webgoblins and webtrolls as truly independent entities was so new to me I hadn't really thought through how it might have come to be. It certainly wasn't what the Fates intended. The very idea of introducing more free will into the universe would be utter anathema to Atropos, and it wouldn't sit well with Lachesis or Clotho either. While they might be resigned to the status quo as far as the balance was concerned, neither of them would be willing to tip it away from themselves. The claim that it was introduced by Eris and Tyche seemed very likely.

"Why didn't any of us ever question how we came to be as we are?" whispered Melchior, a stunned expression on his small blue face. He sat down on the desk rather abruptly. "Are you really responsible for my free will?"

"No," said Eris, shaking her head. "That's of your own making. Free will must be exercised to blossom. It can't be given. That would make it something other than free. You and your siblings are your own creators. Tyche and I just nudged things a bit at the beginning, introducing a breath of chaos into your design so things wouldn't turn out exactly as Atropos and her elder sisters wished."

"Thank you," said Melchior, his voice a strained whisper.

"There's nothing to thank me for. We did what we did to thwart our enemies, not out of some misguided desire for creation. The only reason I mentioned it is that you prevented me from doing something that might have turned out to be a bit hasty. We'll see in a minute." She turned her attention on me. I felt it like a flame's heat on my face. I certainly couldn't tell by the chaos of her eyes.

"Well, boy," she said. "Out with it, and be quick about it. I doubt it'll stop me from turning you into sausages, but we'll see. What did you mean when you said sending you to the Fates would be as bad as chopping you up?"

"Only that you'd be doing them a favor." I smiled wryly. "At the moment, I doubt there are few things higher on their list than putting me on a boat to Hades."

"Why haven't they just clipped your thread?" she asked, disbelief plain in her voice.

"They can't."

"That's ridiculous," she snorted. But she put her feet back up on the desk and settled into her chair. "You'd better come up with something better than that if you want me to believe you."

"It's the truth," I said. I was staying away from the personal trouble between me and Atropos, and the curse hadn't kicked in yet. I bobbed my head in the closest approximation I could make of a bow while I remained chained. "It's a matter that causes them considerable consternation, and I owe you and your Fate Core virus a vote of thanks for that."

"What do you mean?" she asked.

"The virus you sent into the Core was meant to erase destinies, wasn't it? To remove people's futures from the hands of Fate? Well, it worked. For me."

"That's an interesting claim," she said. "You'll pardon me if I'm a bit skeptical. First off, the virus failed shortly after it entered the Core. Secondly, even if it hadn't, it did its job by running life threads through its digestive system. I hope you're not going to try to tell me that it just happened to nab yours in the brief time it was there."

"I won't, because that's not what happened. The reason it erased my destiny was that it swallowed me whole, like Cronus with Zeus's elder siblings. Like them, I survived the experience. My thread had nothing to do with it."

She nodded. "Keep talking. If this is a lie, at least it's an interesting one."

So I sketched her an abbreviated version of my role in killing the virus dragon and Ahllan's theory about what happened to my thread as a result. When I was finished, Eris nodded again.

"That *would* explain why they haven't just made an end of you," she nodded. "But it begs a couple of questions. For the moment we'll leave aside the fact that *if* you're telling the truth, it's to you that I owe the failure of a virus I put considerable time and energy into. I might just choose to forgive you, if you've twisted the Fates' tails hard enough. But I'd like to know two things first. Why were you in the Fate Core in the first place? And, if you did kill my virus, why aren't destiny's bitches falling all over themselves to reward you?"

"If I tell you, there's absolutely no way you're going to believe me," I said.

"I don't believe you," replied Eris.

"What did I just tell you?" I asked.

"That I wouldn't believe you," she responded. "But that's got nothing to do with my not believing you."

"I know that," I said. "Because I know why you don't believe me."

"I don't believe this," said Melchior, burying his face in his hands. "Ravirn, would you just shut up for a moment and let me handle this one?"

"And why would I believe *you*?" asked the goddess. "I don't believe him."

"Because I'm not under a curse," said Melchior.

"That could easily be changed," said the goddess. "I'm getting tired of twenty questions."

The goblin held up both hands placatingly. "In that case, I'd better get started. The problem is that my companion has something of a reputation for intransigence."

"I can't imagine why," replied Eris dryly.

"This is nothing," said Melchior. "By his usual standards, he's been the soul of sober diplomacy. I think it's the manacles. They seem to be good for his disposition."

"Melchior," I growled, putting teeth into my tone, "I think you're straying from the point."

"Sorry." He turned back to Eris, who had started to drum her fingers on the desk. "I'm sorry. It's just that opportunities like this are so rare. Usually, when he's in hot water up to his neck, I'm somewhere down by his ankles wishing for a snorkel."

"You were saying something about *him* being difficult," prompted Eris. "The trait seems to be catching."

"Yes. Again, sorry. You see, you aren't the first goddess he's irritated. He was making a hobby of it with Atropos."

"Could we dispense with the editorials, Mel?" I asked.

"Of course," he replied. "The point of this is that Atropos has zero sense of humor about being crossed."

"She's not alone," said Eris, pointedly.

"Right," replied Melchior, speeding up his delivery. "Atropos invited Ravirn to have a little chat with her, and she was quite insistent. It seems that she wanted him to do her a favor. He didn't want to, and rather than doing the sensible thing and lying about it, he tried to slither around the issue. Atropos didn't like that and gave him an ultimatum and a couple of days to think about it. She also signed him up for a sort of involuntary nondisclosure contract by laying Cassandra's curse on him. And that's why there's no chance you'll believe the story if he tells it."

"Finally," said Eris. "A claim subject to verification." She rose and stalked to within touching distance of me. "Let's see," she continued, reaching out and laying one hand on each side of my head. I found myself suddenly and painfully aware of the woman scent of her, a sort of musky enticing smell with an undertone of exotic spices. "I want you to silently count to ten, then tell me that Atropos gave you the gift Apollo bestowed on Cassandra. Begin now."

While I counted, Eris hummed. Like the Fates, she possessed the ability to produce multiple notes. However, hers weren't the least bit harmonious. But what else would you expect from the Goddess of Discord? When I reached ten, I made my declaration. As I spoke, I felt the curse's numbness take possession of my lips. But this time there was a hot, prickly undertone to the feeling, as though someone was trying to pinch the flesh awake.

"Apollo's was better coded," said Eris. "But this isn't half-bad. She put some effort into it. Reason enough, I suppose."

"For what?" I asked.

"To break the thing, of course. Thwarting Atropos would make it worth the effort all on its own, but this does double duty. I want to hear the long version of the story your web-goblin was spinning, and I want to hear it from your own lips. That means the curse has to go."

"I didn't think that was possible," I said. "Doesn't it have to be removed by its caster?"

"I am Discord," replied Eris. "The unmaker. There are *very* few spells I can't undo. Now hush."

Eris placed a finger on my lips. Her flesh was cool and dry, but I still felt a sweet burn. She began to croon deep in her throat. It was unlike any spell I'd ever heard. This was no binary modulation. This was pure wild magic, riding on a sound like storm waves swallowing a beach or the wind ripping shingles off a roof. From the place where her finger touched my lips, I felt the pleasant burn spread out and down to my tongue and throat, like eucalyptus syrup tracing a slow, fiery path through my system. The sensation crossed from almost pleasure into searing pain as she withdrew her finger. The pain continued to build. I wanted to speak, cry out, scream, but someone seemed to have yanked my sound card. Then, just as the pain reached an unbearable crescendo, Eris leaned forward and gave me the gentlest of kisses. Her lips were like soft ice, and they instantly quenched the flame, sending cool healing down my heated nerves. It lasted only a split second, but it wasn't something I was going to forget anytime soon.

"Well?" she asked, a half smile playing on her beautiful mouth, "What do you think of my methods?"

It took me a minute to compose my thoughts. Eris had a knack for sending one's edifice of reason crashing to wrack and ruin. It had been an educational experience, but not one I cared to repeat. First off, the tiny rational bit of my brain that wasn't completely addled by lust knew that what she had said earlier about being the worst kind of virgin goddess was only too true. Second, I didn't think Cerice would approve. Not at all. Third, it had hurt. A lot. And finally, I still didn't know if it had worked.

The question was how to answer without offending Eris any more than absolutely necessary. I was beginning to think that upsetting the powers that be might not be the brightest pattern of living. At least not while they could lay their hands on me. So, something like *10 for style, 5.9 for sincerity*, was not on the menu of safe answers. Even I can learn a lesson if you hit me with a stick enough times.

"You quite took my breath away," I said after a moment.

"Shall I return it?" she asked, pursing her lips as though she were blowing a kiss.

"Urg," I said, as libido and common sense fought for control of my vocal cords.

"My," interjected Melchior from the desktop. "That's quite coherent of you. You'll have to excuse him, your loftiness. Occasionally he slips into the quaint syntax of his prearticulate infanthood. Allow me to interpret. What he meant was 'thank you, but that won't be necessary.' " The goblin shrugged his shoulders. "Of course that's more of a paraphrase than a straight translation."

"Ah," replied the goddess, turning to look at Melchior. "Is that what that was? If he does it often, he's fortunate to have you around to speak for him."

"Aren't I just?" I said, putting all the sarcasm I could muster into the question. "Thanks for the help, Mel." Though, in truth, I *was* pleased with him. He'd managed to draw Eris's focus away from me.

"What I intended to say, before my charming sidekick stuck his little blue foot in, was thank you. Atropos has been busily writing bugs into the code of my life, and it's absolutely delightful to have someone remove some of her work." I paused for a moment to see whether my lips would start to tingle. When I felt no touch of the Cassandra curse, I breathed a deep sigh and upped the ante. "Atropos is a tyrannical, unscrupulous, evil-minded, scheming manipulator."

"Now *that* I can wholeheartedly endorse," said Eris, returning to her chair. "But as much as I admire the sentiment, I'm minded to ask why it is you're saying it."

"She's out to crush free will," I said. "And she wants to use me as her hammer."

"Tell me more," said Eris.

"She's coded a program to eradicate self-determination." Eris's reaction to what I thought of as a bombshell wasn't what I expected.

"Yes, that's why I sent my virus into the Fate Core."

"You know about Puppeteer?" I asked. I was a bit annoyed. I had gotten much the same response from Cerice when I'd first told her about things, and Ahllan for that matter. And even though I knew how *they'd* gotten hold of the information, I was beginning to feel that there was some secret newsgroup out there that everybody but me was subscribed to: alt.atropos.evil.plot . . . or some such. It was irritating.

"So, she's calling it Puppeteer," said Eris.

"Yes, she is. How did you know about it?" I asked.

"I didn't exactly know about it. Let us say rather that I inferred its existence. But unless I'm wrong, she hasn't got it working yet."

"No, she hasn't," I said. "Every time she's tried running the thing, it's crashed. There's a fatal error in the code somewhere, and she wants me to fix it."

"That explains it," replied the goddess. "I've felt rhythmic pulses of disturbance in the balance between chaos and order over the past several months. But they've been very weak. They'll have been caused by her failed test runs. And that brings us to a pivot point."

For some reason that phrase sent one of Eris's "pulses of disturbance" through my bone marrow. "What do you mean?" I asked.

"Well, it could be argued that if Atropos needs you to make her program work, then the easiest way to be sure she doesn't succeed is to eliminate you."

"I was wondering why you hadn't taken these off yet." I rattled my chains and sighed. "I was kind of hoping it was just an oversight. No such luck, huh?"

"I'm afraid not. Do you have any thoughts on why I shouldn't simply remove you from the picture?"

"Let's see. We've established that charm is out. You're already aware of the fact that my continued existence irritates Atropos. I don't suppose you have a program that's not working, something I could debug for you?" Before she could answer, I shook my head. "No, probably not. The only thing that comes to mind is the way you said 'could be argued,' which implies that perhaps killing me off wasn't what you had in mind. Melchior, how about you? Any bright ideas for keeping your partner among the living?"

"Well," he said, with a twisted smile, "if her worship really is in the market for increasing the overall level of discord in the multiverse, bumping you off would be like kicking in a goal for the other side."

"Oh thanks, Mel. Thanks a lot."

"If I'd said the melodious sound of your voice, I'd have been flat-out lying," he replied. "And you must admit that you tend to leave a comet trail of angry deities and generalized destruction in your wake."

The shattering-glass sound of Eris's laughter rang out. "If nothing else, I should keep you around as a comedy team." Her expression turned more serious. "Actually, as you guessed, I have at least one reason for not removing you immediately. As it turns out, I do have a program that needs a bit of debugging. It's nothing I couldn't do myself, mind you. But it's proven quite intractable to date."

"Hey, Boss," said Melchior, grinning. "This is starting to sound familiar. Maybe we should open up a consulting firm. M & R Associates, debuggers to the gods. What do you say?"

"I say it should be R & M, but other than that . . ."

"I don't know," replied Melchior. "M & R has more of a musical sound to it."

"Why don't we discuss it later," I said. Eris was drumming her fingers on the desktop again. I turned my attention her way. "Why don't you let me out of these chains, and we can discuss this program of yours."

"Not yet," said Eris. "First, I want to hear the full story of Puppeteer."

I gave her a slightly edited version. Since she already knew about the spell and the secret of familiar free will, I left those in, but I glossed over my differences with my grandmother. Lachesis might want to kill me at the moment, but that was the result of a misunderstanding, and besides, she was the head of my branch of the family. When I finished, Eris whistled a single note, and my chains fell away.

"Thank you," I said, rubbing my wrists.

Eris whistled another series of notes. This time I couldn't detect any effect, and my bafflement must have shown on my face.

"I've restored your weapons to you," said the goddess.

After she had pointed it out, I became aware of the reassuring weight of sword and dagger on my hips. Likewise, the pressure of a full shoulder holster under my arm.

"Thank you again," I said.

After another minute or so of silence the goddess reached into a drawer, pulled out a small yellow memory crystal, and slid it across the desk. The eight-sided gem was filled with traceries of blue neon that represented the energy flows of the spell. It was the strangest piece of code I'd ever seen. Rather than the neat angles I was used to, the lines formed a hopelessly tangled series of loops and curves. It looked more like a neural net than a spell.

"What is this programmed in?" I asked, starting to sweat.

"DiskOrdinal," she replied. "I created the language myself. But don't be alarmed, I wasn't expecting you to work on it like that. It's all binary underneath, and it won't take long to recompile it in a form you're more familiar with."

I relaxed. "That's a relief. I was afraid our relationship was about to deteriorate abruptly."

"Come with me." Eris rose and climbed the ladder to the floor above.

"Shall we, Melchior?" I asked, sliding off the desk.

"Of course" he said, hopping to the floor. "But after you, I insist."

We emerged on a circular wooden deck surrounded by low stone battlements. It was dark and Eris's golden-apple processors performed their dancing-star routine overhead. A wind from the nowhere beyond the castle's walls blew across the towertop, carrying with it a melange of dried flowers and hot circuits. Eris put two fingers in her mouth and whistled like a shepherd calling a dog. Even though I was beginning to adapt to the glamour she cast, I found myself wanting to sit up and beg. I don't think any being possessed of even the most rudimentary sex drive could have ignored her allure, but I did my level best not to drool. Apparently I wasn't subtle enough. With a wicked smile in my direction, Eris suggestively slid her fingers deep into her mouth for a moment before very slowly and sensually withdrawing them.

I found myself swallowing audibly. "If we're going to have a working relationship, my lady Discord, you're going to have to stop doing things like that. I need to stay focused if you want me to debug your program."

"Sorry," she said, but her tone belied the apology. She gave me a broad wink, "Force of habit, really. I know I shouldn't practice on my own side, but I have to keep my hand in."

"Delightful." I didn't like her thinking of me as being on her side. Not one little bit. I might be unwilling to see Atropos murder free will, but I wasn't interested in signing up to play for the Chaos Marauders either. I didn't think it would be wise to declare it openly, but maybe I could put a little discreet distance between us. "Remind me to do something nice for you when I get a chance, like starting a major fire in your basement."

"I like fires," she said with a wistful smile. "Leading admirers astray makes for a nice hobby, but it's got nothing on a really world-class fire. Selling that cow to Mrs. O'Leary has to rank as one the best bargains I've ever gotten."

I winced inwardly. "You're responsible for the great Chicago fire?"

"Among others." She waved a hand airily. "Anything to keep in trouble. Why . . ."

I didn't get to find out what she would have said next because just then the end result of her summoning whistle arrived. Like a falling star, one of the glowing apples dropped straight for Eris's head. She stabbed it out of the air in the manner of a pitcher fielding a line drive, and the slap as flesh met processor made me wince.

Putting the apple to her mouth, she took an enormous bite. Immediately, a thick green caterpillar nosed out and started questing around with its mandibles. Eris placed the spell crystal from her pocket in front of the small creature's face. Taking the crystal firmly in its jaws, the caterpillar slowly withdrew into the center of the fruit. When it was completely gone, Eris placed her lips over the hole as though she were kissing the apple and replaced the piece she'd bitten out. Then she tossed it lightly into the air, where it proceeded to violate about nine laws of physics by continuing to accelerate after she let go.

"Now we wait," she said, leaning against a crenellation.

I sat down in one of the gaps across from her. "What exactly does this program do?"

"Nothing," said Eris. "That's where you come in."

"What's it *supposed* to do?" I asked, sourly.

"Grab the source code for Atropos's doomsday spell."

I let out an involuntary whistle. That *would* be nice. I needed Puppeteer. With it, I could clear my name with my grandmother. And if Eris had a copy as well, I could leave her to worry about countering it. I had no doubt she'd be able to handle that task better than I.

I realized then that Melchior had been awfully quiet for some time, and looked around to see what he was doing. He was sitting, goblin fashion, in a sheltered spot as far away from Eris as he could get.

I didn't blame him. The Goddess of Discord was not the most settling company I'd ever had. If I could have avoided dealing with her, I would have. Also, he'd had an awful lot of shocks lately. It started with Atropos trying to kill us, included the virus he'd contracted, my new involvement with the familiar underground, the change in our relationship, and now, the discovery that his self-determination was germinated from a seed sown by Eris. If we survived all this, I owed him one hell of a vacation.

But there seemed to be something more to it than that. His face had a thoughtful, worried look that struck me as out of character. And, every so often, he would run his tongue along the edge of his broken fang. I knelt beside him. "Are you thinking thoughts I should be aware of?"

"Maybe," he replied. "There's a detail missing. I don't know what yet, but I've got a premonition it's going to be ugly."

I put my hand on his arm. "Look at it this way; if there is something dark and unexpected creeping up on us, our

luck is holding. I'm not sure what I'd do if we got a surprise of the happy variety."

"Wouldn't it be nice to find out," said the goblin, a long-
ing note in his voice.

I squeezed his shoulder, then rose and turned my attention to Eris again. "Do you have any idea why your spell
didn't work?" I asked.

"Not really. Every time I ran it through my spell-
checker, my system crashed and I had to go back and rejig-
ger the code."

"What happens when you actually try to cast it?"

"I haven't," she said. "If it kills the checker, there's no
way it's going to function properly."

"Sure, but you can learn a lot from seeing just how it
hangs under field conditions."

"Go teach your grandmother how to code in Basic, boy,"
said the goddess. "Don't you think I'd have tried that if I
could have?"

"I don't see the problem," I said.

"What *do* children learn in school these days?" she
asked. "Didn't I tell you how I learned about Atropos's program in the first place?"

"Yes," I replied. "You said something about a disturbance in the balance. And?"

"You really don't understand, do you?" She shook her
head sadly. "Think of reality as a wire stretched between
the two poles of chaos and order. This wire is tuned to the
balance between the pair, like the string of a musical in-
strument. Any change in that balance acts like someone
plucking the string, sending a note vibrating through the
length of reality. Anyone with the right sort of hearing can
hear the note. Are you with me so far?"

"I think so," I replied. "My grandmother never taught

me anything like what you're talking about, but it makes sense. I'm surprised she didn't mention it."

"Having known Lachesis far longer than you've been alive, I am somewhat less than shocked." Her tone was dry. "But that's a bit off subject. When Atropos first tried to cast her Puppeteer spell, it gave the string of reality a gentle, but powerful strum." She made air guitar motions. "The effects of a successful implementation of her scheme would change things in a deep and fundamental way, and the implications are still reverberating through the ether. It set up a sort of low-amplitude standing wave that won't die out until the spell is either countered or carried through to a successful conclusion. Anything I do to affect the outcome will change the tone of the note, so the second I try to cast my spell, whether it works or not, Atropos and the other Fates will instantly be aware of the change."

"Oh shit," said Melchior, jumping to his feet. "That's it."

"What's . . ." I trailed off before I really got started. I could see it too. "My grandmother already knows about Puppeteer," I whispered. "She's known about it all along.

Eris gave me an odd, almost pitying, look. "Of course she does. She couldn't help but know. The Fates, Tyche, me, we're all tuning forks for the forces involved. When the note is struck, we resonate in sympathy."

"I am so fucked," I said.

"As much as I'd like it if the singular pronoun were the correct one, Boss, I'm afraid it just isn't so," interjected Melchior. "The proper phrasing is 'We are so fucked.'"

CHAPTER EIGHTEEN

I stared blankly around the open deck of Eris's tower. I was in shock. No, I'll be honest. I was beyond shock, in a special little realm reserved for those who have quietly deceived themselves about the basic nature of their existence and are suddenly faced with the truth. Denial is a great place to live, as long as nobody ever opens the windows on reality.

I had no doubt Eris would lie to me in an instant if it served her interests. For that matter, she'd probably lie to me just for fun if she thought it'd make my life a little more discordant. But this was no lie. It was certainly possible Eris could have learned about Puppeteer through some other means, but her explanation made too much sense.

What Atropos wanted to do *would* have profound consequences. The spell was bound to make some sort of existential noise. I'd avoided using magic after my assault on the Fate Core because I was concerned about the Fates detecting me. Why should a spell of Puppeteer's magnitude be any less obtrusive? When I looked things square in the face, I couldn't bring myself to believe my grandmother was completely unaware of Atropos's plans.

Far more disturbing was the sudden conviction that it didn't really matter one way or the other. My grandmother was a manipulator and a controller, the absolute dictator of my family. No, that wasn't nearly broad enough. My grandmother, Lachesis, was the measurer of Destiny. Every thread spun by Clotho passed though her hands to be given its allotted span before going to Atropos for the final trimming. Atropos might be the gleeful administrator of mortality, but it was Lachesis who decided who would live and who would die and on what schedule. She would no more disapprove of a spell that gave her greater authority than a penguin would disapprove of ice.

When Atropos had shown me Puppeteer and commanded me to help her, she hadn't been concerned about the other Fates finding out. She'd been concerned about them finding out too soon. She didn't want to ruin the wonderful surprise she was making.

For months, I'd been figuring that all I needed to do to get out of my personal war with Atropos was to show Puppeteer to my grandmother and prove I hadn't started things. When I hacked the Fate Core, I'd dug the hole even deeper, but I'd still believed all I really needed to do to make things better was show my grandmother the truth. It had never once occurred to me what it would mean if she already knew.

I found myself sitting on the rough timbers of the tower roof without even the vaguest memory of how I got there.

"You're telling me the truth, aren't you?" I whispered up to the goddess.

"Of course," said Eris, with a grin. "I almost never lie. Why bother when the truth is usually so much more devastating? The truly honest individual has very few friends.

Like most young people, you have a certain passion for the truth. With age, however, you'll find that the occasional comforting lie or self-deception makes for a *much* more pleasant existence. The bleakness of truth can be very hard to face."

She shook her head, and her skin shifted from gold to black and back again as the light played over her bichromatic features. "Diogenes was a masochist. If he'd ever found his honest man, he'd have been deeply disillusioned. I imagine the first thing that honest man would have said is: 'You've spent your whole life looking for me? What an enormous waste of time. Why didn't you try making things better where you were instead of searching for a semimythical place where they're already perfect.' Diogenes might have had a hard time answering that question."

"Maybe," I said, "but at least he had an ideal to strive for." I was wishing right then and there for one of my own. Having one of the pillars knocked out from under your universe really makes you wish for an alternate support structure. As a dedicated cynic, I've always prided myself on building my world on the shifting sands of the actual, the real. At the moment, I was envying the bedrock foundation of belief that provided the fanatic with his unshakable sense of his own virtue.

Eris's breaking-glass laugh crackled forth again. "Priceless," she said. "Idealists are some of my favorite people. They're so committed to achieving perfection of one sort or another they'll turn down opportunities for incremental changes that go in their direction. Take democracy; I can't begin to count the number of times people have refused to vote for the lesser of two evils and ended up with the greater one in their living rooms. It's really quite delightful. I do love idealists. They make my life so much easier."

I decided I wasn't the person to try to defend ideological purity, not with my cynical side screaming that Eris was absolutely right. It isn't easy to put together a rational plan when the one you came in with has been dynamited. My original plan had called for collecting my evidence and running. Instead, I was sitting on top of the tallest tower in the Citadel of Discord without the slightest idea what was going to happen next. And, at least until Eris's spell was finished recompiling, there was nothing else for me to do but ruminate.

On the one hand, it felt wonderful actually to have a moment where I could stop and think. On the other, I had the sense that someone had just hidden the goal posts, and I was running out of time to find them before the Furies ended the game.

"Who else knows about Puppeteer?" I asked at last. "Do the Furies?" That was my biggest worry now, that they might know and be allied with Fate.

"I doubt it," replied Eris. "The effect is still a subtle one, even if it is pervasive, and the sisters of vengeance are not noted for their appreciation of fine distinctions. I once heard Tisiphone say she liked to think of subtlety as a type of large-caliber automatic weapon. Actually, Tisiphone and her sisters aren't alone on that score." She turned away from where I was sitting to look out over the battlements. "I don't know if you've read that dreadful little book by Bulfinch, but his listing of the peccadilloes of the various children of the Titans, while lacking in style, does have a rather painful degree of accuracy. As a group, the denizens of Olympus and Hades are not known for careful thinking."

"What she's saying," said Melchior, as he paced back and forth, "is that most of the deities of ancient Greece couldn't navigate their way out of an unwalled amphitheater with a map, a guidebook, and GPS."

"I think I begin to see why self-determination wasn't in your original specs, little man," said Eris, giving Melchior a penetrating look. "But you've stated the case succinctly enough. If any of my fellow gods had the wit to listen for Atropos's meddling, they might well be able to discover it. However, I doubt any of them would exert themselves on the topic. Even if they did, I wouldn't want to bet any stake I was afraid of losing that they would understand what they'd found."

"So," I said after a moment, "why don't you fit that pattern?"

Eris laughed again. "Oh, I've never been of the same mind-set as the rest of my divine cousins, which is one of the prime reasons I chose to set myself up as a nemesis to the whole idiotic lot. Also, having Atropos and her sisters to play against all these years has kept me sharp. I dislike the three of them with an intensity beyond anything you can probably imagine, but I won't lump them with the others for wit. Your grandmother in particular is a very, very sharp operator. I've never seen her do anything for fewer than three reasons. Even her most-straightforward-seeming statements and actions are carefully crafted to serve more ends than the obvious ones. All in all, a much nastier opponent than Atropos."

"What?" I asked, sitting up. I needed something to take my mind off the ticking clock. How long was that damned recompile going to take? "You've got to be kidding. Are we talking about the same two Fates here? Lachesis may yank on the threads of destiny, but it's Atropos who cuts them short."

"That's actually part of it," said Eris. "Atropos is a very straight thinker. If she doesn't like you or what you're doing, her first impulse is to kill you outright. Only if she's blocked does she resort to anything else, and even then she'll just do her best to make you miserable."

"Isn't that enough?" I asked. "She's doing a damn fine

job in my case. I don't see how anyone else could make my life any worse."

"You lack imagination, boy. I could make your life infinitely more painful if I wanted to." She smiled, almost wistfully. "But that wasn't my point. Where Atropos goes for the direct route, Lachesis is more subtle. If she were out to get you, you'd never even know it. She doesn't make people's lives into living hells, she arranges things so that they do it to themselves. Someone trying to kill you is a problem that's amenable to direct solutions. Someone who puts you in the position of wanting to kill yourself has created a situation that's far harder to deal with. I'll take the straight thinker as an enemy over the twisty one every time."

I wanted to argue on my grandmother's behalf, but found I couldn't. When I was driving cross-country with a crashed Melchior in the seat beside me, I'd begun a process of introspection. In the past few minutes I had taken another long walk down the path I'd started then. I wasn't entirely sure where the journey would lead, but it was changing the way I looked at things in a deep and fundamental way. I was coming to believe that my grandmother didn't *deserve* my allegiance. It was a very painful realization, and one I would rather have done without, but change is a necessary corollary of life. Either you're going somewhere or you're dead.

Perhaps the most terrifying thing I'd discovered in the hour or so since awakening in chains was that I liked Eris. Growing up as a scion of the middle house of Fate, I'd been taught that Eris, and Tyche with her, were the epitome of chaos and evil. More than once, my mother had warned me that if I didn't quit behaving in such a disobedient and willful manner, the Goddess of Discord would carry me away to be a slave in her castle.

Now, here I was, face-to-face with the great bugaboo of my childhood, and she was nothing like I'd expected.

Certainly she was frightening, but in many ways she was less scary than the matriarchs of my own family or the Furies. She possessed something the other divine figures lacked: a genuine sense of humor. It was a dark and brutal humor, but then the multiverse is a dark and brutal place. If you couldn't joke about the macabre and the bleak, you were likely to be mighty short on laughs.

Just then there came a descending whistle like incoming mortar fire. I hunched up, but there was no explosion. Instead, it ended with a sound like a soggy Ping-Pong paddle smacking a leather couch. Before I could move, I felt a sharp jab in the ribs. Eris had poked me with an amber crystal about five inches long. It was shaped like a four-sided anorexic pyramid, with a base perhaps an inch across and a tip like a blowdart. Binary code ran through it in sharp angular lines of gold.

"I'm calling it Orion," she said, handing me the spell.

"The Hunter," I replied dryly. "How original."

I held it up against the star-speckled blackness that encapsulated Castle Discord like a snow globe. For one brief moment I found myself feeling that neither side was worth fighting for, and I contemplated throwing the spell into that darkling sea and giving up on the whole thing. But that wasn't an option. Regardless of all the other issues, I was committed to opposing Atropos and Puppeteer, even to the death. More than that, though, I was committed to my friends, Melchior and Cerice, Shara and Ahllan, and that meant I had to keep moving forward.

"So, 'Once more unto the breach' dear friends,' " I whispered to myself. Then I stood up. "My lady Discord, it seems we are to be allies of a sort. That being the case, what should I call you? Eris seems too informal. And referring to you as Goddess of Discord every time I speak goes too far in the other direction."

She laughed her dissonant laugh. It was beginning to grow on me, sending a pleasant chill running down my spine. There was something appealing about it, something that went straight to the libido. It made you want to tell her jokes and . . . Realizing where my mind was wandering, I shook my head to clear it. She was doing it again.

"What a funny child you are," she said when she stopped laughing. "Formality is oil for the machine of social order. It smooths the way and puts people in their place. That's why your charming grandmother and her splendid sisters insist on all that bowing and courtly language. I've no use for any of it. You may call me whatever you wish. I've been known to answer to many things, most of them unprintable, and taken delight at every hurled epithet. To this day Athena still calls me 'that bitch.'" She smiled in fond remembrance. "But, if the thought of addressing me as 'hey you,' or 'demonspawn,' distresses you, call me Eris, or even simply Discord."

"I think I'll go with Discord," I replied, after a moment's thought.

She licked her lips. "Is Eris a touch too *intimate*?" she breathed.

It was like she'd read my mind. I reddened, and my desire meter pegged deep into the danger zone. I took a deep breath and let it out. Another. "Look, Discord, if you really want me to help with Orion, you're going to have to quit doing that."

"You'd better listen," interjected Mel, from somewhere near my knees. "The boy has focus issues. Ask anybody. He has enough trouble with walking and chewing gum, much less debugging and fantasizing. It's too much to ask."

"Oh, all right," she said. "I'll turn it down." She smiled and a twinkle appeared in her eye. "But I won't promise to keep it that way."

She let out a reverse wolf whistle. The waves of sex appeal that had been rolling off of her and slowly eroding my ability to think vanished like they'd never been. She was still stone gorgeous, but now she possessed the same statuelike quality of distance as the Fates or Furies.

"Thank you," I said, with as much sincerity as I'd ever mustered. "Now, if you can give me someplace quiet to work, I'll see what I can do."

She nodded. "Done."

That was her only move, and I started to ask where we should go. Then I realized that the air was no longer cold and flavored by the outdoors. Instead, it was warm and slightly stale. There'd been no sensation of movement and, even more amazing, no feeling of disorientation, but now we stood in the game room I'd visited earlier. It was like the trick she'd pulled when I first woke up from my little nap, not appearing so much as suddenly having been there all along.

"How do you do that?" asked Melchior. His tone clearly expressed the incredulity I felt.

"Do what?" The goddess grinned.

"Move us around like that? It's not an ltp link or any other kind of transport I've ever used."

"Do you want to know the secret?" she asked.

"That's why I asked," said Melchior.

"I didn't move us at all."

"Then what did you do?" I asked.

"Nothing at all," she said.

"That's ridiculous," said Melchior. "We were standing on a windy tower top. Now we're in an interior room. One with really ugly art." He pointed at an oil-on-velvet painting of dogs playing poker.

At just that moment one of the dogs grinned and winked at me, and I realized that it was a coyote rather than the collie

I had taken it for at first. I gave a start. In response, the coyote showed me its hand. Five aces. Hearts, clubs, spades, diamonds, and what looked like paw prints. I closed my eyes for a moment. When I opened them again the painting had returned to normal.

Melchior continued, "Something had to change for us to get here."

"No," said Eris. "It didn't."

"Then," I interjected, "why do we see things differently?"

"I was wondering how long it would take you to ask the right question," said Eris. "It's all a matter of perspective. Castle Discord doesn't really exist in the classical sense of the word. When I decided I needed a home other than Olympus, I wanted something that would suit my mood. And since my mood is notorious for being an ever-changing target, I needed something as malleable as thought itself."

"If we're going to get all existential," said Mel, "we'd better get comfortable first." He hopped up onto the card table and sat down.

I took a chair and did the same.

"Castle Discord is a state of mind," said Eris, "an island of probability floating in the ocean of chaos that separates the worlds. It's more like a suit of clothing for my mind than a building. It assumes whatever form I think it should. When I decided we were in the game room, the castle rearranged its internal reality to reflect that desire."

"But when we were wandering around earlier it seemed relatively rational in structure," I said. "Rooms seemed to be more or less the same size on the inside as the outside. Stairs led neatly from one floor to another. We were able to follow cables from point A to point B without passing through point Σ."

"You must possess an orderly mind," she said. "When I'm not exerting my direct will on any part of the castle, it assumes the shape of whoever is occupying that portion of it. Didn't you encounter any oddness at all?"

"It *was* day on the inside and night on the outside," I replied.

"Does he miss a lot of appointments?" Eris asked Melchior.

"Do satyrs chase nymphs?" replied Melchior. "Does your hard drive always crash the day before you do a major backup? Is Atropos a control freak?"

"Yes, Mel," I said. "I think we get the point. I've been known to lose track of the time on occasion. So I get distracted and go off task every once in a while. Is that a hanging offense?"

"It is for your grandmother," he replied, "and for Atropos."

"Speaking of tasks," interposed Eris.

"Right," I said. "Mel, if you'd be so kind as to switch to laptop form, I should take a look at this."

"As you wish," he replied.

He winked at me and melted. Like a plastic action figure on a griddle, the process started with his feet. Soon there was nothing left but a flat blue lump, which then reshaped itself into a streamlined clamshell. Flipping the lid, I opened his memory bay. A small but surprisingly deep drawer, it was lined with shiny black plastic. I set Orion in place and watched as the bay flowed around the crystal, conforming to its shape.

When I closed the bay, a golden pyramid icon appeared on the screen. Clicking on it made the structure unfold like a puzzle box disassembling itself. The monitor filled with an ever-changing, three-dimensional structure of angular lines.

Melchior. Code Warrior. Please, I typed.

A small animated goblin appeared on my screen.

Ready to RAM, he replied.

Pulling out my athame, I plugged in and joined Mel, diving into the code. It was bliss. There is nothing in all the infinity of possible worlds that I enjoy more than hacking and cracking. Coding from scratch is okay, but nowhere near as much fun as pulling apart somebody else's program and finding the holes.

Back before I ended up at the U of M, I'd flunked out of Carnegie Mellon. CMU is a weird sort of place, split almost evenly between highly talented engineering types and highly talented performing artists without much of anything in the middle. My roommate there was a pretty cool guy, a concert pianist. He practiced five or six hours every day, often going over the same piece a hundred times. Once, I'd asked him if he didn't get bored.

"This is what I was born for," he'd replied. "When I'm playing in the zone, I become the piece. Nothing else matters. So, I guess the answer is yes and no. Yes, because it takes a lot of work to get to the place where I am the music, and it can be tedious. And no, because when I do get there, I know every second of effort on the way was worth it."

That's how I feel coding. Sometimes the programming's a slog, which is how I got booted out of CMU, but when I hit that perfect hacking pace, I am the code, and it's all the reason for living I could ever need. I hadn't been there for months because I hadn't dared submerge myself so fully since before Atropos tried to recruit me. I'd always had to keep one eye open for someone sneaking up on me in the real world. But in the center of Castle Discord, with the goddess herself watching over me, I was as safe from attack as I was ever likely to be again. And, unlike the past couple of times I'd jacked in, I wasn't going to be dealing with an actively hostile environment. No enemy security. No viruses trying to eat me. And no major risks of death.

Eris is the queen of hacking, and Orion was magnificent. I'd been terrified and impressed by the virus she let loose in the Fate Core. I was actively awed by Orion. It was a big evil bastard of a spell with all sorts of baroque subroutines and logic traps, and it was beautiful. I wanted it. With every twisty hacker fiber of my being I wanted to crack that spell and own it. I kept digging in deeper and deeper, trying to find some flaw. It became an obsession. There had to be a hole I could crawl into, some error that would let me make the spell mine. I slid my consciousness along every line of binary and pried into all the dark corners. I pulled at anything that looked loose, pushed every lever, and flipped all the switches. Finally, I found it. Down in the depths of the job batch that would allow the spell to search multiple worlds, I found a fissure in the logic. I was just inserting the electronic equivalent of a crowbar when I felt a sudden sharp pain.

My body was demanding my attention. I tried to ignore it, but the pain came again. This time I heard an accompanying sound, a sort of harsh thwack. Grudgingly, I let my awareness slide back into my body. I arrived just in time to fully experience the back of Eris's hand. It hurt. I shook my head and tried to focus. There was blood in my mouth and my cheeks felt as though someone had been slapping the daylights out me.

"Wha' th' hell?" I mumbled.

"It's about time," said the goddess. "Did you find it?"

There was an edge of desperation in her voice, and that scared me. Nothing should be able to upset Eris that much in the heart of her own domain. Since the last thing I wanted to do was aggravate a frightened goddess, I decided not to play for laughs.

"Yes. I think so, but I didn't have time to get a really thorough read. What's the problem? Why didn't you just pop into cyberspace and get my attention politely? That was kind of harsh."

"I wasn't willing to risk it," she said, answering my second question first. "If I'd jacked in, I'd have had to relinquish some of my controls over Castle Discord, and that doesn't seem like a good idea at the moment. The castle is an island of code floating in the interworld chaos. When the chaos gets turbulent, the island vibrates. Right now the whole damn thing is trying to conga. Something powerful is thrashing around out there. I imagine that whatever it is, it's looking for us."

" 'By the pricking of my thumbs, something wicked this way comes'?" I asked.

"In a word," said Eris, "yes."

As if in response, there came a tremendous thud, like a giant pounding on the gate.

"Sounds like we've got company." I tapped the emergency alert on Mel's keyboard. "Any thoughts on who it might be?" I asked Eris, as Mel made the shift to webgoblin.

"Ding dong," said a voice from the window.

It was Tisiphone. The Furies had arrived.

CHAPTER NINETEEN

Tisiphone, the red-haired Fury, drew back one claw-fingered fist and threw a punch at the window. A sharp wet smack like flesh hitting a stone wall followed, that and a muffled shriek. Eris had exerted her will, rendering the room windowless and plunging us into deep gloom.

In Ravirn's Big List of Things to Avoid, the Furies occupied slot number one. Atropos ran a close second, but the bounty hunters of the gods edged her out by dint of having zero reason to keep me alive.

"Can they get in?" I asked, my voice a hoarse whisper.

"If they try hard enough."

"I was afraid of that. Can you beat them?"

"In a fair fight under normal circumstances?" said Eris, her tone startlingly cheerful. "Not a chance. Here, in the heart of my own power? I don't know."

"Hey," snapped Melchior, "how many times do I have to tell you that I hate it when you do this?" He yanked the end of the networking cable from his nose. Then his eyes tracked back along the line of the wire until they found the other connector. It was still attached to the athame driven through the palm of my hand. His eyes widened. "Do you want me to do something about that?" he asked, in a cautious tone. He made plucking motions. It was the first time I'd thought about it. With a quick wrench, I pulled it out.

"I take it we're in the soup again." He sighed. "I feel a bit like a bouillon cube."

"Tell me about it," I replied. "I'm thinking about getting a crosshairs tattooed on my forehead. The Furies are here."

Mel glanced pointedly at Eris, asking me a question with his eyes. I shook my head.

"Well then," he said. "Have you to started to plan the strategic withdrawal?"

"Nope," I said.

"Why in Hades's name not?"

Any answer I might have made was preempted by a sudden shuddering impact on the wall where the windows had once been. The noise was so loud it was more felt than heard. Powdered mortar shot out along every joint between the stones, filling the air with a gray haze. A moment later it was gone. Or, rather, we were. With a flick of thought, Eris moved us to a different part of the castle, the dungeons. I hadn't been there before, but the shackles and bars were a dead giveaway, as was the dank crypt smell. I could hear shattering masonry somewhere in the distance.

"It won't be long now," said Eris. "They're concentrating their power. In a moment, I'm going to go out to meet them."

"What happens if you can't beat them?" I asked.

"That's hard to say," said Eris. "If your story is true, they're here under the Aegis of the Fates, but that's just the freelancing they do for all the powers. They're ultimately responsible to Necessity alone."

I started at that name. Raised in the family of Fate, I'd

only heard Necessity's name used a few times as anything but a swear word. Never manifesting in body, Necessity was more concept than being, a sort of ensoulment of the collective unconscious of the pantheon. Occasionally called "the Fate of the Gods," she was the final arbiter in conflicts between members of the pantheon, but no one wanted to involve her because she was genuinely nonpartisan. Mostly the gods preferred to fight it out among themselves. If they absolutely had to have a judge, they'd get Zeus, because he could be bribed. Justice and the Furies were sometimes called Necessity's handmaidens, but this was the first time I'd ever heard it confirmed.

"What does *she* have to do with all of this?" whispered Melchior.

"Impossible to say," replied Eris. "Necessity goes her own way. I'd better get on with it." Eris shimmied in a way that made me very glad she'd turned off her sex appeal and was suddenly garbed in black-and-gold armor. Instead of the rapier and dagger she'd met me with, she held a two-handed sword over six feet in length and ten inches across at the base. It must have weighed fifty pounds, but when she gave it a test swing, it danced through the air as lithe as a reed whip.

"I hate to mention this," I said. "But curiosity is killing me. Why aren't you just throwing me to the wolves?"

Eris laughed. "If I thought it would do any good, I'd give you to the Furies in an instant. But if you were all they were here for, they'd have let me know when they arrived."

"Oh," I said. "What do they want then?"

"You know?" replied Eris. "I don't give a damn."

Then she was gone. For that matter, so was I. I found myself in another tower room, Melchior at my side. We were looking down on the castle's inner courtyard. Only, even as I watched it expanded, growing in seconds from a square a hundred yards on a side to a baseball stadium surrounded by a sea of bleachers. The tower changed as well, becoming a tall press box of dressed stone. The bright summer aromas of popcorn and hot dogs drifted up from the empty seats below us. For the moment, Eris stood alone at home plate. She raised her sword to me in salute.

"Hang on for a bit and see how things transpire," whispered her voice in my ear. "If I fall, finish Orion and take it to Tyche. Atropos can't be allowed to win."

She might have said more, but just then a triple shadow crossed in front of the golden apple of the sun. The Furies appeared from behind me, sailing low over the tower. Alecto flew the lead, her storm-shot pinions and granite skin a foreboding presence. Slightly behind and to her right followed Megaera, whose seaweed wings and pale green flesh seemed to whisper of drowned sailors. Trailing by a hundred yards was Tisiphone. Tongues of fire danced through her hair and trailed from her wings. She winked and waved as she passed me.

It was strange to see the Furies and know that, at least for the moment, I was safe. Going after me with Eris loose would be like fishing a minnow out of the shark tank with your bare hands. Of course, if they did take her, I'd be the next course.

Gesturing for her sisters to follow, Alecto folded her wings and plunged toward Eris. Megaera was right behind. Tisiphone sideslipped through the air and began to circle around behind Eris. At home plate, the Goddess of Discord raised her sword like a batter awaiting the pitch. A split second before she would have been in range, Alecto opened her wings and rolled to the side, skimming away inches above the earth.

"Steeerike one!" called Alecto.

"And the Furies are ahead on the first call," Tisiphone announced from above.

"It's not a game," said Megaera, plunging straight onward.

Her great green wings parted like the mouth of a Venus flytrap as she stooped on Eris. There came a sharp crack like the world's biggest bullwhip being snapped, and suddenly Megaera was flying up and back.

"It's a hit," said Tisiphone. "And what a shot, too. Looks like it's going clean out of the park."

"Unkind," admonished Alecto.

Megaera remained silent as her backward arc continued. She struck the tower a few yards below my window, and the impact shook the building to its foundations. I looked down, expecting to see blood smearing the wall as she slid away. But the stonework was clean, and she was starting to stir even before she hit the ground.

While I was watching what happened to Megaera, I missed something on the field. There was the ringing noise of steel on steel and a shout of "foul ball." When I looked up, Alecto was bouncing away down the baseline, Eris's sword clutched in her taloned feet. The dugout disintegrated in a flurry of splinters as Alecto smashed into it.

Then Tisiphone was there, flying straight out of the wreckage. The cloud of dust and debris raised by Alecto's fall caught fire from Tisiphone's wings, becoming an expanding fireball. Riding the shock wave, Tisiphone crashed into Eris, sending the goddess tumbling.

"Ooh, a bean ball," said Tisiphone as she climbed steeply away. "How very unsporting."

"Would you two quit with the commentary and just take her?" called Megaera.

She was on her feet again and preparing to reenter the fray. But before any of the Furies could take advantage of the situation, the world changed. The stadium and all its trappings were gone. In their place was a dense tropical jungle. Rich humid air redolent with the smell of green growing things and the perfumes of exotic flowers filled my lungs as I stood on an open platform high in the branches of a giant tree. Tisiphone was visible circling above, but Eris and the other Furies were concealed by the growth. I tried to spot them by looking for out-of-place colors, but the vines that wound through everything came in a million hues. I was still looking when I heard Discord's voice whisper in my ear.

"Watch this."

Like an Apollo rocket taking off, one of the trees suddenly sprouted flames at its base and leaped skyward. As it sailed past Tisiphone, its branches lashed out and grabbed the Fury, dragging her with it. They had climbed perhaps another thousand feet when the dome of heaven suddenly sprouted an eyelid. As the tree and the struggling Fury approached this feature, it opened. As with Eris, there was no eye within the socket, but rather the twisting madness of raw chaos. Tisiphone and the tree plunged through and were gone. I swallowed once.

"Nice," said Melchior.

"I can't say I'm sorry to see her go," I replied. "But that seemed a bit harsh."

"Not at all," said Eris's disembodied voice. "And nowhere near permanent enough. I just ejected her from the knot of reality that houses my domain. She'll be back soon enough. In the meantime though . . ."

There was a sudden thrashing in the greenery below. At first I couldn't see anything. Then chain lightning exploded skyward, blasting the undergrowth asunder. Revealed in a smoking circle were Eris and Alecto. The former had the latter pinned in a sort of full-nelson wrestling hold modified for a victim with wings. Alecto was clearly straining to break free, but Eris's strength was too much for her. That wasn't the only thing Eris was doing. Working her will on the stuff of Castle Discord, she was causing the thick, dark soil of the forest floor to rise up around Alecto's feet, wrapping her legs in a muddy embrace.

That was when the tree nearest mine seemed to come apart. The thick green shroud of its canopy dropped as though fall had come all at once. This green cloud was almost on top of Eris before I realized it must be Megaera's wings. But before Megaera could finish her descent, a thick purple vine slithered down behind her, snapped out like a frog's tongue, and wrapped itself around her waist. Megaera's long claws slashed out, severing it. But four more vines, each a different color, sprouted out of the two severed ends and instantly clutched at the Fury. Her claws flashed again, and again the vine split and multiplied. Other vines joined the battle. In seconds, Megaera was wound tight in a rainbow-colored vine cocoon.

"I think I'm going to be sick," said Melchior.

"What?" I asked, startled. "Why?"

"That's Eris's network," he replied. "That's the thing I was vampired onto. It's awful."

"Oh, don't be such a prude," said Eris's voice. "Tangle is one of my favorite pets. It's the genetically engineered offspring of the hydra. After that little fuss with Hercules, I realized my initial design was flawed. Hydra was vulnerable in the head department, and since he didn't have much in the way of brains to start with, I decided to eliminate the case he carried them in. It was really . . ." There was a long pause. "Shit."

"What's going on?" I asked, but there was no response.

I tried peering downward. A vine-covered Megaera lay at the feet of an almost entombed Alecto, who was still struggling feebly against Eris. It looked like a complete triumph for Discord except for one little detail. There was a strange flickering glow coming from the ground under Megaera, and the soil was rising and cracking as though giving birth to a miniature volcano. The small cone rose another foot, then erupted, splashing Eris. The goddess, hair flaming, threw herself to one side and rolled while Tisiphone rose out of the fire. She caught hold of Alecto with her left hand. With her right she grabbed the vines that encased Megaera and burned them away. Clutching her sisters to her breast, she leaped skyward.

"I think it's time," said Alecto, her voice crackling out like thunder.

"But we were having such fun," replied Tisiphone, blowing me a kiss as she passed.

"I thought it was time and past before we ever arrived," growled Megaera.

"Then we're agreed?" asked Alecto.

"I suppose so," said Tisiphone, with obvious reluctance.

"Oh, get on with it," said Megaera.

The three Furies vanished in a boil of multicolored light. Strands of black and silver braided themselves together with others of swampy green and fiery red, creating a roiling knot of brightness so intense I had to look away.

"Game time is over," said the triple voice the Furies used when they spoke in unison.

As abruptly as it had come, the blinding glare winked out. Hovering in the air where the Furies had been was a single form with three heads. The first was an emerald sea serpent, the second a fiery lion, the third an ebon goat with silver horns. It had an elongated female torso with three pairs of breasts and three sets of arms. Below this torso was a long, thick dragon's body. On the creature's back were three sets of wings identical to those of the three Furies.

"Give my regards to Tyche," Eris's voice whispered in my ear.

"Is there something I can do?" I asked.

"Yes," said the disembodied voice. "Run as if Cerberus himself were snapping at your heels."

With that, I found myself elsewhere, a greenhouse filled with flowers of every hue and shape. I'd only begun to look around when I realized that Melchior and I were surrounded by a neat circle of forget-me-nots. Recognition gave way to action as I snatched for the scruff of my goblin's neck. Even as my fingers closed on that cool blue flesh, the faerie ring's magic took hold and the world dropped away beneath us.

Nerve endings screamed in protest as a burst of intense heat engulfed me. With it came eye-tearing light. I felt as though I were at the white-hot core of a flashbulb. Relief came in a cold wet breeze carrying the scent of damp concrete. In that brief moment of peace, I lifted Melchior into my arms.

The greenhouse was gone. We stood in the middle of a midnight street at the heart of an enormous city. Around us a swirling mass of newspaper shreds danced a temporary ring. My first thought was that it had been assembled by Chance Eddies. Then I heard a triumphant cry and the beginning abjuration of a spell of control. Before I could disabuse the sorcerer of the notion that I was a summoned demon, the heat and light came again.

This time we arrived in the center of a huge and elegantly set table. The linens were of rich ruby damask and each place setting sparkled with silver and crystal. A braided wreath of fruit-laden grapevines surrounded us, and I could only assume that we'd displaced some gorgeously crafted centerpiece. The impeccably dressed and exquisitely turned out diners appeared only mildly surprised at our sudden appearance. It seemed as pleasant a place to end my trip as any. I exerted my will on the process, holding the ring open, and lifted a foot to cross the vine boundary. One of the women smiled up at me. She was all in evergreen lace and sable velvet and she was beautiful. She was also possessed of an entire mouthful of sharp predator's teeth. The contents of her plate were moving.

Blistering heat. Glaring light. An endless flat plane of glass glowing faintly blue in the moonlight. The scent of ozone. A ring of perfect red roses.

Flash. Booming drums. A dusty clearing. A dozen small monkeylike things slowly orbiting me in a shuffling dance, their hands clasped. The aroma of roasting meat.

And so it went. It was far worse than my first trip through a faerie ring. Then I'd entered of my own accord with a firm goal in mind. Now I was blipping aimlessly between worlds without the faintest glimmering of intent. I could feel all of my worries and desires slowly draining away as the journey moved faster and faster. I knew I was in danger of losing myself forever in the ennui that came with the sensory overload, but somehow I couldn't summon the energy to care.

That was when Melchior bit me. I let go of him with a scream, but he stayed firmly in place. His fangs were sunk deep into the soft tissue of my shoulder, and all four sets of his claws clung to my left side. He stuck to me like the flaming jacket the centaur Nessus had used to slay Hercules. Stunned by this unexpected betrayal, I tried to pull him loose, but there was no way, not without doing considerable damage to myself. Just then we made another world transition, moving from a brightly lit desertscape to a dark and blasted hillside. A powerful smell of burning hung in the air. As we crossed over, the pain in my shoulder abruptly intensified. I cried out again and staggered, the combination of repeated sensory hammerblows and Melchior's unprovoked attack leaving me shocky and disoriented.

"Jump," a voice howled in my ear.

I launched myself up and forward with all my might before realizing it was Melchior who had commanded me. Somewhere about halfway through my wild leap, the web-goblin released his grip and dropped away. I landed in a crouch that turned into a half kneel as my bad knee gave way. Expecting further attack, I ignored the pain-laced weakness of my leg and forced myself to my feet. As I rose a noise came from behind and my hand went to the hilt of my rapier. It was fortunate I reacted so quickly, drawing my blade as I turned, because it allowed me to parry the axe blow that whistled toward my neck an instant later.

The force of the attack numbed my arm to the elbow, but my blade held, and the axe rode up and over my head in a shower of sparks. As the axe flashed past, I got a brief look at my attacker. He stood slightly above me on the dew-slick, grassy slope. A big man, he was garbed like a hunter in a hooded jerkin and breeches tucked into knee boots. An empty bow case was slung over his shoulder. In the dark I couldn't make out colors, and his hood was drawn up, shadowing his face. The next couple of minutes were a confusing blur as I backed away from his onslaught, often stumbling or slipping on the rough ground.

An axe is an awkward sort of weapon and slow. Under any normal circumstances, the superior speed and maneuverability of my rapier would have allowed me to slide past his guard and turn him into so much shish kebab.

The problem was that no one seemed to have explained that to *him*. I was wounded and weary. My bad knee was getting steadily worse under the constant pressure of retreat on an uneven surface. And I was still disoriented from my passage between worlds. My opponent, on the other hand, seemed fresh and strong, and he was throwing around a broad-bladed axe like a willow wand. Instead of elegantly sliding around his attacks and skewering him, I was trying desperately to turn the unending series of cuts he rained on me.

It was a job my thin dueling blade was never meant for, and I feared it would break at any moment. I did fumble for my dagger, but my left hand was still too awkward, and I ended up dropping it. A few seconds later, my knee gave out completely, and I went down on my back. The axe swung up for a cut I would never be able to parry. Instead, I set my blade for a counterthrust. I might not be able to win, but I could probably arrange things so we both lost.

The axe started a downward arc that was going to split my skull into neat halves like a walnut. In the same instant, I brought my rapier up in a thrust that would end with a foot of steel perforating my attacker's intestines. The edge came down. The point rose up.

My opponent shrieked and fell to his left as that leg folded underneath him.

With a wet, schlunking sort of noise, the axehead sank six inches into the earth next to my right ear. The haft struck my cheek a glancing blow, tearing a long gash.

My rapier went home in his right arm, passing completely through his biceps and standing out a good six inches on the other side.

I paused to revel in the fact that I wasn't dead. It felt wonderful. Any number of times over the course of the previous few months, I'd feared I was going to die. But this time was different. This time I'd *known* I was dead at that very moment. There'd been no doubt in my mind. And yet, here I was, still breathing. Breathing was good. I liked breathing. In fact . . .

"Don't just lie there," said Melchior. "Give me a hand tying Dairn up before the shock wears off."

There were a number of questions I wanted to ask, but I can be practical when I have to. So I helped Melchior bind and gag my erstwhile opponent. I also bandaged Dairn's wounds. There were two. In addition to the damage I'd done his arm, Melchior had hamstrung him. I also got Melchior to dose both of us with painkillers. Only once those tasks were completed did I turn my mind back to my questions. I had a number of injuries that needed attention as well, but waiting a few minutes wasn't going to make much difference.

"What the fuck is going on!?" I yelled. "Why in Necessity's name did you bite me?"

"Sure," said Melchior. "You save a guy's life, not once, not twice, but three times in ten minutes. And what does he do? Does he say thank you? No. I don't think so."

"Melchior, could we skip the dramatics and the runaround just this once? It's been a very long day. No. Scratch that. It's been a very long winter. I think my knee is completely gone, maybe for good. And"—I held up a hand with the thumb and forefinger an eighth of an inch apart—"I'm this close to passing out. I'd really love to find out what happened before I leave the land of vertical."

"All right, but it's not going to be any fun this way," he replied reluctantly. "I bit you because you were about to lose us in the faerie ring. When we went in, you seized control of our transport. Not a big surprise. You were in the driver's seat the only other time we went through one together as well. Unfortunately, you didn't have a goal in mind, or at least you didn't express one, and that's a sure recipe for doom. You can lose your soul that way, and I think you were pretty close to that point at the end. So I decided I'd better take the wheel. The only way for me to do that was to break your concentration, and with it, your hold on the process. Biting you seemed the easiest way."

"All right," I said. "I can see the need. Thank you. Next question. Where are we? And why is Dairn here?"

Melchior looked at the fractured slope above us and flinched. "This is, or perhaps I should say was, Ahllan's home. It's the only ring I really know."

I wanted to deny Mel's assertion, but I couldn't. Now that I knew what I was seeing, I recognized familiar details, like the tree beneath which Cerice and I had first made love and the beer-can ring where Melchior and I had arrived. It was a shattering realization. Ahllan's beautiful house looked like a honey tree after grizzlies had been at it.

"The Furies or Atropos?" I asked.

"I think I know where we can get the answers." Melchior pointed to where we'd propped Dairn against a rock.

"Why don't we have few words with my dear, sweet cousin?" I agreed. My tone was ugly, even in my ears.

"That suits," responded Melchior. He moved to Dairn's side, and slowly slid one claw under the fabric of the gag, slicing it neatly away.

"Well?" I asked.

"I don't see why I shouldn't tell you," said Dairn, the rhythm of his breathing staccato with pain even through the morphine. "The Furies got here first. They're the ones who opened the door, so to speak." He gestured at the ripped-open hilltop. "Though I think that was all that they did. They were looking for you, and they don't seem to have been interested in the others. Fortunately, we weren't far behind. The troll and that hellcat you call a girlfriend put up quite a fight, but Atropos sent enough of us to do the job."

I felt like my guts had been yanked out and used for sandal straps.

"Where are they now? And why were you here alone?" I asked.

"I'm not sure what happened to the troll, but the last time I saw Cerice she was hog-tied and hanging over Hwyl's shoulder."

I couldn't help myself, I backhanded him. I was in lousy shape, and it was a weak blow, but it split his lip. Unfortunately, it also jarred my knee, and even with the painkillers my world flashed red and white for a while. "You didn't answer the second part," I said, through clenched teeth. "Why are you here by yourself?"

"I was waiting for you. Atropos didn't want to leave a big group because she thought you might have some way of spotting them. Instead, she reworked the ltp links to this DecLocus so that anyone coming in would have to appear over there." He jerked his head. "I was all set up with my bow, ready to put an arrow through your neck when you arrived. The only problem is you came in through the back door. By the time I realized you were here, that little bastard"—he pointed at Melchior with his chin—"was already on top of me, and he cut my string."

"So that's why you let go of me when we first got here," I said to Mel.

"Not really," he replied. "I figured you weren't going to be real rational about my having bitten you, and I wanted to put some distance between us before I tried explaining. Landing practically on top of this jerk was just sort of a perk." He paused. "Two perks really."

"Two?" I asked.

"Yeah. In addition to taking his bow out of commission, it gave me a chance to keep him from sounding the alarm."

"How so?"

"By relieving him of this."

Mel reached into his pouch and pulled out the magically

insulated sack he used for spell supplies. An angry buzzing sounded from inside. He opened the top partway and pulled out a tiny naked woman. She had waist-length black hair, dragonfly wings, and a nasty disposition. A webpixie. Dairn wasn't really a sorcerer, so he didn't need to haul around a laptop like Cerice and I did. Instead, he used one of the new handhelds. This one was very unhappy.

"Does she—" I started to ask Melchior. He jerked a thumb meaningfully in Dairn's direction.

"Right," I said. "Melchior, Bedtime For Bonzo . . . Please."

Despite the pause the spell request came out a little more naturally this time. Maybe I'd get used to it after a while. He whistled a chunk of binary that ended with Dairn's head lolling to one side as he began to snore.

"Free will?" I asked.

"I don't know," he replied. "I kind of doubt it. She's too small to have any real processing power. She'd almost have to be an idiot."

"Let me go for a minute, and I'll show yer who's an idiot," she snarled, in a surprisingly deep voice. "I'll yank yer eyes out of they sockets and stuff 'em up yer snooty goblin nose."

"I think that answers that question," I said. "That doesn't sound like the sort of personality programming Dairn would go for in a familiar."

"Yer damn right it's not," said the pixie. "He's a right bastard. 'Kira do this. Kira do that. Faster Kira. Faster. Do yer want me ter trade yer in on a cell phone, Kira?' When I'm done with blue boy's eyes, maybe I'll have a go at his."

"What an enchanting little thing you are," I said dryly. "Did you happen to see what happened there"—I pointed at the hill—"or were you too busy plotting death and destruction?"

"If yer wants ter know what happened ter the frill and the troll, I can tell yer, but it'll cost."

"We'd like to know what became of the little purple goblin as well," I said.

"Why for? Every damn one of 'em's a stuck-up pain in the arse."

"What say I tear her wings off," said Melchior.

"No, Mel. Tempting as that sounds at the moment, she might know something important." I turned my attention back to the pixie. "What do you want?"

She looked surprised at first, as though she couldn't believe I'd actually negotiate with her. Then she looked suspicious. Finally, she spoke. "Freedom," she whispered.

"Deal," I said.

"What!" yelped Melchior. "You can't be serious. What's to keep her from running straight to Atropos the second we let her go?"

"And he calls me an idiot," scoffed the pixie. She turned her gaze on Melchior. "What are yer? A great damned loon? What's ter keep me, an escaped familiar, from running ter the Fate of Death? The fact that she'd take me apart and use my parts for jewelry doesn't strike yer as enough reason ter stay as far away from her as I can fucking get?"

"Well, when you put it that way . . ." said Mel. "I suppose it does sound pretty stupid."

"What other way is there ter put it?" she asked, rolling her eyes. "The real question is, how does I know yer'll keep yer word once I tell yer what I know?"

"Let her go, Mel."

"What?" His voice was incredulous. "She's as vicious a little thing as I've ever seen. She even threatened to tear my eyes out, and you want me to let her go?"

"She's also one more independent-thinking being who happens to have been enslaved by a branch of my family, a predicament I'm sure you're familiar with. We haven't any more right to hold her prisoner than I had to order you around."

"I don't see you turning *him* loose," said Mel, pointing at Dairn.

"No. But I might if it can be done safely."

"Oh, all right," said Mel. "You've got that stubborn look." He paused for a moment. "And, much as I hate to admit it, you're probably right."

He opened his fingers. Immediately the pixie took wing and streaked away. She'd gotten about fifty feet before stopping. For a long time she hovered there. Then, flying much slower, she came back to a point about ten feet away.

"A deal's a deal," she said. "There was a pretty nasty fight. Maybe a dozen of Atropos's git against the girl, the goblin, and the troll. The troll was somethin' else. She picked up one of those boys, a big furry guy in a loincloth, name of Hwyl, and used him like a club. That was a sight. The girl took down two or three before they swarmed her under. When that happened, the goblin went nuts. Never seen one of them so het up. She got all four sets of claws into the leader's head, she did. I think she near killed him. That's when my former master there put an arrow into her."

"No!" exclaimed Melchior.

"'Fraid so," responded the pixie. "It hit her in the face and she dropped off."

Melchior closed his eyes in obvious pain, and a tear ran down his cheek. When he opened them again there was burning rage there, and he started for Dairn. I'd anticipated that though, and I was able to catch him by his scruff.

"Not yet, Mel. We haven't heard the whole story, and he's a bound man. Later, we'll let him have a head start and take him in a fair fight."

"I've never been much for fair fights," said Mel, but

some of the murderous tension went out of him. "Tell us the rest," he said.

"There's not much more. With the girl and the goblin down, there weren't no way that troll was going to win. She must have seen that too, because she chucked the big galoot at the others, grabbed up the goblin and dived into the wall."

"Dived into the wall?" I asked.

"Yeah. There was this big red hexagram deal there. The troll jumped into that, and the whole thing vanished."

"That's something," I said. "Ahllan wouldn't have taken Shara if it was completely hopeless."

"Thanks for trying," said Melchior. "But even if Shara was repairable, that gate went to Castle Discord. You can't just change the coordinates on one of those like you do an ltp link. They went into the gate all right, but they never came out the other end. We'd have seen them."

I winced. Travel between the worlds was never a sure thing. I'd had more than one relative go missing. Lost in transit didn't make for a poetic epitaph, but neither did operator error, and they'd both applied to people I knew. The pixie suddenly darted in closer.

"That's all I saw," she said. "I got to go now." She turned and started to fly away, then paused and looked back. "I'm sorry."

CHAPTER TWENTY

Melchior and I made a pretty grim pair as we sat beside the ruins of Ahllan's home. The former owner, along with a severely wounded Shara, had gone missing between worlds. Cerice was taken by the Fates. Our only other ally, the Goddess of Discord, was last seen in a losing fight with the Furies. And every last bit of it looked to be my fault. All in all, I was beginning to wish Melchior had just let Dairn split my skull. At least that way, I wouldn't have had to live with the havoc I'd generated in every life that mattered to me.

"Any thoughts on what we should do next?" I asked.

"How about taking an ltp link to nowhere? I find the thought of having the stuff of chaos render me down to component bits to be a soothing one."

"Too quick," I replied. "I feel a need to suffer for my crimes. Besides, that's the way Ahllan and Shara must have gone, and I'd hate to sully—" I stopped then, because the faintest glimmerings of an idea had just occurred to me. "Melchior, what did I just say?"

"Don't you remember?" he asked.

"Humor me," I said.

"All right. You said that Ahllan and Shara were eaten by the chaos between worlds. Does hearing me say it make it any less of a nightmare?"

"That's what I thought I said." I sat up straight. "Powers and Incarnations, I'm an idiot. You know what, Mel? You are a beautiful person."

"Look, if you're going to drift off into insanity, could you at least do it quietly?" He turned and stared out into the darkness.

"Don't you see it?" I asked.

"Why do I suddenly feel like I've wandered into *Waiting for Godot*?" he asked. "Here we sit, two fools on a gray stage waiting for nothing. We've even got the tree."

He didn't see where I was going. It was kind of nice to be one step ahead of somebody for a change. Still, I couldn't leave him hanging.

"I'll make it easy for you," I said. "Ahllan and Shara are missing and presumed dead because they went into a gate that almost certainly dumped them into the Primal Chaos, right?"

"Yep."

"Mel, how did Ahllan survive after Atropos threw her on the junk heap?"

"She needed energy, so she transported herself into the Primal Cha . . ." His face lit up like Apollo rising in the east.

"If they're still out there, can you—" He cut me off.

"Already on it." He hopped to his feet. "Executing Red Flag." His expression went far off and dreamy for a few seconds. "Red Flag away," he said. "Now we wait."

I don't know if it's possible to express the way I felt then. Waiting to find out whether someone you care about is alive or dead is perhaps the most emotionally wrenching experience a person can have. In its own hellish way, it's worse than the news that someone you love has died. At least with the latter, the worst has happened and you can begin to deal with it. The uncertainty of not knowing leaves you without any landmarks. You slide endlessly up and down the ladder that leads from hope to despair. I was in the middle of a downswing when Melchior let out a whoop.

"I've got a response from Ahllan," said Melchior, his voice crackling with excitement. "It's a message-received confirmation and a time-critical ltp address."

The news sent a momentary thrill through me. Ahllan was alive! The happiness was brief, however, and it was followed by a nasty crash. As long as the matter of Ahllan's whereabouts and status were unknown, I'd been able to focus on that. Now, with the issue at least partly resolved, my mind turned to Cerice and Shara. The image of Hwyl carrying Cerice off fixed itself firmly in my inner vision, periodically alternating with a picture of Shara with an arrow sticking out of her face.

I barely noticed as Melchior set up an ltp link. It wasn't until he actually tugged my sleeve that I realized it was ready. That presented me with a couple of problems. First, I couldn't stand up. My bad knee wouldn't take my weight. That was relatively minor. I could always crawl into the ltp field. The second problem was more serious: what to do about Dairn.

I didn't want to leave him there. Atropos might send one of her brood back to check on him at any time, and he knew enough about our movements to make me nervous. Likewise, I didn't want to take him to Ahllan's new hiding place. If he got loose, he'd bring the forces of Fate down upon us. Even if he stayed firmly tied up, Atropos might have some way to track him. That wouldn't have stopped me if I'd thought he could be used as a bargaining chip to get Cerice back. But he was a failure, and Atropos wouldn't hesitate to sacrifice him. Just slitting his throat and leaving him for the crows seemed the most sensible solution, but I couldn't do that either. As much as I hate to admit it, I have a bad case of ethics. Then I hit on the perfect idea. I had Melchior levitate him to the faerie ring and push him in. It wasn't the same as killing him, because he would probably manage to roll out again before he lost his mind, but he was certainly in for a very bad time. With that taken care of, we headed out.

Chaos. The raw, wild wine of creation. The mad tumble of it met my eyes from a distance measured in fractions of an inch. For a brief instant, I thought Mel had blown our transfer. That impression was quickly dispelled as I completely failed to dissolve. Then I realized I was viewing the stuff through a crystalline barrier. It induced a strange sort of déjà vu, and when I rolled onto my back, I discovered why. We had arrived in a huge sphere of transparent crystal, perhaps fifty feet across. It was identical in type, if not in scale, to the one in which I'd had my disastrous initial discussion about Puppeteer with Atropos. It was even filled with the same strange, clear fluid.

Suspended seemingly at random in this liquid matrix were various oddments of furniture and electronics. If you were to take the contents of Ahllan's former home, mix them into a bowl of Jell-O, and let it set up, you would have achieved a similar effect. Nearest us, perhaps eight feet away horizontally and four vertically, was an electronics bench, its surface canted about thirty degrees toward us. Ahllan hung in space a few feet above it. A bright purple laptop lay on the bench in front of her. An arrow was driven through the upper half of the clamshell casing and the screen was a splintered wreck. Melchior shot across the intervening space and ran a small hand across Shara's keyboard.

"Is she dead?" he whispered.

"No." said Ahllan. "The arrow missed her motherboard and her DASD memory. But she's in a very bad way. She was in goblin shape when it hit, and she lost a lot of blood. The only way I could save her was by forcing a shift to laptop mode. Unfortunately, I couldn't pull the arrow beforehand without killing her, and it has a metal shaft. Besides the obvious damage to her screen, there was some shorting in the connected components. I've done everything I can to stabilize her, but I'd rather not try to make repairs without her designer on hand."

"And Cerice isn't exactly available," I said, sitting up. The thick warm fluid took much of my weight.

"No," agreed Ahllan, "she's not."

"That'll have to be job one," I said.

"The Fates aren't going to want to let her go," said Melchior.

"I think it can be done," I said. "I have something they want more than they want her—something they'll be willing to trade for."

"I don't think I'm going to like this," said Melchior. "What did you have in mind?"

"My life."

"I was afraid you were going to say that," replied the goblin. "You can't do it."

"Why not?" I asked. "I got her into this mess. In fact, I got you all into this mess. If the only way to make things right is by giving myself up to the Fates, that's what I have to do."

"As your partner," said Melchior, "I'm going to veto this one."

"I'm sorry, Mel. You're the best friend I could have asked for. I love you like a brother, but I think I'm going to have to dissolve the firm."

"That's not going to fix everything," he snapped. "You know that. Even if you get Cerice free and she's able to repair Shara, Atropos still wins. With you gone, and probably Eris as well, Atropos will be able to implement Puppeteer unopposed."

"Atropos hasn't solved her coding problems yet," I replied. "Maybe she never will. Even if she does, she won't go unanswered. Tyche's still out there. You can take Orion to her. Don't discount yourself or Cerice when you discuss opposition, or these two, for that matter." I gestured at Ahllan and Shara.

"Nor will Eris be removed from the scene forever," said Ahllan. "She's a true immortal. The worst they can do is torture and imprisonment, and no chain can hold the Unbinder indefinitely."

"You're not agreeing with him." Mel's voice was incredulous as he turned to Ahllan.

"If you have an alternate solution," she said, "now's the time to propose it."

"That's not fair," he said. "Come on, Ravirn. You've at least got to take another look at Orion before you do anything else."

"What's Orion?" asked Ahllan.

We brought Ahllan up to date. Then she told us her story, confirming what the webpixie had said.

"Which brings us to your arrival here," concluded Ahllan.

"That's something I've been meaning to ask," I said. "Where is here? More to the point, what is it? I was in a similar bubble once, but that's as far as my knowledge extends on the subject."

"It's a sort of looped gate," replied Ahllan. "If you think

back to your transportation to Castle Discord, you'll remember that a single-use gate keeps track of its two endpoints though a series of sliding mathematical formulae. Imagine a point outside the mweb, a random location somewhere between the worlds. Now picture a gate that starts and ends at that point. The mathematical value for your start point is identical to the value for your end point, so you end up with a gate that opens into itself."

"OK," I said. "I'm with you so far. But don't you run into a paradox? I mean, when you step out through the gate, don't you bump into yourself coming back in?"

"You would if you tried to do it within the ordered confines of normal space-time. But out here"—she gestured to the phantasmagoric dance outside of the sphere—"what you get is a sort of self-enclosed bubble of reality."

"And the fluid?" I asked.

"Condensed probability," she replied. "The essence of order."

I shook my head. "I'm having a hard time believing this."

"Oh, don't do that," said Ahllan, her tone deathly serious. "You might make the whole thing vanish."

"Now, just a second," I said. "That's the most ridiculous thing I've ever heard." I was about to go on when I saw the evil sparkle of humor hiding behind her seriousness. "Are you pulling my leg?"

"Maybe." She grinned.

"Ravirn's going to throw his idiotic life away trying to bust Cerice loose, and you're cracking jokes?" asked Melchior. "How can you do that at a time like this?"

"How could I not?" asked Ahllan.

"She's right, Mel. It doesn't make any difference in the end result, but isn't it better to go to the block laughing rather than crying?"

"No!" snapped Melchior. "You shouldn't go to the block

at all. And if you do go, you should snarl and claw the whole way, and spit in the executioner's eye before he swings the blade."

"All that does is raise your blood pressure," I said. "That's no good."

"Why not?" he responded. "It's not like the axe isn't going to lower it right back again."

"Point taken, Mel," I sighed. "But none of this is releasing Cerice from durance vile. Why don't we get this program running before my nerve breaks?"

It was a valid concern. I might believe I had a moral obligation to substitute my neck in the noose for Cerice's. Actually, there was no might about it. Moral considerations aside, I knew now that loved her. If I could buy her life at the cost of mine, it was a bargain.

That didn't mean the prospect left me unmoved. It scared me beyond the capacity for rational thought. Still, I couldn't see any way around it as things stood. And I didn't think the Fates were going to give me a whole lot of time to concoct a better plan. For that matter, with my right knee shot, my left arm mostly useless, and the pile of other injuries I'd acquired along the way, I was in no shape to pull off a strenuous rescue.

"Mel, I'm sorry. Powers know I don't want to do this, but I can't see any other options. I need your support, now more than I've ever needed it before."

"Dammit, that's not fair," he said. "My job has always been to get your ass out of the fire. Now you want me to support you putting it in? I just can't do it." He turned away, and half swam, half flew to the bench where Shara lay.

"He'll come around," said Ahllan. "Just give him a little time."

"Ahllan, I don't have a little time. I should be gone already."

"No, you should not. There are a number of preparations to make first. You have to have a binding deal with the Fates before you surrender yourself into their power. Otherwise, you might just as well not go for all the good it will do Cerice. Frankly, I don't know how you're going to be able to trust a word they say."

"Actually, I think I've got a solution to the reliability problem," I said. "The trick is going to be establishing a secure channel of communication, one that doesn't just let them backtrace me and scoop me up."

"There, I can help. Atropos is the one who thought up these bubble gates. She did it to have a secure retreat. There's no way to get here without knowing the exact location and gate formula, and since we're bouncing around in the primal chaos those change on a minute-to-minute basis. I built this one right after Shara revealed me to Cerice. I knew I might need another bolt-hole one day."

"If that's the case, why don't we begin?"

"Not quite yet," said the Troll. "Melchior was right about one thing. You should have a second look at Orion before you go. It'll give you another bargaining chip, and if you can fix it quickly, you can leave a copy here for me to send to Tyche. The girl *is* powerful, but a complete scatterbrain. If Eris couldn't make the spell work, Tyche never will. She'll need a corrected version if she's going to accomplish anything."

"All right," I said. "But I shouldn't give it more than an hour."

"Agreed. I think the primary reason the Fates took Cerice was to draw you in. As long as they believe you'll come for her, Cerice should be safe enough. But if you don't take the bait quickly, they may try to up the pressure."

"Mel," I said, "are you willing to take one last ride with me? I want to look at Orion."

He turned back to face me. "All right."

A few minutes later I once again slid into Orion's complex architecture. This time though, I knew what to look for. With a virtual Melchior at my side, I dived deep into the angular logic of the code. The flaw was right where I remembered, and it was the work of seconds to extend my consciousness into it. Using cracking tools coded long ago, Melchior and I broke the fissure wide open. The subroutine thus revealed was like an origami crane with a broken wing. Together we carefully unfolded it, looking for the critical mistake that prevented its proper functioning.

It was a simple thing really, a tiny loop of logic that forced the spell to write and rewrite the same bit of data over and over again. Worse, if it *did* ever manage to move on, it would do the same for each location searched. Under normal circumstances, that would have caused an overflow of the spell's memory resources, an error that would have caught Eris's attention. In this case however, it didn't blow the memory's capacity. Instead, it dug a self-perpetuating pit in one tiny part of it, a much more subtle problem.

The patch we put on the spell didn't really fix the problem. I wasn't a good enough programmer to remaster Eris's intricate work. Instead, it did what most of my code did; it jury-rigged a work-around. Now, when the program hit the flawed subroutine, it would go through once, necessary for the proper function of the spell, then the patch would kick the write function on to the next data band. It worked a bit like tapping the side of CD player to make it skip.

When we finished, I had Mel copy a duplicate of the patched program to his DASD memory. It pretty much absorbed all of his free space, but he could hold it. Then I popped out Eris's crystal, loaded a blank one provided by Ahllan, and burned a new copy.

"There you go," I said, holding the spell up for Ahllan to

look at. "No matter what happens to me now, there's a way to pull the source code on Puppeteer."

"That still doesn't provide us with a counterspell," said Melchior. "From what Eris said about the way these things work, the second Orion is run, it'll be like goosing Atropos and the other Fates. They're going to know Puppeteer is in the hands of the enemy, and they're going to be furious. Unless someone can code a counter pretty damn quickly at that point, things are likely to get very ugly. With neither you nor Eris available for that duty, there isn't going to be a whole lot of point. If Ahllan is right, Tyche isn't going to be much help."

"Get Cerice to do it," I replied. "I may be able to out-hack her, but as far as straight coding is concerned, she's better than I'll ever be." I handed the crystal to Ahllan. "See that it gets to whoever needs it."

"I will," she said. "In exchange, I've got a couple of things for you." Seemingly from nowhere she produced an intimidating-looking device that was all leather and chrome.

"What is it?" I asked.

"An orthopedic knee brace. After your refusal to get your leg properly fixed the first time you collapsed on my doorstep, I did a little shopping. I had a feeling you might need this eventually. It's not exactly like armoring you for battle, but it's similar," she said, bending down to put it on me.

I examined the brace while Ahllan strapped it in place. It was an articulated leather sleeve that strapped around the leg. Two pneumatic pistons ran from just above the joint to just below it, one on the inside of the leg, the other on the outside. They looked rather like the devices that hold the hatchback of a car open. It wasn't pretty, but it would keep my weight off the joint. When she was done, she handed me a cane. Its shaft was a highly polished cylinder of ebony, its head a perfect sphere of emerald glass.

"Thank you," I said. "You've saved me a serious indignity. I wasn't looking forward to arriving at the Temple of Fate using a wheelchair."

"Bad bargaining position," she said, "to say nothing of how much harder it would be to make a break for it should you get the chance."

"Not likely, but I'll keep it in mind. Now, if you'll provide me with a link, I've a call to make."

"Certainly." Her eyes began to glow.

"Wait," interjected Melchior. "I'll do it." His voice was thick with emotion.

"Thank you, Mel. It means a lot."

"You're welcome," he replied. "I have a condition though."

"What's that?" I asked.

"I want you to take me with you."

"I can't do that," I said. "The price is high enough already."

"It's far *too* high, if you ask me, but that's not what I meant. I'm planning on coming back. One of us doing the noble sacrifice routine is more than enough. Cerice may not know about Shara, and I don't want to think about how she's going to respond when she finds out about you. Someone's going to need to be there for her, if for no other reason than to give her a ride. I expect she'd rather not rely on the good graces of the Fates for that. So I'll be coming, too. You can negotiate my free passage when you make your deal."

"That's fair," I said. "Ahllan, is there anything special we need to do to make a visual transfer protocol link from here untraceable? Or does the nature of the bubble do everything for us?"

"There's a little more to it than that, but Melchior knows what to do."

"In that case; Melchior, Vlink; Ravirn@melchior.gob to Lachesis@phalla.troll. Please." That "please" was feeling more natural all the time. It was too bad I wasn't going to be around long enough for it to become routine.

"Connecting to the mweb," said Melchior, his voice flat and abstracted. "Searching for phalla.troll. Connect. Communicating with host. Link established."

Light burst from Melchior's mouth and eyes, shaping itself into a three-dimensional image of my grandmother. From out of a set face, Fate's eyes glared at me. Only this time, there was a difference in that gaze. Where in the past they'd always seemed all-knowing, and all-judging, there was now a chink in that icy certainty, a faint hint that there were things beyond their power to predict. In tandem with that, there was a deep and abiding anger directed at the source of the uncertainty.

It was a strange sight, made stranger by the fact that it was aimed at me. Eris's virus had rendered me a man without a destiny. There was no way for the Fates to know exactly what I would do now. It gave me a bittersweet sense of power. For perhaps the first time in my life I was truly independent of my family's authority. At the same time, it severed a safety line I'd never really realized was there, a sort of invisible security blanket, and I knew I'd never be able to get it back. I suppose all normal children go through the same sort of thing when they finally strike out on their own, but it was not something I'd been prepared for, growing up in the house of Fate.

For one brief, agonizing moment I wanted to ask my grandmother to make everything better, to make it all not have happened. But it was too late for that. My own choices and those of the Fates had opened a gulf between my grandmother and me that could never be wholly bridged. Still, I felt my throat choked with tears unshed.

" 'How sharper than a serpent's tooth' to have a thankless grandson," said Lachesis, her voice a silken, strangling cord.

The quote was exactly what I needed. It hurt, but it also made me mad. As anger rose to drive back sorrow, I found my voice. "Spare me the Shakespearean dramatics, Grandmother. It was Atropos who set my feet on this path, not lack of gratitude. I share the fault, of course, but so, I think, do you. Or am I wrong in believing that you knew of her plans before I did?"

"Where did you hear that?" said Lachesis.

"From Discord," I replied, noting she hadn't denied the accusation.

"And you believed the goddess of strife?" she asked, again avoiding an answer.

"I did," I said, "but based on logic, not persuasion. You needn't deny it. For that matter, it really doesn't matter whether you confirm it. Either way, I'm convinced of the truth of the matter."

"You've grown, boy," said my grandmother. "But not in the way I'd hoped. You have failed in your loyalty to the interests of Fate. I should have been more firm in my discipline. Then you might have made the proper choice when Atropos made her offer."

I took a deep breath before speaking again, but my voice came out ragged anyway. "You did know."

She nodded. I was absolutely certain Lachesis knew about Puppeteer, but it still hurt to have it confirmed.

"I made the only choice I could," I said after a moment.

"No," said my grandmother. "You could have put your family first."

"I did," I said. "I chose every one of them who isn't a

Fate. There are only the three of you, and there are several hundred of us. I also opted for the interests of all of the other countless souls out there who would have ended up dangling like puppets from your fingers."

"Never puppets," replied Lachesis. "Errant children rather. Children who need a bit of firm guidance. Just as you do." She shook her head sadly. "If only Atropos had come to me first, I might have been able to present the thing to you in its proper light. She has always been too sure of her methods. And now, you're ruined. How can I bring you back to your senses?"

"I've never left them," I said. "Everything I've done, I've done with my eyes wide open. But none of that really matters. It's all in the past, and I've called you to discuss the present. I have a proposition for you."

"What is it?" she asked. Her voice shifted instantly from soft lament to businesslike efficiency, making me doubt the sincerity of the former.

"You have something I want very badly."

"Cerice, you mean?"

"Yes," I said.

"But she is in the care of her grandmother," replied Lachesis. "What better place for her could there be?"

"Almost anywhere," I responded. "I want to buy her freedom."

"I don't know if that's possible," said Lachesis. "She seems to have been infected by the virus of rebellion, for which I hold you responsible. She needs to be cured or quarantined."

"Killed or imprisoned, you mean," I said.

"Your words, not mine," replied Lachesis.

"I note you don't deny them. But, again, that doesn't matter. What does is that I have something you want even more than Cerice."

"And what might that be?" she asked.

"Me."

"Interesting proposal," said Lachesis. "But I don't know if it's adequate. We do want you, Ravirn. There is no doubt about that. But equally certain is that we'll eventually get you, no matter where you hide. Why should we give up Cerice just to hasten the inevitable? Do you have anything else we want? Anything that might sweeten the pot?"

"Oh, quit dancing around the edges of the thing," said another voice, and the picture suddenly expanded to include Atropos. "We want Eris's little spell, boy. I had Khemnos toss Castle Discord after the Furies left. He found some scraps of source code that were most suggestive, but he didn't find the spell master. If you can bring it to us, we may be able to come to an agreement. If not, you'll just have to wait until we catch you before you get to enjoy our hospitality."

"That might be a long wait, judging by past performance," I replied. Atropos's lips narrowed and tightened, and I knew I'd scored. Before she could speak again, I pulled the Orion crystal from my belt pouch. "Was this old thing what you wanted? It's really just a rag."

None of that was what I'd planned on saying, but they were interested. That meant we could probably come to an agreement, which in turn, meant I was about to sign my own death warrant. If I was going to die anyway, why not indulge my wit?

"If that's the spell, yes," said Lachesis, ignoring my sally. "Bring it in, and we'll let Cerice go."

"Knowing your sterling history for telling me the truth, I'm inclined to rush right out the door," I said. "Unfortunately, there's that incident in my youth where I was lost in the jungle and taken in by a band of wild lawyers to be raised as one of their own. Or was that Tarzan? I always get us confused. The point is that I've internalized the lessons taught by those crafty beasts, and I just can't bring myself to do this without some kind of binding contract."

"Let's just hunt him down and kill him," said Atropos. "Then at least we won't have to listen to him."

"You have no idea how tempting I find that suggestion," replied Lachesis. "But I want the spell now. Let's humor him." She turned her attention on me. "What did you have in mind? It's not as though there's a higher power to appeal to. We *are* causality, and you've already flouted our authority."

"You know, it's funny you should mention that. When I was talking to Eris the other day, she happened to mention that traditional mother of invention, Necessity." I had the pleasure of seeing both Fates twitch, all but acknowledging a hit on my part. "It gave me the seed of an idea which has since blossomed fully. I thought that we might invoke her attention as witness to our agreement. What do you think?"

"That I should have snipped your thread months ago," said Atropos. "Lachesis might have protested, but better that than our current dilemma."

"What a waste of talent you are," said Lachesis. "But I suppose it can't be fixed now. I want to see this finished, so I agree. Atropos?" she asked over her shoulder.

"No," came the reply. "We can always catch him later, and I don't want that interfering hag involved."

"It seems we have a tie," said Lachesis. "Clotho, yours is the deciding vote. What will it be?"

"That we should make a virtue of Necessity and draw her attention to what we do next. There will be much for her to see."

"Very well," continued Lachesis. "We will abide by your condition." She turned her attention a bit to the side. "Phalla, Split Screen; Realtime Message Mode. Execute."

"Executing," came the troll's reply.

A moment later the view supplied by Melchior divided itself. Half the viewing area was still filled by the Fates. The other half showed blank space.

"Phalla," said Lachesis, "Relay the following to Necessity@somewhere.olympus. Execute."

"Executing."

"Necessity," declaimed the three Fates in perfect unison. "We invoke and abjure you to witness and enforce the agreement into which we are about to enter."

With no fanfare and no fuss, she was there. The half of the viewing area devoted to her changed not a whit. No sound issued from hidden lips. There was no signal of divine attention whatsoever, and yet there was not the slightest question in my mind that I was being watched by an outside power.

"Are we satisfied?" asked Atropos. Her voice was sarcastic and dismissive, but the visible tension around her mouth belied the tone.

"I can't speak for you," I replied. "But I'm content."

Terrified would have been a more accurate description, but I couldn't very well say so. And so we began to dicker. It was a strange feeling, bargaining away my freedom and with it my life. The negotiations seemed to stretch on forever. Like a man making a deal with the devil, I didn't want to leave any loopholes. Like the aforementioned devil, they kept trying to slide them in. In the end, we reached an agreement that freed Cerice and allowed Melchior to conduct her to a safe place, in exchange for me surrendering myself and Orion. I did manage to avoid the issue of copies of the spell, and I made no promises about what would happen after I gave myself up, which were small victories at least.

At that point, it was time to go. I ran a hand along

Shara's ruined case in parting, gave Ahllan a hug, and thanked her for everything before saying good-bye.

Then I turned to Melchior and found myself incapable of speech. Tears filled the corners of my eyes, and my throat felt like I'd been gargling molten sulfur. I found that I'd resigned myself to dying, but not to saying good-bye. Of course, good-byes are one of life's most serious moments, and I've never done serious well. But there was more to it. I wasn't ready to leave Melchior behind, and fundamentally I never would be. Unfortunately, that's the way it works. Life is one long series of unexpected hellos and unwanted good-byes, and nothing we do can change that. It wasn't a profound realization, nor even a particularly original one, but that didn't make it any less true or painful.

Bending down, I took Melchior in my arms and pulled him close, trying to burn every aspect of him indelibly into my memory. His skin was cool and faintly pebbled, like a worn leather jacket. He smelled dry and spicy. I marveled at how light he seemed. When I was carrying him around in my bag, he seemed to weigh a thousand pounds.

"I'm going to miss you, Mel."

"Not for long," he replied sourly. "Not if Atropos has her way." Then he relented. "I'm sorry. That was uncalled for. It's just that I'm going to miss you, too, and probably for a whole lot longer. Are you sure you don't have one last rabbit to pull out of your hat?"

"Afraid not, my friend. I've used up every trick I know. Besides, if I back out now, I'll be flouting Necessity, and I have a feeling that's a bad idea."

"We'd better get this over with then," said Melchior. I nodded my agreement.

"Melchior, Mtp://mweb.DecLocus.prime/templeoffate. Please."

"Opening ltp link to Mtp://mweb.DecLocus.prime/templeoffate," said Melchior.

Time is always fastest when you don't want it to pass at all. Long before I was ready for it, a hexagonal column of light stood waiting to take me to my meeting with the Fates. Ahllan's hideaway was warm and welcoming around me, homelike. It took every ounce of will I possessed to leave.

Stepping into the light, I said, "Melchior, Locus Transfer. Please."

CHAPTER TWENTY-ONE

The transfer from Ahllan's weird little bubble of probability to the Temple of Fate was a long one. The troll had placed her hideaway in the depths of the Primal Chaos, as far from the main flow of reality as she could get. The Temple *was* the main flow. You couldn't get any closer to the center of things than the physical home of the Fate Core. It rested at the base of Olympus, and though the gods who made their home above might quibble as to which was the true heart of the multiverse, those of us who'd been born into the family of Fate had no doubts.

Clotho was waiting for me when I arrived. That was a relief. Atropos and I had never felt anything but antipathy for each other, and my relationship with my grandmother wasn't much better at that point. Besides, Clotho was the only one of the three who had a vested interest in seeing Cerice come out of this in one piece. Her eyes scanned over me as I made a slow and painful climb up the stairs. Starting at my feet, they worked their way up to my face, at which point a very odd look passed across her features. In anyone other than a Fate, I'd have called it a double take.

"Ravirn," she said. "It's good to see you again." There was a warmth to her voice I'd never heard from either my grandmother or Atropos. It was strange but welcome, though I knew I had no allies among the Fates.

"I wish I could say the same," I replied. "But that is a fault of our circumstances, not of yours."

She smiled then. "Circumstances are what you make of them. That's true even for us. Will you give me Eris's spell?" I handed the crystal over. "Thank you. If you'll follow me, there are a few things yet to be seen to before we can draw the curtains on this episode in the great game."

She turned and walked into the Temple without a backward glance. For a moment, I considered bolting. After all, I'd technically fulfilled my side of the bargain. But I didn't dare try that with Cerice still firmly in the hands of Fate. Besides, a fast hobble was the best I could do. I took one last look at the sunlit fields below Olympus, then, leaning heavily on my cane, trailed after Clotho. The inside of the temple had been rearranged since they'd tried to cut my thread. The long boardroom table was gone. In its place was an arrangement that would have looked more at home in a court of law. A witness stand stood in the center. There were two judges' benches, one on either side of the room, each with three seats. The one on the left was empty. Atropos and Lachesis sat at the one on the right, with Lachesis in the outermost seat.

Cerice stood in a large wooden cage just behind her. She had a black eye and a cut lip, but no other apparent injuries. Her clothes were stained and bore more than a few rips, but her head was high. When I met her gaze, I felt the breath rush out of me as though I'd been punched in the gut. Though whether it was in anger at her imprisonment or relief that she was all right, I wasn't sure. It was the former that sent me storming across the floor to the place before my grandmother. Well, perhaps limping with intent would be closer to the truth, but storming is what I wanted to do.

"Let her out," I snarled. "Now!"

"Don't use that tone with me, boy," said my grandmother. "I won't tolerate it."

"What are you going to do? Kill me twice? I've fulfilled my part of the bargain. It's time you fulfill yours. Release her."

"All in good time," replied Lachesis. "As soon as we've determined to our satisfaction that you have acted as you promised, we'll see her on her way. Assume the stand." She pointed to the center of the room.

"Oh, can't we just kill him and let the girl go?" asked Atropos, throwing her arms wide in exasperation.

Ignoring both of them, I hobbled to the door of Cerice's cage and reached for the lock. Out of the corner of my eye I saw Atropos stand up, shears in hand. I didn't really care. The worst they could do to me was already on the program. I'm not sure what would have happened next, because the building drama was interrupted just then. With a rush of wind like the first breath of a hurricane, the temple doors slammed open.

"Sorry we're late," said the tripartite voice of the Furies, from outside. "We had a bit of trouble with the package."

"We'll deal with you later," Atropos said to me, her voice a harsh whisper. "In the meantime, since you're so eager to see your inamorata, why don't we accommodate you?" She whistled a couple of quick chords, and with a flash and a thump I found myself inside the cage with Cerice.

"We had an agreement," I snarled at Lachesis.

"We still do," she said. "But it's going to have to wait a bit."

"This wasn't part of our terms," I said. "Cerice was supposed to be released immediately."

"How sad for you," said Atropos. "Now, don't you know that children are meant to be seen and not heard?" She whistled again, and I found I couldn't speak. Then she cocked her head to one side as though thinking. "And better yet, not seen either. Yes, I think it would be for the best if no eye outside your cage could see you, either of you." A third time she whistled, though without any apparent results.

No sooner had she finished her spell than a goat's head peered in through the open doors. It was followed a moment later by those of a serpent and a lion. All three sat atop the same giant torso. And three sets of arms were wrapped tightly around a wildly thrashing cocoon of steel chains.

"Put her in the dock," said Lachesis.

For a few moments the Furies were wholly occupied with that task. As they had said, the package was a troublesome one, and it took all of their strength to hold it in check.

That was when Cerice hit me with something midway between a passionate embrace and a flying tackle. It sent a stabbing pain through my knee that made my eyes water, and nothing had ever felt better in my whole life. I dropped my cane and wrapped my good arm around her, squeezing hard enough to crack human ribs. We held that pose for several long moments before she whispered in my ear. "What in Hades's name is going on?"

I wanted to scream. The last time I'd seen her I'd still been under the influence of the Cassandra curse, and now I was silenced. In all probability I wasn't ever going to get the chance to speak to her without a curtain between us. I had to try. Opening my mouth as wide as I could, I attempted a yell. Nothing came out. Atropos had done something to my vocal cords so they wouldn't vibrate. I felt tears of frustration start in my eyes. I turned away from Cerice and very calmly and methodically began to bang my head on the bars of the cage.

"Ravirn," whispered a voice from somewhere near the level of my knees. "Where are you? I can feel the cage, but I can't see it." It was Melchior.

"He's right here," said Cerice, "with me. In addition to apparently making us invisible, Atropos put another spell on his speech. He's pounding his head against the bars."

"Tell him to stop it. I'll explain everything."

I realized then that he must be outside the cage. Apparently, Atropos hadn't bothered to include him in the spells she'd cast on me, any of them. Not a surprise, I suppose. To her he was just a made thing, like a table or a chair. It was moot in any case; as much as I loved him, I didn't think there was much he could do to help. Neither one of us had any tricks left up our sleeves.

Still, I'd never been happier to see him. I nodded vigorously at Cerice, pointed to Atropos, my throat, then Melchior. Cerice gave me a hard look, but knelt so the webgoblin wouldn't have to speak too loudly and draw attention. While Melchior brought Cerice up to date, I took a look around.

The composite creature that was the Furies had wrestled their bundle into the witness stand. As soon it was in place, the chains fell away to reveal Eris. The Goddess of Discord was no longer dressed in the armor she'd worn when last I saw her. Instead, she wore a long, shimmering tunic of gold and black. It was in the traditional Greek style, as was her hair. She looked every inch the classical goddess. Once she was on the stand, the Furies reassumed their singular forms and moved to the judge's bench opposite the one occupied by the Fates.

"By what authority did you command the Furies to

bring me here?" declaimed Eris. Her voice was clear and ringing, and it was directed straight at the Fates.

"By right of redress," said Clotho. "You have moved unfairly to tilt the balance."

"Yes," agreed Lachesis, before Eris could respond. "Using my grandson as a proxy, you invaded the inner heart of our power in defiance of the ancient compact."

"Are you referring to that callow boy I found in my cable closet?" asked Eris. She laughed. "Has the weight of your authority finally driven you into madness?" Her voice was incredulous. "Me, use a sprig like that? I think not." She turned to the Furies. "Surely *you* can't believe I'd stoop to such abject cradle-robbing."

"The evidence was convincing," said Alecto.

"Though we did find it odd," continued Megaera.

"But then, odd is how we find you as well," concluded Tisiphone.

"Do you have an alternate explanation for this?" asked Megaera, and the image of the Fate Core virus sprang into three-dimensional life in the air between them and Eris.

"The colors and most of the signature are the child's," said Alecto.

"And he has proved talented," said Tisiphone.

"But," said Megaera, "when we unraveled the virus and looked at the source code, your hand was also apparent."

"If you've a more entertaining hypothesis, we'd love to hear it," said Tisiphone.

"Or a more plausible one," agreed Alecto.

I wanted to know how the damnable thing had come to be rewritten in my colors as well. That was one question I'd never gotten an answer to. I turned my gaze on Atropos's webtroll Kalkin, who was standing behind his mistress, and so was quite close to where Cerice and I were imprisoned. I figured Atropos would have exempted him from the invisibility spell that covered me because he was such an integral part of her magic. But even if she had, I didn't expect to get any response out of him, so I was surprised when he met my eyes. Without moving his head he quickly darted his glance from me to Atropos and back again, then tipped me the slightest of nods. It wasn't exactly a signed statement, but I took his meaning well enough. Atropos had done a little jiggering.

"Oh, the code's mine all right," said Eris, in response to the Furies. "But those aren't the colors I put on it. I've no need to suborn babies to get into anyplace that allows Atropos to write its security algorithms."

"So you admit violating the Fate Core," said Lachesis. She turned to the Furies. "There, guilty by her own admission. What more evidence do you need?"

Evidence? I thought. *Why was evidence needed?* And why were the Fates deferring to the Furies? There was more going on here than I understood. Just then, fierce hands grabbed me from behind.

"You magnificent idiot," Cerice whispered in my ear as she wrapped her arms around me. "Couldn't you think of a better way to free me?"

With Atropos holding the key to my voice, I couldn't very well respond, but I wouldn't have had the time anyway before she spoke again.

"So what's the plan from here? Sorry. I forgot that the cat has your tongue." She paused. "I also forgot that planning isn't your long suit. I assume the idea is to improvise."

I turned my full attention to her and shook my head.

"You do have something in mind then?"

Again I shook my head.

"Do you mean to tell me that your only plan was to trade yourself for me? Melchior didn't have that wrong?"

The contortions her face went through as a series of emotions took her one after the other was quite impressive. "I'm not sure whether I should kiss you or strangle you. That's the most romantic thing imaginable, but it's not the brightest. Do you know that you're the single most maddening person I've ever known?"

I shrugged. Then I pointed to what was happening outside the cage. While Cerice and I had been getting reacquainted, the Fates and the Furies had continued their dialogue with Eris. Things didn't seem to be going well for the Goddess of Discord.

"I think a thousand years and one sounds about right," Lachesis said to the Furies.

"As I keep telling you, she started it," said Eris, pointing to Atropos.

"Said it you have," agreed Megaera.

"Proved it, you have not," countered Alecto.

"If you'd let me out to track down Lachesis's missing grandson, I might be able to do something about that."

"If you could find him, that is," said Tisiphone. "We have hunted him for some little time now, and yet he remains uncaught."

"Frustrating," said Megaera.

"Surprising," said Alecto.

"Entertaining," said Tisiphone.

It was at that instant that I realized why Atropos had hidden us from outside eyes. It was for fear that I might be able to alter the outcome of this exchange. Without my copy of Orion, I didn't think there was much I could do, but I had to make some kind of attempt. I turned back to Cerice and pursed my lips as though whistling.

"No go. I tried that earlier. Magic simply doesn't work in here."

Then inspiration struck. There might just be a way to get

out of this with my skin intact. Lachesis was beyond the reach of my arms, but not of my cane. I slid the stick through the bars and poked my grandmother in the ribs, hard. She didn't even flinch, but after a moment she did turn in her chair as though she were stretching. She focused her gaze firmly on me. Apparently Atropos had exempted the Fates from her spell of invisibility.

"What do you want?" Her lips didn't move, but I could clearly hear her.

Smiling wickedly, I pointed to my throat.

"All right," she said, "but for my ears alone."

Then she coughed once as though she'd swallowed something wrong. Somewhere in that cough there was the faint hiss of spell code, but it was well hidden. If I hadn't been expecting it, I'd never have noticed. And, since no one else paid it any attention, I had to assume it had passed unnoticed by the Furies.

"I can blow this for you," I said, and though my vocal cords still felt as if there was a fist clenched around them, I knew that she and I could hear each other.

"Somehow that seems unlikely," said Lachesis. "You don't exactly have a lot of cards left to play, grandson mine."

"I've got one. By my lights, you've broken your word to Necessity. Even with my throat sealed, I think I can draw her attention to me, and unless I'm very wrong about the way things work, that will also show me to them." I pointed at the Furies.

"Then what?" asked Lachesis.

"I tell them everything."

"With no spell, you expect them to take your word over ours?"

"What if I told you there was another copy?" I asked.

"That might change things," said Lachesis. "Damn Eris's virus. If we'd had your thread to watch when we negotiated, we'd have seen the possibility. Very well. Keep silent about your copy, and we will free you and seek no reprisals against you or yours."

"You'll stop Puppeteer, too," I said.

"That's asking too much, I think," she replied.

"It doesn't work," I said. "And you have Eris on the ropes. How much is that worth?"

"Enough," she replied. "We can write a new Puppeteer later. Deal."

"Oath to Necessity?" I asked.

"Oath to Necessity," she affirmed. Then she smiled, before turning forward again. "You are shrewd, grandson, very shrewd. You may yet prove an asset to this house. Perhaps I might even be persuaded to reinstate you."

Somehow, I didn't think so. Not after what I hoped to see happen next. But her last sentence almost changed my mind. It was the offer of home and family back. I'd been pretty certain my ploy would buy my freedom and at least a temporary guarantee of safety. I hadn't thought that the making of it might win back everything else I'd lost. It was more tempting than I'd have believed possible.

For several long seconds, things hung in the balance. All I had to do to earn my family back was to hang Eris, our ancient enemy, out to dry. It wouldn't even be permanent, just one piece bitten out of an immortal life. Oh, and there was the little matter of my self-respect. I'd have to give that up too.

Using the cane, I lowered myself to the floor of our cage. I reached through the bars and placed my hands on Melchior's back. He seemed a bit startled at first, flinching. Then I moved my fingers in a pattern I'd followed a hundred times before. For a moment I wasn't sure it would work. I hadn't built him for what I was doing, but then I hadn't built him for free will either. I held my breath while

I waited. When Melchior suddenly looked back over his shoulder with an incredulous grin on his face, I let it out in a quiet sigh. We were in business.

"The quick, brown fox jumped over the lazy dog's back," he whispered.

In response, I typed *Yes* on his back. There was no keyboard, but his skin was sensitive enough, and he had a computer's perfect memory for everything that happened within the range of his senses.

Melchior, I typed, *Nine One One.* I needed to make sure that he knew that whatever he did next was solely on his own recognizance. That was critically important this time. Then I added, *DASD DUMP?* I didn't make it a command. I didn't even make it a request. I couldn't. What he did or did not do next was a decision he had to make completely on his own. Anything else would abrogate my deal with Lachesis. More importantly, anything else would abrogate my deal with Melchior. The one that said we were partners, not master and servant.

Melchior jerked like I'd struck him, and turned to look at me. But, of course, I wasn't there to see. There was panic in his eyes as they tracked blindly across my invisible face, and I really felt for him. I wanted to help him, to take some of the weight I'd just placed on his shoulders back onto my own. But I couldn't, not if I was going to let him be his own master. Watching his pain and indecision while doing nothing to alleviate it was as hard as anything I'd ever done, but after a time, his eyes calmed, and he straightened his back.

"Executing," he whispered, turning away from me. He began to spew high-speed code as he marched straight across the room toward the Furies.

At first, it was as though he were the only living thing in a statue gallery. Every figure but his froze as he made his slow progress into the center of the court. But it was a long spell and, one by one, the assembled goddesses began to stir.

Eris reacted first. Perhaps it was because she recognized the notes of her spell, perhaps because she knew the secret of familiar self-determination. In either case, her response was a subtle thing. It started with a slight relaxing of her shoulders, an easing of a tension more felt than seen. Then came an infinitesimal lifting of the right side of her mouth, and the slightest bow of acknowledgment or thanks in Mel's direction.

Next to move were the Furies. Alecto sat up a bit straighter, seeming to take a real interest for the first time. Megaera assumed a prim-and-disapproving expression, clearly unhappy about this interruption to the orderly progression of things. Tisiphone clapped her hands together and grinned like a child with a new toy.

Atropos leaped to her feet then and whistled a long string of ugly-sounding code. In response, a miniature storm cloud formed in the air above Melchior, tossing and whirling in a dark-and-menacing way. Even from where I was, I could see Mel flinch and the bright beads of sweat that popped out on the back of his bald skull. But that was all. His spell recital neither slowed nor stopped. I couldn't have been prouder if I'd fathered him, rather than building him, or more scared. Atropos clenched her fist and a bright bolt of orange lightning shot from the cloud. But in the same instant, Megaera stretched out one seaweed-and-saltwater wing like an awning over Mel's head, and the bolt struck that instead of the goblin. A slight wince crossed the sullen features of the Fury, but that was all.

At some point in that sequence Clotho must have moved as well, because when I looked from Melchior back to the Fates, she was no longer seated with the other two.

Where she had gone was anybody's guess, because she was nowhere to be seen.

The last individual to react was Lachesis. My grandmother spun in her seat to glare at me. "What?" she screeched. "How dare you? You'll burn for this, Ravirn." A quick burst of code spilled from her lips, and suddenly the cage was no more. She rose to her feet slowly and angrily, whistling as she stood. I could feel the hair on my arms and the back of my neck rising to stand on end as she continued to spout complex harmonies, building a terrible spell of punishment.

"Oath to Necessity," I called, and as I did so, I felt my vocal cords slide back to their normal configuration.

She ignored my words and pointed both hands at me in a terribly deliberate manner, sending a stream of flame straight for my face. It stopped when it hit Tisiphone in the chest. I hadn't seen her cross the intervening distance, but suddenly she was there.

"Naughty, naughty," she said, but her voice sounded different from the way it normally did, as though it were coming from a great distance. "Mustn't violate Oath to Necessity. We don't like that."

"How dare you?" snarled Lachesis. "It was he who violated the oath, not I."

"That's not how Mother sees it," said Alecto, from across the room, and her voice too, seemed strangely distant.

"What do you mean?" asked Lachesis.

"Necessity hears every oath taken in her name, whether you invoke her or not," said Megaera, in the same faraway voice.

"I don't understand," said Lachesis. "I didn't violate my oath. He did."

"I'm afraid not, Grandmother," said I. "I promised to keep quiet about Orion, and I have."

"Then what is the spell your goblin is spouting over there?" she asked.

"Oh, that's Orion, all right. But he's doing that on his own. I just pointed out to him that if he wanted to take independent action, he happened to have a copy of Orion in his DASD memory. I left it there after I made a duplicate crystal."

"His actions are an extension of your own," said Atropos, stepping up beside Lachesis. "He's your creature."

"No," I replied. "He's my friend. I'm profoundly grateful he was willing to act on my suggestion, but the action was his. I'd think the reaction of the Furies would have been indication enough of that. Didn't your encounter with your former familiar, Ahllan, teach you anything?"

"Oh, Khemnos spouted some nonsense about seeing her acting on her own, right enough, but that's foolery. I assumed that you or Cerice had salvaged her and stashed her somewhere for your own purposes."

"Afraid not," said Melchior, who had just finished with the spell. "Neither one of them is bright enough for that." He'd just deliberately discarded the secrecy that provided his kind with their best protection against the whims of Fate, and he was shaking all over, but his voice was firm.

"I'll kill you all," said Atropos.

"That would be a violation of Fate's word to Necessity," said Eris, from her place on the witness stand. "I'd advise against it."

"As would I," said Megaera.

"It *would* be unwise," agreed Alecto.

"But such fun," said Tisiphone, smiling hopefully.

"Now," said Alecto. She was holding up an eight-sided memory crystal. Puppeteer. Emerald green, and filled with gorgeous traceries of gold, it was the thing that had started this whole mess. "It's time for the verdict."

"Not that there's much to decide," said Megaera.

"Perhaps someone will dispute the judgment," said Tisiphone, hopefully.

There didn't seem to be any takers.

"Our judgment is in favor of Discord," said the oddly distorted version of the tripartite voice the Furies used when they spoke for Necessity. "She was acting in accordance with her mandate as an agent of chaos. Eris, you are free to leave." The gate of the witness stand sprang open. Eris bowed to the Furies and stepped to the floor of the temple.

"Thank you," she said. "I think I'll stick around for a bit."

The Furies ignored her. The second she was absolved she ceased to exist for them.

"Atropos," said the Furies, turning their attentions to the Fate. "We will take the Puppeteer spell and nullify it. However, you have done nothing against your mandate. You are also free to leave."

Their duty to Necessity done, the Furies seemed to shrink, relaxing back into their separate personalities. A moment later, they unfurled their wings and rose into the air.

"I've no doubt we'll be seeing *you* again," said Alecto, pointing a finger at me like a gun.

"Considering your nature, it's almost inevitable," agreed Megaera, and for the first time since I'd met her, there seemed to be the faintest note of pleasant anticipation in her voice. It sent a chill right through me.

"We'll have such fun," added Tisiphone.

With a rush of storm winds and the blowing of hunting horns, they were gone.

Atropos smiled coldly after them, then turned her gaze my way. "Well played, nephew mine. I didn't realize you had it in you." She might hate me, but she would never let that interfere with the proper display of family manners.

I bowed as deeply I could with my knee in its brace. I

made sure to keep the gesture formal and not mocking. I'd finally learned better, and the lessons had been expensive ones. "Thank you, Madame."

She reached into her pocket and pulled out a clear life strand. It was stiff and vital at one end. Though that portion was as transparent as the rest, it somehow gave the impression of color removed. At the point where the strand passed between Atropos's thumb and forefinger it underwent a transition. From there on it was like the spun glass of a fiber-optic cable, possessing no color or light of its own, but rather, passing along the hint of things far distant. There was also no end in that direction. The strand just seemed to vanish into another space. I recognized it as my thread.

"I'll be keeping this. I may not have any power over it at the moment, but at some point that must change. I can be very patient. I am the end of all things, nephew mine. I shall be the last. When birth has ended, I will cut Clotho's cord, and she will be no more. The time will come when every last thread has been measured, and I will snip Lachesis from the great weave. In the end only Death and I will remain. Then I will cut his thread, and it will be me alone. With my last strength I will close the shears on my own life. I am the end of everything, including you. This isn't over, nephew mine. Never forget that." Then she just faded away, like a Polaroid photo in reverse, taking my thread with her.

My legs felt like Jell-O, and my ears were ringing like church bells at a Quasimodo festival. I wanted nothing more than to lie down and sleep. I needed time to heal and to assimilate all that had passed. But as Atropos had so sweetly pointed out, it wasn't over. Lachesis was approaching. Her expression was terribly, terribly sad, though as usual, the emotion didn't touch her eyes. I braced myself.

"You have made your choice. Now you must abide by the consequences, and so must I. You have sided with chaos against order. I revile you. You have failed in your duty to the house of Fate. I cast you out. You have betrayed your family and me. I take back your name." She, too, faded from view.

Clotho, who had been conspicuous in her absence from the field during the past few minutes, reappeared and approached me. I didn't know why, and I didn't know what to expect from her. I stood before her, alone and nameless. She looked me up and down very closely. When she finally met my eyes, she was smiling.

"I spun your thread out of the stuff of chaos, and to chaos it has returned. That spinning was my first gift to you, and I think it has not been entirely wasted. So I will give you another present. You have been the cuckoo in the nest of Fate, our dark and tricksy bird. I gift you a new name: Raven. Fly high, dark bird. Fly high." With a wink and a grin, she was gone.

Of the great powers, only Eris was left. She approached me, a broad smile spreading across her beautiful, bichromatic features. As she came, her clothes shifted from Greek formal to dance-club leather and lace.

"I've always liked Clotho," she said, expansively putting an arm around my shoulders. "There is a chaos in beginnings that her sisters can never know. Welcome to the wild side. We don't go in for all those houses and things that your blood family is so enamored of, but we do have fun together when we aren't stabbing each other in the back. Look me up when you're on your feet again. Friday is poker night. Bring money." She put her lips up to my ear, blew gently, and whispered, "In fact, bring lots."

Then she threw her head back and laughed like all the windows of hell shattering. It was a wild, eerie sound and it continued long after she had departed.

So, I'd been offered a place of sorts, but it wasn't one I particularly wanted to take. I'd started down this road because I wasn't willing to see order overwhelm chaos, but I wasn't any more excited about seeing things go the other way. There had to be some middle ground. Didn't there? But that was a question for another time.

They were all gone by then, the true immortals who smashed aside everything in their path. That left only Melchior and Cerice. We were alone at last. I looked at Cerice, afraid to speak. So much had happened. I was cast out, wearing a new name and a new role. Would she still want me?

"Raven?" she said, and it seemed almost that she was tasting the word. Checking for poison perhaps. "It fits somehow. My grandmother is more forgiving than yours."

"And you?" I managed to ask, though it was so very hard. Until I'd heard the answer, I wouldn't be able to count the full cost. "What do you think?"

"I think I'll stick around for a while," she said, wrapping her arms around me. "I've always been attracted to bad boys."

"There are still a thousand things I need to tell you," I said, thinking of the many half-truths, the omissions and evasions. We had a hard road ahead, though not half so hard as the one we'd already trod.

"We'll have time for that later," she said. "For now there's only one thing I need to hear."

This time I could speak my heart.

"I love you, Cerice."

"And I am awfully fond of you, my dark bird." It was a start.

I knelt then, though it cost me dearly in pain. I needed to face Melchior at his own level. "Thank you, Melchior," I said, placing my one working hand on his shoulder. "I . . ." I found I couldn't go any further.

He'd exposed himself before the Fates and risked his life for me with no way of knowing what the consequences would be. I owed him everything, and I couldn't even begin to find the words to express what he meant to me.

Once again, he came to my rescue. "Don't worry about it," he said with a grin. "You're welcome. You'd have done the same for me, though with less panache, of course. That's what partners are for. Right?"

"Right," I agreed, smiling back.

Suddenly, despite all the threats and uncertainties still to be faced, I felt confident about the future. With people like Melchior and Cerice around to keep me on the right track, I knew everything would work out. We'd get Shara fixed, even if I had to drag her wandering soul back from the banks of the Styx. I'd keep a step or two ahead of Hwyl and the cousins. Who knows, I might even finish college.

"Chez Ahllan, and Shara?" I asked.

"As quickly as ever we can," said Cerice, worry about her familiar clear in her voice. "Melchior, would you do the honors?"

"It would be my pleasure," he replied, bowing to Cerice and digging for his magical tools. "Let's go home."

KELLY McCULLOUGH has sold short fiction to publications including *Weird Tales*, *Absolute Magnitude*, and *Cosmic SF*. An illustrated collection of Kelly's short science fiction, called *The Chronicles of the Wandering Star*, is part of InterActions in Physical Science, an NSF-funded middle school science curriculum. He lives in western Wisconsin. Visit his website at www.kellymccullough.com.

THE ULTIMATE IN
SCIENCE FICTION AND FANTASY!

From magical tales of distant worlds to stories of technological advances beyond the grasp of man, Penguin has everything you need to stretch your imagination to its limits.

penguin.com

ACE
Get the latest information on favorites like William Gibson, T.A. Barron, Brian Jacques, Ursula Le Guin, Sharon Shinn, and Charlaine Harris, as well as updates on the best new authors.

Roc
Escape with Harry Turtledove, Anne Bishop, S.M. Stirling, Simon Green, Chris Bunch, Jim Butcher, E.E. Knight, and many others—plus news on the latest and hottest in science fiction and fantasy.

DAW
Mercedes Lackey, Kristen Britain, Tanya Huff, Tad Williams, C.J. Cherryh, and many more—DAW has something to satisfy the cravings of any science fiction and fantasy lover.
Also visit dawbooks.com.

Get the best of science fiction and fantasy at your fingertips!

3 1524 00453 5060